Marty spun around and advanced on Vie, her arm raised.

Vie took a step back, as an image flashed through her mind: in the kitchen, in Brooklyn, Marty punching her in the chest, screaming *I hate you!*

Marty's arm fell to her side. "I've never been as good as you, have I? You thought I was scum, and you convinced Armand to do the same."

"That's a lie! I was the one who always took care of you. I was the one to bail you out of trouble. If it weren't for me, you would've gone to prison. I made the money to pay for your private school, and I put you through college."

"Guilt money," spat Marty. "You always wanted to be rid of me. The money meant you were in charge of everything. What do you think happened to Armand? I bet I know: you took away his pride. You treated him the way you've treated me, as a hanger-on."

Vie was trembling. She felt nauseated. "Please stop."

Marty looked at her for a long time. "Okay," she said at last, "I'll stop. But I know things about him you don't. About your mother, too. . . ."

SCENTS

The bestselling novel of passion,
ambition and revenge by
Johanna Kingsley

SCENTS

A Novel

JOHANNA KINGSLEY

Bantam Books
Toronto • New York • London • Sydney • Auckland

SCENTS
A Bantam Book / January 1985
8 printings through April 1987

ISBN 0-553-26583-0

Published simultaneously in the United States and Canada

Bantam Books are published by Bantam Books, Inc. Its trade-
mark, consisting of the words "Bantam Books" and the por-
trayal of a rooster, is Registered in U.S. Patent and Trademark
Office and in other countries. Marca Registrada. Bantam
Books, Inc., 666 Fifth Avenue, New York, New York 10103.

PRINTED IN THE UNITED STATES OF AMERICA

O   17 16 15 14 13 12 11 10 9 8

SCENTS

I

NEW YORK

1

Fall 1983

"Make way for the Queen!" a man's voice called out.

The guests looked up, champagne glasses in hand, their silks and taffetas rustling in the breeze of a warm October night above Central Park.

Vie Jolay stepped out on the terrace strung with miniature Japanese lanterns. She smiled as endearments and praise rose from all sides, telling her she'd done it again, she was a darling, she looked stunning; her new fragrance was divine. The soothing babble of the fashion world, she thought, but couldn't dismiss her feeling of triumph. The new scent had been an instant sellout when it previewed in Dallas and Beverly Hills.

In a long fluid column of muted silver, one shoulder bare, small drops of diamonds at her ears, Vie lived up to her nickname. To her customers, she was simply Madame Jolay, but to those who knew her in the trade, she was Queen Vie (rhyming with "bee"), ruler of a private kingdom that some thought magical.

"I want to thank all of you for coming here tonight. It's the support of people like you that keeps me in business."

"Rubbish, darling," interjected the familiar voice of Vie's old friend and mentor, Philippa Wright. "It's you who does it all. We're just the cheering section."

Vie smiled at the tiny woman in her sixties, still the dynamo she'd been as vice president of New York's most elegant department store. "You more than anyone, Phil. You single-handedly dragged me up the ladder when I was starting out."

Philippa flushed with pleasure at the public avowal, but

her natural spikiness asserted itself. "Pushed, you mean. I was behind you, remember, heaving you up in front of me. Thank God you didn't slip. Would've crushed me completely."

Laughter made the guests relax, and the promotion party became more like a family occasion. Mike Parnell, Vie's personal lawyer, put an arm around Philippa and squeezed. He admired the woman greatly. She had a sixth sense about fashion; Philippa had always been able to predict the trend and prepare her customers for it in such a way that each considered the new style an expression of her own individuality.

Vie Jolay did the same with fragrance, Mike reflected. Every woman who used her perfume felt it as an enhancement of herself. A Jolay customer believed the liquid she dabbed behind her earlobes or between her breasts would bring out a hidden self, mysterious and beautiful.

Vie's promotional genius was an important factor in her success. Giving the promotion party in her own home was typically brilliant, providing an intimacy that couldn't be felt in any public place. The penthouse was luxurious and original, particularly with its greenhouse, where lush tropical blooms and exotic trees grew in the heart of New York City. Vie had designed her penthouse herself; the whole apartment was an extension of her personality and taste. Here she offered guests exquisite delicacies and fascinating company in a setting of white marble, pale wood, and large skylights. Her new fragrance, O! de Vie, spouted from small marble fountains.

The guests, rich or famous, occasionally both, and dressed by the most important designers, came to impress others and ended by being impressed themselves.

Vie whispered conspiratorially to Mike, "Enemies in our midst. Lauren's wearing Joy and Dyan has on the newest Yves St. Laurent, not on the market yet."

"You're fantastic, Vie."

"Just professional." She shrugged her shoulders lightly, making ripples undulate along her soft metallic gown.

"Who's the woman in purple?" he whispered back. "And what's the stuff she has on?"

"A vice president at my bank. Over seventy, but refuses

to retire, and nobody can think of a reason why she should. I don't recognize the scent, probably custom made."

"God-awful."

Vie laughed. "I can't get too close myself, but I doubt it's the fault of the fragrance. She probably doesn't realize that her sense of smell has faded, so she keeps dabbing on scent until she can detect it herself. By that point, she's reeking. Like a blind woman selecting clothes—except she *knows* she's blind and gets someone to guide her. This woman wouldn't accept a guide. She goes on relying on her senses without realizing, probably, that at least one of them is betraying her."

"Mad queen," said Mike affectionately. "What her nose knows knows no other."

"That's good! You just make it up?"

A round man with only an aureole of hair lightly encircling his baldness planted a loud kiss on Vie's cheek. "This is some do, sweetheart. Best lox I've had in years."

"It's Scotch smoked salmon, Murray."

"Lox where I come from, love, and it's terrific."

Murray Schwartzman was Vie's old sales manager, had protected her like a watchdog for years, adored her, and was one of Vie's favorite people.

"What do you think of Jolay's expansion?" he asked suddenly.

"I don't know." She was instantly serious. "My sister's a good businesswoman. We're making much more money than we ever did. But *you* know how I operate, Murray. The years we spent working together were good. I felt I knew everything that touched Jolay. Now it's so spread out . . ."

"Where *is* your sister?" Murray asked. "Isn't Martine going to make an appearance tonight?"

Vie felt a twinge of apprehension. She'd been asked the same question after their father's funeral. And Martine had never showed.

"She'd better turn up," said Vie bluntly. "She's the feature attraction for the second act."

"Watch out she doesn't upstage you," Murray said abruptly and walked away.

An old cherub with soft, fluttering hands called her

over. "Delicious lady, you have surpassed even yourself tonight."

"Thanks, Piero," she said to the fashion photographer.

"Those models! My dear, wherever did you find them? Each one I would like to spend days shooting. Visions, they are. What is that shine you've put on them?"

The six models—three white, two black, one Eurasian—had been hired for the evening to circulate among the guests offering sample bottles of *O! de Vie*. They were dressed in shimmering ivory, and their exposed skin was dusted with the same iridescence that lay at the bottom of each bottle of perfume. "Mother-of-pearl," Vie told him. "We've been pulverizing it for months."

"You are a genius, no doubt about it whatsoever."

Vie smiled and moved on. The thin trace of mother-of-pearl was the "magic" touch that enabled them to sell at $150 an ounce.

"Cute name," said Don Garrison, Vie's banker. His formal hug reminded Vie that he was attracted, but would remain firmly in control. "You'll make millions." She'd known him since the time Nina left their lives and she'd started in business. He was her Rock of Gibraltar, who'd had the imagination and guts to back her with a bank loan when she was still a teenager. He'd even had the dignity not to act surprised when she paid him back months before her twenty-first birthday.

"How'd you pick the name?" Don asked her.

"It's a play on words," Vie said. "The *O!* is mysterious. It's ecstasy, wonder, a closed circle, an incantation."

"By you."

"Yes, but that's the beauty of it. Since vie is French for 'life' it implies all sorts of things, though it also echoes an elegant, faintly exotic after-dinner drink."

"I'm not up to all that, honey. Just a humdrum financial wizard, but I say it's cute, and it smells great. You've got yourself another winner. Where's Martine, by the way? She's working on this new campaign with you, isn't she?"

"Of course," said Vie with a confidence she didn't feel. "I'm expecting her any minute." She turned away from Don before he could detect her anxiety.

*　　*　　*

A few people were beginning to leave. Elaine Smollett, Vie's secretary of more than fifteen years, bore down on her, dispersing whoever stood in the way.

"What do I do with these camera buffs?" she asked. "They've finished off the salmon, they're half-pissed on champagne, and they want to go home."

"Tell them stories," said Vie. "Give them more champagne. Anything. They've got to wait."

"I told them that, boss. I told them they had to get a shot of the Jolay sisters together. But half of them are kids in safari suits, and they're so pleased to have shot a few biggies that they're ready to decamp."

"Hypnotize them," Vie said worriedly.

At that moment a hubbub rose from the direction of the hall. Thank God, Vie thought, she's finally come.

"Hey, you guys," Martine Jolay protested laughingly to the photographers, "let me at least run a comb through my hair."

They took no notice. Martine's dark gamine looks were as camera-perfect in their way as was the regal blondness of her half-sister Vie. Martine was smaller, more buxom, with a crackling restlessness that contrasted dramatically with Vie's calm intensity.

They posed together as the Jolay sisters, though neither woman had taken the company's name as her own. To the camera eye they presented a study in opposites: Liz Taylor and Grace Kelly. Martine's emerald dress, an opulent creation by Oscar de la Renta, billowed beside Vie's classic silver column by Adolpho. Whenever Piero d'Angelo did a major shooting of them together, he called it his Polish Portfolio, because they were poles apart.

Piero was pleased with his joke. But Martine and Vie had learned that each had her own magnetism, fields of force that attracted or repelled the other.

"All right," said Martine when they'd posed long enough, facing each other, looking out at the cameras, the perfume standing between them or each holding up a bottle. "Knock it off, guys." She leaned toward Vie and whispered, "I've got to talk to you."

"Thank you," Vie said to the photographers. "Please don't forget to take a bottle of *O! de Vie* home with you."

She turned to her sister and whispered back, "Meet me in my bedroom." It would take a few minutes, she knew, for each of them to work her way upstairs through the crowd.

As she extricated herself from the well-wishers, Vie wondered what excuse Marty would give. It was unusual for her to come late, especially when the press was there. For the past few years Marty seemed to be everywhere ahead of Vie. Moving too fast. Ever since Marty had entered the business, she'd introduced concepts of management and expansion that made Jolay Perfumes, Inc., a wonder child of the industry. But Vie had fought to keep it family owned, as it had been since she'd founded it.

Then things began to change, not to Vie's taste at all. Offering public stock on the New York exchange had been Martine's idea, and she'd pushed it through the board of directors.

At the time Don Garrison had said, "It's an essential move—the only possible next step." Almost everyone who had opinions on the matter sided with Martine. Philippa remained neutral; Elaine Smollett muttered deprecations of the action until Vie asked her to stop.

It was done. Though Vie's veto had prevented the entire company's stock from going public, two-thirds of all shares were offered for sale. Martine's analysis proved correct. The company did become stronger, and the new funds had been invested in raw materials used for fragrance compounds.

But Vie saw to it that the company remained under her control. Like tonight's party: she operated best in her own arena, where she could be fully in charge. Going public had meant a weakening of authority and, in Vie's eyes, a loss of direction.

"Whew!" Marty said, slamming the door behind her. "What a bunch of toadies out there."

Vie stiffened. "A lot of good friends, too."

"Didn't stop to chat." Marty plopped down on the satin-covered bed as though she were wearing jeans. "I bet you were in a state about me not showing up. Sorry. It was important. Very important." She put her hands up under her head, watching Vie carefully. Vie waited beside her Georgian wardrobe.

"I was on the Street," said Marty slowly, "gathering intelligence. Talking with some of the insiders to get the story of our stock jump during the past week."

"It's *O! de Vie*. The success has been greater than any predictions. In Dallas alone—"

"That's not it," Marty cut her off. "Of course a successful new product doesn't hurt, but do you know who is buying Jolay?"

"We have a survey of investors—"

Again Marty interrupted. "And that doesn't tell us one hoot about this week's rush. It's all coming from the same source, from Motek." She propped herself up on her elbows to study Vie's reaction.

Vie was shaking her head. She knew that Motek, the multinational conglomerate, owned many different types of products and services, but nothing vaguely touching fragrances. She knew she didn't want Motek, or any corporation resembling it, to be buying heavily into Jolay. "They don't have cosmetics, toiletries—not even health products!" she objected. "They have nothing to do with our business."

"And they're obviously interested. They're buying up large blocks now, preliminary to acquisition."

"We won't let them!" Vie was nearly shouting.

"Why not? The value of our holdings would zoom."

"But we'd belong to them! Impossible. We personally still control thirty-three percent of the company stock between us, and we can prevent them from acquiring more than that."

Marty gave a slow smile and got off the bed. "Maybe you can't."

Vie stared at her, suddenly realizing what Marty might do with her stock.

"Think of the money you'll have, Vie—enough for half a dozen penthouses like this one."

Vie shook her head angrily. "You're playing with my life, *my* business, and I'm going to hold on to it!"

Marty walked up to Vie until she was nearly touching her. "I'm tired of taking orders from you, sister dear. It's time I was giving them. In case you haven't noticed, I've turned this company around since I got into it. And I'm not going to let you ruin it for me. You're too old-fashioned, Vie. You're living in the past. But it's my world now—and I'll prove it to you!"

Vie shrank back from her sister's menacing closeness, though her voice still held its authority. "You've always tried to get everything your way, Marty. You've been trying to take over since you were a child." She strode to the door and yanked it open. "But you couldn't get ahead of me then, and you can't now!" Vie marched out of the room, and then started to run, away from her sister—back to her own party.

2

1951

Although only four, the child was a block of unyielding dead weight. Her father tightened his grasp and dragged her along.

Armand Jolaunay, known as Armand Nouvel, was walking down the Brooklyn street on a hot Saturday in late November with a small daughter on either hand and a list of rooms for rent in his pocket. Men in shirt sleeves, drinking beer on their front stoops, shouted over to friends on other stoops; women in short-sleeved flowered prints strolled by with groceries and baby carriages. Most of the women looked like Medusas, he thought, with their hair sectioned and rolled over cylinders of metal or plastic or fastened tightly to their heads with sharp-pronged clips.

The air was rich with odors, some almost overpowering to his highly developed sense of smell. The pungency of garlic, the sharpness of oregano filled his nostrils, followed by heavy sauerkraut spiced with caraway. He took out his handkerchief, still holding on to his younger daughter's hand, and blew. Vie, his older daughter, was wrinkling her nose.

In addition to the painful assault of odors, the unnatural heat of the day made Armand uncomfortable in his gray wool suit and tie. He didn't know the term Indian summer, he'd never been in Brooklyn before, and he felt ill at ease in this false season in the New World.

Garbage was scattered over the sidewalk where it had been overturned by foraging animals or dumped by indifferent people, and he steered his children around islands of old coffee grounds, soggy newspapers bleeding with last night's tomato sauce, beer cans, and cigarette butts.

"Come here!" he said sharply to Martine, who once again had edged from his grasp and seemed prepared to wander off.

"Gimme *that* hand," she whined, pointing to the one that now held her sister's.

God save me from little girls, Armand thought as he led Martine over and across to the left hand. She took it, sticking her tongue out at Vie. "Assez!" he said sharply. "Enough!"

"Smell that, Papa," said Vie, smiling. "Delicious."

From behind a frame house came the odor of burning leaves, smoky and rich. "It is fire," he told her. "Very dangerous." Someday he'd tell Vie about the fire that had destroyed his business and his future. But there was time enough; she was only seven.

Martine was still trying to free herself. His arm ached as she became wooden. He was surprised by the heaviness of a small child who resisted him. But he held on tightly.

"Why is she such a brat, Papa?" asked Vie.

He smiled at her. She could pick up his moods like a seismograph; they were two of a kind. Sometimes Armand let himself spin out little dreams of the two of them together, just Vie and himself, the king and the princess, with no dark imp around.

"Papa," said Martine, "Vie stinks."

"No she does not. You are not to say that." He didn't mean to take sides between the girls. Martine was only four, after all. She was not at fault for having been born. The fault was his alone, his weakness that had made him

turn to another woman after the death of Anne. Golden
Anne, the image fixed in his mind, her face lit by the sun,
her skin fresh as earth after rain.

"She stinks, and so do you," Martine insisted.

The picture of Anne disintegrated like a soap bubble. He
yanked the child toward him and slapped her quickly on
the buttocks. She began to scream. He felt people turning
to look. His suit and tie made him conspicuous. They'd
see him as a foreigner, hurting a child.

But an old woman caught his eye and nodded, endors-
ing his strict discipline. He looked away angrily, reaching
for the slip of paper in his pocket. He studied it and
looked up at the houses they passed, to avoid any further
contact. Martine's screams diminished to whimpers.

He stopped in front of a dark-green house with a large
porch. "You must both behave yourselves now," he told
the girls. "Not be like puppies who run into everything
and make commotion."

Martine gave him a dark look, to show she hadn't forgiven him.

"If you are good," he bribed, "I will buy the ice cream
later."

"Chocolate," bargained Martine. She knew Vie loved
vanilla.

"Anything you wish. Two lumps."

"Scoops," corrected Vie. "Two *scoops*." She'd picked up
the language as a duck learns swimming, Armand thought.
Even Martine used phrases that made her sound like an
American child. Armand's English, learned in France, had
been charmingly effective for his British and American
customers; once, in his shop, the Duchess of Windsor had
said she'd rather hear Armand speak than Chevalier sing.
But in America he often had to defer to his children on
linguistic matters. That was as it should be; he'd insisted
on English from the moment they'd left Marseilles, confident that the girls would grow up in the United States.

Finally, last month, they had arrived, after nearly a
year in Canada. They came down over the Quebec border,
the safest route. Nevertheless, immigration officials looked
him up in a thick book. Had he ever been a Communist?

He'd answered no, truthfully, while smiling to himself at the irony of the question.

His forged papers held up under the investigation, and he was released to set foot on New York soil, under an assumed name, his cloudy past evaporating in sunny hopes for a new life.

Yet, it was dismal, trudging through Brooklyn looking for a place to stay. Les banlieues this would be called with contempt in Paris: the outskirts, where "they" lived, those people who weren't part of the glamorous mondaine city.

"You must behave," he repeated to the children, though he doubted that their behavior would have anything to do with the outcome. At the last place they'd gone to, the landlady had said, "No children," but he'd seen half a dozen girls and boys in the backyard. The real response, Armand knew, was "No foreigners"—or at least no foreigners of a kind these women couldn't place. His dress was somehow wrong—perhaps the cut of his suit gave him away, or the European shoes, with their high shine. He couldn't disguise his accent or his characteristic mannerisms. And then, he was a man alone with two children. All these, he decided, added up to an undefined suspicion in the good ladies of Brooklyn who turned him away.

The children weren't the problem, though it wouldn't hurt if they were well-behaved. Vie's blond looks were enchanting—her hair in blue ribbons that she'd learned to tie herself—and Martine's dark curls and black-brown eyes made strangers smile and call her a little doll.

They walked up the wooden steps to the peeling ochre door. Armand rang the bell and waited nervously.

A faded woman with pale plastic rims to her glasses opened. Her dress hung on her, its hemline ending like a dangling apology to both fashion and attractiveness.

He held out the newspaper clipping. "Mrs. Murphy? I have come about the rooms. My name is Armand Nouvel," he said, holding out his hand. She didn't respond, and he let it sink back to his side. "These are my little girls, Vie and Martine."

"Pleased to meet you," she mumbled.

He smiled into eyes that seemed to have gone through

too many washings, the blue remaining only as a trace in the gray.

"Won't you come in?" she invited listlessly.

He followed her, noticing the dowdy white shoes: a nurse's sensible footwear. For the first time since setting out that morning, Armand felt cheered. He could handle this one.

Opposite the entrance chipped stairs led directly to the next floor. Mrs. Murphy turned right and opened the door to a living room whose flavor was immediately familiar to Armand. Over the piano, a tasseled throw embroidered with gold threads. Over the mantelpiece, china cats crouched next to garish madonnas and glass elephants. All around the room, trashy bric-a-brac was displayed as though they were treasures.

His second wife would have felt at home here, Armand thought, with her plaster saints, her atrocious taste. The sudden memory filled Armand with hatred toward the woman who'd nearly killed his child.

"Won't you have a seat, please," said Mrs. Murphy, gesturing to the sofa, a stolid, pale-green affair covered with pillows displaying baby animals. When he sat down, the landlady placed herself at the far end, to insure the greatest distance between herself and Armand. The children flanked them in armchairs.

"What do you do, Mr. Nouvel?" she asked shyly, her back pressing against the sofa's arm.

He leaned toward her. Her voice was soft, and he had trouble hearing. His nerve deafness, which he'd had since childhood, meant that he'd instinctively learned to read faces, or lips, and could usually catch what people were saying as long as he could see them clearly. Women's voices were more difficult than men's, and he was not yet accustomed to the facial movements of people speaking English. "Perfume," he answered. "I have been a parfumeur—somebody who makes perfumes."

"Oh." Like most people, the landlady was unaware of Armand's hearing deficiency. When he moved closer, she blushed in the unexpected awareness of physical intimacy. "I didn't know they were made by men."

She'd never thought about perfumes before. They were

out of reach, like orchids or champagne. Even their names—*My Sin*, *Joy*, and French words you couldn't pronounce—were like secret messages from another world, where everyone was rich and elegant.

"In France all the great parfumeurs are men," he told her.

"Oh yes," she agreed, feeling the warmth of his eyes on her lips. "You come from over there?"

He nodded.

"And your wife, the girls' mother, she's over there now?"

"Dead," he said, pressing his fingertips gently together to form a little shrine with his hands.

"I'm sorry. . . ."

"It is over," he said mildly, wondering how to forestall her questions.

"I'm a widow myself. My children are grown, though; I don't see them much anymore."

"A pity," he commiserated while beaming inwardly. A frumpish woman without a husband, who was already—he could tell the signs—interested in him, and who missed having children around: what could be more perfect? "What do you do, Mrs. Murphy?" he asked to be polite. In America, he'd heard, it was considered rude not to ask someone about his job as soon as you met.

"I run the house, you see. I have four tenants here, and then I go out and take care of a few elderly people, a few hours a day. . . ." She stopped, afraid of boring him.

"What a good person you are, madame! Your work brings happiness, it is important." Her shoes told the story, he thought: a dreary life between bedpans and arthritic joints.

"I suppose it is," she said with surprise. She removed her eyeglasses and looked at him a moment before lowering her gaze modestly to the floor. "Would you like a cup of coffee? And the girls—some chocolate milk?"

"You are too kind, too kind," murmured Armand, rising when she got up. He noticed that she moved with the gracelessness of women who regard their body as something that gets in the way. Again he felt optimistic; his charm was one of the few things he could still rely on.

Going into the kitchen, Frances Murphy was surprised

at herself. She'd never done this for a prospective tenant before. But there was something about this man—the long, sensitive mouth with narrow lips, his strong cheekbones, the hint of pale fire in his eyes. The physical closeness he insisted on when they talked. His formal clothes, a little strange but elegant, with the white triangle of a handkerchief in his breast pocket, smelling faintly of lavender when she got close.

Her hands shook as she put the kettle on. If he would stay, she would give him Jurgens's room. Jurgens had described the Alps to her. She'd been young then, but she hadn't forgotten anything. She'd relived the scenes over and over again, the snowy peaks, the fine hairs on the back of Jurgens's hands. If this elegant man would stay, she could visit him in his room. Frances closed her eyes and smiled.

Armand stood when she entered the room and took the tray from her hands. He held her eyes until she looked away, her lashes fluttering.

They drank their coffee in silence while the girls sipped chocolate milk with perfect decorum.

"Would you like to see the upstairs apartment?" Frances Murphy blurted out.

He smiled slowly. The rooms were his. The next challenge was to have her waive the two months' advance mentioned in the ad. Without the waiver he couldn't do it, and they needed a place immediately. The hotel's daily rate was eating up his paltry funds. And he had to be able to leave the children somewhere while he went job hunting. Taking them along was worse than merely hellish—it was hell with chains.

"Alors, mes petites." He summoned the children as he got up. "We go with this lovely lady to see the rooms."

Dutifully they followed the grown-ups. Alongside the stairs the wall was hung with faded black-and-white photographs of lonely seascapes, where whitecaps lay sandwiched between wide slices of sky and sand. No people, no living things appeared in the pictures. "I took those," said Frances, "long ago, on a trip to Atlantic City with my mother."

On the landing of the first floor stood an enormous white

ceramic scallop shell. A monstrous thing, Armand thought, but instinctively knew she was waiting for his praise. "What an interesting sculpture."

Frances beamed, her face turning pink. "Really? You think so? I got it three weeks ago, a sort of present to myself. I'd been in love with it for weeks, passing by the garden shop every day to make sure it was still there. I'm so glad you like it."

Horrible, Armand thought as they continued up the next flight. The rooms were on the top floor, small but sunny. At $58 a month, they would do. He would have to resign himself, Armand realized, to living in a house of suffocating vulgarity.

Blushing, Frances asked if he'd mind putting down two weeks' rent in advance. He assured her it was no problem; they'd move in tomorrow. $29 instead of $116! He beamed as they shook hands at the front door.

When Frances closed it, she remained there a moment, catching her breath. A prince was coming to stay at her house, a man of true culture.

Halfway down the block, Vie said, "Her dress was awful, like a big sack."

"I am sure she is a kind woman," Armand said.

"That doesn't help how she looks," Vie insisted. "Or the stuffy way she smells."

My daughter, he thought, and Anne's. At seven she has standards, she has taste. Armand wished he could meet the expectations he had encouraged in her. "Let us hope all is for the best," he said lamely.

"Ice cream," Martine piped up.

"Yes, you have earned your scoop. You were good."

"*Two* scoops."

"Two; yes. And also for you, Vie."

As he led the girls to the soda fountain, Armand thought about the unspoken agreement he'd just entered into with Frances Murphy. She would expect his attentions and, later, his affection. She would be modest at the beginning, encouraging him to coax her. If he did, she would capitulate instantly and then be grateful, probably effusive. She'd soon expect more than he was willing to give.

He knew the little drama well; he'd played it out often.

He'd always been interested in women, even as a boy in his teens, and they responded by finding him irresistible or, at the very least, charming. His genuine interest in women meant that he flattered them without thinking about it, a trait that often proved handy and one he could rely on when the rent fell due. But he'd have to move carefully.

When he came back the next day, the rooms looked smaller and dingier than he'd remembered. But at least, he consoled himself, it was a place to live.

A year ago, boarding the ship at Marseilles, he'd pictured a spacious Manhattan apartment, very modern and American. Something designed by Frank Lloyd Wright with large panels of glass and a skylight, overlooking the Hudson. Or he would envision a pretty little house in the country, near enough for him to commute to work. Fruit trees blossomed in the spring, a dog leaped down the path to greet him every evening, and a nearby stable offered the girls daily riding lessons.

His vision of life in America was like that of many who had immigrated to her shores: an individualized version of the American Dream, where people prospered by their talents and industry. But Armand wasn't merely an immigrant, he was a fugitive; and though he was sure of his talents, he could produce no proof of them.

Instead of the country house or Manhattan apartment, he was forced to retreat to the boroughs with his girls. His lofty dreams ended in this chicken coop, he thought bitterly: a boardinghouse, a tiny cluster of rooms that opened on a dark corridor, creaking steps, and a hideous scallop below.

He sweated from the effort of carrying their baggage up the stairs. When he brought the cases into the children's room, Armand saw that the beds were already rumpled. Vie was flushed with anger. "Do something," she pleaded.

He was tired, he wanted peace. But the child's command was that of a princess to her knight. He sighed, looked around, and understood what the problem was.

The twin beds stood opposite each other, one against each wall. They were made up identically, with candy-striped sheets, bleached through launderings, covered with pink blankets. Martine's panda lay on one bed, her tiger on the other.

"Ça va," he said soothingly. "We will make the choice now. Which is the bed that you want to have, Martine?"

"Don't care."

"And you, p'tite Vie?"

She shrugged in a gesture that reminded him of Parisian boulevards, a shrug meaning, "I don't give a damn."

Taking a penny from his pocket, he held it in a fist behind his back. Vie went first, chose the hand with the penny, and selected the bed beside the window.

Martine's little face was contorted. "Not fair! *My* bed." She sat down on it, hugging her panda.

"Yours, then. Vie, take the other." Armand felt Vie's intense hazel eyes inspecting him. He wanted to apologize for the constant little betrayals, painful but unavoidable.

Her eyes released him. "I like this one better anyway, it's more cozy."

"Mine!" shouted Martine, running to it and hugging the tiger in her other arm.

Vie didn't look at her father. "You can have it," she told her sister contemptuously. She took her stuffed poodle off the window ledge and placed it on the pillow beside the window. It was the bed she'd decided would be hers when they'd first looked at the room yesterday.

At seven Vie had already discovered that she could almost always get what she wanted. It was a matter of observation and strategy. She couldn't explain it to herself that way, of course, but she was able, as if by instinct, to evaluate situations, pinpoint what she wanted, and then let nothing distract her as she went after it.

What she told herself was, "I'm the most important person in the world. Mama is an angel, and I'm one, too." Saying that made her feel strong, and she didn't mind not having playmates or pretty dresses.

But sometimes being the most important was terrifying, and she'd become petrified by thoughts or images of death. She'd cling to her father, trembling, while he stroked her hair and tried to ease her fears with little songs. She didn't like his doing it, didn't like the way the familiar tunes would keep getting at her until the words and rhythms made her forget the important things she was thinking about. Sometimes Papa didn't understand her, Vie felt.

The picture of her mother that always stood beside his bed interested her only vaguely. A blond woman with eyes laughing into the sun, in a summer dress, sitting in a meadow of lavender. A stranger's face, holding no knowledge of her, Vie's, existence.

She could remember the other woman, though, her stepmother; but she hated to think about her. A dark, angry face, rough movements, shrill voice. Vie remembered being all alone in a jungle, wild animals coming to eat her, their faces the same as that woman's. It was fuzzy but real, and Vie hated it when her thoughts started moving back to certain places, because she'd feel like crying.

She knew that mothers were strange. They died or ran off screaming, and they didn't like little girls. Papa loved her, Vie knew, but she didn't feel safe.

Frances Murphy stood at the door of their room. "Is everything all right, girls?" she asked nervously, blinking at them.

"Yes," said Vie, without looking up.

Martine didn't answer. She was making her stuffed animals fight each other. She preferred the panda, and it always won.

Frances moved on to Armand's room while the panda and tiger pounded each other viciously. Martine urged them on with fierce little cries. Suddenly she lost interest, and the toys fell to the floor. She didn't notice; absorbed now by an image only she could see, she stared straight ahead. Vie picked up the panda and hid it under her own bed.

Silence in the children's room relieved Armand as he continued to unpack.

"Anything I can get you?" asked Frances.

He noticed that her hair was teased. The fragrance she had on—for his sake, he suspected—was a cheap gardenia smell that brought a funereal aroma to the room. "Thank you, no," he said. He didn't want her hovering, examining each item as he brought it out. Some things were private, and one or two almost sacred.

"You are most kind, dear lady. You have more important things to be doing. I shall not be long, and afterward perhaps you will allow me to bring a bottle of wine to your parlor, and we shall drink to health and good fortune in your house."

She nodded, pliant with happiness, and left the room. Probably to splash on more gardenia, he thought spitefully.

How long would it take to get a job? Armand wondered, noticing as he put it away that his best shirt was frayed at the collar. If the situation became desperate, he'd be forced to look up old contacts from before the war. Twelve years ago. It would be hard to track them down, and even now, even in America, it could be a deadly risk. Better to start again in a lowly position, tell no one who he was, and trust that his gifts would shine forth, lighting his way back to the top of the profession.

It would take time, and the girls needed someone to look after them. An English nanny, a French governess would be more appropriate, he thought ruefully, but for the moment there's only this Mrs. Murphy. He was glad he'd had the foresight to pack a bottle of sparkling wine.

Armand locked up the suitcase, empty of everything except his most important possession, took the wine by its neck, and went downstairs, telling the girls to be good.

Martine couldn't find her panda anywhere and was becoming frantic. Vie, lying on her bed, was pretending to read.

"Panda!" Martine wailed. Vie took no notice.

"You awful!" Martine screamed. "You nasty!"

"Don't call me that. Shut up."

"No! You shut up."

Vie got off the bed slowly, advancing toward her sister. "You want that stupid panda? Crybaby, crybaby."

"I'm not!"

"Crybaby, crybaby," Vie taunted. "Stick your head in gravy."

Martine leaped at her and began pulling her hair.

"Stop that!" Vie shouted, hitting her on the side of the face. "Brat!"

With her teeth Martine grabbed a piece of Vie's upper arm and bit down with all her might. Vie went on hitting her but couldn't loosen the hold. She felt she'd soon start crying from the pain, and she hated to cry. Martine's eyes were shining, her face flushed as she held on, ignoring the blows, biting down as hard as she could.

"Stop!" Vie begged when she couldn't stand it any longer. Her eyes were unbearably hot, aching for tears. "Please, please. It hurts. Stop!"

Martine bit harder.

"I'll give it to you, I'll get your panda, please stop."

Martine let go her hold. The drops of blood high up on Vie's arm outlined the teeth marks. "Panda," demanded Martine.

Vie couldn't help crying now that it was over. She got the panda out from under her bed. Martine grabbed for it, but Vie was stronger and held on to the animal. She felt humiliated by her tears.

"Mine!" shouted Martine, lunging again.

"You love it. You love your stupid panda," Vie accused her. She took the panda's arm and pulled on it as hard as she could. Her eyes and nose were streaming, and she hated Martine for seeing her like this, for doing this to her when she was only a four-year-old.

The arm remained firmly attached to the panda's trunk. Martine caught hold of a leg. As she tugged at her toy, Vie moved back abruptly and the seam loosened. Martine yanked the leg from its socket and fell back onto the floor, the torn-off limb in both her hands. She screamed in shock.

Vie, holding the trunk, began to pull out the stuffing, reaching inside to tear away the plush until the animal was hollowed out, its insides scattered over the floor in clumps.

Martine stared with horror, picked herself up and ran out the door screaming. Vie followed her out into the hallway, close behind her down the stairs. When Martine ran into the scallop shell, Vie stumbled over her.

The adults heard a crash and came running. They found the girls on the floor lying among the smooth white shards of ceramic. The children looked up at them with frightened expressions, but neither girl was crying, and their cuts appeared minor.

Armand helped Vie up, then Martine. He was about to begin scolding her, but stopped when he saw the expression on Vie's face.

She looked happy, as though she'd accomplished something. He heard Frances Murphy's woeful cries behind him and gave Vie a little smile of complicity. This would remain their secret: the hideous scallop was rightly destroyed. It made the house a bit more bearable. Ugliness should be eliminated.

Vie stood like a miniature queen, surveying the ruins. She was so like him, Armand thought, as self-assured as he once was, before the world crashed around him.

II

FRANCE

1

1921–1931

Armand had always felt he'd be a perfumer. By the time he was thirteen, he was sure. Seeing his father work at the perfumer's bench, inhaling the aromas that would blend in the final composition, Armand became inspired and eager to begin experimenting with them himself. Most ingredients were too expensive or rare, but Armand begged spices from his mother and gathered armloads of wildflowers. He placed the petals on glass trays he'd first covered with fat, leaving the petals there until the oils in them had been absorbed by the fat. He used the resulting pomade as though it were an essential oil.

Armand's father, Maurice, was touched by his young son's attempt at enfleurage, an ancient process for extracting flower oils. He gave the boy lessons on the history and nature of perfume making. More important to Armand was his father's occasional gift of samples of animal fixatives and essential oils. He experimented with these, combining them with cinnamon, fresh mint, and rind of lemons—anything at all that gave off a distinctive aroma. His dream was to someday accomplish in fragrances what Mozart had done in music.

He'd had such dreams even as a younger child. They hardened in 1921, just before his fourteenth birthday, when *Chanel No. 5* was launched.

What would become the world's most famous perfume caused an immediate sensation when it first appeared. The golden fluid in a simple container beckoned like a magic potion. Its name, a stark numeral, resonated in the unconscious, suggesting mystery. The staying power of the scent had never been formulated before.

Until 1921 women, and men also, had to douse themselves in fragrance, reeking strongly at the beginning of the evening, if they hoped to retain even a lingering scent later on. Chanel's stable formula incorporated aldehydes, volatile organic compounds; reacting with other ingredients in the fragrance base, they allowed the wearer to apply just a dab of perfume and depend on the scent to last for hours.

In addition, *No. 5* was the first perfume to move away from purely floral scents. No longer did a woman have to choose between smelling like a rose, jasmine, or heliotrope if she used scent. The new formula was more subtle, an elusive accord that lent its user desirability and mystery.

The perfume was formulated in Grasse, France's—and therefore the world's—center of perfumery. Gabrielle Chanel had commissioned it as an accessory, like her long ropes of pearls, or cloche hats, to set off the simplicity of the clothes she designed. The chemists in Grasse gave her five samples. With the help of Maurice Jolaunay, her consulting chemist at 31, rue Chambron in Paris, she selected the one that would become *No. 5*.

Maurice had been working at Guerlain when Chanel spotted him, handsome and slightly unkempt, his mustache in evident need of a barber's attentions. "Are you a bohemian?" she asked him.

He shook his head, coloring slightly. "Then you will be my stable groom," she announced. Through inquiries Chanel had learned enough about him to know she wanted to lure him from Guerlain's stable to her own. And Mademoiselle, as she was always called, had never wanted anything she didn't eventually get.

Jolaunay was a prize. The family he came from had been perfumers for centuries, since the reign of Charles VII in the fifteenth century, when they'd received the perfumers' arms. In the seventeenth a Jolaunay made perfumes for Louis XIV and his court.

The diminutive ruler of fashion took delight in astounding Maurice with her knowledge. She deliberately set out to flatter him by being able to recite his family history.

"And Claude, your great-grandfather, was perfumer to Napoleon and Josephine," she finished triumphantly, looking fixedly at him from across her desk.

He blinked at her, shaking his head in admiration.

She flashed him a wide smile. "But you must tell me the rest. After Claude, the déluge, hein? We hear no more about the Jolaunays of the golden nose."

Maurice patted his mustache for comfort. "Claude Jolaunay was the first among my ancestors to establish his own parfumerie. He was to die in it when the shop caught fire. Some say the fire was set by his rival, Guy Montalmont." Maurice shrugged. "I cannot say. But for two generations the nose was retired, until my father—"

"Became chief chemist at Guerlain," supplied Chanel. "And you were his apprentice, no?"

"That's correct, madame."

"I am Mademoiselle," she said with a stern look. "There is only one. That is how you must address me, Maurice. I will pay you two times whatever it is you're getting from Guerlain, and you will work for me."

It was a command; he was not asked, simply told. "Your great-grandfather," she said, "was working to develop a perfume of floral essences combined with an organic compound which was to retard oxidation and make the scent last longer. Am I not right?" she crowed.

"Absolutely, madame—I mean, Mademoiselle."

"You have the formula?"

"Almost. That is, I am not sure that we have the original, but we do own a formula for such a perfume compound."

"Excellent! You begin work for me tomorrow."

"But . . ."

Her small hand waved away his interjection. "You need an apprentice? Have you a son?"

He smiled at the tiny, fierce woman who looked like a girl. "He is only thirteen. I must wait a few years."

"Good. You may take him on when he's ready. Adieu, Maurice." She gave him a strong handshake. "We shall set the world spinning on its nose, hein?"

Barely a year later they did just that, with *Chanel No. 5.*

*　　*　　*

In 1924, the year of Chanel's leathery-toned *Cuir de Russie*, Maurice called his son into the study to talk about his future. Armand was tall for his age, with ruffian good looks that women were beginning to notice.

"Another year and you will have your bac," said Maurice. "Then you will come to work for me and Mademoiselle Chanel."

"Yes, Papa," said Armand dutifully, tugging at the lapel of his schoolboy's jacket. He didn't want to work for his father. Not because he didn't like the idea of perfume; on the contrary, all he wanted was to work at the perfumer's organ, choosing from the vials that were its pipes one ingredient after another, blending these "notes" into a harmonious "accord," the perfumer's word for a composition of fragrances.

He knew that the only way to his goal was through apprenticeship, and yet the prospect of working for his father dismayed him. He'd visited 31, rue Chambron and had seen that his father's position was similar to that of a headwaiter or a butler—someone who could exert influence but was never entitled to take initiative.

"You understand that it is a great honor," Maurice said to his son. "Chanel is perhaps the most important maison de couture in Paris, or the world."

"Yes, Papa, but she is not a nose."

"Watch what you say! There are thousands who would jump at the chance."

"Perhaps, Papa, but they do not have my talent."

"Insufferable boy! Leave this room and mend your attitude! No more insolence from you!"

"Yes, Papa." He backed out of the study.

The following year, on schedule, he came to work at Chanel, in the expanded lab of his father. He was remarkably adept. Within weeks it became apparent to everyone who worked with him that the boy had inherited "the nose." Maurice felt pride in his son's sense of smell, which he readily acknowledged to be even finer than his own. A visiting chemist who spent an hour with Armand at the organ called him Stradivarius because his discrimination at the workbench was so refined.

After the first six months of apprenticeship Armand was

sent to supplement his natural ability with technical knowledge of scientific methods. He attended courses at the Polytechnique in addition to working a full day at the lab.

During his second year at Chanel he was permitted to sit in while Mademoiselle and his father conferred. That year, she brought two new fragrances on the market— *Bois des iles* and *No. 22*; the first woody, the second floral.

Mademoiselle liked to tease Armand about his emerging handsomeness. "Mon petit civet," she called him, "My little civet cat." He knew, by the way she smiled and opened her eyes wide when she saw him, that she was fond of him and that the term was an endearment. But it made him uncomfortable to be called civet by a woman older than his mother. Civet, one of the valuable animal fixatives, was taken from a pouch near the sexual organs of civet cats and gave off a musky, erotic odor. He remembered becoming embarrassingly aroused once in the lab while sniffing it.

But he couldn't think of Coco Chanel in those terms, even though her love affairs were common knowledge and added the tantalizing whiff of scandal to her image. Her current lover, the Duke of Westminster, was rumored to be the richest man in England. Armand knew some of the fabulous stories: emeralds sent in the bottom of a grocery hamper, orchids arriving out of season, Scotch salmon dispatched by private couriers. Chanel was a legend whose private life brought additional spice to the paprika personality who'd gone from convent girl to autocrat of fashion, acclaimed throughout Europe and even in America. To Armand, entering his twenties, her amorous adventures were nothing compared to her extraordinary independence, her freedom to design what she liked and to dictate to a waiting world.

He dreamed of doing the same. She became the model for him that Maurice could never be. Armand had long ago evaluated his father as someone who would always remain an employee, most content in a world controlled by others, where he had duties and a sense of safety. Armand's mother was more adventuresome in spirit. But she had no outstanding talent and, obeying the dictate of middle-class society to stay at home, she did no more than invent unusual meals and, to Armand's dismayed discovery, take lovers that Maurice never learned about.

His father sensed that Armand didn't admire him enough and became stricter and more critical of his son. When he found him idle for even a moment, he pounced. "Out, out of the clouds. You are not here to make daydreams."

Armand was thinking of his ancestor Claude, the only entrepreneur among the Jolaunays. Why not himself? He had the skills.

For the past three years Armand had been leaving the house an hour earlier than Maurice every morning. He enjoyed the luxury of being alone and of not having to rush. Often, strolling down the Boulevard on the way to rue Chambron, he let himself imagine that the future was already present, and he was now walking toward his own perfumery. The happiness on his face attracted the women he passed, and lowered lashes, frank stares, slow blushes would add up to a dozen or more feminine tributes by the time he arrived at work.

He noticed every one, and what clothes the women were wearing, how their hair was styled. But mainly he was aware of their scent, distinctive with each woman, regardless of whether the smell was her own or one she had dabbed on.

On an autumnal Tuesday in 1931, spiced lightly with cold and the aroma of roasting chestnuts, Armand took his time, smiling at a pretty girl whose coat was too thin for the roughening weather. Soon, he thought, she'd be in furs.

He arrived at the lab in a happy mood, removed his outer clothing, and put on the white smock. Then he set to work on his current task of translating a perfume compound into a formula more suitable for toilet water. It was close to noon when he was interrupted.

Maurice came into Armand's section of the lab holding out two pieces of impregnated blotting paper. "Tell me what you think."

Armand looked at him, surprised and a bit uneasy. Why was Maurice so unaccustomedly asking *his* opinion? Was it a test of some kind?

He sniffed each paper, then returned to the first. "Too intense," he said. "It would overwhelm anyone who wore it." The second was more subtle, leading with oriental notes, a pale reminder of Guerlain's *Shalimar*. "It lacks a clear motif," he told his father. "It's top-heavy, needs more body, and I can hardly detect the sillage." Without that—the lingering scent—no perfume could be considered important.

"Nonsense," said Maurice. "You are hypercritical. With the first you may have a point, but the second is good. You think faultfinding is a sign of sophistication."

"Neither of them works," Armand insisted.

"Stubbornness, that will be your downfall. I should know of what I speak, I have a lifetime's experience," he said, drawing himself up to his full height, an inch and a half less than Armand's.

"And I have the evidence of my senses," Armand answered angrily.

Maurice was about to deliver a withering retort when Chanel strode into the room with a horsewoman's gait. "Good day, gentlemen," she said in English.

Maurice kissed her hand. "You must do something about that mustache of yours," she told him affectionately. "It scratches horribly. How are you, little civet? You're looking like a rain cloud. Never mind, I have only a moment. Bring out the samples you have for me."

Maurice brought three: those Armand had just criticized and one devised earlier, with a green topnote. "Not bad," she said, "quite fresh. But too young for me, I think. It's for girls, not women. Still, play with it and bring it back to me."

"Yes, Mademoiselle."

"Now this one is impossibly heavy, like being smothered in a velvet drape. This—perhaps. No, wait—as I'm smelling it, the scent disappears. Poof! This is skywriting, no substance to it."

"As you say, Mademoiselle. We will try again." Watching his father's discomfort gave Armand no pleasure.

"I want," said Chanel, "something with the freshness of the first, but heavier. For a woman who wears a redingote:

frank, natural; at the same time it must have authority. Give me an empress on horseback," she ordered, laughing.

"How poetically you put it!" cooed Maurice.

"*L'Air d'Écosse*," Armand suggested, knowing that Chanel loved riding to hounds in Scotland.

"Bravo! Too bad you are not older, or rich," she told him flirtatiously. "Au revoir, then, gentlemen, à bientôt." She cantered out.

Maurice whirled around to Armand. "Back to the workbench. We will stay late tonight."

"No, Father. It is better to start fresh in the morning."

"I say now! And you do as I say!"

"I will not!" A moment ago, his father had been bleating like a little lamb. Now his roars sounded like nothing more than wind. Armand tore off his apron.

"You work until I dismiss you!" shouted his father. "We stay here until midnight."

"You don't understand," Armand said evenly. "I'm leaving. Not for the day. I'm leaving to go out on my own. I am not working for you any longer."

"You are insane."

"I've thought about it for a very long time. You know as well as I that a Jolaunay nose is worth a fortune—yet only once did a Jolaunay dare to work for himself. Why? Why didn't you try to set up your own shop?"

Maurice's face was dead white. "Child. Madman. You've been apprenticed for six years, and you think you know everything."

Armand abandoned the appeal he was making to his father. "I know this: that I have a strange gift, something like an alchemist's, and with it I can transform basic oils into the gold of perfume."

Maurice was trembling with anger. "And who will pay for your 'alchemy'?" he shouted. "Who will you find to subsidize your craziness? Not me, not a cent from me. And don't try crying in your mother's lap, either. I'll never give you anything. You have disgraced me."

"I wouldn't accept anything from you," Armand said, tight with fury. "You'll see, I'll do it, and a time may come when you ask *me* for employment."

He saw he'd gone too far. He realized, too, that Maurice

would have to face Chanel's anger on his own. She was a
jealous ruler, who didn't tolerate defection. Her stable
belonged to her until she decided otherwise.

Armand let a few minutes go by, to soften the harsh
exchange. Maurice was still shaking. "Papa . . ." Armand
began tentatively.

"No! You will not call me that. Since you are leaving,
go. And find yourself a place to live. You are not welcome
in my house any longer."

"As you say." Still he waited, hoping for a reconcilia-
tion or, at least, truce. "My intention is not to hurt you or
Maman," he said sincerely. "Please, try to understand. I
must have the chance. If it comes to nothing, I will start
at the bottom again. But if I succeed, the world will know
the name of Jolaunay!"

"Armand," said his father in a gentler tone. "You know
nothing of business. You have extraordinary ability, yes—
greater than my own. But this is Paris, the fashion center
of the world, a city of capital and power, where a young
man like you can't hope to succeed without money or
patronage."

"I *must* try."

Maurice turned his back and said gruffly, "Go then."
But his voice was no longer angry.

Armand rented a tiny apartment on a small street in
Montmartre, between the Sacré-Cœur and Place Pigalle. It
was a mistake. Though the quartier was lively and colorful,
he learned quickly that it was totally unsuitable for him.
Bearded artists with berets, chanteuses and leggy show
girls straggling home at dawn, pushcarts piled with fruits
and vegetables making their way past hennaed prostitutes
standing with black silk-stockinged legs apart—this was
Montmartre. Here Toulouse-Lautrec had found his subjects,
and the narrow streets provided material for Utrillo's
brush, but to a man hoping to embark on a business
intended for the rich and powerful, Montmartre offered as
much opportunity as the cemetery of Père-Lachaise.

Forfeiting two months' rent, an act that made his landlady stare with hostility, Armand found more appropriate
though duller lodgings on the Boulevard Haussmann,
within walking distance of the Place Vendôme and the rue

Chambron. It was November, and his savings were down to
pocket money. The only luxury he allowed himself was
breakfast at a small café-tabac near his apartment, where
he ordered a petit pain and café au lait, occasionally a
croissant or a brioche. Other meals—snacks, really—he
took at home or while walking along the street: bread and
a piece of fruit, sometimes cheese or a cheap rilette made
with chunks of pork.

The city was cold, his room colder. But Armand was
twenty-four, in love with life and his own expectations.
Just being on the streets excited him: the warm smell of
freshly baked bread, the clean printers' ink on newspapers,
men puffing on Gauloises, the shoeshine boy's saddle soap,
ladies in their furs suffused in fragrance. Sometimes he
followed them; sometimes he struck up an acquaintance.

He was young, ladies found him charming, and he was
sure of his talent. The world was waiting for him; all he
needed was money.

The owner of the café-tabac offered him a job waiting
on tables. Since there were only four, Armand also washed
dishes, cleaned the floors, and went on errands. His salary
was tiny, tips were virtually nonexistent, but he often
received a meal there and a few glasses of wine.

His earnings provided for survival, nothing more. Three
weeks before Christmas a habitué of the café offered Armand a source of income by delivering packages. From
then on he began work before six o'clock in the morning,
making deliveries until noon, when he came to the café
for another ten hours' work.

Two days before Christmas, bleary with fatigue, he felt
overcome. His legs barely held him up. For the first time
since leaving home he was depressed, particularly if he
thought of Christmas Eve, when he'd be alone. The holiday spirit had penetrated the café, where old customers,
who counted out their centimes when they paid the check
throughout the year, were now ordering the best brandies.

Bringing out a tray of Armagnacs, Armand was hailed
by a voice from the past. "Jolaunay! Could it be you?"

Newly seated at the window table, plump and smiling,
with dimples in either cheek and a snub nose over a fair,

thin mustache was a man who could still carry off his old nickname of Putto, a Renaissance cherub.

"Pierre Du Près!" Armand served the brandies quickly and rushed over to embrace his old school friend, a cabinetmaker and the son of one.

Putto kissed him on both cheeks, pummeling his back. Then he held him at arm's length. "Mon pauvre gars! How you look! What has happened to you—you, the splendid Jolaunay, jewel of the lycée, our brilliant boy snatched up into the empyrean of Chanel?"

Armand laughed and hugged his friend again. He realized he hadn't laughed in weeks, and a great relief swept through him, clearing out the fatigue. He took a seat and recited his history, finishing by explaining his reasons for leaving Chanel and his determination to make perfumes of his own.

"Bravo!" said Pierre when he'd finished. "A new Chanel in the making! Younger, much taller, and a different sex, of course, who doesn't have the advantage of turning bedfellows into patrons. . . ."

"That's not fair!" Armand defended her. "She is a genius!"

"Yes, yes," Pierre agreed smiling. "Not to attack the lady's honor. But you are a genius, too, are you not? Of course. So where, then, is the duchess who provides you with a yacht and buys you a perfume shop?"

"I wish you'd find her for me, Putto. She seems to be hiding, though I've looked everywhere." He grinned, feeling tremendously cheered by his friend's banter.

When the owner called Armand back to work, Pierre grabbed him by the sleeve. "You may not go," he said, "until you give me your solemn promise to spend Christmas with us. It will make my parents very happy. They have always held you up as a shining example of the Republic. So much so, in fact, that I've been forced to point out to them that you are not Joan of Arc."

With a quick embrace Armand left him, promising to be there Christmas Eve.

The goose, with its chestnut stuffing, was so good that it brought tears to his eyes. This was the first time Armand had sat down to a family meal since being disinherited.

Madame Du Près refilled his plate, and Monsieur poured more of the La Tache into his glass. The wine was voluptuous, deep garnet, with a full body that lingered in a musky aftertaste. "If I could make a perfume as sensual, as harmonious as this wine," Armand said, "the world would be on its knees before me."

"A pretty sight," said Madame Du Près, laughing. "A sacrilegious thought for Noël."

"Forgive me," he said hastily, but Madame placed her hand on his arm and was smiling at him with affection.

"You make that perfume," said Pierre, "and I'll drink it."

In boisterous spirits they continued the feast. In addition to Armand, the guests were Pierre's sister, her husband, and two delightful children; an eccentric old aunt with an ear trumpet and sapphires blazing at her throat; an old gentleman who never spoke but smiled throughout; and a middle-aged bachelor who was referred to as The Philosopher and who quoted from Voltaire, Kant, and Hegel.

When they finished, Pierre's mother lighted the candles on the tree, and the children were given their presents. Afterward, happy and protesting, they were carried up to bed by their parents, whose return twenty minutes later signaled the time to go to mass.

In the church they sang hymns and carols. A group of schoolgirls, dressed all in white, came slowly down the aisle carrying lighted candles toward the nativity scene at the altar. In high voices, they sang.

> *Un flambeau, Jeanette, Isabel-le,*
> *Un flambeau, courons au berceau. . . .*

When they'd come to the end and picked up the song again, the congregation joined in.

> *. . . C'est Jésus, bon gens du hameau,*
> *Au moindre bruit, Jésus s'eveille. . . .*

Armand felt the wonder, the miracle. His heart was full and suffused with light.

When mass was over, they hurried out into the cold, back to the warm house with a fire blazing in the fireplace, the candles burning on the tree.

Monsieur Du Près poured pale old cognac from a crystal decanter and also offered vintage port to anyone who wished to celebrate Christmas "à l'anglais."

The adults now brought out their presents for each other. Armand was nervous about his offering. Lacking money for a fine gift, he'd concocted scents for each member of the family, labeling the small store bottles with "Madame," "Monsieur," "Putto," and "Claire," Pierre's sister. He hadn't known there would be other guests and apologized to them. Each had brought him a small token—candied fruit from the aunt, cigars from The Philosopher, a print of the Battle of Waterloo from the smiling old gentleman. They all assured him it was nothing, and Armand felt like a spoiled, happy boy in the bosom of a family.

Armand gave his present to Madame first.

"Fantastique!" she exclaimed, sniffing and dabbing it immediately behind her ears. "You are a psychologist! The perfume—c'est moi!"

"Extraordinaire," said her husband, smelling his private cologne and looking thoughtful. Claire kissed Armand on both cheeks and said that he understood her like a brother, while Putto simply grinned with pride.

"That is for you," he told Armand, pointing to an immense package near the tree. "It comes from all of us. Open carefully, please."

Armand gave him a questioning look and then began to undo the wrapping. Underneath he found clouds of tissue paper. He parted them with care, and gasped. Before him stood a miniature amphitheater in dark cherry wood, with perhaps a hundred small glass bottles held in four tiers, a perfumer's organ. Pierre and his father must have worked on it night and day to finish in time. It stood gleaming, the polished wood and glass catching glints from the candlelight. Armand knelt before it, weeping like a child.

"Come now," said Monsieur Du Près, pleased and embarrassed. "It's nothing. Take your cognac and come along with me." He signaled Pierre to follow them.

Armand didn't understand why they were leaving the others, but he went along to the workroom. Monsieur closed the door behind them. "We have something to talk

over with you," he said. "Pierre and I have discussed it,
and the presents you gave us tonight have convinced us
absolutely. We believe in you, in your talent, and we want
to invest in you."

Armand could think of nothing to say.

"My father and I," Pierre assured him, "have been very
fortunate this past year in our work. We've been able to
accumulate some capital. . . ."

"You are too good!" Armand blurted out.

"Not good, practical. We want to see our capital grow,
so we have decided to invest wisely. You cannot make
perfume out of air—though who knows? You probably
can do even that."

"In any case," Monsieur interrupted, in a businesslike
tone, "would ten thousand francs help you to purchase the
ingredients?"

"Ten thousand! But . . ."

"Settled. Now let's go back for another nip."

They returned to the warm room and, in the early hours
of Christmas Day, raised their glasses to toast the birth of
the enterprise.

2

1932–1942

During the twelve days between Christmas and Epiphany,
on January 6, the pace of Paris turned sluggish as its
fashionable residents recuperated in the soothing air of
the Côte d'Azur after the rigors of dress fittings and hair
appointments. In the stores, stocks were depleted after
Christmas buying. Shopkeepers kept lackadaisical hours,
and Armand couldn't impress anyone with his need for
haste. He waited impatiently for his order from Grasse

while continuing to work at the cafe and spending his free hours transforming his room into a laboratory.

When his supplies finally arrived, he was like a race-horse at the starting gate. Except for his afternoon hours at the cafe, and snatches of exhilarated, dream-filled sleep, he charged ahead on his plotted course.

First he analyzed perfumes already on the market. He'd done some of this at Chanel, but mainly to disqualify them. Now he tried to dissect the scent in finest detail, identifying each ingredient, even if it was only a soupçon of essential oil, animal fixative, or synthetic material. Usually it was impossible to derive the exact formula of the original compound before distillation, but Armand noted down his educated guesses in a black leather-bound book which he referred to as his bible.

Analysis, though interesting, was simply "foundation work," essential to his smell education but with none of the exhilaration that came when he was experimenting on his own. Sometimes he'd devise a fragrance that was rich, various, elusive, and he wanted to run into the street and stop each passerby with the news. But two hours later the scent had changed drastically or vanished. He thought of Chanel's "skywriting," and he knew he still had a long way to go before he produced a stable perfume.

Sometimes he lacked a particular ingredient, like guaiac-wood or ylang-ylang, without which he couldn't express the ephemeral character of the scent he had in mind. Then he'd send in a new order and return to foundation work while he waited helplessly.

More than a year went by before Armand formulated his first perfume, *Nuits Blanches*. Mme. Du Près gave it the name, inspired by her reading of Pushkin's stories set in Petrograd's white nights. She also suggested to Armand that he package the scent in a delicate white glass bottle with a silver stopper. "A woman," she told him, "likes to handle pretty objects. When she goes to her dressing table, each woman feels like a queen. She sits down to the important work of making herself more beautiful. In that moment she is not vain at all, she is serious. She is at work. When she reaches for her powder or her perfume, it must be in a beautiful container. That's part of the magic.

The beauty of the object will transfer itself to the user. *She* will become more beautiful."

It was a lesson Armand never forgot.

He was able to sell a few dozen bottles to parfumeries in the most elegant sections of Paris. Most orders were renewed, a few increased, and Armand hired an assistant to help with *Nuits Blanches* while he worked on a new formula.

In 1934 he created *Âme*, based on strong oriental notes. The perfume was contained in a small bowl, reminiscent of the designs of René Lalique, a stunning black lacquer etched with gold, the outer form as wonderful as the soul—âme—within.

He rented a small servant's room in the building as his bedroom, and another room next to the lab which became his shop. The Du Près' designed it and made all the furniture, for which Armand insisted on paying full price. The pieces were solid, graceful, and gleaming. The delicate white bottles and the exotic black gold bowls that stood everywhere around the room complemented each other like innocence and experience.

Engraved invitations were sent a month in advance. Mme. Du Près ordered a new dress; Armand's mother, delighted to be invited, sewed a new lace ruffle on her navy blue silk. The Moët & Chandon was ordered. Armand lived in a sleepless daze, awaiting his shop's grand opening.

It went flat. Though Claire waltzed in wearing a pale-green creation of Madeleine Vionnet, she represented the high fashion point of the evening. Suppliers and shopgirls turned up. The owner of the café-tabac downed five glasses of champagne in happy succession. Armand's mother embraced him sympathetically. It was painfully apparent that no one from the haute monde had deigned to accept Armand's invitation. There was not a person at the party who could help him in launching Parfums de Jolaunay.

The people were beginning to leave when Maurice arrived, alone. He stood near the door, fingering his mustache and looking around at the guests. When Armand came over to him, Maurice said quietly, "I expect you'll be looking for a job soon."

Armand had no answer.

* * *

He gave himself until summer before accepting defeat. Two weeks after the opening the Baronne de Vincennes appeared in his shop, accompanied by a frail woman who appeared to be her companion or maid. The Baronne was of an uncertain but advanced age, heavily rouged and apparently drowning in her voluminous clothes. She surveyed the room like an eagle, pounced on a bottle of *Âme*, and declared, "Pretty." Without smelling it, she asked for three bottles and indicated to the smaller woman that she should pay.

The Baronne de Vincennes was fabulously rich, a well-known hostess, and the mother of a cabinet minister. Unfortunately, as Armand discovered, the grand lady was anosmic: she could smell almost nothing at all.

It was ludicrous. Still, she might recommend him to friends, at least on the basis of his containers, Armand thought ruefully. But no more aristocrats came to his shop. He was forced to give notice to his assistant. Money had run out once again, and Armand had still not fully repaid what he considered his debt to the Du Près'. He himself would have to look for work, as Maurice had predicted. In six more weeks it would be summer, when annual closings in all of Paris would mean the end of Armand's venture.

In June two smart young ladies came into the shop. The prettier one, with large yellow eyes like a cat's, smiled coquettishly at Armand and asked to buy a bottle of *Âme*. "My great-aunt, the Baronne de Vincennes, gave me a bottle for my name day," she told him in a charming, breathy voice. "I a-dore it, simply heaven."

When he sold her the bottle, she looked up at him through thick, pale lashes and said, "Don't you forget me, now. I'll be back soon. Toodle-oo." She waved at him while skittering out.

True to her word, the Baronne's grandniece returned a few days later, accompanied by a bevy of chattering young women almost as pretty as herself. They all bought *Âme*, and a few of them also took a bottle or two of *Nuits Blanches*. They kept their eyes on him, and he could hear their comments as they appraised him. "Mignon," said one, "he's cute." Another said he would look wonderful on horseback, while the girl with the yellow eyes whispered loudly to a friend that he was "a savage inside—wild and uncontrollable." Armand gave no indication that he heard any of this, but he was flattered, and amazed at the thought that his looks, and not his products, could attract customers.

On Thursday of that week a small, dynamic woman in a large hat came to the shop alone. She had a formidable air, and Armand thought he recognized her from somewhere. Her gaze landed on every object in the room. She picked up a bottle of *Nuits Blanches*, unstoppered it, and sniffed the tiny cork. She looked at *Âme* without touching it. "Excellent design," she said to Armand. "My compliments. The other one is good too." She gave him a large smile and held out her hand. "Happy to make your acquaintance. I am Madame Greco."

He kissed her hand, mumbling, "I am honored, madame." In fact, he couldn't believe it was she. The first time he'd seen a Greco design, he had been stupefied by its elegance.

Mme. Greco designed as from a Greek temple; her dresses were liquid and classically elegant, like a soft, moving column.

"How old are you?" she asked suddenly.

"Twenty-seven."

"I see." She reflected a moment. "Listen to me, I am about to make you a great offer. I know that you worked at Chanel, with your father." Her eyes twinkled. "My spies tell me you left of your own accord."

"That is correct."

"Good. And now I ask you, of your own accord, to come and work with me. You will have your own laboratory and whatever assistants you need. You are free to create what you like; I retain only the power to veto. Your perfumes capture the spirit of my clothes. They will be like the signature to my designs."

He was overwhelmed. That an artist like Greco should recognize him! "You honor me," he told her, "and I hope you will forgive me, but I need time to consider your generous offer."

"But of course. That was part of my calculations. In ten

days you will bring me your answer. No later; we close before Bastille Day. Au revoir, M. Jolaunay."

Pierre urged him to accept. "A fabulous opportunity, a magnificent coup. This woman," he said, "is the duchess you've dreamed of, arriving in a large gray hat. Let her raise you to the skies, place you on her pedestal. . . ."

"On a Greek column, you mean."

"Whatever. Follow her! She's your fate."

Yet something held Armand back. Two days before he was to give her an answer, he still didn't know what it would be.

Customers had been coming into the shop all morning—women en route from hairdressers, dressmakers, masseuses. Armand's shop was both charming and centrally located, a place to catch one's breath in perfumed surroundings.

The women flirted playfully with Armand and chatted together, each woman investing abundantly in compliments to the others in hopes of receiving flattering returns. Most were users of Jolaunay perfumes, but bottles lasted a long time, and there were many occasions—birthday, name day, Christmas, the opening of the opera—for their husbands or lovers to present them with fresh supplies. The women themselves rarely bought anything when they came to the shop.

Sales were steady, but not impressive enough for security. Armand knew that his independence was precarious. Going in with Mme. Greco would assure him income and a place in the world of fashion. Nevertheless, he wavered between the logical choice and his desire to do it alone.

At lunchtime the women deserted his shop for their rendezvous, giving him airy kisses and flutters of gloved hands as they left. Only one woman remained, someone he hadn't noticed before, in a mannish suit and a hat with a veil. He watched her now as she went over to a bottle of *Âme*, picked it up, and withdrew the stopper.

When she lifted her veil to smell the perfume, Armand drew in his breath quickly. He knew that woman. It seemed he had known her face a long time and memorized it. But from where? When? Had he dreamed her? She was almost too beautiful to be real.

She returned the stopper to the bottle and replaced her veil, striding softly toward him.

The puzzle came together, and Armand felt himself blushing like a child. In front of him was Garbo.

Armand bowed but didn't dare kiss the hand held out to him. He made change for the large banknote, bowing again as he gave it to her. He escorted her to the door, and she turned a moment, held up her veil and smiled. Then she was gone. Not a word had passed between them.

He stood looking after her. Garbo, the eternal female, the mysterious woman, had stepped out of legend and come to his shop. It was a sign. Armand knew he would follow his own dream.

By 1935 a trip to Paris was incomplete without a stop at Armand's "enchanting little salon," as it was known. La Maison de Jolaunay became a haunt for the rich and powerful. The Duchess of Windsor told friends how cozy and tasteful it was, one of her absolutely favorite spots across the Channel, where you inevitably ran into someone of your own set.

Though Armand distributed perfume to a number of select stores, many of his customers preferred to buy in the intimate exclusivity of his shop, where they could be protected from the curious and the common folk. He had expanded into two adjacent rooms, which he furnished in the same style as the original one. Next to the shop he retained the small lab, used solely for research and experiments. Orders for his fragrances were filled in a factory to the north, at Clichy, where chemists made up the bases and distillations according to formula.

Coffee and petits fours were served in the shop throughout the day. The latest fashion magazines lay on low rosewood tables. Three afternoons a week young models or actresses walked, and sometimes danced, through the rooms, wearing creations by hopeful new designers, to whom Armand offered his salon as a showcase.

It was an exciting place to be, and customers had the sense that fashion was being made before their eyes. It was also safe and respectable. The Princess Royal called it "my club in Paris," and the concept stuck with British customers.

Armand worked on improving his English, to better converse with some of his regulars. American clients were particularly charmed by his speech. "If my poodle could speak," Jean Harlow told a journalist, "he'd sound like Armand Jolaunay."

That quote appeared in an article in *Harper's Bazaar*, where Armand was described as "the young prince of fashion" who possessed the perfumer's rare gift of a "golden nose," and whose "silver eyes" were shown in close-up. After the article came out, he received fan mail and love letters from romantic American housewives, some of whom offered their services; others, their hand in marriage.

Not to be outdone, American *Vogue* sent a photographer to the salon to shoot models in bathing suits. They were, said the text, "veiled mysteriously in Jolaunay fragrance." The point was made: perfume had become fashion, and no well-dressed woman could be without it, even on the beach.

Rumors of Armand's love life were constant. He arrived at the opening of the Paris opera with a stunning auburn-haired singer wrapped in black broadtail. Was she the one? A week later he was seen at Deauville with a handsome, though slightly mannish, novelist who owned a racing stable. To the New Year's party given by the Countess of Moët & Chandon in her château at Épernay, Armand brought a statuesque woman of such dazzling blondness that she was dubbed The Viking Queen.

People talked about him, and stories of the salon circulated through Parisian society. The account of the Shah's visit was a particular favorite.

When the Shah of Persia arrived early one afternoon with his retinue of twenty-seven, he demanded to buy up Armand's entire stock. Armand bowed deeply but refused, saying that he needed to keep enough on hand for his regular customers. "But if you care to wait a few weeks, Your Majesty, I shall have an order made up for you, of however many bottles you wish."

"To wait?" His Majesty repeated disbelievingly.

A bearded minister stepped up and handed Armand a small silver cask filled with emeralds.

But Armand declined the bribe, insisting that he was obligated to his customers.

His Majesty then pointed to one of the women in his entourage. Her skin was a pale coffee cream, her eyes midnight blue. "Take her," said the Shah, pushing her forward with a slight prod.

"I cannot, Your Majesty," answered Armand.

The Shah glared and left with his company.

Armand was more celebrated than ever after that incident. And when he received the telegram from Teheran asking for two thousand bottles each of everything he made, his devotees roared with delight.

Soon after the outbreak of war in September 1939, many businesses closed their doors. Exempted from the draft because of his hearing loss, Armand kept his factory running and continued to serve coffee and cakes in his salon. Foreigners, landlocked in their respective countries, no longer assembled there, but through the first year his French customers came for refuge against the invaders threatening their country and their way of life.

"I don't understand how you're doing it, old man," said Pierre. They were sharing a bottle of cool white wine at a table outside the Café de la Paix. It was June 1940, more than nine months since the war had started, a month after the Germans had invaded France. The government had defected to Bordeaux, and Paris had been declared an open city. "Everybody else seems to be losing his head or his fortune. Look at your old boss Chanel—she simply locked her doors and took herself to the south."

"She stayed open during the last war," Armand reminded him. "War is dreadful, but it's good for business. *Some* business. Dismal times make people want luxuries more than ever. Do you remember reading of the stock market crash in America?"

"Of course. Men jumping from windows, making little orphans everywhere."

"Right. But the cosmetics empires of Arden and Rubinstein went on prospering. Why? It's carpe diem: live today, for tomorrow you die."

"When the world around her stinks, a woman wants to smell like an untouched flower."

Armand smiled at his friend's aphorism.

Pierre sipped his wine thoughtfully. "As long as the Germans leave Paris alone, we may pull through. I wish I could believe there's a chance for that to happen. Those bloody Boches! They're barbarians. Hitler is a madman. I'm afraid"—his voice dropped and Armand leaned close, watching his lips—"I'm afraid for Maman."

"Is she ill? I hope . . ."

"She is Jewish," he said very softly. "Born Grossmann."

"What difference does it make?" Armand asked. "Many of our leading citizens are Jewish. Look at the Rothschilds—look at every industry in France."

Pierre shook his head, a sad smile on his face. "Old man, you are a wonderful artist. But your nose doesn't let you smell danger. I tell you, if the Germans come here, we are—what is their word?—kaput."

Armand picked up the nearly empty bottle and poured out the remains evenly in both glasses. When he put the bottle back on the table, it exploded. He stared at it, but the bottle was intact. Then he realized that the sound was of doors slamming as people rushed out from the café, and a waiter shouted to them, "It's happened! They're here! The Germans—they've taken Paris!"

"Oh my God," said Pierre, and downed the last sip.

Within a week the city was deserted, or seemed to be. Terrified of what the future might hold in the hands of the Nazis, Parisians closed their houses and shops; many fled.

Armand's parents came to see him at his apartment in the Place Furstemberg. Maurice walked past Georges, the valet, without greeting him. "When do you close?" Maurice asked his son curtly.

"Close?" Armand went to kiss his mother, inhaling her familiar smell of lilacs.

"Of course. Everyone is. The maisons de couture are all shutting down."

"I have no reason to. It would mean throwing people out of work at the factory and the shop."

"You're foolish, Armand," said Maurice in anger. "Your stubbornness will destroy you."

"You said that to me nine years ago, when I left Chanel," Armand told him, "and I've not done badly for myself."

Maurice glowered. "All right, you little cock, crow now. There'll be nothing to crow about in a few months."

"Please," Mme. Jolaunay said softly, holding Armand close to her. "Come with us to my brother's. They have room. You will be most welcome. Take a rest."

"Thank you, Maman." He patted her shoulder. "It's better if I stay." He saw tears come to her eyes and added, "I'm sorry, Maman. I must keep open for the workers. I must see this through."

They left abruptly. "So," said Armand to Georges, "we stay on to hold the fort."

Georges looked at him darkly. "No parties this summer, I'll bet."

He was right. Almost everyone of Armand's acquaintance had left town, and so many workers took leave from the factory that he was forced to close it down temporarily.

Armand worked by himself in his little lab beside the shop, experimenting chiefly with synthetic materials, which, he suspected, would soon become the only ingredients he could rely on getting. His supplies of natural essences and extracts were running low already; many came from distant places. Distribution problems, war priorities, and shortages would make replenishing them difficult if not impossible.

Some synthetics he'd used from the beginning; Âme was, in fact, based on ethyl vanillan, a synthetic vanilla. Synthetics had been used in perfumery for the last fifty years at least, not as substitutes, but as complements to natural oils. Now, however, wartime dictated that Armand find chemical compounds to use in place of the plant and animal extracts originally incorporated in his formulas.

He was still experimenting, not yet satisfied, when summer came to an end. He opened the factory again and resumed production. In late September he gave his first small dinner party since the occupation.

Pierre arrived early with a buxom, humorous-looking woman called Marie-Louise. She'd been a dress designer

until a few months ago, she said, but now couldn't find
anyone to employ her in her profession. "I am selling in a
food store instead," she told Armand. "Wines and cheeses
to placate the beast."

"The Germans?" Armand asked.

She nodded. "They are greedy as children at a carnival!
Maybe they were deprived in the field before they came to
Paris." She shrugged. "Who knows? Now that the stores
have opened again, they are buying everything in sight—
even perfume, I understand."

"Perhaps as gifts when they go on leave?" Armand
suggested.

"Did you hear?" Pierre asked. "They caught a man who
was pretending to be a German soldier. Though his uniform was correct, it was obvious that he was an impostor.
You know why? He wasn't carrying a parcel under his
arm!" Pierre laughed grimly.

Marie-Louise heaved her large, well-shaped bosom.
"Sometimes, when they are grabbing up everything, it
looks to me as though they are ravishing her."

"Who?" asked Armand.

"Paris. She is like a beautiful courtesan openly displaying her wares, and all the Boches are having her."

Armand looked over at Pierre questioningly. Marie-Louise
was obviously bright, and lively, but strong talk from a
woman made him uneasy. Pierre, however, was gazing at
her with such admiration that Armand wondered if Cupid
had been pierced by one of his own arrows.

The other guests arrived then, and Armand had no chance
to speak privately until much later in the evening, when
Pierre drew him aside. It was not, however, to talk about
Marie-Louise. "I thought you should know," he said. "My
parents will be leaving soon. We are all afraid. They will
be going away permanently—or for as long as this stink-
ing war lasts. We don't want to attract attention, of course,
but you are such a good friend, I wanted to tell you, so
that you can say good-bye."

"When do they plan to leave?"

"Next Wednesday."

"I'll come by the day after tomorrow—if that's convenient."

Pierre nodded.

On the following day Madame Du Près went out to buy the fresh beans her greengrocer had promised to save for her. She didn't return. By late afternoon Pierre and his father went to look for her. All they could learn was that she'd been forced into a truck by a German soldier.

"He had a gun in his hand," said the grocer. "Imagine! What will become of our dear Madame?"

M. Du Près began to cry while Pierre patted his shoulder helplessly.

Disconsolate and feeling totally helpless, M. Du Près became like a child in his dependency on Pierre. Within a week of his wife's disappearance he was an old man. He wandered through the rooms of his house looking for her, calling her name. He couldn't cook for himself and didn't care whether or not he ate. All he wanted was to die.

"You must have hope," Pierre told his father, though he himself had none. In place of hope he put survival. He and Marie-Louise married in a clerk's office and three hours later left, with his father, for the house in the country. Ten days earlier, Pierre thought, the move might have saved his mother. Now it would save him, the son of a Jewish woman and therefore, though baptized, regarded by Judaic law and by Hitler's as a Jew.

Armand was the only witness at the wedding ceremony. Afterward he saw them off, and Pierre whispered to him where they were going. "If things get too hot, come to us. God willing, we'll still be alive."

Armand kissed him on both cheeks. "Good luck."

"We'll all need that," said Pierre. Attempting a smile, he added, "Keep your nose out of trouble, old man!"

Then they were off, and Armand felt he missed his friend already. And Madame! The Du Près had been his family, and without their support he might not have succeeded, might not even be in business now. He'd paid back the original investment, but that was nothing. Now the family was in danger, and there wasn't anything he could do to help. Someday, he vowed, he'd repay them.

But he heard nothing from them and had no specific address to which to write. In any case, it would have been too risky. More and more, and with increasing openness, Jews were being dispatched from the streets and even from their own homes.

They had the worst of it, but other citizens of Paris were also suffering. Starvation settled like a disease on the city. Food became the only conversation, and rationing was seen as simply a way of depriving everyone equally. People picked up half-starving cats from the streets and cooked them for dinner. When a health ordinance warned against the dangers of this, crows were shot to make stew.

Most of Paris starved, while a few continued their lives more or less undisturbed. They went to hear an opera or see a play at the theater. They arranged banquets in restaurants and went to a nightclub afterward. Some, like Armand, had enough money to get whatever they wanted through the black market.

Armand's prediction that people would buy luxuries in dreary times came true, and he was a prime beneficiary. In the two years since the occupation, other perfumers had closed down. The house of Montalmont, old rival to the house of Jolaunay, had locked its gates. Armand's fragrances were in demand. German officers, priding themselves on being able to appreciate finer things, bought Jolaunay perfumes for their wives at home or for the pretty collaboratrices they slept with in Paris. For themselves, they bought colognes, to scent their handkerchiefs or to refresh themselves after shaving.

French officials followed their example. *Âme* was a favorite at Vichy, used discreetly by Mme. Pétain, more lavishly by other wives, some of whom congregated in Armand's salon, nibbling cakes or the fresh fruit Armand bought through private channels.

On his mother's birthday Armand went to the house with a goose, two hams, smoked fish, chocolates, and a bottle of whiskey.

"Nazi food," said his father, turning away, but his mother accepted the gifts gratefully, explaining to her husband, "I've been famished for so long!"

Maurice put up no battle but told Armand, "I must talk to you."

"Fine," Armand said in feigned innocence. He was sure he knew what his father had to say.

"Not here. I'll meet you tomorrow at four in Les Halles," he said, and described the particular corner where he'd be standing.

When Armand arrived at the appointed place, Maurice was waiting. "Let's go," he said. "It's better to walk while we talk."

They passed among the stalls toward a little cafe where Armand had ended many evenings, himself in tuxedo, with a woman in evening gown, eating the rich onion soup at dawn. "You are in danger," said Maurice bluntly. "People say you are a collaborator. They see Germans coming into your shop. They know you sell to the enemy."

"Why say 'enemy'? We are occupied, they are living with us. Should I bite off my nose to spite them? I'm simply doing my own work, the same work I learned from you."

Maurice paused to look after two huddled figures with large yellow stars stitched to the front of their shabby jackets who hurried past. "It's them," he said, "then it will be us. Poor devils."

Armand said nothing. The figure of Madame Du Près was before him, with her kindness, dignity, intelligence. He went on walking beside his father. "What can we do to help?" he asked.

"Refuse to cooperate."

"How? By closing down our businesses and sending people out to starve? By punishing those the Nazis haven't punished enough?"

"Henri Montalmont closed down within minutes of the occupation and has made it known along certain lines that he will work in the Resistance until France is free. To him, to people like him, you are nothing but a traitor," Maurice said bluntly.

"I can't help that. It's not true. If all perfumers closed shop, we'd only end up by sabotaging our own industry. Perhaps it is more useful to be loyal to French citizens than to France herself."

Maurice looked at him questioningly. "I don't understand."

"It may be better to infiltrate than to resist."

"What do you mean?" Maurice asked sharply.

"Only that a wise fool may be of more service than an ignorant one."

Maurice could make nothing of the remark. "I don't know which kind you are," he said, "but it's certain you're a fool. You deafen yourself to what people are saying. You blind yourself to what is happening in France, through networks of resistance building up here or sponsored by London.

"Perhaps I know you're not a collaborator," Maurice went on softly as Armand moved closer to his father to hear, "but I think you are dangerously ignorant. You don't understand the violence that nurtures many of our best people. The underground is growing, Armand, and in time will reach out to destroy not only the Germans and the Pétainists, but also people like you, whose giddy optimism becomes as intolerable as oppression. You'll see: they'll make no distinctions between an SS man and a stupid little shit like you."

He'd never heard such words from his father before. "I do my work," he said, "that's all." How else could he hope to accomplish anything? Only by having friends in the occupation army could he save lives. He relied on their information, for which the price was silence.

"Do what you like," said Maurice, still keeping up a regular pace. "But don't come to visit us again. You bring dishonor on your parents. Go your way. I am ashamed to call you son."

"You don't understand . . ."

"I understand," Maurice told him. "You are a fool, selfish and stubborn." He stopped a moment, patting his mustache. "Adieu, Armand."

"Couldn't we say au revoir?"

"No," answered Maurice. "We shall not meet again. You have made your own grave." He started walking away, rapidly, and Armand stood watching until he could no longer make out his father in the distance.

Then he headed for home, where Georges had laid out his evening clothes on the bed and prepared a glass of sherry on the silver tray. "Georges," said Armand, looking at him carefully, "Do you know where I'm having dinner tonight?"

Georges shrugged.

"With the Germans."

Georges stiffened, but his face was inscrutable. "Will that be all, monsieur?"

Armand sighed and nodded. When Georges was gone from the room, he went to the mirror, steadying himself with both hands on the lace-covered dresser. Armand looked across at the image of a man who'd become perplexing to himself at times, sometimes even hateful. He accused himself now as though he were his own father: You spineless creature. Espèce de merde.

He came to his own defense: You don't understand; I hate them too. That's why I can't let them destroy me. Look what I've built up, against all odds, against your censure. . . .

Armand shook his head. There was such a thing as morality. Men had standards they lived by. How far could one go in stilling one's conscience for the sake of success?

In his anguish he could no longer make out the image in the mirror. He turned away. "Damn you," he said aloud. "You told me I was too weak to do it on my own. You never had any faith in me. It all had to come from myself. But I showed you, didn't I? Became my own man, restored the name of Jolaunay. I'll stand up to anyone. Not you, and not those Boches, will take it away from me."

He fumbled for his clothes and put them on slowly, fastening the onyx cuff links without help from Georges. He scented his handkerchief with *A.J.*, the cologne he'd formulated for himself. Armand was ready, but it was still early. He decided to walk to the Tour d'Argent; the fresh air and exercise would clear his mind.

Passing along the quai, he looked down at the Seine and pictured the river gently uncurling from the mouth of the Channel to the vineyards of Burgundy. Moving waters—on a map the stream would be etched like a blue vein, running through the heart of Paris. The river was life; Armand felt the metaphor with fresh insight.

Ahead of him, on the Île de la Cité, stood the Cathedral of Notre Dame, dark and sooty as though in mourning.

Notre Dame, he thought, Our Lady, to whom at every moment prayers were being sent for deliverance.

Stop these thoughts, he told himself. He raised his chin, straightened his shoulders, and walked at a lively pace in the direction of the restaurant.

"The others are upstairs, monsieur," said the headwaiter, bowing. "Shall I take you to them?"

"Thank you, Jacques. I know the way."

Armand walked up and knocked softly at the closed door. No one answered. He could hear the laughter coming from within and knocked again, more boldly. Finally he turned the gold handle and walked in.

Oberg spotted him at once. "Ah! Der Jolaunay ist da! Entlich—komm, komm rein!" He gestured him over.

Karl Oberg was the newly appointed SS Police Chief of Paris. Pink and sweaty from too much celebrating, he pounded Armand on the back and led him around to meet the other guests.

"This is the great perfume maker!" Oberg introduced him. "The man who makes pussies sweet enough for us to stick our faces in! Ha, ha! How is it you have not come to our other gatherings, Jolaunay? You know," he complained jovially to a stout, elaborately decorated officer, "I have invited this scoundrel dozens of times—hundreds. Always he is busy with something." Turning to Armand, he said, "I was beginning to think maybe you don't like me. And I was beginning to feel that this is a very sad state of affairs, which I must take measures to remedy. Here, drink up! Heil Hitler! Drink to my new post! You have come to congratulate me tonight. Me, the new Uberleitner of Paris! When I think how far I have come, from my humble beginnings!" He paused a moment, reverently. "I was nothing as a young man, and now Paris belongs to me! We must celebrate, my friend. Here, another glassful. Prosit to me, to the Supreme Head of the Paris SS!"

Dutifully Armand raised his glass and drank. "Come, that is not enough!" shouted Oberg, linking his arm through Armand's. "We are brothers, Germany and France; you and me! We will drink Brüderschaft!"

Armand cringed but knew he couldn't refuse. Yet he felt

disgust and even a slight fear as he watched himself take part in the ceremony of brotherhood. With arms interlaced, each man drank from his own glass. Then they extricated themselves and clinked. "Servus!" said Oberg, kissing Armand on both cheeks.

"Servus," he replied dully. He knew that the Latin word, meaning "your servant" or "at your service," signified that from now on they would call each other "du" or, in French, "tu," the familiar form of "you" used by friends or comrades.

"Good," said Oberg, smacking his lips. "That's done. You've come to honor me tonight. Everyone is coming, even the unspeakably influential Obergruppenführer"— Oberg's eyes gleamed at Armand, but the expression in them wasn't of pleasure—"my boss. Come to make sure I'm doing a good job. His Hochrat finds it difficult to swallow that a crude country boy like me has landed such an exalted job." Then, as though he'd suddenly been caught telling tales out of school, Oberg gave Armand a sharp, hostile glance. "You Frenchmen. You think we have it easy, trying to establish order here. It is a city of delinquency, of vandals. Your kind doesn't know what order means! But we'll teach you—you'll see!"

His words, and the tone in which they were delivered, were menacing. Armand felt real fear, as though he were in the presence of a dangerous animal.

To Armand's relief, he was rescued by the announcement of dinner. The twenty-four men took their seats at the long table. "Women," said Armand's neighbor to the right, "are invited for boring evenings only, not when we are celebrating and in high spirits." He winked. "That would interfere with the little pleasures we like to take afterward."

The toasts were in champagne, which they drank with the hors d'oeuvres. Then they switched to Margaux 1929 with their pressed duck. Strains of Wagner accompanied the meal.

Armand held up the brick-red wine and sniffed. Its bouquet was full, elegant, and sensuous. For a moment he was almost happy.

"Wunderbar," said his neighbor to the left. "Nicht wahr?"

"Très bon," Armand agreed politely. The man had been introduced to him as Obergruppenführer Something, a name he didn't catch. He apologized and asked for it again.

"Obergruppenführer Rauchmannsberg, at your service. It is for me a great pleasure to be in Paris again. I have always admired your city for its culture and refinement. Take your wine as an example: the aroma! What bliss to smell something so refined, so subtle, after the stink I'm used to in the East. Ah, and this duck," he said, bending over the plate and inhaling deeply, "how civilized!"

Armand turned his attention to it, the specialty of the house. It was an elaborate dish, requiring long preparations in which the animal is skinned and boned, its flesh forced through a press to extract all the blood.

"Your work is in the East?" Armand asked politely.

The commandant was a corpulent man, and the lower part of his large face glistened with grease. He wore his napkin tucked in at the neck, like a cravat, and raised it to wipe his mouth and chin before answering. "Yes. I am on leave for a few days. A relief, I tell you, back to civilization after those filthy Jews. And you, monsieur . . . ?"

"Jolaunay."

"Not *the* Jolaunay? A pleasure, a pleasure. I have just bought a few of your white bottles for my sister. You are a man of taste, Jolaunay, a connoisseur. Your cologne on my handkerchief has saved me many times."

Armand took another sip of the opulent wine.

"I beg your pardon?"

He laughed. "The stink can be so overpowering when the wind blows in a certain direction, that even a strong man like myself can become faint. Therefore, I always carry a scented handkerchief to protect myself."

"From what? Where does the stink come from?"

His neighbor looked at him in astonishment and then laughed, slapping his thigh. "That's good! The stink of bodies, of course."

"Bodies?"

Now the man frowned and looked at Armand suspiciously. "Jews," he said curtly. "Decomposing filthy Jews." He met Armand's stare, then abruptly turned his back and began talking to his other neighbor.

Armand felt nausea. The duck on his plate was a piece of dead, tortured meat, the wine sickeningly bloody. The man must be mad, he told himself. He saw Madame Du Près's face in front of him. His father thought he was shit; Pierre had accused him of naïveté. Yet at least he'd taken the advice of an old acquaintance, a colonel in the French army, who'd come to the shop soon after the occupation and warned Armand about his Jewish employees. He'd thought the colonel was being alarmist, but nevertheless— thank God!—he had acted immediately. That was just before the disappearance of Pierre's mother. At least those people were safe through his intervention, Armand reminded himself. His position meant that he was able to protect them. But they were only a handful.

"Meine Herren, messieurs. Achtung!" came a stern announcement. Instantly the room fell into a stiff, correct silence.

"You will all now rise for the entrance of SS-Obergruppenführer Reinhard Heydrich!"

The men rose as one, their arms stretched in the rigid Hitler salute. Heydrich strode in with two aides-de-camp at his side. His bearing was erect, his chiseled features held a formal smile as his eyes made a quick inventory of the room.

Armand was not offering the salute. Heydrich's glance fell on him a moment, then moved away. "Heil Hitler!" said Heydrich. "At ease, everyone."

He went over to greet Oberg first, then circulated easily from person to person, shaking hands, listening with attention, and saying a few words before moving on.

When he was introduced to Armand Jolaunay, Heydrich's eyes twinkled. "So," he said, "you are the man who perfumes the High Command. But you are not very fond of us, I see."

Armand stiffened in alarm.

Heydrich was smiling and laid a hand on Armand's shoulder. "Of course a French citizen is not obliged to salute the Führer. However, it would be a sign of politeness. More than that: I would recommend it as a *politic* gesture.

You will remember that?" Heydrich gave him a nearly imperceptible wink.

When he left the party a few minutes later, all arms were raised in salute, including Armand's.

Less than a month later, Armand received a special safe-conduct pass, via the High Command, to inspect his fields of lavender in Grasse. On June 4, 1942, Reinhard Heydrich was assassinated near Prague by a group of Czech patriots flown in from London. Though Armand didn't hear the news until later, he'd remember the date all his life. It was the day he first met Anne.

3

1942–1944

The girl was dancing through the lavender, bending now and again to pick a blooming stalk and sniff it. She was dazzlingly blond. Fairer than The Viking Queen, Armand thought, remembering the Scandinavian beauty for the first time since they'd parted. This girl was younger and moved as though to distant music. She stopped still and embraced herself. Watching her from afar, Armand grinned with surprise; it was a gesture he could never make. Her obvious delight in herself was the most spontaneous thing he'd seen since the war began.

When she turned and he knew she'd seen him, Armand held his breath. He wanted her to go on as before, thinking herself alone, acting without self-consciousness. But she froze like a rabbit in view of hunters. He didn't want to frighten her, and yet he knew he couldn't walk away, perhaps never to see her again.

He came up slowly, and she didn't move. He was afraid she'd bolt at the last minute, like a forest creature who

senses at a particular cue that camouflage will not protect
it. But she remained like a statue as he came close.

Her skin was the rose of apple blossoms. Her eyes were
green and slightly slanted. She was so pretty he hardly
dared speak.

She didn't look at him. "Mademoiselle . . ." he began
tentatively, in case she didn't understand French. She
seemed to soften. "Mademoiselle," he repeated. "I hope I
am not disturbing you?"

She gave him a little smile, and he wanted to touch her.
"I frightened you," he apologized.

"I thought you were German."

"No, I'm a Parisian. I thought *you* were German."

They smiled at each other. "Do you have your papers?"
she asked.

"Yes," he answered, puzzled. "This is my field. Are you
working it?"

"Me?" Her laughter burst like a brook released by first
thaw. The sound was magical. "Oh no, monsieur, I don't
work in fields. I didn't know it was yours. The lavender
brought me here! I, too, come from Paris."

He wanted to take her in his arms, press her against
him. Instead he asked, foolishly, "Are you down here on
business?"

"Yes," she said seriously, "my own business. And you?"

"Armand Jolaunay." He held out his hand, but she shrank
from him. Oh God, he thought, what has she heard about
me?

"Jolaunay perfumes?"

He nodded, dreading what she would say.

"I adore them! You're a famous man!"

His relief was so strong that he couldn't stop laughing,
and she joined him, laughing at nothing in particular, just
for the joy of it.

When they'd subsided, she said, "I got my first bottle of
Âme in 1937, when I came to Paris. It was so beautiful I
couldn't open it at first. I got it from a man who was
trying to seduce me, and he did. But after about a week I
saw that he was all body and no soul. I said to him, 'You
gave me *Âme* because you have none. You are nothing but

a lovemaking machine. I care for the perfume more than for you.' So I kept it and sent the man packing."

He was amazed that she could be so open, like a child. For some reason he didn't mind that she said things he usually didn't like to hear from women. Instead of cooling his interest, her frankness increased it.

He strolled along with her, bending when she did to pick lavender. Her name was Anne, she told him, Anne Larbaud, born and raised in Alsace. Armand could hear Alsace in her French, a light Germanic lacing to her cadences. "I came to Paris to be a great mannequin!" Laughter bubbled through her words. "Silly me! I was never beautiful enough."

"You are very beautiful." Painfully so, Armand thought.

She went on as though he hadn't spoken. "First I worked at Schiaparelli, then I was a model for fashion photographers. I could never get to the top," she told him earnestly, "because I don't have the je ne sais quoi—you know, the mystery, the aloofness."

"Thank God for that."

Her eyes sparkled when she laughed, her lips parted, and he saw the perfect teeth, her tongue darting between the rows, teasing him. He couldn't take his eyes off her mouth. "Anne!" he cried.

His tone stopped her laughter. She stood next to him, her arms full of flowers. His too; Armand felt immobilized by them. She looked at him, her eyebrows raised in question. He leaned down and kissed her. Her lips were soft as petals.

Her eyes smiled at him from a mock-solemn face. She threw open her arms, flinging the loosened bouquet over him. Armand tossed his flowers toward her, and they were both drenched in tiny blossoms. Her laughter rose, intoxicating the air.

They walked into town, unable to speak, their hands brushing against each other.

In the store they bought a picnic of fruit, cheese, bread, and wine and then carried it back to the field. Anne arranged the food on the ground and stretched out beside it, propping herself up on her elbows. She looked up at him, her eyes squinting in the sunlight, and broke the silence. "I like your face," she said. "It hasn't been occupied—by them."

He removed his jacket and tie without taking his eyes off her. "The shirt comes off too," she said softly, her fingers moving down to the buttons at the front of her dress.

Armand threw himself down beside her, and she opened her arms to him. Her tongue quickly explored his chest, moving up to his neck, along his jawline, until it came to his lips and slipped between them. She undid her dress while she kissed him and with both hands pulled his head down to her breasts.

He inhaled the smell of her skin, the faint musk of her sweat, and the scent of lavender. He took off his remaining clothes as she made herself naked. She arched against him, pulling him toward her, letting out a soft cry as he entered her. Her eyes were closed, her face flushed and perspiring, the blond hair spread around it. Watching her, hearing the music of her cry, smelling her body's heady arousal, Armand couldn't control himself.

Afterward he apologized. "That was too fast."

But Anne was smiling, her face radiant. "We have time," she whispered.

They lay together silently, naked in the sunlight, and contentment flowed between them. "How did you come here?" Armand asked at last. "How did you find me?"

Again her soft laughter embraced him. "But no, you were the one to find *me*. I was afraid of you, staring like that."

He kissed her bare arms, remembering the sight of Anne embracing herself. "How did you come here?" he repeated.

"From Paris. I saved up my money and made my escape."

"You mean you're in Grasse illegally?"

Her mouth pouted enchantingly; he kissed it. "I hid in the back of a truck," she said, "and jumped out when I sniffed freedom. The truck was moving quickly, and I twisted my ankle in the jump, so I had to go hobbling like an old woman into the bushes."

"Poor angel."

"What poor? I was free!" She gave him a triumphant smile. "I came into Grasse. The people here, they don't give a sou where you come from. You can drop from the sky or from a tree—it's all the same to them. No questions. They know I'm a runaway, but I'm safe with them." She spoke with the conviction of a child who knows she's loved, Armand thought. No wonder the townspeople were charmed by her.

"I work at the tavern in the evenings, and the landlord has given me a room of my own upstairs. You will visit me tonight?" Anne asked.

"Of course." It had been out of Armand's hands since their first kiss.

After she finished work, they sipped brandy together in the tavern. Armand knew the owner from previous trips to Grasse, and neither he nor Anne wanted to antagonize him by spending the night in her upstairs room. Planning ahead, Armand had taken along the front-door key of his hotel. The door was locked at eleven; guests who returned later had to ring for the night porter.

After midnight they slipped past the sleeping porter without waking him. They spent the rest of the night awake, making love, talking, lying together in silence. Their bodies understood each other with a simplicity and need Armand had never known. And when they were satisfied, words cascaded in. By dawn Armand knew Anne more intimately than he'd thought it possible to know anyone.

Later that morning he was able to get his permit extended by five days, claiming urgent business. But he canceled all his business appointments, and for the rest of his stay he and Anne spent every moment together except for the hours when she worked.

On her day off they went to Nice and walked barefoot along the beach, picking up shells. She told him about her life in Paris. "I was a Zazou, and all my friends were Zazous."

He'd heard the term but wasn't sure what it meant. "We were called that because of the music, I think," Anne told him, "the jazz we were always listening to. Mainly we were bohemians—very rich bohemians, with flashy clothes, furs, jewelry, even perfume." She gave him a coy look and laughed. He took her hand. "We collected whatever was scarce or frightfully expensive. I had a wonderful collection of Billie Holiday records. A few Louis Armstrongs, Duke Ellingtons. . . . Sold all of them to get here.

"We were out for ourselves only, and against many things. Against the Boches, of course, and the old fogies in Vichy, and against anything bourgeois or traditional or conformist." She kicked up sand as she enumerated. "Against property, too, though we were always buying things or trading for them. And marriage! Despicable, we called it, a capitalist, bourgeois institution. *We* believed in free love, which meant you had to go to bed with anyone who asked or you'd be a prude."

Armand winced.

If she noticed, Anne paid no attention. "People asked you to go to bed the way they asked for a dance. And you'd go with him for a little while—an hour, a few days. Light entertainment."

He let go of her hand, feeling torn apart. He didn't want to hear any of this, and yet he didn't want her to stop. He had to know everything, despite the pain it gave him. "Am I," he asked bitterly, "the current performer?"

She gave him a puzzled look and then, in a voice full of reproach, answered with a question. "How can you ask me that?"

"Forgive me."

"You want to hurt me?"

He stopped and took both her hands. "Never. I'm—I'm just confused. I never met a woman like you, and I suppose I'm—jealous."

"Of the past?" she asked incredulously. "How can that be? With our first kiss we wiped it out and forgave each other everything. Didn't we?"

The determination in her look thrilled him. "Yes," he agreed fervently. "Everything is forgiven."

As they walked back to the hotel, they passed a newsstand where headlines blazed: HEYDRICH ASSASSINATED!

"I met him once," Armand told her. Anne looked at him questioningly. "At a large party. He was exceptionally good-looking."

She didn't ask further. He bought a paper, and they

went to their pink hotel room, where he threw it, unread, on the dresser.

They made love on the large brass bed, taking more time with each other now. But, whenever he looked down at her face, oblivious to him, damp and glowing in its own pleasure, he couldn't contain himself, couldn't hold back, and he'd have to come into her then, riding the insistent waves of her orgasm as though he were simply a thing of her desire.

At dinner, in a garden restaurant off the palm-lined Promenade des Anglais, Armand asked Anne to tell him more about her life.

"But you didn't want to hear," she reminded him, stabbing a fat scallop in her Coquille St.-Jacques.

"I was stupid, and that was in the past. Forgive it."

The lush flora that surrounded them gave off only a hint of scent, subtle and yet emotional. It would be a challenge to recreate, he thought. "Anne's hair," he labeled the smell to himself before placing it in the back of his memory. He leaned toward her.

"Buying, selling, jazz, clothes, men. One morning I woke up and the sun was coming through the blind in fine sheaves. I said to myself, 'You are a piece of stupidity. Stupid person,' I said, 'you are wasting your time. It isn't *things* you want, it's freedom. Why buy another bottle of something that has a springlike fragrance? Go out and get the spring.' So I sold all my razzle-dazzle things, and I made a pile of money, which I used to bribe people and get myself freedom."

He was watching her mouth as she talked. In two days he'd have to go back. He couldn't bear the thought of not being able to hear her voice, not looking into green eyes laughing back at him. "Come with me. Come live with me," he said.

"And lose it all? Go back into war?"

"It wouldn't be the same," he pleaded. "You'd be with me, not the Zazous. You'd live well. Please, Anne," he begged, his need breaking through his voice. "I love you more than anything in this world. Say you'll come."

"Even if I'd want to, I couldn't," she said softly. "I'm here illegally. I don't have travel papers."

"I can arrange that."

She cocked her head but accepted what he said without questioning him. She took his hand in both of hers. "You know that I love you. At least it feels like love. But how can we be sure, either of us? One week that we've taken out of life. It's not real. When you're in Paris, you'll look back on a dream."

"But you're dreaming the same one, my darling! We're in the dream together."

"Yes, but we may wake up separately."

He became angry. "You can't throw this away! It's unfair! It's madness!"

"Maybe you will come back again to Grasse?"

"Who knows?" he said, with intentional brutality. "Anything can happen." She was treating him like another of the men asking for her favors, he felt, toying with him. She was still a child, just a willful little girl.

When they returned to the hotel, they didn't make love. Next day they drove back to Grasse, and the following day Armand left for Paris. When he kissed her on the side of her neck, the fragrance of her hair and skin made him tremble. Whoever she was, and whatever she wanted to do, he knew he was hers. "I'll be back," he whispered.

She kissed him fiercely on the mouth and then pushed him away abruptly, as though she couldn't trust herself. "Better make it soon," she told him and ran toward the field.

Three weeks later Anne was coming out of the kitchen with an order of beer and sausages when he walked into the tavern. She gave a shout, dropped the tray on the nearest table, and raced into his arms. He lifted her off the floor as she shouted, "Yes! Yes! I don't want to live another minute without you!"

Anne's papers couldn't be arranged until the fall, and when she finally arrived, her exuberance vanished in the grim atmosphere of occupied Paris. To Anne it was more dismal than ever. Food was in even shorter supply. People were either discouraged or angry. Paris had become a city of the poor, colonized by hunger, coiled violence, and the frustrations of poverty. She was afraid of what would happen to herself and Armand here. Love might be taken prisoner or left to die as a casualty of war. But she resolved to believe in it and to hope.

She refused to marry Armand, however, though he kept trying to persuade her. "This is not the time," she told him.

"If we'd stayed in Grasse, would you have married me?" he persisted.

She thought for only a moment. "No. I would turn into a piece of property if I did that."

Her motto was, "If not I for myself, who then?" It was a saying she'd learned one evening at the house of her closest school friend, Rachel Weiss. Anne had lost track of her since then, but she often thought back on evenings when Mr. Weiss would read from the Torah and from Talmudic scholars. "And being for myself, what am I? And if not now, when?" Wise words; hearing them, Anne had resolved to try living by them, remaining free so she could be true to herself. Whenever she thought about the Weisses, she repeated the words as an amulet to insure their safety.

When she fell in love with Armand, Anne discovered that freedom was a slippery thing to define. With him she felt more herself, and without him she was lonely. The freedom to be lonely, she learned, didn't make you free.

But she couldn't accept his proposal. "These are strange times," she said. "People should marry only if they want children, and who would want a child now?"

Her decision saddened him, but he realized he had to accept her terms or lose her. He would have preferred marriage, but at least they were living together, in his apartment on the Place Furstemberg, with Armand's valet.

Georges served both of them and buffed Anne's shoes to the same high polish he gave Armand's, but true luxury was no longer possible. Armand wished he could provide Anne with some of the extravagances he'd taken for granted before the war. Then his apartment, with its original blend of modernity and the antique, his eclectic collection of furniture, the pieces always harmonizing with each other and with the room, had been featured in the pages of *L'Intérieur*, a magazine devoted to home design. The article was headlined, "A Son Goût"—to his taste—which the writer praised lavishly, calling it both elegant and amusing.

Now the apartment was falling into disrepair and looked almost shoddy. It needed a complete overhaul. Paint was peeling in the bedroom, plaster had fallen out of the living-room ceiling. The parquet floors had dark scuff marks, and a few of the windows were scratched. But repairs had to wait until the war was over. "Après la guerre" became a popular expression in Paris, the rallying cry for a return to order. "Meet me at La Coupole seventeen minutes after the war," people would say, in a mixture of irony and hope.

"Après la guerre," Anne told Armand, "we will be married. Après la guerre we'll eat steak, buy new curtains, have a baby." For the duration they'd live together, trying to hold on to their love in the embattled surroundings.

Armand's mother came for a visit but wouldn't stay to have a meal with them. She was polite to Anne, nothing more, and she whispered to Armand when Anne was out of the room, "The girl's very pretty, but take care. She's probably the flighty kind, who goes after the men."

Armand listened to his mother with tight lips. You should know, Maman, he thought bitterly—birds of a feather.

She told him that his father was ill. "You must come to see him."

"He has disowned me," he reminded her. "He wouldn't want me there."

But a few days later his mother sent a note to the apartment saying that Maurice's condition had turned critical. His heart was very weak, and he could no longer get out of bed. "We'll go," Armand decided. "It may be the last opportunity for you to meet him."

Anne chose a demure pearl-blue suit and pinned her hair up in a chignon. "Don't I look like a schoolteacher?" she teased, parading around Armand.

"One that every schoolboy dreams of ravishing," he said. "Let's go."

Maurice was too weak to sit up. His face was the same color as the pillow, and his hair had turned white with streaks of pale gray. "So it's you," he said when his son entered the room. "And what's that?"

"This is Anne, Papa."

"Looks like a German," he spat. "Get her out of here."

"I go with her," warned Armand.

"Then go. Leave me alone; I've had my fill of you."

They left the house but returned later the same evening. Preparations had to be made; Madame Jolaunay was close to hysteria and needed her son to comfort her; Maurice was dead.

In the second week of December, Anne discovered that she was pregnant. Armand was overjoyed. "Now you will marry me," he said happily.

They were in bed when she told him. He kissed her eyes, her lashes, the line of her hair from one temple over to the other, and Anne, sinking into his love, knew she couldn't have an abortion. His child, a child conceived by the two of them, couldn't be scraped out and thrown away. If the price of its life was her personal freedom, she had no choice, Anne knew, but to pay.

They were married a week later, just before Christmas, in a quiet civil ceremony attended by a few friends. Afterward they all went to lunch at Lapérousse. Anne was so stunning in a cream satin suit and small cloche with veil that the waiters mixed up their orders and Armand couldn't take his eyes off her. "She's the most beautiful woman who was ever born," he kept saying. "And I'm the happiest man."

"Long live Armand!" their friends toasted. "Long live Anne!"

And the baby too, she thought, smiling in bridal happiness on her wedding day. She felt, as she looked into the adoring eyes of her new husband, that they'd outwitted war through their love, which would last forever.

Ten days into 1943, three weeks after the wedding, her baby died. Anne fought against the lashing cramps, determined to hold on to the fetus. But her will gave out when the first thick clots seeped out of her, and in a despairing voice she asked Armand to get her to a hospital.

The doctor could find no particular cause for the miscarriage. "It's been happening a lot over these past few years," he told Armand. "Something like an epidemic, probably due to the stress of war." He assured them both that he could find no deformity in Anne and advised them to try again.

But Armand was afraid. Though Anne quickly recovered her health and beauty, there was something profoundly sad about her which he couldn't reach. "Nonsense," she told him, trying to dispel his worry. "It was just a mass of cells, nothing vaguely human. Who could grieve for that?"

Yet he knew she was feeling the loss. He did himself— and not the loss of the child so much as of Anne's intense vitality. Since the fall of 1942, when she'd come to live with him in Paris, her liveliness had become muted and her eyes only rarely laughed at him with astonished joy. She'd come alive again over the baby, and now that was gone, too. She languished through the spring and into the summer. Armand blamed himself. He'd plucked the wild rose because he couldn't bear to leave her, and now she was wilting.

Sensing his concern about her, Anne was determined to cheer him up. She gave little parties at home, arranged for an evening a week at the opera or the theater, and forced Georges to take a day off every weekend, when Anne and Armand could have the apartment to themselves, stay in nightclothes for most of the day, and take lunch in bed. In September, without telling him, she stopped using contraception, and by late March 1944 she was certain she was pregnant again. She kept it to herself until the time had passed when she'd lost the other. In early June she felt she was safe and told him the baby was due in October.

Armand was pleased but cautious. "I wish I could stay home and take care of you," he said.

"Rubbish. You'd make me feel like an old lady, with your fussing. And what would happen to your business? People have babies all the time without closing down their shops."

"I could leave Mercier in charge of the factory and get someone in to the salon. . . ."

"Mercier is unreliable," she said of Armand's foreman, "and if the ladies didn't find you at the shop, they'd cancel their orders. They come for your silver eyes, my cabbage, not for your golden scents. Now enough chitchat. It's your day to be in the factory, and you're late already."

He took a sip of cold coffee from the breakfast tray, still reluctant to leave. "We can call him Claude."

"Who?"

"Him," Armand said, stroking her nearly flat belly. "We'll name him after my ancestor."

"And if he's a girl?"

"Impossible." After a pause, he said, "Claudine?"

She made a face. "Get off to work. Your ideas are terrible."

He went at last, taking the metro as he always did, because it was the fastest way to travel. The metro had been running smoothly and efficiently throughout the war. Probably because it's underground, Armand told himself, smiling lightly at his own joke.

At the factory a predictable crisis was in full swing. Predictable, because despite the priority status given to Parfums de Jolaunay, supplies were always running out. Today it was bergamot. The expected barrel hadn't arrived. "And this is June sixth," Mercier pointed out with agitation. "More than two weeks after the promised date!"

"Let me think about it, I'm sure I'll find a solution," said Armand reassuringly as he walked into his office.

Oil extracted from bergamot mint provided the fruity note in *Grâce*, a fragrance Armand had devised the summer before last, when he had been waiting for Anne to join him. Its name was a deliberate pun, a plea to the officials and an evocation of Grasse. He'd tried to reproduce the scent of the little garden where they'd dined, but he hadn't been able to create a match. *Grâce* was an approximation only, but the samples he'd tried on his customers at the salon brought enthusiastic approval and immediate orders.

What to substitute for the bergamot if the shipment never came in? He looked down at his hands as if they could provide an answer.

Shouting came from inside the factory, and Armand got up to see what caused it. At the threshold of his office door he collided with Mercier, and for a moment he thought it must be the bergamot—the cheer welcoming its arrival.

"They have landed! The Allies are in Normandy!"

Armand stared at his foreman. Workers were running over to shake hands, repeating the news in loud voices, grinning and congratulating each other. Suddenly they fell still, and a single voice began singing, "Allons, enfants de la patrie." As one, all the workers joined in the "Marseillaise."

"Take the rest of the day off!" Armand called out when they'd finished. "Celebrate with your wives!"

He rushed out of the factory, pursued by fear.

Letters of threat and warning had been arriving in his apartment for a number of months. "Collaborator, your days are numbered!" read one. Another informed him that his name was in the hands of the Resistance, "who know what measures to take with a traitor." Others simply abused him or expressed the hope that he would die.

He burned them all, but a few times Anne was able to catch a glimpse of their contents. She firmly believed her husband had done no wrong, though she knew the Germans were his patrons. But she agreed with him that it was important to continue running the business and to go on paying as many employees as possible. She encouraged him to maintain his dedication to the work he did so brilliantly.

Though they'd talked on and off about leaving Paris for the baby's sake, each ended by convincing the other that flight was not necessary. "Those letters come from crackpots," Armand said airily, to reassure her.

"*Dangerous* crackpots." Then she gave a little laugh and said, "But we won't give them the satisfaction of seeing our tails. Besides, I have the blanket to finish." She was crocheting a lacy white covering for the baby and, because she'd never crocheted before, it was taking a very long time.

But when he opened the door on June 6, Anne threw herself into his arms. "I think it's time, Armand. Maybe we should start running."

He led her into the living room and poured each of

them a large measure of cognac. "If we leave now," he said slowly, thinking it out as he talked, "it might seem that I was trying to escape from the Allies. Those in doubt about me would be convinced I had crimes to hide."

She sipped thoughtfully. "Après la guerre," she said, "everyone will know what was right and what was wrong. Everyone will say he did the right thing from the beginning." She gave him a pointed look. "And what 'right' means will depend on who is finally the victor in this pile of manure."

"My darling Anne! I brought you into this mess."

"You certainly did, and I thank God for it."

"My angel. And what do you say now? Shall we fly?"

In answer she brought out the blanket, not yet large enough to cover a doll.

By August she was nearly finished. More threats had been coming in the mail, but Anne burned any suspicious-looking letter unopened, before Armand could come home and find it. The growing terrorism in Paris spread in all directions as scabs of war were ripped open.

Armand had gone to the shop and factory until the time of the annual closing. Then he stayed home with Anne except for hours he spent in the lab. They didn't entertain anymore, or go out in the evenings. Anne was often tired, her ankles and knees were bloated. Food repelled her, and any drink stronger than wine nauseated her. "I never knew having a baby could be so much trouble," she complained mildly. "It's almost worse than the grippe! And in this heat, too—I wish someone could put a stop to summer."

Two days later someone did. French and American troops entered Paris, setting her free as Parisians danced in the streets, kissed strangers, and staged the biggest open-air party the world had yet known. The "Marseillaise" sounded from every street and rooftop as anti-German feeling burst like a balloon of poison gas over the city. "Vive la France! Death to the traitors! À bas les Boches! France est libérée; France is free!"

Anne and Armand stayed home listening to the radio, neither of them able to express their jumble of feelings, which ran the gamut from joy to fear.

They went to bed early, though neither of them could get to sleep. "Our baby will be born a citizen of free France," Anne whispered. In the dark Armand couldn't hear what she was saying, but he heard a new note of happiness and felt grateful.

Toward morning he fell asleep. When he woke later, Anne was gone.

Walking slowly because of her swollen legs, Anne felt refreshed by the still-cool air of the crimsoning morning. Her dreams, whenever she'd dozed briefly, had jerked her awake in fear. They were all bloody: a fetus emerging from the vagina as coagulated lumps; a monster with two heads, bleeding from one eye; a field scattered with amputated limbs. She woke each time with her heart pounding in her ears and her body covered in sweat. When dawn signaled through the curtains, she got out of bed in relief.

She was hungry for the first time in months and decided to go out for fresh croissants. She'd be back before Armand woke, and she looked forward to having a surprise for him.

Walking along the peaceful streets was a rare treat for Anne, who could barely remember when she'd last been out alone in Paris. The Zazou years were ancient history, belonging to a different person in another era. Now she strolled slowly, seeing the gray buildings silhouetted against a salmon sky, with the steeple of Saint-Germain-des-Près rising over the rooftops like a stately periscope. The streets were nearly deserted, except for a few men who walked by carrying newspapers under their arms, cigarettes glued in the corners of their mouths. The gray was melting into warm peach, and Anne felt as though the city was hers, almost as though she'd given birth to it.

Seven more weeks. She tried to imagine what the baby looked like now, curled inside her, attached by a thick cord. The only image that came was of a tiny old man, a wrinkled homunculus. Would it be perfect, she wondered. Or blind, crippled, mentally defective? These thoughts had been plaguing her in the past month. Please, she prayed toward the steeple, don't let any of that happen.

She caught herself at this foolish prayer and admonished herself silently. "Stop. You are a silly business, you are still a piece of stupidity." Then she stopped walking, standing stock still as she felt a sudden movement in her womb. She placed both hands over her stomach and a clear image came to her of what she was carrying: a chubby baby, bathed in light, like early Renaissance paintings of the infant Jesus surrounded by gold leaf.

Smells trailed out from the bakery on the rue Jacob, and she began moving toward it. Inside she gave way to temptation and, after selecting the croissants, bought brioches and a slender honey-brown baguette, still warm in her hands. She pictured Armand when she brought them to him, raising his head to inhale the aroma.

Cradling the breads under her arm, she was smiling as she walked out of the shop. "Good luck with your baby, Mme. Jolaunay!" called the baker. The women in the shop turned and stared at her. When she'd gone only a few steps, the same women rushed toward her and encircled her quickly, their voices rising to shrieks of anger. A heavy woman with a dark shadow of mustache seized the parcel and threw it to the ground. She took hold of Anne's arms and pinned them behind her back. Another woman, wiry and menacing, grabbed a fistful of Anne's hair and jerked her head back violently.

"Traitor's bitch!" she shouted and spat into Anne's face. "Jolaunay's whore!"

The others began to hurl their insults.

"Pig of a fascist!" said a high-pitched voice.

"Collaborator's whore!" came another.

"Pig! Sow!" they yelled, and those nearest began kicking her.

"My baby! Get away from my baby!" With a powerful wrench Anne freed herself for an instant. Then she was set upon again and grabbed by three women who kept her in a painful hold, pulling viciously on her hair, until she thought they intended to snap her neck. Murderous fury blazed on all the faces. They're going to kill me, she thought. "No!" she screamed. She didn't recognize her own voice, distorted by terror. "Save my baby!"

"Whore's baby," hissed the leader of the group and pulled Anne's head back as far as it would go.

Her wrists and arms were burning in the vise of the
large woman's grip. Her legs felt rubbery, about to give
way. Her eyes, staring out to the side, watched the wiry
woman advance slowly, her face flushed with hatred. Something was glinting in her right hand. She brought it up
and Anne saw the sharp, narrow blade of a razor. An
insane smile came over the woman's face as she drew
nearer until her body was almost touching Anne's. She
raised her arm, bringing the razor up over Anne's neck.

Anne closed her eyes and screamed.

4

1944

Georges saw her from the kitchen window, weaving
along the sidewalk clutching her stomach. Her head was
bald, the scalp bloody in places.

He ran down, but when he came up to her, she shrank
away. "Please, madame," he urged, looking nervously
around for her assailant. "It's me. Georges. Let me help
you."

"It's you," she repeated dully and let him support her,
giving over to him her full weight. After a few laborious
steps he paused, and Anne whispered, "Don't tell him,
don't let Monsieur know."

But Armand was running toward them, his face a mask
of disbelief. "Darling, darling," he choked. "My angel.
Anne." He folded her into his arms. "What happened?"

"They don't like blondes."

He brought her to the house, up the stairs, and into bed
while Georges prepared strong tea laced with brandy. In a
tired voice that trailed off whenever the scene came back
in terrifying detail, Anne told the story. Armand sat on the

bed, listening with horror while he stroked her face, not daring to touch the raw, naked head. He could see a few cuts where the razor had nicked her skin, but there were no deep lacerations.

"I'm calling a doctor."

"No." She took hold of his arm. "Too dangerous. I'm all right. They only shaved me, after all—and frightened me a bit."

A bit—he couldn't help smiling at what was so typically Anne. But the assault terrified him; he couldn't understand the violence and cruelty of those women.

"We must get out of here," he said with urgency. They'd survived the war, but liberation stood a fair chance of killing them, he thought grimly.

"Yes," she agreed in a faint voice. "But let me rest a little. I feel very tired now. And the baby. . . ."

"How is he?" Armand just now remembered him.

"Too much workout. Needs rest." She fell asleep while speaking, and he stayed watching her, the uneven breaths racking her body, the twitchings of her mouth, the restless shuttle of her eyes under the fragile lids. From time to time they burst open to reveal a wild, floundering look, and then slowly the pupils would narrow as she focused on him. She'd give a sigh and fall back into sleep. Armand watched, wanting to protect her, realizing it was too late for that now.

When her breathing became more regular, Armand got up softly and went to his study to begin packing for their flight. First his black leather-bound "bible," the book of formulas and notes; then their cash and jewels from the safe that also held numerous papers, all worthless. Their passports could be of no use for travel; the authorizations for special favors were better burned. Now that Pétain and his government were being held prisoner in Belfort, signs of "cooperation" with the former invaders could bring danger from all sides. Armand didn't expect he'd fare much better with the French or Americans than he would with the Maquis.

Georges had entered the room and stood silently as his employer put a match to the papers. When the fire died, leaving a fistful of ashes, Georges spoke. "I am offering my resignation, monsieur."

"Wise of you," Armand replied, poking at the ashes. "You were brave to wait as long as you did." He walked over to his escritoire and opened a small drawer. "Thank you for the loyalty you've shown to us both." He came back to Georges and placed a hand on his shoulder. "I accept your resignation, and here"—he handed him a stack of bills—"is your severance pay. But I must ask you not to leave just yet. We ourselves will be going away very soon. I must attend to certain matters in my business, and madame cannot be left alone in my absence."

"Of course," said Georges, bowing. "I understand. You will tell me when it is convenient for me to depart." As he left the room, Armand realized that they'd lived together for six years and would probably never see each other again after tomorrow. How quickly everything falls away!

He went to call Mercier, to arrange to meet him at the factory right away on an urgent matter. Then he looked in on Anne, still sleeping behind fluttering eyelids. How lovely she was! Even the brutal shearing couldn't blunt her wild beauty. He blew a kiss, turned to leave, and heard her call him. "Please come, come over to me, Armand."

She took his face in both her hands, looked at it a long moment, and pulled him toward her, kissing his mouth with hard insistence. He inhaled the milky skin with its lingering trace of *Grâce* and became aroused, returning her kiss passionately. Then he drew away abruptly.

"Not yet?" she teased.

"Very soon," he promised, startled by their sexual need, rising even in a time of peril.

"Godspeed," she wished him, though he hadn't told her he was going. "I'll be here."

Armand kissed her again and left the house, the scent of her still on him, spiced with *Grâce*. As he entered the metro, he was still conscious of desiring her.

But *Grâce*—the time of grâce was over. They'd stopped making it after the bergamot crisis, two and a half months ago, on the day when the Allies landed in Normandy to launch the chain of events now yanking them from their roots in Paris.

As he came in sight of the factory, Armand sensed that something was wrong. A crowd was milling around the entrance, even though the factory was officially closed.

As Armand approached, one of the men caught sight of him and gave a yell. Others took up the shout and began hurling taunts. "The collaborator's coming!" said one man.

"The pig is showing his face!" called another.

"A face that's kissed a lot of German ass!"

"Right, and spits the shit on us!"

"Stop it!" Armand shouted. He looked out at the sea of faces, all of them familiar, most of them men he could name. "Listen to me! You must hear what I have to say!"

A man close to him nudged his neighbor. "Isn't he a regular little Hitler?" he said in fake admiration.

"Listen! I've been your employer throughout the war. Each one of you took home decent wages while tens of thousands of people were unemployed." Though a few mutterings and catcalls continued, Armand had most of the crowd's attention. "I never collaborated. We made perfumes and colognes and sold them to whoever would buy...."

Mercier, his sleeves rolled above his elbows, stepped in front of the crowd. "It's too late, Jolaunay. We won't stand and listen to your speechifying. We know you for a traitor."

"Not you!" he cried. "Mercier, you worked with me all this time. You were—"

"Don't try throwing the blame. A cheap fascist trick. I am a veteran, and I would have fought in this war, too, if it hadn't been for my bad knee. But you, no. You can't fight for France. First a coward, then a traitor."

Armand felt a strong urge to hit him in the face. His broad, fleshy face that had often smiled with unctuous greed as Armand held out to him gifts of beef, bacon, fresh eggs, grapes from the south. Mercier was the one most implicated. That's it, Armand understood: because Mercier was in charge of the factory, he was turning the anger away from himself, onto Armand.

Once more he tried to address the workers. "Every week you brought home paychecks, and you received more benefits than those working in any other factory...."

Mercier again interrupted him. "We wouldn't have taken them if we'd known they were coming from the Boches. You pulled the wool over our eyes. We should have suspected at the beginning, when you fired our Jewish comrades."

"But that was for their—"

"Silence! Enough lies and dissembling! We made your perfumes, and you used them to cover up the stink of the Nazis. You made us into their flunkies and gave them the fruits of our labor. No more! The factory is ours. Everything in it belongs to us!" The crowd cheered wildly as Mercier let them into the building.

They stormed it like invading soldiers, kicking over the vats of essential oils, smashing the bottles to the ground, avenging themselves on the machinery, destroying the perfumers' organs, ripping apart the chairs.

"No!" shouted Armand, trying to restrain one and then another. But they pushed him aside in their rampage of destruction.

Oils and alcohols, fragrance compounds as costly as gold, were spilling into the streets as people came running out from nearby houses to watch the reeking devastation. The stench was so awful that people coughed and choked, held handkerchiefs or pieces of clothing up to their noses, their eyes red from the fumes. A triumphant shout sounded from inside, and then everyone rushed out of the factory just before a thunderous explosion.

Armand ran to safety with the others and stood watching the fire take his factory, sending up tongues of brilliant color. Then bursts of thick smoke erupted through the flames, poisoning the air with a rank, terrifying smell, an overwhelming stench of decomposition.

He stood hypnotized until he became aware of the men around him staring with pleasure at the cremation of the building where they'd worked for years. Reflected flames lit up the cruelty of their faces. Armand had an image of Anne being attacked by the mob. Stealthily he made his way out of the crowd and then ran, fast as a fox from its hunters.

*　　*　　*

When he reached home, Anne was dressed to leave, a kerchief covering her head. She was looking very pale, and he was afraid for her; but they had no choice. "Quick," he said, taking her arm. "There's no time left."

She picked up her large handbag crammed with medicines, toiletries, underwear, and he led the way, balanced between two heavy suitcases. At the bottom of the stairs Anne touched his arm. "Wait here, I'll be right back." He swallowed his protest as she made her laborious way up the stairs again. When she returned, the lace wool blanket was folded over her arm like a headwaiter's serviette.

"Come now," he said lovingly but impatient. Delay could be fatal.

Anne's movements were so slow on her painfully swollen ankles, and with the weight of the child, that he was beginning to feel panic. Troops were everywhere. Only occasionally did Armand pull Anne into a doorway to dodge a crowd of soldiers. Otherwise they braved it, traversing the city through small streets and alleyways. It was a long, devious route. They knew they had to avoid the southern exit from Paris, where American troops were confronting German lines.

Dusk fell: it was night when they finally came to the boundary of Paris, and crossed it.

From there they walked. For the next three hours they didn't exchange a word, needing all their strength to keep moving. Armand's arms burned with the weight of the suitcases, and he was painfully aware of the strain Anne was under. He could hear her shallow breathing as she tried to keep up with him in the darkness and wished there were something, anything at all, he could do to relieve her. "Courage, my darling," was all he could say, feeling the absurdity of his words as they came out. She'd shown greater courage than he would be capable of, he thought. But she nodded in response, chewing her lower lip.

It was after midnight. They were still alone on the road. Since leaving Paris, they'd met a few starving dogs, but no humans at all. Anne called his name in a faint voice. He went back for her and she rested her head on his shoulder, gasping, "I can't go on."

Armand took her handbag, slipped its handles over his

neck, transferred one suitcase to his side, clasping it with his arm, while his hand carried the other. He guided her off the road, his arm around her waist. At the first clearing she sank to the ground.

His strength exhausted, Armand fell asleep instantly, as Anne did, and both slept through until morning, when they woke to a pale light illuminating a nearby copse of small trees and bushes. It was a lovely sight. They smiled at each other. Armand pointed to an apple tree. "Shall I get us breakfast?"

"Please."

When he came up to it, he found a single premature fruit on a low-hanging branch. He plucked it and brought it back to Anne. "A good sign," he told her, bending to kiss her neck.

"Maybe we've woken up in Eden," she suggested, smiling, as she sank her teeth into the green apple. She winced. "Terribly sour," she told him. "Must be from the tree of knowledge."

He sat against her, a hand on her belly, her scalp against his cheek. " 'Ye must not take thereof, sayeth the Lord,' " he quoted from childhood lessons.

"Unless you're hungry," said Anne, offering it to him.

Cheered, they started on their way again.

For the next two days, pausing to rest ever more frequently, they made their way. When they passed through a town or village, they bought food. Anne drank the milk at the shop, so they wouldn't have to carry glass bottles, and they took along only loaves of bread, a hard sausage, fruit.

At the end of the second day a farmer pulled up to them in his wagon and offered a ride. They accepted gratefully, trusting him through instinct or weakness, because they were at the end of their strength. He asked no questions except when the baby was due and where they were headed. Armand gave the general area, and the farmer said gruffly that he'd drive them part of the way. Armand thanked him, offered to pay, but the man shook his head. "Long walks no good for women in that condition," he stated, and took them past Fontainebleau into St. Florentin and beyond the town.

On the third day they reached the Du Près'.

Pierre's father, though barely sixty, appeared like a man in his eighties. "We got word," Pierre whispered, "Maman was sent East, probably to Poland, to some kind of camp."

Monsieur Du Près seemed to live in his own world, indifferent to his surroundings. But he greeted Armand warmly and asked why he hadn't been to visit them. "The Christmas goose, do you remember?" he asked, smiling. "How good it smelled!" Then, with sadness, he continued, "Those were times, my boy. Their like will not come again. The world has become savage." Noticing Anne at last, he said, "Ah. You've married a Jewess!" Anne's kerchief had come askew, revealing her baldness. To Pierre's father, it was the shaved head of an Orthodox Jewish wife. "But you must have a wig made, my dear," he said, embracing her. "Never mind, you are welcome as a daughter, O Rose of Sharon."

Marie-Louise kissed them on both cheeks and took Anne off to her own bed, the one she shared with Pierre. "I'll bring you apple vinegar with honey. Drink it and rest, mainly rest. You'll tell us about your adventures later, if you care to. Armand is Pierre's dearest friend, one of the family, so you are nearly my sister." Anne protested against taking her bed, but Marie-Louise was adamant. "Having a baby is a serious matter. No amount of pampering is enough."

Exhausted, Armand instantly fell asleep on the couch and slept for several hours, until Pierre woke him with the announcement of dinner.

Despite food shortages, Marie-Louise had prepared a feast: thick garlic soup followed by ragoût, salad, goat cheese, and a large fruit tart she'd baked while her guests were sleeping. Two jugs of wine—one red, the other white—stood on the cheerfully striped tablecloth.

Anne wore a pale smock Marie-Louise had lent her, and a rosy silk scarf to cover her head. Still too fatigued to eat, she made an effort to taste at least a mouthful or two of each dish. She said it was wonderful, and when she smiled, Armand saw traces of the lost radiance lighting up her face.

He, too, could do no justice to the meal after their long

fast, but the look on Anne's face, the friendship he felt around him, and his sense of having reached a haven made Armand say, truthfully, "This is the best dinner of my life."

The Du Prèses asked no direct questions, but their curiosity and concern were obvious. Anne and Armand were willing to tell their friends about the nightmare they'd undergone but were reluctant at first, not wanting to upset the child. Josette, a merry girl of nearly three, was a miniature of her mother. She doted on her grandfather, picking out the tastiest morsels from her plate between two chubby fingers and offering them to him. He always accepted, with a look of near reverence that made him suddenly appear his own age or even younger. "He lives for her," Pierre had told Armand before they went in to dinner. "Thank God he has a grandchild—otherwise he might no longer be with us."

He refilled their glasses. "Don't hold back on Josette's account. She's too young to understand most of it. She understands only what she has already experienced—though I often feel that's too much."

When Armand finished the story, the Du Prèses had tears in their eyes. Monsieur was crying openly.

Marie-Louise embraced Anne. "You must stay here as long as you like," she said. "There's a wonderful midwife in the town, an old woman who's seen every kind of birth and always knows what to do."

"She's a witch," Pierre agreed. "She delivered Josette. We'd been here for less than a year at that point. People were extremely kind to us. They accepted us without question, they brought us food. . . ."

"And things for the baby," Marie-Louise added, "and they came to chat with Grandpapa. We've made friends, and we're quite cozy here. Except that I've had to take up sewing. Dreadful work, but what else to do for a living?"

"You could join me in the fields," her husband retorted.

"Yes," she agreed laughing. "But who would make the dinner? Or play cards with Grandpapa?"

He blew her a kiss. "No one can replace you there. You see? As I've always said, a woman's place is in the home."

"Traitor!" she shouted at him, then turned immediately to Anne and Armand. "Oh, I'm sorry. I didn't mean. . . ."

But Anne was laughing. "Right you are, Marie-Lou! A man who says something like that deserves to be strung up."

Pierre brought out an old eau-de-vie he'd been saving for a special occasion. "None could be more special than this," he affirmed, holding up his glass for a toast. "To you, to your miraculous survival. To your health!" They all took a sip, while he remained standing at the head of the table. "And to my mother. L'chaim!" He looked over at his father, and both of them downed their glasses.

After dinner Josette was moved into her grandfather's room, chirping with delight. Pierre and Marie-Louise would share Josette's bed. When Anne and Armand protested, Marie-Lou ordered them not to oppose her. They accepted, but Anne felt constrained and told Armand later that they would leave as soon after the birth as possible.

When they'd been at the Du Prèses for nearly three weeks, both of them noticed that something had changed. An uneasiness had sprung up. Something unspoken hung in the air, and though their hosts were as cordial as ever, Anne observed to Armand that the animation and cheerfulness they'd felt at the beginning had ebbed away, and it seemed that humor had been sucked out of the household. Armand agreed: a shadow had fallen. Neither of them could figure out where it came from or what it portended.

"You must speak to him," Anne instructed her husband. "Pierre is your best friend. You must force him to tell you what's happened."

But Pierre was evasive. First he told Armand he was imagining things; then, that everything moved in cycles and even the moon had to wane at times.

Dissatisfied, and unwilling to drop the matter, Anne resolved to get at its crux through Marie-Lou.

Next afternoon, when the two women were shelling peas in the kitchen, Anne observed casually, "Since we arrived here, you've been home every evening, and you've had no visitors."

Marie-Louise concentrated on her vegetables and mumbled, "We don't go in for much company."

"Yet you told us the first evening we arrived that you've made friends in the town."

Reddening slightly, Marie-Lou muttered, "They'll keep."

Anne abandoned the peas and looked directly at her friend. "You've been like a sister to us both, and Pierre like a brother. You *must* tell me, Marie-Lou. I know something's wrong—I feel it. Whatever it is, you must let me know it, if you care for me at all."

"If I care for you!" Marie-Louise raised her head and Anne saw that she was crying. She slid her chair across the floor and embraced her.

"The people . . ." she began.

"Yes?" Anne encouraged,

"Oh, people are stupid!"

"Some are, certainly," Anne agreed. "And some are even wicked. But what," she asked with sudden insight, "have they been saying about us?"

"I said you were our relatives. Cousins. They wanted to know why you had come so suddenly. I said it wasn't sudden, we'd planned your visit for a long time. They asked why now, when you are so heavy with child? Why didn't you have your baby at home?"

"Reasonable," said Anne, feeling a premonition of what was to come.

"They. . . ." Marie-Louise broke down in tears. Anne stroked her until she was more composed. Then Anne insisted, "You must tell me the rest."

"They don't know who you are, but they suspect you're collaborators. Someone must have sneaked a look at your poor head—they know you've been shaven. And there've been threats—oh Anne! I don't know what's come over these people. They were so good to us, they were so gentle to Grandpapa and the baby!"

"And now," said Anne, making the instant decision, "you are in danger. Who is threatening you?"

"I think . . . I'm not sure, but cells of the Resistance have been working in the town and in the hills. They hid some Jews among themselves. They're fierce patriots. I think the Maquis are out for revenge." She hugged her friend with all her might and whispered, "It's Josette. I'm afraid for her."

*   *   *

When the Du Prèses sat down for their evening meal, the Jolaunays had gone. They left a note expressing their gratitude and love and their hope that all of them would be reunited soon. There was special love for Josette and a ring of white gold, set with an oval sapphire, to be given her when she reached the age of thirteen.

Nobody ate that evening. Their thoughts ranged across the dark fields, searching for their friends.

A pale moon bleached the tall grasses they walked through until they came to the far end of open land, where a small path led down to a stream and followed alongside it. Three hours after starting out they were forced to take cover and rest. Armand rolled his jacket into a pillow for Anne, and they slept on the mossy ground, soothed by forest vapors.

At dawn he made them start out. They washed quickly in the stream, they drank the tea they'd brought in a flask, and Armand chewed some of the heavy country bread. Anne didn't want to eat. She needed Armand's help to get up off the ground, and her movements were slower, in greater pain than before. Her back hurt so much she couldn't straighten it, but she forced herself to move ahead, concentrating on the chestnuts Armand kicked in front of him as they walked.

By afternoon, despite their frequent stops, she was conscious of nothing but pain, sharp and commanding, like thick needles jabbing into her spine. When they came out of a forest path, she raised her head and saw a small cluster of houses standing on a hill, apricot-gray with the light behind them. "Isn't it beautiful! Like a little stage set. . . ." She doubled over with a strong contraction. "Oh, God."

"Anne! What is it?" But even as he asked, another wave of pain pitched her forward and she went down on her knees.

"Forgive me, Armand. I think it's coming."

"No!" he cried to the trees and hills, to God. The baby wasn't due for at least two weeks. How could she be having it out here, in the open, with no one to help? He

turned, about to tell her that it was impossible and that
she had to try once more, but he saw that her eyes were
closed and she was pitching back and forth, grasping her
stomach and moaning softly.

He looked around wildly. On the hill a church steeple
rose over the houses. Next to the church a light switched
on. "Wait here," he said.

"No. Don't leave me alone, Armand. Please." Her face
contorted as each new spasm took hold. She was panting
and her mouth was open, her lips white and cracked like a
sun-dried riverbed.

Armand could make out a dark structure close to them
on the left. Hurling his suitcases under a bush to hide
them, he picked Anne up in his arms and carried her
there.

It was a barn, empty except for a pile of straw to the
right. Tottering under her weight, he put her down on the
straw. "My back!" she screamed. "My legs! They've got to
be higher. Please, oh please."

He piled straw under them, making a hard pillow. He
saw how heavily she was perspiring. "Water," she breathed.
"Please, God, help me. I need water."

Armand was icy, nearly paralyzed with fear. On the
wall above her head someone had scrawled in white
paint; "Vive la France!" and, under it, "Vive de Gaulle!" He
realized that the barn was a meeting place for a cell of the
Resistance.

He kissed her wet forehead. "Take deep breaths," he
told her. "Count to one hundred. Grab hold of my handkerchief—here. Hold tight; I'm getting help." He raced up
to the house beside the church.

He returned with a priest, who placed candles around
Anne and lit them. Her cramps were regular now, spaced
close together.

"Water!" she begged.

They'd brought it from the house, and Armand rushed
to get it, but the priest commanded, "She must not drink.
Take this sponge"—he withdrew it from his cassock—
"moisten it, and put it to her lips."

He did as he was told. Then the priest instructed Armand,
"Help me raise her."

He unfolded the newspaper he was carrying and spread it on the straw under Anne. "A disinfectant," he explained. "The ink sterilizes."

Anne's breathing was short and shallow now, each breath overlapping the last. Her water burst, suddenly, and she propped herself up on her elbows, her knees bent and legs apart. She was bearing down with an expression Armand hadn't seen before: fixéd, removed, almost demonic.

The little flames on the candles swayed and flickered in the breeze. Armand saw the priest bending over Anne, the sleeves of his cassock pushed up toward his armpits, his hands between her legs.

Armand heard a wail, then a scream. The priest was holding a blood-soaked infant upside down by its feet. The wail swelled into a loud cry. "Good!" he exclaimed, righting the child and handing it to Armand.

It was a girl, he registered, but he didn't look at her. He was staring at the thick blood seeping from between Anne's legs. He realized Anne was screaming.

"The afterbirth," said the priest. "Quick. Tear the rags. Bring water."

Armand placed the baby on the straw next to Anne's shoulder and ran for the jug. The screams became louder, bounced from the walls. The room was suddenly brilliant with light.

Armand whirled around to see the flames leap up where a candle had fallen on the straw close to Anne's head. The priest grabbed Armand's jacket, threw it onto the fire and flung himself on top of it. Armand poured the water he was carrying over the straw. He picked up the squealing child and heard the priest say, "Her leg. It's burned the child's leg."

Blood was seeping through the straw, changing its color from champagne to burgundy. Screams mingled with cries. The bed grew dark with blood, the priest's voice was urgent. Everything reeked of blood. So much blood, Armand thought wildly. Is there no end to the blood? It would drown them all. Suddenly there was silence.

From a far distance Armand heard a voice say, "She's gone, my son."

He didn't understand. He felt a hand on his shoulder

and the voice came again. "Your wife is dead. May she rest in peace. The Lord giveth, and the Lord taketh away."

The screaming began again. He was cradling Anne in his arms, and the room stank of blood and paraffin. The screams continued; they were his own. The priest left with the child, saying something about cleaning, caring for the leg. . . .

Armand rocked Anne back and forth, feeling nothing at all, his senses dead. Above her head blurred white letters swam.

A long time later they began to come into focus. "Vive . . ." he read dully. He looked down at her face and kissed her open lips. "Anne!" he shouted, kissing her again and again, "Vive Anne! Vive! Vive!"

When he came up to the house hours later, a nervous woman opened the door. She looked him over and, without speaking, led Armand to the bathroom to wash. When he'd finished, he put on the robe prepared for him and passed through the sitting room. His baby was sleeping in a wooden box, covered with a small, harsh blanket.

In the next room the priest stood waiting, arms folded over his chest. Behind him the curtains hadn't been drawn. Armand looked out on the small stone church with a cemetery in front. "We must bury her now," he said.

"Not possible. It's nearly midnight."

"Tomorrow morning."

"You will need a stone, a coffin. . . ."

"Doesn't matter."

"You must register the death. Our village is too small for a registry office, but two kilometers from here. . . ."

"No! We must do without that."

The priest, still standing with arms folded, stared at him, and Armand suddenly recalled the look on his face when he had first entered the barn and had seen Anne's head, with its fuzzy down of new hair.

"You do not want to register your wife's name?" he asked slowly.

Armand had no recourse but mercy. "Please, Father, bury her. She was an angel." Tears ran down his face. "You must believe me. She was innocent as an angel."

"I'll see what I can do. Calm yourself, my son. I promise I shall bury your wife. But you must tell me who you are."

"Armand Jolaunay."

The priest's eyes moved to a figure standing in the doorway. Armand hadn't noticed the housekeeper's presence. She gave a bare hint of a nod, stepped back. "You promise to do it?" he asked the priest.

"I promise. She shall be buried at dawn."

The housekeeper signaled Armand to follow her to his room. They passed his sleeping infant on the way, but Armand didn't notice.

Next morning at dawn, shrouded in mist, beside the open grave, the priest intoned his words in Latin. Anne was lying in a pinewood coffin he'd been able to provide from the cellar. The church, Armand thought—always prepared for death.

He tried to concentrate on the words, but he couldn't reconstruct them from the lessons he'd been given as a boy. A twig snapped. He heard a sound like footsteps. Armand stiffened.

Two shadows passed in the gray mist. The priest was making the sign of the cross. Armand knelt. He could sense someone close behind him. He tensed.

Before he could spring, two men rushed at him from either side and grabbed his arms. The priest looked up and nodded at them.

"What is this?" Armand shouted, trying to wrench free. He was held tightly. The priest left his place beside the open grave holding Anne's coffin.

"Members of the Maquis," he said, joining the men. "Comrades in the struggle to free France from the fascist oppressor."

"*You?*" Armand asked. "You called them?"

The priest nodded.

"But you gave me your promise!"

"To bury your wife. I've done that." His eyes narrowed, he drew himself up. "You are a traitor to this nation, Jolaunay. I never promised to protect you. . . ."

Armand cried out in protest.

"You are scum, Jolaunay. You and your kind carry the

contagion that perverts our noble purpose. The Nazis have been crushed, but we men of the Maquis will continue our work with the help of God Almighty until the stain of your filth has been wiped from the land." He nodded at one of the men, who dropped Armand's arm, pulled out a pistol, and pressed it against his side. "You will go quietly, Jolaunay."

"My daughter!" he remembered.

"We are not vindictive. The child will not be made to suffer for the sins of her father. She will be raised by nuns in the foundling hospital."

Armand tore his right arm free, grabbing the hand with the pistol. The gun went off, the bullet whizzing close to the priest's ear, and Armand and his captor were on the ground, wrestling for the gun that both of them held. The other men stood back, jumping away from the gun's range. Armand jabbed the butt in the man's stomach. The man's hold loosened. Armand stood up, holding the gun in front of him.

"Up," he commanded. "All right, all three of you: march."

He led them to the house, walked them through to the back of it. "Where's the cellar?"

"Cellar?" the priest repeated dumbly.

"Don't play games!" Armand brought the gun to the head of one of the Maquis. "Cellar. Underground. The place where you hid all your pure resisters. Quickly!"

The priest jutted his chin toward a door beside the larder. It was padlocked. "Key," Armand commanded. "Don't be smart. I don't care if I blow off one of your heads—or all of them."

The priest held it out. Armand ordered him to unlock the door. Then he pocketed the key and forced them downstairs.

He had them sit in a corner, their backs toward him. The one whose gun he'd taken turned suddenly and lunged. Armand squeezed the trigger.

It got him in the chest. The man's hands flew up, and he dropped to his knees. "Bastard!" he shouted and sank to the ground.

"Shut up!" Armand yelled at the priest, who had been intoning a litany. "Both of you, flat on the ground."

They obeyed, and Armand ran up the stairs, closed the door behind him, and locked it. Waving the pistol above his head, Armand made a quick search of the house. The box in the sitting room was empty. He couldn't find the baby in any of the rooms and wanted to call out to her, but he had no name. "Vive Anne!" he shouted as he dashed into the hallway, "Viveanne, where are you, Viveanne?"

The front door was standing open, and he saw people running up to it. Armand raced to the back, leaped out through the kitchen window, flung the pistol away, and ran.

5

1945–1951

Near the old walled town of Carcassonne, on the river Aude, Mme. Glouzet got up from her rocking chair to answer the knock on the door. She moved slowly because of an injury to her back from a flogging she'd been given by her stepmother's steel cane when she was five. The knocking came again and she muttered angrily, "Calluses to your knuckles!" She opened the door on a bearded man holding a small child. The man asked whether the room was still for rent.

"How long you planning to stay?" she asked suspiciously.

"That depends, I. . . . May we come in?"

"I need a deposit," she told him, opening the door wide enough for them to come through. "The child—does it make much noise?"

"She's very quiet and good."

"Long as she stays that way. They're more trouble than dogs, lots of them." She looked the man in the eyes, noticing they were the color of lead or unpolished silver. "I do not permit dogs here."

"I understand."

The woman had a harelip and a few of her teeth were missing. "I like cats," she continued, leading him to the room. "They're good, don't talk much. But dogs are only trouble. Won't have them. You bring a dog in here, you're out."

Armand handed her the deposit. She scowled at the money, then slipped it into a pocket of her trousers. "That child—how old is she?"

"Eighteen months."

"Mighty young." She squinted at Vie. "What do you feed her?"

"Anything." She'd lived on bread and milk the first few days after he'd stolen her from the orphanage, six months ago. Later, when he judged they were far enough away from the town, and after he'd rinsed her hair with a brown dye, Armand took her into cheap restaurants, where he fed her from his own plate. She amazed him by eating everything he gave her.

"She yours?"

Startled, Armand nodded.

"Where's the mother?"

"Dead."

"Must've been pretty." On that gracious note Mme. Glouzet left them.

Vie's hair was now back to its natural white-gold. That, and the ugly area on her thigh where the candle had burned her, were the marks that had identified her the night he'd broken into the nursery and shined his flashlight on the sleeping infants. The room was hot, and most of the babies lay uncovered, nightgowns bunched up at their middles. His beam had caught the mark on her leg. He'd been afraid it would have healed during the time— nearly a year—since her birth; afraid that he wouldn't be able to distinguish his child from others.

But he'd been granted the sign. Creeping up silently, he'd taken her in his arms and wrapped her in the blanket. He escaped out the window, holding on to the ledge with one arm while his feet groped for footholds on the rough stone wall. From there to the ledge of a second-story window. Then scaling down the wall again, until Armand felt he was close enough to the ground to jump.

He'd miscalculated the height and fallen awkwardly, on his back, but without injuring himself. The baby in his arm made no sound, as though she sensed the need for silence. Despite the risk, Armand turned on his flashlight to make sure she was all right. She was looking up at him with a steady gaze. It was the direct, unwavering look of her mother.

Since then they'd been moving south slowly, stopping at inns and boardinghouses on the way. Now they were practically as far as they could go while still remaining in France, close to the border with Spain and the tiny mountain republic of Andorra. If they had to, they'd flee over the Pyrenees. But for the time being, Armand would take the chance on settling. He'd had more than he thought he could bear of running and hiding. And Vie needed regularity in her life.

Within three months of arriving at Mme. Glouzet's, Vie began to talk. Though she'd been able to walk when Armand had kidnapped her, and moved with the grace of an older child, by the time they came to their present home her only words were *papa, bébé* (meaning drink, not baby), *lait* and *leur*, for "fleur," flower.

She made friends with a kitten in the house and called it *Mi*, short for *ami*, "friend." She addressed Mme. Glouzet as "mam," and then in short order began picking up more words, new ones every day, and soon was arranging them in an order that approximated skeletal sentences.

"The child is all right," admitted Mme. Glouzet to Armand. "Minds her own business. Like a cat." The landlady was cranky and eccentric, but she seemed to have developed a fondness for Vie and even for him. Sometimes she prepared a special dish for them, scowling fiercely when he tried to thank her.

Armand began to relax, after nearly two years when he'd never felt himself out of danger. He worked with farmers, peasants of the Languedoc, who kept their own counsel, paying little attention to him or to Vie. They

were people who worked the ungiving red earth at the
foothills of the Pyrenees, speaking a sharp, guttural French
and fearing nothing except God and the mountains. They
showed Armand a rough kindness, offering to share their
wine or cheese with him, teasing him about the child who
came along wherever he went. He was able to believe that
they intended him no harm.

He worked through the summer, into fall. In winter he
did what he could, anything at all, but even the most
menial jobs were scarce, and in January he was lucky to
find employment for even two days of the week.

In Carcassonne, he thought, perhaps he could find something that would pay a living wage for him and Vie. He
hated spending money on trips to the town, but nevertheless he determined to begin a regular schedule of going
there every week.

Waiting for the bus, he shivered as a cold wind slapped
him. He realized Vie's coat had become too small. He'd
bought it in the autumn, for her second birthday, not
realizing a child could grow so much in a few months.
With a job, a real job—maybe even skilled work, he
fantasized—he could buy her warm clothes, a little rabbit
fur, with a fur bonnet and matching muff. Everyone would
take her for a princess.

"Why you smile, Papa?" asked Vie sternly.

"Dreams, little one. I see you as a fairy princess living
in a palace made of flowers. The flowers are gold and
silver, yet their fragrance is that of living flowers, growing
wild in a field." She looked at him with wide eyes, and he
elaborated the story, bringing in gentle raindrops that
turned into glistening diamonds when they reached the
flowers. The rapture on her face inspired him, and he
invented more and more, stopping only when the bus
came in sight. Then he noticed that a young woman stood
behind him, must have been standing there a long time.
She'd been listening to his story and gave him a charming
smile as he stood back to let her board the bus ahead of
him.

Her smile made his stomach contract sharply. Since
Anne's death he'd had nobody. As he watched her climb
into the bus, he noticed how tightly the material of her

skirt stretched over her hips. Her calves were strong and beautifully shaped in their sheaths of dark stockings; her ankles small. He felt himself swallowing hard. God, he thought, I need her. I'd forgotten how it feels to be around a pretty woman.

But he took a seat far away from her.

The woman was looking at him, a quizzical smile on her lips. Armand closed his eyes, but behind the lids he saw her soft mouth, the row of teeth, the slight opening and a hint of deep pink glistening inside her lower lip. When he opened his eyes again, she was looking out the window and Vie was pulling at his jacket, asking for the story to go on. He put her on his lap and didn't take his eyes off her until they reached Carcassonne. Then he waited for the woman to walk past them and smiled at her. He'd become so unsure during these years, so distrustful of everyone, that he was unable to trust himself.

Vie's solemn baby eyes were studying him. He reached for her hand and began walking from the depot toward the main square, not wanting to look at her now because she was so like Anne, and he was feeling that he'd betrayed her.

Unreasonable, irrational, probably close to being out of control, he told himself. He shared the room with his child, and a gorgon was his landlady. Sex had no way of entering his life. He didn't even dare stroke himself on nights when he woke, his body like a cobra about to strike. Afraid the child would notice if he touched himself, he lay rigid, his hands rolled into fists at his side.

"Papa, we go maycan store?" Vie pleaded.

"Of course, little angel, we always do." She meant the large grocery; "maycan" referred to the American canned goods on the shelves, their contents usually inedible. Evaporated milk, powdered eggs, something called Spam.

"Terrible," confided the grocer to Armand, as he did each time they came. "Americans, they are cannibals." He gave Vie a hard red candy wrapped in cellophane, which she popped directly in her mouth.

Armand fished for it, extracted it painfully and, after removing the paper, dropped it back in. Their next stop was the kiosk, for a newspaper, and then the cafe where

Vie had her lemonade and Armand studied the notice board to see if anyone had answered his short ad or if there were other announcements of job openings. Then he joined Vie, ordered a coffee, and looked at the classified section of the paper.

Afterward they followed leads, if any, and every trip to Carcassonne ended at the pharmacy, near the depot, where the rows of bottles holding colored liquids, the dried herbs, the little silver scales to measure prescriptions, all made him feel at home. The smells of the shop—soap, medicine, lotions, powders—always held a predominant note of lemon or pine.

The woman behind the counter was roughly his age. Yet she greeted him playfully whenever they entered. "Voilà, Monsieur le papa!"

"Bonjour, Mademoiselle Benoit. Ça va?"

She shrugged. "It goes. Always too much to do for a woman alone."

"Perhaps you could use a helper?"

"I suppose." She shrugged again.

Glancing toward the back of the shop, Armand could see the old man in his wheelchair, drooling slightly. His daughter had said she always put him there so she could keep an eye on him while she worked. A hard life, Armand thought, commiserating with the plain woman who never complained openly but whose pinched expression revealed the arduousness of her existence. He knew nothing about her except that she seemed kind and dutiful.

"What about me?" he asked. She stared at him blankly. "I mean, I could help you in the shop. It would be easier on you." And just the right job for me, he thought.

"But you know nothing about a pharmacy!"

He took a deep breath, then spoke rapidly. "I worked for Chanel many years ago. As a perfumer's apprentice; I worked with natural and synthetic materials, helping to formulate compounds."

"I see. Why did you leave Paris?"

"My wife was killed there."

"By the Germans?"

Damn. He hated interrogations of any kind, particularly in front of Vie. His lies had to be consistent, and he would have to remember them. "She was caught in cross fire. The nationality of the bullet was not determined. I was left alone with Vie and, as you can imagine, I was brokenhearted. A cousin of mine, with whom I've been close since childhood, invited me to come stay with him and his family. They live in the region."

"And you are with them now?"

"Alas, no! The mother of my cousin's wife was taken ill, critically ill, in America, and they decided to join her there. She's now much better, but they plan on remaining." Armand almost let out a sigh when he finished. He was perspiring heavily.

"Poor man," said Mlle. Benoit tenderly. "I'll see what I can do." Her voice changed abruptly. "But you understand, I cannot pay very much."

He nodded.

"Very little," she added. Forcing down the price of everything was natural to her, a real pleasure. "But I'll see," she promised. "Come back next Tuesday, M. Delarue, and you'll have my answer."

Odile Benoit smiled after they left; she'd drive her best bargain yet, with that man. He was attractive, well-mannered, a widower—and willing to work for her! She smiled broadly, breathing on her glasses and polishing them with the hem of her skirt. He was lying about his past, she was sure of that. So he had something to cover up. Fine. She'd always been a clever one; she'd ferret out Armand Delarue's secret and have a hold over him to use if necessary. She fitted the glasses back over her ears. You'll see, she promised herself. Things are about to change.

She laughed out loud, and at the sound her father uttered a cry of alarm. She turned to him in disgust. "What a life you've given me!" she accused. Since he couldn't speak, she never knew if he heard or understood her. "You've tried to make me into a freak like yourself. I've wasted my youth, become a laughingstock—unmarried at thirty-six! It's hard, terribly hard, for a woman to live on her own. No one to care for her, no one to turn to for comfort or strength." Self-pity came as naturally to Odile as miserliness. She was too clever to believe her own complaining, but she enjoyed its doleful luxury.

She was unmarried for the simple reason that no one had asked her. Before the war, when she was in her late twenties, she still had hopes. Then the men disappeared, possible husbands had turned soldiers. Many died or vanished. Her father had his stroke, followed two months later by the death of her mother. Olile's spinsterhood became one of the side effects of war. Her frustration led to anger and then settled into deep hatred for her father, on whose terrified form in the wheelchair she heaped the blame for her unfulfillment.

When Armand came into the store on Tuesday, he noticed she'd done something new with her hair. As he came close to her, the *Muguet* she was wearing reminded him of Marie-Louise, who loved lilies of the valley. She wore them in their season, then pressed them between pages of books.

Odile's hand reached to her head in a girlish gesture when Armand complimented her hairdo. "Look at *that* hair," she said, tousling Vie's. "Pure silk. You must lend me your beautiful daughter one day. I have no children of my own. What a lovely child!"

Armand smiled at the warm, motherly woman. He invited her to an early supper, a light meal before they caught the nine-fifteen bus back home. She said she'd close up shop and be ready in a few minutes.

Over dinner Odile told him that, after making her calculations, she realized she couldn't afford to hire an assistant after all. What she needed was a partner, with whom she'd share profits—though she didn't indicate how they'd be divided and who would bring in capital of his own.

There, she thought, I'll find out if he has money, and how much.

He jumped at the chance. For this opportunity it was worth selling some of the remaining jewels, perhaps the pearl-and-ruby necklace, the piece of greatest value. Anne would understand, he was sure. An investment like this could mean a proper life for Vie.

* * *

He'd sold a few of the jewels when the money ran out while he was still on the road with his baby. He'd had to sell them for a fraction of their value to former black marketers, now turned smugglers or swindlers in peacetime. He'd told himself that as soon as he found a place for them to settle, they'd live on whatever he could earn, saving the rest of the jewelry for the eventuality that they might have to escape again.

Going back for the bags the day after the murder had been a wild risk, but he had been grateful ever since for the stubborn impulse that forced him to return to the hamlet. He had crept into the cemetery in the early hours of morning and made his final adieu to Anne before covering her coffin with earth. Looking up from the grave, Armand could see the house where he'd killed the man, where his child lay sleeping. Or perhaps she'd already then been sent to a foundling home.

He thought of trying to find her, but in the clarity of mind that follows shock and grief, Armand realized it would be suicidal. How could he feed a newborn? How keep her warm and safe while he was on the run from his pursuers? And if they caught up with him . . . ? He had no choice but to leave her wherever she was.

His lucidity of thought had then directed him to find the bags. In them lay the only hope of survival, if and when he should eventually retrieve his daughter.

He had crept back toward the barn, searching the bushes with blind fingers in the black night. Nowhere. He heard a sound and sprang up. His left foot hit something hard. He bent down and felt the suitcases. Armand grabbed them. The sound was not repeated. He moved away quietly and wasn't followed.

For months after, he didn't come near human habitation. Running. Running from his hunters. Running away from his memories. Months of living in the woods like a wild man, his beard knotted and filthy, his clothes transformed to rags. The days grew shorter and colder. He found a shallow cave and dug it deeper, scooping out earth and stones with his fingers until they were numb and bruised. He rested, dug again, and made a shelter for the winter.

All his senses became more acute, even his hearing. But his sense of smell was that of a bloodhound as he tracked small game with an improvised slingshot. Staying alive took all his energy. Often he gave up the search for food because he was too tired. He slept by day and again at night. He longed for death but wouldn't let himself give in. He had to stay alive for his daughter, child of love, his life, Vie.

Winter had ended as streams gurgled and the woods were renewed with incipient birth. Snowdrops, then violets blooming in the moss. Still Armand had remained hidden, not knowing where he was or how far he'd come from the little village.

When he had first ventured out of the forest, the light and colors of the meadow dazzled him. Intense cornflowers, scarlet poppies, and the brilliant white of wild carrot sparkled in the grasses: blue, red, white. The colors of the tricolor, he realized, the flag of France.

But still he waited. It was summer when he dared approach a village, dressed in the rags he'd washed repeatedly in a stream and dried in the sun. His skin was hard now, rough but very clean. His hair, despite his attempts to cut it with a sharp stone, remained long and ragged.

The first person to catch sight of him ran away. Armand was starting his retreat back to the safety of the woods when a dog came running toward him with a young boy racing behind, shouting at it to stop. When the boy reached Armand, and had the dog by its neck, the child smiled, seeing nothing to fear in a figure who looked like many of the illustrations he'd seen in the children's books he'd only recently put away.

"How do you do, monsieur?" he asked politely.

"Tell me. . . ." This was the first time he'd spoken to anyone but himself in all those months, and Armand's voice cracked like dry twigs. "What is the date?"

"I'm not sure," the boy answered. "But I know it's August."

"What year?"

"1945," he said with assurance.

"And the war. How is the war going?"

"It ended a long time ago."

"When? Do you remember exactly, mon garçon?"

The boy smiled and recited proudly, "May 7, 1945."

"Who won?"

"We did, of course. Hitler is dead."

Armand bent down to hug the child. "Bless you," he rasped. "Perhaps you have saved my life."

The boy beamed with self-importance and then ran off again after his dog, who'd picked up a scent and was following it with tail wagging and loud yelps.

It was three weeks later when Armand tracked down the hospital where Vie must have been placed. The only foundling home within fifty kilometers of where Anne was buried; he'd been sure she hadn't been sent somewhere more distant, expensive, and arduous to reach in wartime.

He and his child traveled through the countryside, through towns and villages for nearly six months, using up the cash and then having to pawn the jewelry or selling it quickly for a fraction of its value.

Odile smiled, her thin lips stretching over large teeth, when he'd said he'd take up her offer. Within a week—two at the most—he would have thirty to forty thousand francs, he promised.

"That will do nicely," she told him, letting her hand rest lightly on the sleeve of his jacket. "Next week I will make dinner. You are invited to my house," she said. "You may come even if you don't have all the money on hand yet," she added magnanimously.

The small house, with a facade of whitewashed stone, stood against the rough surface of a cliff. Odile served them aperitifs in the living room. The chicken she brought out, garnished with petits pois, new potatoes, and small onions, looked festive and tasted delicious. He complimented her extravagantly.

After dinner Vie fell asleep on the flowered couch. Odile covered her tenderly with a knitted blanket, and the gesture brought tears to Armand's eyes. It was the first time he'd seen a woman tend to Vie. When Odile straightened up, Armand put his arms around her and kissed her, feeling a great wave of relief.

They went upstairs to a tiny room, where she made up his bed under a giant crucifix that covered most of the wall. Bringing in two cushions from her own room, Odile improvised a bed for Vie on the floor.

She removed her glasses. He kissed her again, in gratitude for all she was doing for them. She unbuttoned her blouse, undid her skirt, and let it fall to the floor. Armand wanted to stop her, but the intimacy of her womanly movements aroused him. Her ripe body stood before him in a soft pink slip. He was amazed by it—the curve of belly, weight of breasts, outline of plump thighs pressed together, the line between them reaching up to the soft, triangular folds.

His body took over, commanding him. He forgot his reluctance as he reached out to the sweet promise of flesh, not noticing the determined, calculating look on Odile's face. Ignored for so long, his body rushed to satisfy itself. As he entered her, he climaxed.

"I'm sorry," he whispered a few minutes later in shame, reaching to embrace her. Odile shifted to avoid his touch. She looked up at the ceiling with a triumphant smile.

A wave of loneliness, terrifying in its volume, crashed over Armand. He'd never missed Anne so bitterly.

Odile stepped out of bed carefully, picked up her clothes, and put her glasses back on. She looked down at him. "Now," she said, "we will get married."

It was a command.

Barely two months after the wedding Odile pulled Armand into the back room of the store. "Dr. Mallaquin examined me this morning. I'm having a baby," she announced. "Aren't you pleased?"

He heard the news with dread. Another pregnancy and childbirth; another child to provide for. But he was afraid of his wife—his jailer. "Very pleased," he mumbled, not meeting her eyes. "You should be taking things easier. I'll look after the shop."

He was already doing that. Now he increased the number of hours he spent there, remaining after closing time and coming in on Sundays. The hours when he tinkered with substances from the storeroom or with the new supplies of essential oils and fixatives that he'd ordered in small quantities brought him nothing but contentment. Only when he was immersed in work could Armand push away his worries about Vie and the future.

Vie was becoming more beautiful every day, he felt, but she was strangely silent and would often concentrate on something with such unswerving attention that she seemed like a little yogi, meditating on its essence. "She's not normal," complained Odile, but Armand thought Vie was simply withdrawing from things she couldn't understand or control, especially her stepmother's insane jealousy.

Armand had entered the marriage on command but willingly and, to some degree, happily. That is, though he could feel no pleasure at the thought of intimacy with his wife, he told himself that habit would soon convince him. He wanted a way of life that resembled the normal. He was grateful for the anchor thrown to him by Odile, and he crawled up to the safety of marriage like a shipwrecked man finding shore. He didn't love Odile, but her presence meant he belonged to a family. In gratitude he gave her kindness and tried to act the part of a loving husband.

But Odile wasn't an anchor. The comfort she seemed to offer was merely a lure, and once she had caught Armand, she was determined to gut him. She had to have everything from him. Though she loved no one, Odile felt entitled to being loved. Her consuming passion for Armand was jealousy—of his daughter, of anything that elicited his love and therefore, as she felt it, stole away what was her due. She was jealous of Armand, but not through love. She hated him for depriving her of her last chance at happiness.

Armand tried to protect the child by hiding his love for her when Odile was around. But sometimes the barrier he'd erected against the show of affections would collapse and he'd hold Vie in his arms, drink in the smell of her young skin, run his lips over her hair.

Surprising them like this in the kitchen, Odile erupted with fury. "That's right, you disgusting man—fondle *her*. A little child, your own daughter—but that's the way you are, isn't it? You do with your own child what you will not do with a woman!"

Vie looked at her with large frightened eyes, and Armand wondered what she understood, fearing what she might remember in future years.

On a Monday morning in late January, Armand was working in the little lab he'd set up at the back of the pharmacy, so engrossed that he'd forgotten to open up the store. By the time he was aware of hammering at the door, he'd put the magic touch on the formula: a dab of rosemary. Fresh, warm, with a hint of something savage, the fragrance bloomed in his nostrils with its own authority. *Anne*, he would call this. No, he couldn't risk that—*Zazou*, then. He gave a little laugh as he went to answer the door, drenched in joy at the birth of his perfume, his *Zazou* for Anne.

"Where were you?" asked a neighbor of theirs crossly when Armand opened the door. "Your wife has just had a baby. A girl."

Dr. Mallaquin agreed to be the child's godfather. As a close friend of her parents, he'd known Odile since she was a little girl. A severe, heavily bearded man in his late forties, the doctor was proud of his work in the Resistance as a member of the Maquis. He'd disliked Armand at first sight and distrusted him, encouraging Odile's attempts to find out about his past. He agreed to hold the child at the font, however, because she was old Benoit's grandchild. The girl would be christened Martine, after St. Martin, who brought Christianity to Gaul in the fourth century.

When they came back from the christening, Odile asked Armand where Vie had been baptized.

"Nowhere," he said curtly.

"She lives in sin."

Armand said nothing.

"A sinner," she insisted. "And you a worse one, taking a German to bed to make a little heathen."

"What do you know about my wife?"

A shower of hatred came over Odile when he said "my wife." In that moment she vowed vengeance—on him, on the dead woman, on his child. Since their marriage he'd abused her, Odile told herself—by ignoring her, turning away from her body even when she put up no resistance, when she would have permitted him to have his way. He'd moved out of her bedroom during her pregnancy.

Odile repeated to herself that she'd let him into her house, her shop; she'd shown him every wifely consideration; and yet he spurned her, turning instead to thoughts of the dead woman. Odile's hatred shifted easily from the vegetable in the wheelchair, on whom she'd daily heaped invectives, to the living monster who was depriving her of everything she deserved.

Odile committed herself to revenge. Because he didn't love her, she wanted Armand to suffer. She was a woman without gentleness or generosity, except to her own emotions. To them she gave in wholeheartedly, and she fanned the hatred burning in her until it filled her thoughts as well as feelings and began to destroy her reason. Because Armand loved his daughter, she would torture him by killing Vie. Odile didn't know how it would be done, but she thought about it obsessively. Her growing madness began with thoughts of revenge and spread to thoughts of murder.

Customers accepted samples of *Zazou* with suspicion at first. They were not accustomed to receiving anything free. Odile, coming into the shop for the first time in months, was outraged. "How dare you give away what it costs good money to buy? Cheating me out of profits—that's the sort you are!"

He let her remove the tiny vials lying on the counter, but the giving out of samples had already produced its effect. People came back asking for more. Armand used his time in the lab to distill the scent into eau de toilette, pouring it into bottles labeled with his own hand. He'd decided not to produce the denser perfume just yet, since its price might take it beyond the reach of his customers.

Each batch of eau de toilette sold out the day he made it. By altering two of the ingredients, Armand discovered a variation of *Zazou* that worked well as a cologne for men. But he was kept too busy filling orders for the original scent to make up the men's cologne. He needed an assistant, realizing Odile would never agree to such a thing. All he could do for the present was continue with *Zazou* and hope that, somehow, he'd find a way to convince her that an employee in the lab would increase their income.

He closed up shop on a Saturday evening and walked home through gentle twilight in lingering traces of the day's heat. The pale moon stood above the sinking sun. Trees, touched with yellow, were already beginning to shed their leaves. A flock of geese made their way home, flying in two streams behind their leader, forming an almost perfect V against the darkening sky.

Vie—how could he change the bitter, improvised life he'd made for her? He followed the geese with his eyes. He and Vie could fly off to a new land, holding hands as the wind carried them over rooftops, Vie in a long dress with a small crown in her hair. Like a Chagall painting he'd seen in Paris. The geese became specks and vanished. Dreamer, Armand told himself; you're a stubborn fool and a dreamer.

When he came up to the door, he heard strangled crying. He rushed in and ran to the tiny bedroom he now shared with Vie. She was huddled on the floor beside the bed, her eyes wide and terrified. He knelt down, begging her to tell him what happened, but she wouldn't answer. Finally she took her arm from behind her back and slowly brought it out for him to see. From wrist to elbow the skin was a deep purple bruise.

When he scooped her up in his arms, she spoke. "Go to baby, Papa. She cries and cries."

The sounds he had heard on entering the house hadn't stopped, Armand realized. He'd forgotten the other, thinking only of Vie. Carrying her, he walked into Odile's bedroom and found the baby lying on her stomach in a pool of vomit, crying and choking. He put Vie down, picked Martine up against his shoulder, and carried her to the bathroom to clean her. Vie patted her sister's back, murmuring, "Mustn't cry, little doll, mustn't cry."

A door slamming below made Vie stiffen in terror.

"Odile?" he called out.

No answer, but he could hear the sound of movement on the ground floor. Clasping both children firmly, he started down the stairs, meeting Odile coming up.

She seemed not to notice the girls and barely glanced at him. "My father died," she said harshly.

She pushed him aside and went up to her room, locking the door behind her. He knocked and called to her, but she didn't answer. Armand took the baby into their minuscule room, making a bed for her on the floor so she couldn't fall out. Vie would tell him nothing about her arm.

Armand knew he had to leave, for the safety of his child. Perhaps both children—Odile was so unstable that she couldn't mother her own baby. Vie was able to care for herself and get food when she needed it, but Martine was still helpless.

Armand tried to devise a plan for their escape. But his imagination balked. He could run with Vie perhaps, though still a fugitive, but could he in conscience leave behind another child of his, whose mother might neglect or even abuse her in insane rage over her husband's abandonment?

He pondered and got nowhere.

On a Sunday morning Odile took the children outside of town, along the steep banks of the riverside. She walked grimly, carrying the baby who, at ten months, was already a substantial weight. Odile had left the carriage on the side of the main path in order to follow a steep, narrow trail leading up to the highest part of the escarpment. She walked with a fixed purpose, telling Vie to walk ahead.

When they reached the high point, Odile ordered Vie to the edge. But the girl stopped still and wouldn't budge. Odile laid the baby on the ground and came toward Vie. She grabbed an arm, pulled Vie out to the brink of the precipice and with a quick, violent shove pushed her over. She stood a moment listening to the scream. Then she went back to her baby and began the descent toward the main path.

He'd been unable to get to sleep until dawn. Then, the faint light dispersing his black fantasies, Armand fell into a sleep so profound he didn't wake until nearly noon. When he did, he found himself alone in the room. The children were gone. He jumped up, running through the house, calling Vie and Odile. Her door stood open. They were gone, all of them.

They didn't come home for lunch. Armand tried eating something himself but was too worried. He imagined terrible things, then told himself that his imagination had always been too powerful, everything would be all right, there'd be a reasonable explanation for their absence. But something was pulling at his stomach, and his hands wouldn't stop shaking.

At nearly three in the afternoon, he leaped up as the front door opened. Odile came in with the baby.

"Where's Vie?"

Odile's look was hard and triumphant. "Wandered off, wouldn't come when I called."

"Where were you?" he shouted.

"Taking a walk. Just a nice walk, but the little devil ran off. Of course I tried to find her," she said in a voice of obvious lying. "But the baby was nearly starving by this time, and I had to bring her home."

"Where? Where?" He was beside himself.

She merely smiled. "I must make Martine some lunch."

He grabbed her by the shoulders, ready to shake the life out of her, if necessary, to discover where they'd been, when he heard a knock and ran to the door.

Vie was lying in the arms of a tall man, her clothes badly torn, her skin a network of bloody cuts. "My God!" Armand shouted, taking her from him.

The man followed them into the house. "Found her by the river, could've drowned. Must've fallen off the cliff there. Real high one, a miracle she made it."

"Stay here beside her," Armand ordered as he went for a basin of warm water. He returned quickly and very gently removed her tattered garments, using a soft sponge to wash off the mud and the dried blood. Vie wasn't crying. As he bathed her, Armand saw that the cuts were all small. Dozens of them, but none much deeper than a scratch.

Odile came into the room. Vie gave a loud scream.

"Back, is she?" Odile said harshly. By the way she looked at the girl Armand suddenly understood.

* * *

Running again, her screams still echoing in his ears. "Nazi! Murderer! I'll have my revenge, you monster. Friends in the Maquis, they'll torture and kill you. Yes, and her, too, with a traitor's blood in her veins!" Odile, insane with rage, grabbed Martine out of the basket she'd been rocking in and threw the baby at Armand. He caught her by a leg, and Odile went on screaming. "That one, too, tainted by her father's blood, a monster you made me carry in my womb. They'll bleed you to death, they'll slaughter you like a pig. Yes, I'm telling them everything!" She'd run screaming out of the house, and Armand emptied the safe, threw some clothes in a rucksack, picked up both children in his arms, and turned fugitive again.

Running and hiding, with two children this time as he made for the border. Picking up work where he could find it, for a few hours or days, knowing Odile could make good on her threats. The open safe, the missing children would convince even those who recognized Odile's madness that he was a thief and kidnapper.

At four and a half, Vie was forced to mother Martine, feeding and washing her, singing her to sleep. Sometimes Armand had to leave her alone with the baby while he worked or foraged for their dinner.

For nearly a year the nightmare ground on, as they criss-crossed the border, hiding out in caves, abandoned shacks, makeshift shelters he dug or constructed. Finally, in Marseilles, among the peddlers, Armand learned that Massud, the light-eyed, stringbean-thin vendor of carpets, was willing to sell other things as well: papers and passports.

Armand turned over to him what was left from the safe, keeping only Anne's wedding ring, a brooch he'd had made for her when she agreed to marry him, and his black leather-bound book. True to his word, Massud procured what they needed within six weeks.

Two days later, with new names, forged visas, and only enough money for food on the crossing, they boarded the ship that would take them over the Atlantic to a new world of forgetting and of beginnings.

III

NEW YORK

1

1952–1954

At eight, Vie Nouvel, as she was now called, had been taking care of her sister for what seemed her whole life. In the strange caves and shacks they'd lived in, Martine was the doll she had to wash, feed, burp, and keep warm. When they'd reached Canada, Vie told her father to find them a mommy, so she wouldn't have to do dumb things all the time. He promised to try, but even now he hadn't been able to find one. Since they'd come to Brooklyn, Vie had met many women her father had brought home, and she didn't care which one of them would stay, as long as the woman would take over Martine.

But they all disappeared after a few days, and she'd even forget what they were called. Mrs. Murphy was often around, but that wasn't much help—she'd babysit for both of them when Papa went out in the evening, but she'd put them to bed right away and go down to her own room. Vie was always stuck with Martine, who wasn't even a doll anymore. She was nearly five and a brat.

As she turned on the bathroom light, Vie wished Martine could disappear like those ladies. But when she was sitting on the toilet thinking about it, she remembered that she loved her baby sister, and she wished there were some way to get loved back by her.

Coming out of the bathroom, Vie noticed a dim pool of light edging out from Armand's door. She crept up and through a crack could see her father at his table in his faded dressing gown, an empty bottle and wineglass beside him, his arms resting on either side of an open book. She gave the door a little shove, and he grabbed hold of the book, pressing it tightly against him as though someone were trying to take it away. Then he saw it was Vie and relaxed, laying the book back down. "What is it ma p'tite?" he called

"Martine was crying again, it woke me up."

"Why is she doing that, darling?"

She walked over to the table. "Something she dreams, I guess. She does it an awful lot." Seeing displeasure on Armand's face, Vie switched to her sister's defense. "She's just a little kid. She's bad a lot, but she doesn't mean to be. That's how she is."

Armand shifted in his chair, bringing his legs out to the side. Vie mounted his lap and curled into his embrace. "What's that book?"

"A secret."

She leaned over and looked at it more closely. It wasn't like any book she'd seen before, with its strange writing that didn't look like words, and numbers all over the page separated by peculiar signs.

"I know. It's a magic book," Vie suggested hopefully.

"Yes." He nodded, smiling. "It is magic. It tells you how to make gold."

She looked at him in amazement.

"Gold," he went on. "Liquid gold, made from the oils of flowers, spices, even animals. Gold that comes in a little magic bottle."

"What can it do?"

"It makes your dreams come true. Drops of the potion can turn an ugly woman into a desirable one. And a beautiful woman, like your mother, like you will be, turns into a queen."

"And a king marries her?" she asked in wonder.

"Yes. And she rules his heart. Where she walks, there is beauty and love."

Vie stared at the book. "It's all in there?"

Holding her closely, Armand pointed to the open page. "These secret words and numbers tell you how to make the potion. They're called formulas. This one is for a perfume called *Âme* that I made a long, long time ago."

"Make me some!"

"Someday," he said dreamily, "I will make a fragrance

as light as your hair and intense as your eyes. For your mother I made a perfume called *Grâce*, and it smelled like her. But no scent could match her own. She was"—his voice cracked—"an angel!"

"Don't cry, Papa," she said, stroking his cheek. "It's bad to cry."

"I won't, little Vie. Someday I will teach you how to read the magic signs. But," he said firmly, "you must promise never to tell *anyone* about the book. If you do, it will lose its powers. You understand?"

"Yes, Papa."

He turned his head in the direction of the room she shared with Martine. "You must give me your promise, Vie. *Nobody* shall know."

"I promise," she said with conviction.

"Good." He kissed the side of her face. "Now back to bed. You have school tomorrow."

When Vie pulled the covers over her, she knew that something very important had happened. In the bed by the wall Martine was sleeping quietly. Someday, Vie promised herself, I'll make her love me. I'll make everybody love me, because I'll have the magic. . . .

Armand Nouvel stayed awake through the night, poring over his old notes, hoping that something would revive his dormant powers, inspire him to try again. Finding a job seemed to be an impossibility. Small offices, dark storerooms, and poorly equipped labs passed in short takes through his mind: places he'd applied for work. Nothing: they all asked for references, employment records, papers of officialdom required for dismal, mindless jobs he would have rejected even as a boy. The only offer had been selling cut-rate supplies to small hairdressing shops—and he'd said he couldn't possibly accept.

But he hadn't paid the rent this month, and though Mrs. Murphy said she could wait, he saw no prospect for next month, either. He owed more than rent—she hadn't received anything at all for looking after the children, and Armand felt she'd become careless about them.

Either he'd have to forge papers detailing a past that never existed, so that he could be offered jobs he didn't want, or he'd have to accept the tawdry sales job. He looked up from the book toward his bedside table and met Anne's laughing eyes in the photograph. Her voice came to him clearly: "You must not be a piece of stupidity, my cabbage."

It gave him a jolt—clear as though she stood next to him. He nodded agreement. Surely he'd earned a chance for freedom after these horrendous years. For her, freedom had been escape from Paris into lavender sunshine. If only he'd left her there! No point in that now, he told himself; and if Anne had stayed in Grasse, Vie would not exist. Still, Anne had remained a free being to the end. She accepted no chains on her spirit. If she were here now, she'd tell him to be true to his talent, to dedicate himself to the part of himself that was an artist and would always be free.

Yes, my darling, he answered her ardently, but how? The inspiration's gone, I'm tired, I'd like to give up.

But you just can't!

Again, it was a clear voice. He wondered if he could be going mad. More likely, his imagination was playing tricks. It had always been powerful—too powerful.

He knew he had to go on trying, even though a sense of failure permeated every aspect of his life. No work, no money, no ideas, no kind of life for Vie, no woman for her to turn to.

Not even that, though he'd tried with dozens. Each of his bedmates left behind only her scent, and usually he'd remove that by changing the sheets as soon as she was gone.

They liked his looks and his accent. A few begged to stay with him, claiming they'd fallen in love. He suspected it was loneliness instead, but didn't care either way. He'd grown indifferent; a woman, to Armand, was simply something you needed from time to time, like red meat, and you consumed it quickly, without emotion.

His eyes refused to focus on the pages any longer. A week, he told himself; give it one more week, and if nothing happens, go back to the cut-rate beauty supplies. He got up, closed the book, and put it in its cardboard box. This he placed in the suitcase, locked it, and returned it to the back of his closet. Then he showered, shaved, put on his only suit, and prepared breakfast before waking the girls.

He walked them to school, as he always did, and then took the subway into Manhattan for his nine o'clock interview.

Two hours later Armand was back home, a transformed man. He didn't even feel the effects of his sleepless night, and he could hardly wait for Vie's return to give her the news. He had to tell someone right away. He ran down to Frances Murphy, kissed her on both cheeks, and told her he'd be starting work next day as assistant chemist in a fragrance lab for soaps, bath oils, and detergents. She went pink with happiness at his attention, her eyelashes fluttering rapidly as he ran upstairs again to his room.

He picked up Anne's photograph and kissed it. Maybe, he told her silently, the old book *is* magic, after all.

A week later he lost his job. It was simple, really: his stubbornness again.

He'd told the chief chemist, "This compound smells like something that is dying. It's terrible. The sweetness is decomposition. I will not work on it."

"You were not hired for your opinions. Your job is to follow orders," came the reply.

Armand took off his apron. "Then my job is finished," he said.

And that was that.

Vie was playing on the porch with two cats when he came home, drenched from the cold rain. "You're early, Papa," she said happily, not getting up off the floor.

"Better come in, it's cold here," he answered, remembering how pleased she'd been for him a week ago. He didn't want to have to tell her that he'd left and what it meant.

"Not yet, we're playing school. I'm the teacher and Jewel and Tiger are the class. I can't decide which one should be the teacher's pet. What do you think, Papa?"

"I think you should come in now." He didn't care about the cats one way or the other, but he remembered that Vie's first "friend" had been the kitten she called Mi, at the house of eccentric Mme. Glouzet. She'd hated to leave it when they moved to Carcassonne. Who knew, maybe she still missed the little animal. "Five minutes," he relented. "But no more."

When Vie came up to the apartment, he was looking at the mail with the expression he always wore when he did that. Bills made him frown, and his mail, he told her, was nothing but bills.

"Here's a note from your school," he said, holding out a sheet of blue-gray paper.

"What does it say?" she asked, before taking hold of it.

"They want me to come there and speak to your teacher."

She read the important words, printed except for blanks which were filled in by pen. She saw her own name, handwritten: Viveanne Nouvel. It was followed by a request for her parents to come in on Friday at 8 A.M. to meet Miss Michaelson. "You'll come, won't you?" she asked her father hopefully.

"I don't think I will be able to."

She swallowed hard, deeply disappointed. Then she remembered she had to be grown up. "It's because of your job, isn't it, Papa? You'd be late for work. But maybe," Vie suggested, "you could get to see my teacher earlier."

"It's not the job," he answered curtly. "That's over."

"Then why won't you go!" she flung at him, seeing in his announcement only an admission that he had no excuse.

"I am not very good in these things, Vie. I am not accustomed to the American education. Perhaps Mrs. Murphy will go to meet the teacher."

Vie's eyes blazed. "She's not my mother!"

She ran from the room and Armand followed, but she wouldn't speak to him. She turned her head away and stared out the window while he apologized. When he'd repeated for the third time that he *would* make the appointment, she looked at her father lifelessly and her voice came out flat. "It doesn't matter to me."

She thought she'd never forgive him. He made her feel like an outcast, different from the others. In that moment she hated everything about him that was foreign.

The teacher, a stern little woman with a body flat as a ruler and a stiff walk, told Armand that, though his daughter was doing well as far as her grades went, she was having trouble integrating with the other children. He didn't know what it meant.

Miss Michaelson tried to explain. "She doesn't volunteer comments in class. She doesn't engage in social interaction with her peers."

Still he didn't answer and the teacher, mistaking his unfamiliarity with the jargon for ignorance or lack of education, switched to simple words, which she articulated slowly as monosyllables: "Your child does not get along with the other children. She has no friends."

He shook his head sadly, thinking she'd never learned to make them and that her early childhood had taught her to trust no one. Like himself, she was proud, secretive, and creative. He saw Vie as a solitary genius, a lonely ruler— and didn't understand that she was a child in desperate need of affection, who didn't know how to ask for it.

She was terribly lonely, as was Martine. But the younger child grasped at anything to fill her need, while Vie accepted her hunger with stoicism.

Armand became a salesman of hair dyes, treatments, and nail polish, servicing beauty shops in Brooklyn and Queens. During the first year he worked for three different suppliers, finally settling into his job at Alamode, where he was accepted despite the obvious drawback of his accent.

His English speech, so charming to customers in prewar Paris, had become a liability in the boroughs of New York by late 1953. McCarthyism was at its peak, and many shopowners were fearful of the Communist menace. In Richmond Hill the owner of a three-dryer shop listened to Armand's cadences and said, "You're a foreigner, ain't you? I don't buy nothing from foreigners. Don't deal with no Reds."

The Richmond Hill shop was scratched from his rounds. Armand tried to find humor in the irony of becoming a suspected Communist after escaping from those who pursued him as a Nazi, but the joke was too black. Once again he was living in a world of witch-hunts. Old fears returned, his dreams brought back horrors, and for a while he was nearly catatonic. He hardly spoke, simply holding out his samples and order sheets, thereby gaining sympathy from some regular customers, who thought he'd suffered a mild stroke.

McCarthyism in America, Armand felt, was a return to the persecutions of the war: Nazis murdering Jews, followed by the terrorism of the Resistance. He remained in a deep depression, barely touching his food, uninterested even in what Vie told him, until he was brought back to life by the United States Army.

He watched the congressional hearings to investigate Senator McCarthy's charges against the Army on Frances's TV in her living room, amazed by the firm dispensation of justice, delighted by the wit of Joe Welch, hypnotized by the mad outbursts of the senator and his counsel, Roy Cohn. He cheered at the outcome, his faith in humanity almost restored. The Army–McCarthy hearings gave Armand his first sense of pride in America and her democracy, and because of it, he filed naturalization papers that would allow him and his children to become American citizens.

Some measure of confidence restored, Armand applied to Margaret Pearson, the enormous cosmetics company rumored to be about to enter the fragrance market. He had heard the gossip where he worked, and wrote instantly to the company, saying he had an attractive proposition for them.

Ten days later he received a letter thanking him for his interest and promising to be in touch sometime. It was signed by Seymour Levy, Executive Vice President in charge of marketing.

He began to fantasize. Every evening he rushed to look at his mail, but no letter followed after the first. A month went by and his fantasies faded. Another month, and he stopped thinking about it.

In May, Frances Murphy stopped him as he came through the door and told him a Mr. Levy had phoned to ask if he could be at the offices of Margaret Pearson tomorrow at three o'clock. "I said you'd be there—was that right?"

He kissed her, and she knew it was.

Next morning he phoned Alamode to say he couldn't come in because of a dreadful toothache. Then he went out to buy a new shirt. By one o'clock he was riding into

Manhattan, to the Fifth Avenue main office of Margaret Pearson.

He didn't dare enter the building until two minutes to three, and then had to wait five minutes for an elevator. When he came up to the receptionist, it was six minutes after three.

Before he could take the offered seat, Mr. Levy's secretary came to escort Armand to his office.

"Nouvel?" Levy barked as they entered. "Right, sit down, tell me what you've got."

The secretary left. Armand lowered himself into the leather armchair facing Levy, took a deep breath and answered, "About perfumes I know everything."

"Good. That's a start." Seymour Levy grinned appreciatively. He was a balding man in his forties and looked to be of medium height. His face, too fleshy, gave signs of self-indulgence, but his eyes were like drills boring below the surface. As he looked at him, Armand could feel his intelligence, his impatience, and his arrogance.

"Where've you worked before?"

"In France."

"Paris or Grasse?"

"Both."

"Who for?"

"Myself." It slipped out in the artillery of their exchange, ricocheting back to Armand like the stroke of doom. "That is," he amended quickly, "I have worked in the big houses as chemist."

"You got references?"

"Destroyed. In the war, we have had much destroyed."

"I know that," said Levy impatiently. From his breast pocket he drew two cigars. "Smoke?"

"No, thank you."

"Won't ask if you mind, you're in no position to. One of the advantages of running the show." He laughed gruffly as he unwrapped the cellophane.

"Take this fragrance venture, for instance." He stood up, smaller than Armand had estimated, bit off the end of his cigar, spat it out in the wastebasket and stood with his back to Armand, looking out at the city beneath him. "It's my baby. I figured the time's ripe, branch out from the nailpolish-and-lipstick image, get into something more intangible, high class. Of course"—he turned around, puffing, his hands in his pockets—"we're not letting that drop, you can bet your balls. Pearson is *color*, coordinated lips and nails. The American woman depends on us. Our images are classics. *Blazing Ice*, that was our biggest. *Peach Melba*, *Midnight Sun*, *White Heat*—all of them my babies.

"I don't spend time sitting on my ass, Nouvel," he said, pacing. "I make my score and get right back out there. The name of the game is hustle. What do you say to that, Nouvel?" He was watching Armand carefully while he spoke.

"I am not sure."

Levy gave a laugh and took a seat again in his swivel chair, tilting it back until his head rested on the wall behind him. "You don't know why I'm doing all the talking, right? You figure you're the one looking for a job, not me. So why am I selling to you? Right?" He laughed again and brought the chair forward abruptly. "Because I'm not selling you a damn thing. Nobody who's being interviewed ever says shitsworth, and I don't have the time to be figuring out what he's really saying under the crap. They all come in sounding like God's gift, dishing out a pitch they've practiced for weeks. Tells me shit."

He leaned forward, close to Armand's face. "So, instead, I do the talking—about me, the company, projects I want to get going. And I look the man over very carefully, Nouvel, like I've been doing with you. The way he listens tells me what I want to know about him. I feel I've got him by the balls.

"But I'll admit I don't have you pegged yet, Nouvel. Can't get a grip yet on how it's hanging. But I'm not worried, we got some time." He let a thick ash fall on the carpet and stared at it.

"What I'm after now is fragrance, luxury. Not perfume, the French have that cornered. They got the real status, the high prestige that's out of our ballpark right now. We leave that to Guerlain, Patou, Lanvin—say, you're French. You remember Jolaunay? Top of the pyramid, classiest stuff anywhere. Clever bastard, that guy, went for rarity value instead of distribution, and it worked. Wouldn't anymore, of course, but it was right for its time. The Koh-i-noor of perfumes."

"I know him. I mean—I was working for him, before the war."

"No shit!" Levy's eyes sparkled with interest.

"Yes. Next to the salon was a lab. There we made *Âme.* . . ."

"A classic! Never had a whiff of it myself, but I'd lay odds that if you had any of that stuff on you now, you wouldn't be here. You'd be worth a fortune. Whatever happened to old Jolaunay?"

"Died," said Armand faintly. "In the war."

"Died. Oh yeah, I remember something about him being a Nazi. Shows you can never tell—the sweetest rose and all that. But I'm impressed, Nouvel, I gotta say that. You worked for Jolaunay."

They were both silent a moment, each reflecting in his own way on Armand's perfumes.

Levy started again. "We can't use that sort of thing here, of course. Top of the line will be cologne—and even there we're not predicting much in the way of sales. We need it as our image builder. But we'll rely on the basic grub of fragrance: soaps, dusting powder, deodorants, maybe bath oils or crystals. We'll be directing the line to That Pearson Woman, the one whose fingertips are inky with *Midnight Sun.* We'll be pushing along the lines of 'out spoken,' 'audacious,' addressed to the woman who always gets her man. What can you make out, Nouvel?"

Armand let a few seconds go by, despite the impatience he read on Levy's face.

"Well?" Levy prompted.

"I am thinking of spicy notes. A touch of cinnamon, maybe ending on a note of jasmine. . . ."

"Tropical garden, heady but spiced. I like it." He positioned himself next to Armand's chair. "You'll turn his head."

"Pardon?" asked Armand nervously.

"As slogan: 'You'll turn his head.' Maybe not. 'Bali Ha'i'? No good, we'd have to pay the guys who wrote the song.

'Island in the Sun'? No, we'd have to fork out on that one, too.''

Armand couldn't follow Levy's instant associations and didn't recognize his allusions.

"We'll call it *Dare*—how about that? Never mind, we'll put Research on it. Could be it's too strong, threatening." Levy paced again, observing his feet as he walked. He paused at his intercom. "I want Burt to meet this guy. Yeah, Nouvel." He reached across the desk for a file, glanced at it, and added, "Armand. Yeah, he's ready now."

Levy switched off. "OK," he told Armand. "Josie'll take you to meet Burt Mangello. He's head of our lab, he'll report back. A real pleasure," he said smiling and holding out his hand. "I got a feeling we'll make beautiful music together, Nouvel. Long as you come up with the notes." Laughing heartily, Levy went back to his desk, picking up a stack of papers.

Burt Mangello wore a long white surgeon's coat over his tall, nearly emaciated frame, and his face above it was gaunt, with the large imperfectly hooked nose of an ancient Roman. He was deferential to Armand, as though some of Levy's power had rubbed off on the Frenchman.

Armand moved in a dream, hardly daring to believe what was happening. *Dare*—that was the fragrance he'd be working on soon. How appropriate, he thought—thank God for the inspiration that led him to say he'd worked for Jolaunay. With that, Levy had considered him an equal, Armand was sure. The world of Margaret Pearson would open up to him: elegant dinners, charming women, important men. He was returning to his own sphere.

"Sorry," he said to Burt Mangello. "I did not catch what you were saying."

He repeated it in a soft voice of apology: the lab was up in the Bronx; he himself was in the Manhattan office only because Mr. Levy had called him down this morning, asking him to be on hand in case any of the people he'd be interviewing today seemed promising enough for more intensive briefing. Could Mr. Nouvel arrange to look over the lab in the next few days? They'd just opened the new fragrance wing. Their main organ could accommodate two hundred, maybe two hundred and fifty ingredients, but they were still stocking the lab—he'd see for himself.

Two days later Armand visited the lab, with its immaculate counters and floors, its basins and beakers, the empty bottles that would soon be filled with essences from around the world; the empty stacks that promised to become the "library," where compounds and competitors' completed fragrances would be stored, offering the nose a chance to browse and find inspiration.

"Beautiful," he said to everything. "It is very beautiful."

"Mr. Levy thinks highly of you," Burt Mangello told him. "I'm sure he'd like you to start right away, but of course there's the red tape to get through."

"What is that?"

"Oh, you know," he said off-handedly. "The loyalty oath and then the background clearance. Always takes longer than you expect."

A week later Armand called Levy and left a message. When the call wasn't returned, he tried again. He called Burt Mangello, who was also not available.

Persistently Armand phoned each of them every day, only to speak to secretaries. By the end of the month Mangello took pity and came to the phone. "I'm sorry, Mr. Nouvel," he said. "You just didn't make it."

"Why? What is wrong?"

"I'm not in a position to say. Good-bye, Mr. Nouvel."

Armand stared at the dead receiver. He'd suspected this, of course, when they were both unreachable. But why? The security clearance? Had Levy discovered something? He was as sharp as a fox.

Frances Murphy came up quietly behind him. "I didn't get the job," he told her, putting the phone down.

"Poor dear," she said soothingly. "Maybe it's because you're not a citizen yet."

To Armand it was a final judgment, offering no appeal. He'd come full circle to a dead end.

2

1958–1959

The gun gleamed against navy velvet in the shop window Martine was fogging up with her breath. She rubbed the steam away, making a watery blur and took a step back to see it more clearly. Polished, inviting, the gun was begging her to take hold of it. She could almost feel it in her hands, despite her frozen fingers, naked and chapped because she wouldn't wear mittens at her age. Going-on-eleven was much too old for that cockamamie baby stuff.

She wanted, she *needed* a BB gun! Other kids had them—though she had to admit only The Duke and Casey owned guns, and they were both thirteen.

Marty was the youngest in her gang, by more than a year. The other kids accepted her because she never ran away from a fight, and she was smart.

They were The Saints; their main rival, The Bulldozers, though they'd scrap with other gangs. But with The Bulldozers they'd rumble. Two of them were colored, the rest had Irish or Italian names, and The Saints, the only gang with a girl in it, fought them over territory each considered its own. The contested area was a small concrete lot next to the handball court. On it, skin had been torn, noses broken, heads cut open. Marty had seen a few real bloody fights, ending only with the arrival of cops, but Casey, The Saints' leader, kept her away from them. She was protected from real danger mainly because the gang couldn't risk the possibility of her defeat. Casey set her loose only on the weaklings—The Bulldozers' "professor," a scrawny, red-headed kid with freckles, or his twin brother, who didn't look at all like him, a kid they called "Fruit."

The gang was home to her. Marty hung out with them every chance she got. They were her true family, she felt; her father and Vie belonged in Squaresville and couldn't even make out what was going on. She hated being in the apartment, and though she'd have to face terrible scenes when she came back late, Marty stayed out with The Saints on most nights. She wished they would all live together and nobody would have to go home at all.

When she suggested it to Casey, he only laughed and told her she was a little kid who didn't know nothing about the truancy laws or anything else. She made a face and shook her fist at him, but he just went on laughing at her.

Even when he teased her, Marty worshiped him. There wasn't anything in the world that could make Casey afraid, she figured. He wore his hair shorter than any of the other guys, and nobody dared rile him over it. He was big, with light brown hair and moss-colored eyes that had slivers of gold in them. He kidded her a lot, and sometimes he threatened to drop her from the gang if she didn't stop acting like a baby, but Marty could feel that he really liked her. He knew what she was like, she could talk to him about things that really mattered. He wasn't anything like the dumbbells she lived with—Casey was smart, and he cared about her even though he was wise to her.

She told Casey about the BB gun, how it was begging for her to have it. He didn't say anything about her being a girl, and listened attentively as she described every inch of it. When she finished, he said, "Sounds good to me. You better tell Santa."

Christmas was a week away. The most she could hope to get was a pair of warm gloves.

Christmas Eve, The Saints all went to church. When Marty got home, after midnight, she found the front door locked, so she walked back out to the street and over to Casey's house. She threw snowballs up at his window but kept missing. Finally she made a hit and got three in succession. Casey opened the window and called out softly. Marty whispered, "It's me," and he whispered back that she should go wait by the basement door.

After only a minute or two he opened up and took hold

of her hand, to guide her through the blackness to the stairs. When they were up in his room, he locked the door. "Sit there," he told her, pointing to the bed, "and close your eyes."

When she opened them again, she was holding a large box in her arms. She opened it and there, gleaming against midnight velvet, lay the gun.

She just stared at it. She couldn't even touch it.

"Merry Christmas, kid," Casey said. "Be careful with that thing, it can get you in trouble."

It turned out that he could have been talking to himself. The day after Christmas, Casey was arrested for burglary. His right-hand man, The Duke, was put on probation. With both of them gone, the gang split up.

At Alamode's Christmas party, traditionally given in a large hall rented from the Unitarian Church, Armand was suffering from the concentrated fumes of cigarettes, alcohol, and cloying perfume. He'd just decided to leave, despite the early hour, when a small, buxom woman dressed in forest green came over and gave him a hug. "Merry Christmas!" she said gaily. "Joyeux Noël. Did I get it right? I've been practicing."

"Hello, Nina," he said, smiling at her. "You are looking like a Christmas tree." The satin dress clung to her body, its deep decolletage revealing two pale globes gleaming like silver balls against the deep green. Her hair was pinned up in a French twist, auburn tendrils curling at her neck and at the sides of her face, framing its cherubic features. A Victorian Christmas angel, rosy-cheeked and innocent, with the body of a seductress, Armand thought. He had to keep telling himself that this apparition was the same Nina Maggiore he saw regularly at The Top Knot, a shop he supplied, where she worked as manicurist.

Tonight she was Cinderella at the ball, transformed from her usual ordinary, even plain, self into a charming creature of the night, not beautiful even now, but lovely, with her sparkling eyes, her gleaming skin. She smelled of pine cones and tinsel. Armand shed his discomfort as he stepped into the role of Prince Charming. "You must dance with me," he said, bowing slightly.

He whirled her through tinny strains of "The Tennessee Waltz," waltzing in the European manner, round and round, always in the same direction. When the song ended, she grabbed hold of him, laughing, to steady herself. "You sure know how," she told him, her eyes shining, her face damp and flushed to a pale raspberry color.

The next number was a fox trot, slow enough for them to talk while they danced. He listened, smiling, to her chatter, the words seeming to bounce out from between her lips. She refreshed him with her child's enthusiasm, the astonished burble of her laughter.

They danced well together, he noticed. She didn't hold on for dear life as so many American women did. Nina maintained the distance between them and yet followed his lead with sensitivity that seemed to indicate they'd been dancing together for years. He felt young again, almost carefree. She reminded him of Anne, though nothing about her appearance was faintly similar.

"When I was a little girl," she told him during the rumba, "a friend of mine had a beautiful mother. I mean, stunning! I was a fat, overgrown lump then, but I wanted to be just like her when I grew up. I thought I'd never be able to get a man—I must've been about ten or eleven, and if a boy would talk to me, I'd feel myself getting beet red and I couldn't answer. Then I'd dream about him afterward, 'cause I was boy crazy, but it was all hopeless." With his hand at her waist, Armand could feel her hips roll to the music.

"This gorgeous mother of my friend came into my room one night when I was sleeping over at their house, and I asked her how to get a man. She told me it's simple: all you have to do is compliment him on something he's wearing. 'Men are very vain,' she told me, 'and women always forget that. Tell him you love his tie. Touch the material and say it's marvelous.' The point was to compliment him on his taste. 'He'll think you're very original,' she said, 'and charming.' It took me a few years to be able to act on her advice," Nina confessed, laughing, "but I never forgot it."

He whirled her away and, when he caught her, said, "But you did not comment on my tie. Do you not intend to charm me?"

The music stopped. She reached out to touch the silky material, looking into his eyes. "It's the most beautiful tie I've ever seen," she said with ringing conviction.

He brought her against him and kissed her lightly on the lips.

When they pulled back, Nina said, "You see? It works every time."

"A wise woman, your friend's mother," Armand told her as they started on the next dance, both of them laughing softly, sensing the promise ahead.

A man's voice called out to her, "Hey, Nina, how about sharing the wealth? You going to dance with the same fellow all night?"

"Looks that way," she called back, her eyes never leaving Armand's face.

They were among the last to leave. Armand picked up some of the decorations that had fallen to the floor—a sprig of holly, two miniature pine cones, a clutch of tiny bells—and wove them through fingers of fir into a wreath around her head. She protested, laughing, as he continued his work, altering and adapting until he was satisfied with the crown he had made for her. "You are Queen of the Night," he proclaimed when he'd finished.

"And I'm never going to wake up," she promised

Armand bent and kissed her beside her left ear. "Then I will have to sleep also. With you," he whispered.

Nina put her arms around his neck and held on to him, eyes closed. They swayed, then began to dance slowly across the floor to no music, the last couple left, dancing cheek to cheek in the silent hall, holding each other tight.

When Nina woke up the next day, it was nearly noon. The first thing she did was grin; then she hugged herself. It was Sunday, she didn't have to go to work, and she was in love. All she wanted to do was stay in bed and go over each moment of the night before.

But the buzzer rang from below, and she had to throw on a robe and go down. The intercom hadn't worked since she moved into the apartment and never would. She opened the front door and found no one there, but halfway down the street a young man in a wind jacket was carrying a large parcel. She called out to him; he turned around and came back to her. "You Nina Mangi?" he asked.

"Yeah, Maggiore."

"For you. Sign here."

She could feel it was a flowerpot as she carried it upstairs, and she set it down on the linoleum-covered table before tearing off the wrapping to reveal the cream-colored poinsettias, their papery leaves delicately traced with veins of bluish white. On the card was written simply, "Dream on."

He was a prince, she thought, different from the others, someone who'd stepped out of a faraway world to place a crown on her head. She remembered the touch of his lips, how she never wanted to let go of his mouth, how beautiful he'd made her feel.

She whispered his name, then said it aloud. Armand Nouvel. She wanted to hear the sound again and again. Armand Nouvel. She'd met nobody like him, not in all her thirty-four years.

When he'd brought her home, Armand had kissed the side of her neck. He wouldn't come in, he didn't ask to see her again. But here, only hours later, were the flowers, and he had whispered, "Then I will sleep also—with you." Just remembering that made Nina close her eyes as desire, love—whatever it was—surged through her.

She didn't hear from him that day and didn't have his home address. When she called him at work on Monday morning to thank him for the plant, he was cordial but distant. "When will I see you again?" she blurted out.

"Soon, I hope," he answered in the same polite tone.

"How about tonight?" It came out by itself, and she bit hard on her lip while waiting for an answer.

"That will not be possible, I'm afraid. Perhaps I may give you a call in the next few days?"

She nodded miserably at the telephone, and then called upon her old spunkiness to come out with a cheery, "That'll be great." When she hung up, she couldn't figure out what she'd done wrong. He sure wasn't like the others, damn him.

Armand puzzled over the girl, not trusting his feelings. She wasn't as beautiful as most of the women he'd had in New York, but her charm was electric. Within moments of their meeting at the party she'd switched on something in him he'd thought was buried with Anne, and though he'd felt amazed by his attraction for her, he refused to give in to it. His prospects were dead; hope was the most dangerous thing to feel; he didn't want to rake the ashes, to stir up expectations.

He'd taught himself to ask for nothing from a woman except her body, paying back in kind to prevent both debt and investment. But little Nina Maggiore wafted through his thoughts. After saying good night to her, Armand had walked home, and during that hour's walk images of her hair, her breasts, the earthy smell when he kissed her neck assailed him and filled him with longing.

The next morning he woke after three hours' sleep and went down to send her flowers. By afternoon he regretted it, telling himself he'd been hypnotized by the night. She was a simple manicurist, the kind of girl who could probably be had by any man. Hadn't she, after all, come up and hugged him, thrown herself on him nearly? Yes, the loose kind, a girl for hire, certainly not a woman to introduce to his daughters.

Vie had turned fourteen two months earlier, and though she hadn't yet developed a woman's body, she was so mature in other ways that he hesitated to bring anyone home anymore. She wouldn't comment, but her eyes reproached him. Marty either ignored his guest completely or would say something he found unbelievably vulgar for a child her age.

In all, the situation had become so embarrassing to Armand that he hadn't brought a woman to his apartment for the past six months. He'd been chaste for nearly as long as that and had recently felt the satisfaction of discovering that he rarely thought about sex. He'd decided that he could look forward to a life free from the indignity of sexual need.

But Nina Maggiore threatened his equanimity. After a week, when neither the sound of her voice nor the smell of her skin had diminished in his thoughts, he called and invited her for dinner, promising himself to get her out of his system the way he'd done with other women. Her place if possible; if not, he'd have to risk taking her home. After a night of their acrobatic lovemaking, he'd be free again.

But when she opened the door for him, his heart sank. There was something intensely fragile about her, something that made him want to take her in his arms and protect her from the world. "I am so happy to see you," she said with the candor of a little girl.

"And I you." They stood smiling, not touching, unable to hide the happiness they felt. Not beautiful, Armand reminded himself as he grinned and stared at her. But her face was incredibly dear. He wanted to hold it between his hands and never stop looking at it.

They went to dinner, laughed, held hands, and walked back together arm in arm. Nina invited him up, but again he left her at the door.

For the next three evenings they repeated the procedure: Armand picked her up, they went to dinner, they kissed good night in front of Nina's door. But with each evening Armand came to know her better.

Her parents were both dead. She'd hardly known her father, who deserted her mother and herself when Nina was four. Her mother, a woman Nina remembered as always looking old, worked in a garment factory. She was devout and strict, with a strong antipathy for men, liquor, and entertainment. "I guess she loved me," Nina said, "but I could never feel it. She gave me whatever I asked for, even if she couldn't afford it—everything except affection. I guess that's why I started dating seriously when I was fourteen and a half. Aldo was sixteen. We'd sneak off together and read aloud from books we both loved. He wasn't a brain, but he was crazy about books and read anything he could get hold of."

She smiled at Armand, then took another mouthful of

spaghetti and continued. "When the Japanese bombed Pearl Harbor, we'd been going together a little more than two years. He got drafted and asked me to marry him before he was shipped overseas. I still had a year of high school, and I told Aldo it would be better to wait until he got back, but he said no, he might never make it, we had to get married before." She stopped. "Did I say something wrong? You're looking strange."

"Nothing, chérie. Please go on."

"You sure?" she asked dubiously.

Armand placed a hand lightly over hers. "You must tell me everything about yourself. So, did you agree to marry him?"

She nodded. "It was sort of a compromise. I said we could get engaged, and then we'd marry as soon as he got his first leave."

"And then?" Armand prompted.

"He was killed in the Pacific. I never saw him again. You know . . . I've never said this before, but I didn't like the sex. It hurt, it wasn't what I'd expected it to be— loving. Romantic. I wanted to break off the engagement right then. But I didn't say anything, and a few weeks later, when the telegram came, my first thought was— thank God we did it. Strange, isn't it?"

"No," Armand said, stroking her hand. "Not strange at all. What happened afterward?"

"Everything at once. Aldo got killed, my mother died, I graduated from high school and went to work for Aldo's father. I didn't have the thousand hours—you know, the beautician's certificate—but Mr. Viaggi let me do shampoos and comb outs. I guess I was the janitor, too." She laughed. The waiter came with menus again, for dessert, and Armand told him they'd order in a few minutes. He turned back to Nina, asking her to go on.

"Nothing much after that. I started doing manicures, and I'm still doing them. You could say my life's been held together by nails." She laughed at the joke, but he caught the forced tone in her laughter.

"Did you never want something else?"

Her gaiety fell off suddenly, like a mask. "Oh, yes," she said in a low voice. "I wanted much more. I was going to buy the shop from Mr. Viaggi when he retired, make it my own. Somehow, though, it never worked out. I couldn't get the money together. . . ." Her voice trailed off.

Armand called the waiter over and ordered zuppa inglese for both of them. When it came, rich in custard and cream, Nina tasted it with great care, pronounced, "It's great!" and fell on it like a child with an ice-cream sundae.

While she ate, he watched with fascinated interest, like someone observing a bear devour a honeycomb. She was spontaneous, direct; a creature like Anne when he'd first met her.

Nina finished and picked up their serious conversation of a few minutes before the way others might retrieve a handkerchief. "You know, Armand? All the things you want that never work out, all the dreams people have— they're not worth thinking about. *This* is life: this very moment."

"But it's only through dreams that you can go on living, sometimes," he told her.

She thought a moment. "I guess that's right. But if you hold on to them too long, they get to be nightmares. I had to let go, let them fly up. Pouf!" She made a little gesture with her hand.

"You must teach me," he said, half dreading what was to come but unable to resist the temptation of letting her vitality carry him away.

When they left the restaurant, Nina leaned against him and said simply, "I want you."

He kissed her there, on the street under the overhanging light, feeling her body supplicate his while it commanded him. They stopped for breath, and Nina told him, "You're coming home with me."

He took her arm and they walked quickly, stiffly, not speaking, both of them intent on the love they wanted to make.

Three days later Vie was pouring after-dinner coffee when Marty walked in, wearing the baseball jacket she'd inherited from one of her old gang brothers, stained and unshapely. She glanced at her sister and father, stopped dead, and looked Nina over. "Another one," she said in disdain. "I thought you'd given up, old man."

"Marty!" Vie cried, shocked.

Marty turned to her, hands on hips. "Yeah? What's the pitch now? A new mommy for the little orphans?"

"Stop it!" Vie almost shrieked. "Come and meet Nina."

"Thanks, but no thanks." She turned and went out.

"I'm sorry . . ." Armand began, holding his hands palms upward.

"It's nothing," Nina said, trying for her old tough image. Turning to Vie, she explained, "That's not it, you know, honey. I'm not trying to be your mommy. Just a friend."

In her embarrassment, Vie couldn't answer. She'd understood immediately that this woman was someone special. She was different from the others, not stand-offish and cold like those women—most of them blondes—who came home with Papa and treated her and Marty like stuffed toys they paid no attention to or else like little servants they'd order around. Nina wasn't that way. You could sense her friendliness right off, a warmth that made you feel you'd known her a long time and she knew all about you.

She wanted to take Nina to her own room and show her everything—schoolwork, clothes, the books she had, even her pet poodle and other toys from childhood, now discarded. She didn't know why, there wasn't much, really, to show off with, but she wanted to spread her whole life in front of Nina in hopes that Nina would accept it and maybe even take it over.

When Nina was getting ready to leave, Vie asked shyly, "Will you come back tomorrow night? Could you—please?"

Nina's face lit up in happy surprise. "Bless you, Vie," she said, looking over at Armand but unable to read his expression. "I'll try," she promised. "I really will." She gave the girl a warm kiss.

After they'd gone, Vie raised her hand slowly to her cheek. She'd never been kissed so lovingly by a woman. It was different from Papa's kiss, even stronger than his but much softer, leaving behind a scent of crushed violets. She felt the warmth glowing from her skin and wondered if people could see, if the kiss had left a mark. She'd never wash her face again, Vie decided; she loved Nina.

Vie felt so good when she awoke that she almost forgot to get annoyed at Marty who, as usual, wasn't anywhere around when it was time to set out for school. She couldn't be trusted to get there on her own, and the truancy slips they'd been getting had ended two months ago in a warning that she would be suspended. Vie walked down the stairs, carrying her books and lunch, knowing that even if she did find Marty outside, she'd have to wait for her to run up and get her own things. But she didn't care this morning. She didn't care if they were both late or if Marty never showed up.

Marty leaped from the bushes by the porch, making Vie jump so sharply that she dropped what she was carrying. "Go to hell, Marty," she muttered angrily, picking up the math book with two rumpled pages, the French book whose cover had gotten torn, the lunch bag with its smashed hard-boiled egg and squashed banana.

"I really got you this time," Marty said gleefully.

"Get your stuff and let's go. Right now!" she barked with such authority that Marty obeyed.

On the way Marty observed, "The new broad isn't much on looks, is she? But what's the difference." She shrugged. "Won't last."

"What do *you* know?" Vie snapped.

Marty leered at her. "A roll in the hay, that's all he cares about."

"Don't say that! She's wonderful. And don't talk about Papa that way either."

In answer Marty grinned. After a few steps in silence, Vie said, "You know, Marty? I sometimes wonder what it's like having a mother."

"Yeah."

"Do you ever think about it?"

"Yeah. But I got an older sister, that's just as bad."

"I wish *I* had one."

"You'd hate it."

"Maybe. Still, I wish Papa would ask Nina to live with us."

"You know what I wish?"

"What?"

"I wish you wouldn't call him Papa. It's so babyish."

"Too bad," Vie answered, stung. "I'm not a grown-up."

"You could try," Marty told her, dashing ahead to her school. She couldn't let on to Vie, because she wasn't clear about it herself, that she felt the need of a mother *and* a father. She had no mother, she was sure her father hated her, and though Marty was too young to understand the mechanism of guilt, she was led by it. Marty had made herself into an urchin of the streets, desperately searching for affection and approval from those she recognized as being outcasts like herself.

Vie waited until she could see her sister actually enter the building. Then she continued on to her own school, the junior high, letting her anger at Marty subside as she thought about Nina, and started making plans.

If Nina was coming tonight, Vie would bake a cake, set out the candles, make a real celebration. And after dinner the two of them would sit together, and Vie would ask Nina questions about all the things she couldn't ask Papa, all the mysteries of being a woman. It was scary to think of: getting breasts and then having babies. Nina could tell her things about her period. All Papa had said when she got her first one a few months ago was that she shouldn't be frightened, it only meant she'd entered her womanhood. Then he'd sent Frances Murphy in, and she kept talking about the moon and tides. She'd tried to show Vie how to use Kotex, but that was so disgusting Vie just closed her eyes. Nina would say something that made sense, Vie was sure, not some garbage about the moon.

As she walked into her homeroom, making the bell by a few seconds, Vie was looking ahead to the evening as an event she'd remember all her life, her entry into the world of women through the heart-to-heart she and Nina would have, something like a talk between mother and daughter.

She had to wait a long time—until the spring—as Nina and Armand kept shifting positions in their relationship. Though Nina was sure she loved him, she was reluctant to commit herself. She'd lived alone for all her adult life. The men who'd come and gone had left her with a sense of transience about any affair. She confided in Armand, relaxed with him, revealed more of herself to him than she had to anyone before, and yet at some undefined point she drew back. In the way that an amputee can feel pain in his missing leg, the emotional scars of Nina's life, those that had led her to erect a facade of toughness, made themselves felt whenever Armand pressed for commitment.

Other times they reversed roles. When Nina wanted them to live together, Armand argued that Mrs. Murphy would not permit her to move in there, and Nina's apartment was too small for four. But both Nina and Armand knew this was an evasion. Armand was afraid. His past had left scars of even greater mistrust than hers. He remembered his second marriage. He thought of the faceless stream of women. He was afraid both of being unable to love and of loving too deeply, which would mean a betrayal of Anne. Nina would be a good mother for Vie, he felt sure. She was a delightful, interesting companion and a passionate lover. Armand wanted her to pledge herself to him, but whenever she was willing, his doubts attacked him and made him look for escape.

When they'd been seesawing in this manner for nearly three months, Armand decided to end the tension. He told Nina they would not see each other anymore.

The news stunned Vie into silence. She picked at her food, hardly eating anything. She didn't answer when spoken to. Though Vie was a grown girl of fourteen, Armand saw again in her the child of Carcassonne, with solemn eyes that observed everything silently—except that now she seemed to take no notice of what went on around her. He didn't let Nina know about Vie's condition; he knew she doted on Vie and wouldn't be able to stay away.

On the Sunday that marked the ninth day of their decision to separate, Nina was trying to make herself do the household chores she'd hoped she would never find time for. So far she'd managed to read half the funnies and devour an entire coffee cake, which was making her feel slightly ill and extremely annoyed with herself. When the buzzer rang from downstairs, she panicked, looking at the mess her place was in, realizing she hadn't brushed her hair or her teeth, and that the remains of night cream were still on her face. If it was Armand, having second thoughts, the sight of her in this hovel would drive them instantly from his mind. I won't answer, Nina decided.

But when it rang again, she knew she'd never be able to stand the suspense. Pulling the belt firmly around her robe and grabbing a Kleenex to wipe off her face while she ran down, Nina went to the door.

Vie was standing in front, her face dead white, tears streaming down. Her lips moved, but no sound came. In her arms she held the bloody remains of a cat.

"My God," Nina breathed. Blood had stained Vie's jacket. It was all over her hands. Nina knew she wouldn't let go of the animal. "Come on, baby," she said, putting an arm around Vie to help support her as they went up the stairs.

In the apartment Vie wouldn't sit down, wouldn't give up the cat, wouldn't even raise her eyes to look at Nina. When she did, her first words came out. "He's goddamn dead."

"Vie!"

"Car killed him. Jewel was following me, following me to your house. I told him to get back home. He wouldn't. I bent down to pick him up. He ran away. Right into the street. Car skidded. Killed him." She was now crying piteously, with dry sounds like someone who doesn't know how to cry. "Bastards. He was my friend. Best friend."

"Baby, baby," Nina tried soothing her, reaching up to stroke Vie's hair. "I'll find a box. You'll lay him in it and get cleaned up. OK?"

Vie nodded. Nina got a heavy cardboard box from the kitchen, brought it out, and realized it wasn't enough of a coffin. She knew Vie would want it lined.

The rags under the sink were no good. Only silk or satin would do. Nina looked in her drawers, then her closet. She hesitated only a moment before reaching out for the green satin. She pulled down the back zipper all the way, yanked at the seam until it gave. Vie gasped as Nina tore the dress, then took a scissors from her top drawer to cut a rectangle of material. This she placed in the box.

Vie walked over and slowly lowered Jewel into it. "Poor darling pussycat," she said softly and turned to Nina, surrendering herself completely as Nina took off the jacket, brought Vie to the kitchen sink, washed her hands, dried them, and led her to the bathroom. She quickly ran a bath, removed the girl's clothes, and helped her into the tub. Nina washed her, shampooed her hair, and then dried her with a large towel, powdered her body, combed out the wet hair, and gave Vie a nightgown of her own to slip on.

When they'd finished, Vie said quietly, "Now we can bury Jewel."

"Yes, in a little while. I'm making you some tea."

Vie began to cry again, and Nina could only murmur helplessly, "There, there."

"No one's mothered me before!"

Nina stared at her, taking in for the first time what Vie's life must be. Vie went on, "I was coming here to ask you to make up with Papa. I can't stand it." At that, Nina started crying, too.

When they left the apartment a few hours later, Nina was bathed and scented, her hair pinned up in a chignon. They'd buried Jewel at the back of the house, stealing a few snowdrops and crocuses from next door to put on his grave. On the street Nina hailed a taxi, and they went home.

Armand put up no argument. He'd missed Nina, dragging himself through the days since their separation, feeling only half alive. He kissed her and led her to his bedroom.

After they made love, they discussed the details. Nina would give up her apartment. They'd offer Mrs. Murphy a supplementary rent, which she'd undoubtedly accept.

Lying beside Armand, Nina felt absolutely sure she'd done the right thing. She loved Armand, although she knew it was Vie who had brought her here to live.

3

1960–1961

Windsor, a line of cosmetics sold door to door by housewives who referred to their commissions as "pin money," was the largest cosmetics company in America, and probably in the world. In 1960, when Nina became a Windsor Lady on weekends, the company had franchises in Europe, the Far East, and South America. Helena Rubinstein referred to it as the hot-dog company because its products were cheap and universal. But its profits soared above her own and above those of her rival queen, Elizabeth Arden. Avon couldn't match it, and neither could the image-setting companies of Revlon and Margaret Pearson.

Windsor's secret was simple and well known: cut advertising and risk. Compared to the 85 to 95 percent of their budget that large cosmetics companies spent on advertising and promotion, Windsor spent almost nothing. It printed a catalog listing its merchandise, which Windsor Ladies had to buy from the company to show to their customers. The catalog displayed toiletries, deodorants, hair and bath products, skin treatments, and moisturizers and a line of makeup priced low enough for every woman to splurge and try something new. And if she didn't like the aqua shadow or purple eyeliner, she could return it the next time the Windsor Lady came to call.

Though Windsor's prices were low, they were not so low that they represented or even reflected the actual cost of making the product. Windsor executives never forgot the maxim that price indicates value and knew that they couldn't sell—probably couldn't even give away—a face cream for fifteen cents that had cost ten cents to make.

So, prices were held artificially high enough to give the customer a sense of luxury and to give Windsor the highest income and the most shareholders of any cosmetics company.

Nina started her rounds on the second Saturday in November, four days after John F. Kennedy was elected president. She'd voted for him, as had Armand—his first vote as an American citizen. After the victory they'd meant to go out and celebrate, but money was so tight now that they were forced to toast the new president at home, with American wine.

Starting out, Nina felt optimistic. The weekend job would relieve the pressure of money, let them go out to dinner once in a while or buy a steak to broil at home. She was sure the job would be fun, too. In the training sessions she'd been going to on successive evenings, Nina learned that the products would sell themselves, that women were dedicated to Windsor, maintained loyalty, and seemed to spend their time waiting for the Windsor Lady to show up so they could fill out order forms.

On Saturday Nina went out with her valise of samples, a small stack of catalogs, and a big smile. By evening she was exhausted, but she'd made a commission of more than $30, and she'd enjoyed herself. She liked people and got a real kick, as she told Armand, out of making them feel good.

Sunday she made another $30 and had been invited to coffee and cake by five of her customers. "What I don't get in dollars, I'll make in pounds," she told Armand, kissing him on the top of his head. Despite her physical tiredness, Nina was exhilarated by success and that night, for the first time in weeks, she and Armand made love.

It was always good when they did it, but during the past year they had made love less and less frequently. And as their sex life diminished, they grew further apart, immersed in their own problems, meeting over bills. Preoccupations with work, rent, phone bills, and what to have for dinner made them insensitive to the reasons that had brought them together. They didn't realize they were sacrificing anything; they saw their existence as real life, forgetting that the body and the imagination were real, too.

But on that Sunday the old desire surfaced and then burst out, obliterating the dreariness that had settled on their lives. Nina undressed slowly, in semidarkness, stretching her soft body toward him, exposing her breasts, thrusting her pelvis, exhibiting her nakedness to him.

He became more and more aroused, watching her slow striptease. Her uncovered body was amazing, the most desirable thing he'd ever seen. He'd forgotten how *naked* she could be, so erotically naked that he was trembling when he touched her.

She got in beside him and lay barely moving. Her inaction made her skin seem even more alive as he stroked her shoulders, the ripe, plump breasts, down over her willing belly to the tiny jungle of hairs. He slipped his fingers into the dark slit. He felt the hot welcoming stickiness and drew his hand away. She moaned, begging him to go on. He bent down and ran his tongue from her navel to the dark triangle, outlining it with his saliva. She thrust up at him and he tasted her juices, sucked on the erect little knob until she gave a small cry, grabbed a pillow and silently screamed her orgasm into it. Quickly he penetrated her, driving into her contractions, and came immediately.

"That was great," she said later. "We should do it more often."

"You would become addicted."

"I am anyway, and I can't kick the habit."

He smiled, kissed the side of her forehead, and knew it would be a long time before they made love like this again.

He was too preoccupied, too tired. The debt he had incurred had become a permanent cloud over him, sapping his strength. Armand couldn't blame anyone but himself, he knew, and yet he felt a persistent resentment against Nina. Without her, he would never have dared to try again. His hopes had died with Margaret Pearson, he'd buried them, and then this young woman had started scratching away, exposing him to hope once more.

Nina had encouraged him to believe in his dreams. She told him he was magical, brilliant—all sorts of rubbish, he thought, smiling sadly—and she'd given him the pernicious gift of renewed self-confidence. If he'd never met her, he'd be better off. At least he'd be able to keep his full salary. As it was, one-third of it went to the Grosvenor woman in what seemed like a futile attempt to pay back even a fraction of the money she'd invested in him.

Fifty thousand dollars. He'd run into Judy Grosvenor by chance on Fifth Avenue. She was shopping with her daughter and recognized him, after more than twenty years. "This is Armand Jolaunay," she said to the girl. "A genius. All of us were crazy about him in Paris, long before you were born, Bunny."

She'd been one of his American clients, married to an Astor then. Now, she explained over tea at the Palm Court in the Plaza Hotel, her fourth husband, Matt Grosvenor, had died, leaving her his Texas money and property. She wanted to do something creative that would use up some of her time and energy and was thinking along the line of fashion. A boutique in Dallas, maybe.

When they met again, she'd decided to do something more original than a clothing shop. It would be called Stuff of Dreams, a boutique that carried only elusive, ephemeral, inessential items. Fabergé eggs, a wave captured in a bottle, cloth of gold, and Armand's perfumes.

Nina urged him to accept. He rented a loft and set up his lab. He tried to reformulate his old fragrances. But he was blocked, as though with a permanent cold. His nose could no longer detect scents. Six months later Judy Grosvenor was very impatient, and a month after that threatened litigation. She gave that up, though, when Armand explained his financial situation to her. She could recover maybe two-thirds of her investment through tax relief, she told him. The remaining third he promised to repay.

And now they were practically living like beggars, he thought resentfully. If Nina had never led him to futile hope, at least they would be having wine with dinner. Taking a last chance had made Armand feel more impoverished—in spirit, in talent, as a man—than ever before. He was hollow, he was nothing; and only once in a very long time could he play out his remembered passion.

*   *   *

Nina's first weekend of selling was her most lucrative. She never again brought back $60 for two days. Her profit dropped to $50, then $45, $40, and finally settled at about $35 a weekend. The drop reflected her waning enthusiasm. Though she wanted to make money, needed it, she couldn't keep up a patter of interested cheerfulness.

Mainly it was Armand. After that Sunday night's love-making he hadn't touched her again. It was now months. The fire of their life wasn't replaced by ice, but by luke-warm water.

Then there was Vie, loving as ever, growing into a lithe beauty, but with a remoteness about her that disturbed Nina. The two of them were close as sisters, but Vie seemed to have no other friends, and she didn't share the interests of people her age. Sweet sixteen she wasn't; rather, stately sixteen, solitary sixteen, and still never been kissed. She paid no attention whatever to the admiration on the faces of boys or men when they looked at her. When Nina took her to a party given by one of her col-leagues at the beauty parlor, Vie refused to dance and responded to any male who spoke to her with monosyllables.

Armand was depressed, Vie shut into an ivory tower. That left Marty, a problem Nina didn't even know how to approach. She had no ties to the girl and no influence over her. Nevertheless, Nina wept for her inwardly; for the lost, rebellious child who rammed into her thirteenth birthday with the toughness of an army truck. Nina knew something about the need for toughness, about making an armor to protect yourself from loss and disappointment, but she couldn't get through Marty's even far enough to say she understood.

Marty was rarely home. She moved with a crowd of older teenagers. The three of them at home avoided talk-ing about her, afraid of discovering what she was doing with and to her life.

Living with Armand now made Nina feel helpless. It was a great struggle to retain her vitality, and she often gave up. Working seven days a week left her tired down into her bones, and she didn't have the strength or will to try to liven up the household

She remembered how love used to feel, like a bird flapping giant wings and carrying her off. She remembered, too, how Armand had opened her up, showing her things and making her experience them for the first time. Wine, for instance. She'd always found it sweet as liquid candy, but never as good. Armand gave her sips, then little glassfuls, teaching her to pay attention to what the wine was doing to her tongue, her palate—and to notice the return of taste after she'd swallowed. Now she'd learned to love it, she missed it.

Food, too. Nina had always eaten with gusto, but Armand refined her natural gluttony into a deep appreciation. Again, he'd taught her to pay attention to everything about a meal. How the different courses went together; how textures, colors, and tastes blended. She learned to distinguish the ingredients in a composite dish and to mourn with him the waste of flavor in overcooked food.

Wine, food, her personal appearance: not to overdress. But most of all, he'd made her aware of smell, a sense she'd never paid attention to before. He taught her to take the world in through all her senses, not only her eyes and ears. She sniffed the air when she woke. "Smell is the most subtle and the most individual of all the senses," he told her. To Nina, Armand's body smelled like fresh almonds.

But with all that, she didn't even try, anymore, to seduce him. The flapping wings of love had grown still. In memory of them, and as a kind of payment for what he'd brought her to, Nina continued her exhausting schedule, noticing that she was growing fatter but unable to do anything about supervising a body that Armand no longer seemed to want.

Walking back from the flower shop where she'd bought a yellow rose for Nina's birthday, Vie couldn't understand why she wasn't happier. Everything had turned out so well, just the way she wanted. In Nina she had a mother who wasn't really a mother, the best possible situation. They were equals, they could talk about anything at all, and yet Nina would do wonderful things, like brush her hair out for hours, make her a special treat, change her bed when she was in a rush for school.

Vie frowned. No, the problem wasn't there. Nina was absolutely the best thing that ever happened to her.

Then what was wrong? Marty, of course, didn't fit in, but she'd always been a problem, an outsider. Now that she was older, and since Nina had moved in, Marty was less of a weight on Vie than she'd ever been. "Doesn't fit in," Vie repeated to herself. Fit in to what?

She felt she had her finger on something sensitive, still nameless, that would begin to hurt if she went on probing. What was there to fit in to? Of course! She had it now, and swallowed hard: a family. Marty didn't fit in because there was none. Vie and Nina shared the closest tie. Even Nina and Armand didn't really fit together; tomorrow was her birthday, and Vie was certain her father hadn't bought anything. How could they be a family if they didn't act like one?

The summer was hot and long, lingering heavily into the fall. Nina had gained fifteen pounds since she'd started on the Windsor route, and they clung to her as persistently as the hot weather kept its hold on the air and vegetation. She hated herself like this, her body feeling like a sausage in its tight skin of clothes, the perspiration making her face shine.

On a September Saturday she invited Vie to come along on her rounds. Vie was delighted; she'd been asking Nina to do this for months. She picked out her prettiest summer dress, a gauzy gray sleeveless shirtwaist patterned with tiny roses. They'd bought it together at the thrift shop one Thursday evening, when it stayed open until eight, and next day Nina brought home a wide rose satin ribbon for Vie to use as a belt.

"A vision," Nina said, thinking how young Vie looked, and vulnerable, with her pale long arms, the slender neck, her face free of makeup and framed by gleaming, healthy hair. Vie was at the age when what she wore determined how old she appeared. In a black sheath, she was taken for a young woman. Now she was a girl, showing the promise of later beauty, still on the verge of bloom.

The regular customers couldn't place her. The Nina they knew was too young to have a teenage daughter. "My adopted sister," said Nina, laughing. "Can't you see the remarkable resemblance?"

Vie smiled, and saw nothing incongruous about the remark. Though she was tall and slender, Nina short and chubby, though Vie was blond and Nina dark, though Vie's features were modeled in alabaster and Nina's in coarser clay, Vie felt complimented, hoping that everyone would take them for sisters.

In a faded blue living room, the heavyset woman with chartreuse rollers in her hair asked Nina, "You got something to make me look like that?" pointing at Vie.

"Well, let's see," Nina answered, holding the pencil's eraser to the tip of her nose. Then she shrugged and grinned. "Aw, Mrs. MacCauley, you don't really want to be sixteen again, do you?"

"Guess not," the woman answered dubiously. "But it sure wouldn't hurt to take off a few years and some of these wrinkles."

"Right! And that's just what we're going to do." She brought out the catalog and began explaining to Mrs. MacCauley the virtues of a particular cream, a firming lotion, an abrasive soap to unclog pores and scrub away the outer layer of dead skin, revealing a pink, glowing youthful complexion. The woman listened attentively, nodding her appreciation from time to time, while Vie watched carefully, hearing Nina's spiel, noting changes in the woman's facial expression. She went from harsh to soft, and by the time Nina finished, she was smiling, looking younger and happier than when they'd come in.

On their way to the next customer Vie asked Nina to teach her the secrets of selling.

"No secrets," Nina said, chuckling.

"But you had to go through training to do this, didn't you?"

"Part of the hocus-pocus. It all boiled down to three simple rules. One: get your foot in the door—and that means *literally*. Two: flatter her. About anything at all, and if she's a complete dog, then flatter her furniture, her tablecloth, or her canary. Three: work on her insecurities. . . ."

"What do you mean?" asked Vie, alarmed.

"For instance, you tell her that her skin is delicate, but it's crying out for moisture. She never knew that before, but she always suspected her skin wasn't somehow *right*. You have just the cream, you say, a cream specially formulated for *her*."

"Do you?"

Nina winked. "Who's to tell? Most customers reorder and tell you it's the best product they've ever tried."

"Anything else you have to know?" pursued Vie eagerly.

"Let's see." Nina reflected a moment, then burst out laughing.

"Tell me," Vie implored.

"You won't believe this one, baby, but part of the indoctrination they put us through was to tell us"—she had to pause for laughter—"that we must think of ourselves"—again her own guffaws made her unable to speak—"as though we were doctors." Nina squeezed the last word out before a new wave of laughter came to drown it.

Vie was infected by the laughter, but soon asked unbelievingly, "What?"

"I promise you. *Doctors*. Making house calls, with our valises. Inside the valise was everything to make a person feel better—that's how we were told to think of it."

"How very peculiar."

"Don't I know! Still, it was fun having those sessions to go to." The laughter disappeared suddenly, replaced by a pensive, almost sad expression.

At the next apartment they were met by an overpowering smell of curry, in which Vie could distinguish the pungency of cardamom and savory coriander. A West Indian woman in a white nurse's uniform greeted them. Nina inquired how her patient was doing. "Coming along," the nurse said pleasantly, tilting her head in the direction of his room. "Poor dear isn't much in the way of taking exercise, but noways is he off his food." She laughed heartily; Vie loved listening to her melodious accent, the flowing lilt of her words. "Eating! Like it was going out of style! Come, you all, sit. The kettle's boiling for our tea and I baked us some banana bread."

"Now, Naomi," Nina reproved her. "How many times must I ask you not to fatten me up even more?"

"Fat folks is cheerful," she said, going to the kitchen.

While she was getting their tea, Nina prepared a little display of makeup for Naomi. "She loves blues," Nina whispered to Vie, setting out aquamarine shadow, navy mascara, *Heavenly Blue* liner.

"How nice!" Naomi exclaimed, setting down the tray. She went immediately to the mirror over the mantelpiece and started applying the cosmetics. "How do I look?" she asked when she finished and turned to face them, her blue lids like exotic butterflies that had settled on her face.

"Beautiful!" Nina told her.

"I'll take it all," Naomi said. "Now we'll have a bite of something."

Again Vie watched and took in the gestures and nuances as Nina sold her rouge and lipstick and another blue shadow—*Midnight Shimmer*—for evening wear.

On what evenings would she put it on, Vie wondered, trying to picture the woman's life. Why was she ordering all this? For whom?

When they left, each with a little package of banana bread that Naomi had wrapped for them, Nina tried to answer. "Every woman we've met today, baby, is living on dreams. She's got a hard life, she's by herself, or she's got a husband who treats her like shit or else doesn't notice her. If she has kids, she can't manage them. Every day's the same, and no matter what she does, she gets complaints. She's asking herself, 'What's wrong with me?'

"Then I come into her place with my bag of tricks and I offer her something. I pay attention to her, look at her. I say, 'If you try this or use that, it's going to make a difference.' Deep down, I don't think she believes me, but she reaches out for it anyway. Because she's got to hope for something. Naomi lives with that paralyzed old man day in and day out. Mrs. MacCauley has a husband who's an alcoholic.

"Nobody," Nina said wistfully, "can live with the thought that there's no way out."

They went up to other doors, into more dreary living rooms and rancid kitchens. Sometimes a woman said she didn't need anything more, she still had a lot of stuff from the last time, but usually they bought.

"My best day yet," Nina told Vie after her twelfth sale of the day. Two sales later she said, "Quitting time. You've been my rabbit's foot. Let's go celebrate—I'll buy you a drink." She linked her arm through Vie's as they walked toward Lenny's, a place Vie knew only from the outside, its neon sign missing the *e.*

"You know, Nina," she said, "you're doing the same thing Papa used to do. He's told me about the time when he had a perfume shop in Paris, and he said the women came to buy dreams."

"Not quite the same. . . ."

"Oh, I know, he had duchesses and actresses and all kinds of famous people, really glamorous. But what I mean is, they weren't buying something *real*, like a piece of cheese or rubber galoshes, they were buying magic. The magic in the perfume was going to make them different. Just like the people we saw today."

"Your father's daughter," Nina said, hugging her arm tightly. "You've got it, baby."

"Someday," Vie told her with intensity, "I'm going to bring magic to people, too."

"Yes."

"I will, Nina! I'll do something to make people feel happy, and rich—as though they'd found a pot of gold."

"You'd have to bottle the rainbow," Nina said with a smile.

"I'll do it!"

"Yes," she said slowly, hearing the conviction in Vie's voice, "I think you will." She steered her to the door. When she drew back, Nina gave her a light shove through the swinging doors.

Vie was nervous about ordering a drink, because she was underage and because she was afraid of what a drink might do to her. She'd never tasted hard liquor.

"Two pink ladies," Nina ordered from the bored waiter who looked at neither of them and walked away without giving any indication that he'd heard. But in a minute he was back with their cocktails, and Vie took a small, hesitant sip. Then she smiled broadly. "This is great!" It was delicious and sweet, like an ice-cream soda, only better.

Nina looked at her in silence, her head to one side, trying to prolong the moment when she would have to speak. When Vie's drink was almost finished, Nina cleared her throat. "Do you think you could take over my route?"

Vie saw the seriousness on Nina's face and felt frightened. "Yes. I'd love to do that. But what about you?"

The moment she'd been dreading was upon her. Reaching out for Vie's hands, Nina said softly, "I can't go on."

"With Windsor?" Vie asked, to forestall the presentiment she was feeling.

"I don't know how to tell you. This is the worst thing I've ever had to do. I love you, Vie, you know that. I love you very, very deeply. But my life"—she stopped until she could speak normally again. "My life doesn't make sense anymore. Armand and I loved each other, I'm sure of it. But I've become invisible to him. Even though"—she tried feebly for a joke—"there's more of me now than there ever was."

"You're going to leave us," Vie said coldly, feeling sick.

"Vie. You'll be seventeen in a month. You're graduating from high school next June. Things would have changed in any case. You'd go—"

"Never!" she said fiercely.

"Baby. Please, please try to understand. I don't want to go away from you, ever. But I'm turning into a fat old woman with no life of my own. Soon I'll be forty—and what then? Too late to have kids, get married. . . ."

"Kids?" Vie repeated, disbelievingly.

"I don't even know if I want a child. But I want a chance to do something with myself before I get too old."

"I see," said Vie in a glacial tone. Then suddenly she was out of the booth, running through the door, running in the pale gray light. Nina finished what she had to say— "I'll die if I don't go away"—but no one was listening.

She called the waiter over, paid, and walked out, feeling very old and very tired as she started her slow, heavy walk back to the house.

When she reached the front walk, she saw Vie standing to the side of it. "Baby?" she asked hesitantly.

Vie's arms were around her, holding tight, and Vie was crying, as she hadn't done since the cat was killed, the day that Nina came to live with them. "I love you," she said, letting her tears fall on Nina's neck, "and I don't want to understand!"

Her cry tore through Nina's heart as she held the girl, her own eyes closed. When she opened them, she saw the window of the room she shared with Armand, its blind down. She knew she couldn't go back.

"Wherever I am, Vie, is your home. Always."

"Thank you." She started extricating herself slowly. "Thank you," she repeated, "for everything." She took a step back. "I guess nobody can live without a dream."

"No," said Nina softly. They went up the walk with their arms around each other. When they reached the porch, Vie said, "The only time I felt as bad as this was when Jewel got killed. But don't worry, Nina, I'll be all right. I *know* you have to get out—even though I can't *feel* it yet."

A fighter, thought Nina, holding the door open for her; Vie is stronger than any of us.

IV

VIE'S CLIMB

1

1961–1962

"You are asking the impossible!" Armand shouted.

"I want you to make perfumes," Vie repeated, in the clear, determined voice of an older woman. They were standing in the tiny kitchen space, redolent with brewing coffee, as they faced each other like antagonists. Father and daughter, each born with the same astonishing talent, now found themselves locked in battle because of it.

"Yes, I heard you, and I say you know nothing. You don't know what you ask of me."

"You made them before," she insisted.

"Yes"—he was still shouting—"and once I was an important man. Once I was married to your mother. Once there was a world before the war. It is all buried, and I will not permit that you ask me to dig up old graves!"

"It's our only hope," she reminded him softly. When their rent was three months overdue, Vie knew they'd have to do something drastic. Without Nina's contribution, it seemed, they could barely survive. Vie's Windsor rounds brought only a pittance. Women wouldn't buy from Vie as they had from Nina; they'd pinch her cheek and tell her she was a pretty girl who didn't need anything for her skin. She couldn't win their trust, and the most she could rely on were standard reorders. Vie was rarely able to make as much as $12 a day. Sometimes it was only $5 or $6, and she needed all her will power to go on with the rounds, despite her sense of futility, of energies wasted.

Armand hadn't received the raise he'd hoped for from Alamode. He was still paying back his debt to Judy Grosvenor. In a few months, after graduation, Vie could go out to work full time. But they needed the money before then, and both she and Armand were determined that she should finish high school. Without a diploma she could never hope to find a decent job.

"Do you understand, Papa? We need money to pay the rent. Otherwise we'll have no place to live."

"I've lived without a home before," he said stubbornly.

"Yes, and so did I and so did Marty. Is that what you want us to do? Go off to school in the morning after sleeping in an alley or on a park bench?"

He'd never felt the force of his daughter's anger so strongly before. "Vie, I know you mean well for us all. Please try to understand. I cannot make perfumes anymore. I know that. Even my nose has betrayed me. I cannot go backward. I am not a crab."

"All right, then," she said matter-of-factly. "That's that, I suppose. What'll we do instead?"

"What we are doing now."

"And where will we live?"

"I don't know, we'll see."

The coffee was ready. Vie looked at it angrily before yanking the pot off the stove and pouring out two cups. She thrust Armand's at him with such force that the coffee spilled, overflowing the saucer, on to the floor. She sponged it up quickly, grabbed Armand's cup from his hands, and replaced it with her own, again managing to spill a little. "See? What's there to see? Look out the window—snow on everything. I guess you think some miracle will come along, but miracles have gone out of style. Unless you make them happen. But you—you don't care!" She turned her back to him, her shoulders shaking. "You don't care about anything anymore—not even about me!"

He was shocked. He put down his cup and came up to her, placing his hands at her waist. "Vie, please. . . ."

"Please what?" She whirled around to face him. "Can't you tell the difference anymore? Don't you know what's real and what isn't? The snow is real, and we'll have to go out into it unless you do something! Or at least," she said, with a touch of softness, "unless you give me some help. You've *got* to help me!"

The solemn hazel eyes, intense when she was a baby,

were now almost violent. Armand could feel that she needed him. His child, who'd slipped into maturity without his noticing it. But he'd taken it for granted and depended on her, often forgetting her actual age. Now, despite the determination in her voice and eyes, Vie seemed fragile, unprotected, like a delicate spring blossom in an icy downpour. He saw her again as his little girl, his *child*, for whose sake he'd abandoned thoughts of death and whose life was in his trust.

He embraced her and held her a long time, until the stiffness of her resistance ebbed and she put her arms around his neck. "Papa," she said, "mon gros, you must try one more time. You can't let this happen to us."

He smiled at the endearment. She'd first started using it at eight or nine, whenever he called her "ma petite." "Little one," he said now, delicately stroking her silky hair, "I would do anything in the world for you—even, I suppose, try to make perfume again. But in any case, I cannot afford the ingredients, and I cannot make it from air."

She gave him a child's smile. "Remember, Papa, when you told me about the liquid gold that could turn frogs into princesses? You promised to make some for me."

"Did I? Did I? Vie, my little angel, I would, believe me, I would make a fragrance for you if I could."

"If you had the ingredients, you mean?"

"Yes, if I had them," he said placatingly.

The door slammed, and Vie jumped away from her father's arms as though theirs was an illicit embrace. When Marty walked into the kitchen, she found them both silent, looking at the floor as though inspecting it for termites.

"Nothing beats a warm welcome," she said.

"Hi, Marty," said Vie. "You have dinner?"

"Yeah. Pretty lousy, but it beats the stuff I get here."

"Really? Why don't *you* try making dinner once, for a change?"

"Thanks, sis, I prefer eating out."

"On what money?" Vie asked heatedly.

"Useless," Armand said. "Leave her—she is lost. Your sister is hopeless, a wild thing."

Marty turned on her father as though she would strike

him. "And you're a dead thing! Dead, dead, deadhead. You can't throw a ball, you can't make money, you're too dopey to know what gives. You're a phony as a father."

Armand slapped her hard across the face. "Shut up, you little whore. Nothing but trouble, like your mother. A lunatic. I should have left you. . . ."

"Stop!" Vie screamed. "Both of you stop! I can't stand it."

But Armand paid no attention. "Yes," he went on to Martine, "you should not have been born. I saved you. I carried you off with me, away from your crazy mother who was trying to kill you, both of you. . . ." He stopped with mouth open, realizing what he was saying.

The girls were looking at him with a horrified interest, waiting for him to go on. But he shook his head and quickly left the room.

"You satisfied?" Marty sneered. "You can see how he hates me." Tears welled up, flowed over, and ran down her face with astonishing volume.

Vie held out her arms and moved toward Marty to comfort her. The girl raised a fist and, with all her strength, hit Vie hard in the breast. She staggered back from the pain as Marty ran out the door shouting, "I hate you too. I hate you both!"

Holding her chest where her sister had struck her, Vie felt a sudden insight into the depth of Marty's pain. She felt abandoned. Vie understood that Marty saw *her* as the thief of their father's love.

But how could she make up for that? Later, Vie thought vaguely, still trying to catch her breath; right now there was hard work to be done. First she had to get hold of ingredients for the making of perfume.

Vie did her homework in the mornings before breakfast, so she'd be free after school to hunt down clues that might lead to the treasure she sought—perfumery materials. Her schoolwork wasn't brilliant, and in fact her marks had been falling regularly throughout her senior year, but Vie's average remained in the B– to C+ range, good enough for graduation, and that was all that mattered.

She had lots of other things to do besides school. The

basic running of the household, for one; her Windsor route on weekends; and now her free moments were taken up with going from store to store, trying to find her way to the essential oils, fixatives, and chemicals they needed. She didn't ask Armand, fearing that if she presented him with anything less than a fait accompli, he would withdraw the faint promise he'd made to her. Instead, Vie asked people who worked in drugstores and hair salons, most of whom she'd known since she was little. They were moved by her earnestness. They wanted to help the slender girl with buttercream hair, and gave what advice they could.

She wrote what they told her on a little pad. Sometimes the addresses they'd given simply led to another drugstore or a larger beauty salon. The first true perfume supplier she came to was D&G, where the receptionist looked at Vie as though she must be coming to sell magazine subscriptions. The office was cold gray marble. The antiseptic atmosphere held no trace of scent. It could have been a hotel lobby or a hospital receiving area, offering no hint of the aromatic substances hidden behind the sterile facade.

"Yes, Miss?" the receptionist asked archly. Her hair was steel blue, in perfect complement to her surroundings.

When Vie explained her purpose, a faint smile came to the woman's face. "How many vats will you be needing, dear?"

"No vats. Just a little bit of each."

"I see. You're thinking of something like a chemistry set. I'm afraid we don't make up sample kits, my dear. We sell by the pound or kilo. Wholesale only."

"Thank you," she muttered, almost running out.

Though her experience with Windsor had hardened Vie to an extent—she'd had to accept rejections, even rudeness, and go on to the next door—this new adventure left her quaking. She was intimidated by marble walls, polished receptionists, formidable offices. At other suppliers, like Otto's in Queens, Vie was more angry than intimidated. She hated the eyes of men appraising her, the laughter in their voices when they talked to her patronizingly while giving her lewd looks. She forced herself not to show the disgust she felt, and her ladylike manner soon tamed them.

But everywhere the answer was the same: wholesale only. Even the few times she found someone willing to sell her small amounts, the prices were out of reach, in the same realm of fantasy as the items themselves. Yet people were often kind and suggested other places she might try.

Two weeks of the quest were enough to demoralize Vie almost completely. She'd handed over all of her Windsor earnings to Frances Murphy, in return for a promise that they could stay through April. By then, Vie had assured her, they would be able to meet the rent and start paying back what they owed.

We'll never do it, she thought, walking through the garment district on a busy Monday afternoon. Carts and trolleys of clothes stood at the curb while men unloaded their trucks, pausing to whistle or call out crude invitations to Vie as she passed.

On Thirty-seventh Street, halfway between Fifth and Sixth avenues, Vie opened the cornflower-blue door of In Essence and walked in.

Her heart lifted at the sight before her. The small room looked like a magic cottage, its walls lined with gingham, its shelves holding bright bottles of translucent liquids in blues, violets, apricots, yellows, greens, ambers. The air held a rich potpourri of scents, languorous as incense. She felt like a child in Mr. Baker's candy store, down the road at the corner, where bottles held butterscotch, licorice, strips of pressed fruit, red spice drops, sour balls, and chocolate babies, and the smell of the place, though different from here, was also a blend of so many different ones that it was nearly impossible to distinguish the ingredients. At Mr. Baker's store Vie had once bought a big red Valentine heart filled with chocolates for Nina.

"May I help you, young lady?" came a soft, lilting voice behind her.

She turned to meet the darkest eyes she'd ever seen, so dark that she couldn't make out the pupil from the iris. "I'd like to buy essences," she said.

The tall, slim man smiled. His full hair was completely white, his skin the color of fresh-cut pine. "Chandra

Ghannikar at your service," he said, bowing slightly. His voice lifted and fell, like smooth waves on high sea. He was a wonderful-looking man, Vie thought; something like pictures she'd seen of Mahatma Gandhi.

"My name is Vie Nouvel. I have a list here"—she extracted it from her pocket and handed it to him—"of materials I need. For my father."

He studied it for a few moments, then nodded. "I believe we can fill your order, Miss Nouvel."

She smiled; but others had said the same and then shattered her hopes by giving the price. "Do you know how much it will cost?"

"I must do my calculations," he said seriously, folding her paper in his hands. Vie stared at them. They were the most exquisite hands she'd ever seen, the fingers incredibly long and slim, tapering toward the ends. They looked as though music could flow from them.

"But it is now my teatime," he told her, smiling. "Perhaps you will join me in a spot of tea? It is a more civilized way to discuss your requirements than by standing in the showroom."

She nodded and followed him into the back, where they entered a small, richly patterned room with a little table, set for tea, at the center. The tablecloth was damask, the cups and plates of fragile china with tiny azure flowers against an ivory background. The silver glistened. "I am always hoping for company," he explained. "And I always set for two. Otherwise I find it a bit dismal. Usually my companion is invisible, but better than none at all. I am enchanted to have you here."

He seemed overgrown in this little fairy room. "It's lovely," she said in wonder, taking her seat and fingering her napkin, made of real cloth. He brought out a silver platter holding little seed-covered cakes. Vie laughed, picturing herself as Alice sitting down to tea in Wonderland.

"Earl Grey," Chandra said, pouring the tea. "We are partial to it in my country, a taste we inherited from the English."

"Have you been here long?" she asked politely, lifting the teacup as though it might shatter at her touch.

"Since 1956, when my native Kerala became a state. A

distressing story, my dear, and one I shall not pour or trickle into the charming cockles of your ears."

She was fascinated by the lilt of his speech. She watched his hands dance from teapot to cup. His face, under the white hair, was fine-featured, almond-shaped. "I thought Indians were dark-skinned," Vie blurted out and immediately lowered her head to hide her embarrassment.

"Quite right, my dear. Our millions teem with color—except for the handful of us who've been put through countless bleachings to be made fit for rule. You have read Kipling? No? Not to worry. The British brought their white man's burden to India, bearing the message that the palest shall lead. Though we didn't need them for that lesson," he said bitterly. "We'd been practicing discrimination for centuries.

"My father is a maharajah, who bequeathed to me the noble pallor of his genes. However, they were not white enough to remove the stain of illegitimacy, and therefore my rule is limited to the tiny dominion before your charming eyes." His own showed merriment, but Vie was confused. She'd never met anyone like this man; he seemed to step out of a magic kingdom, with his liquid voice and chocolate eyes.

"Have another seedcake, my dear. Do. And tell me why you have come to grace my small shop with your custom. Are you a perfumer yourself?"

She answered in monosyllables at first. But after her second cup of tea, feeling the kindness of Chandra's interest in her, Vie began to relax and told him a little about her life. She said that her father had been a great perfumer in France but was forced out by the Nazis. Chandra nodded in sympathy. She had no mother, Vie told him in answer to his question; she lived with her father and younger sister.

She told him about the Windsor route, about Nina, who had left, about their lack of money and the overdue rent. She left out nothing except Armand's black book of formulas, from which she'd derived the list she showed Chandra.

"Why is it that you are coming for the supplies and not your father?"

Vie studied his face before answering. He was a stranger, and she'd already revealed unusually much to him. But he looked so distinguished and kind—even wise, she thought—that Vie felt she could trust him. "My father's worn out. He doesn't want—he's afraid to try again."

"And you, young person, intend to give him courage?"

"Yes," she said, full of conviction.

Chandra stood up, grazing the ceiling with his head. "I am a wizard mathematician," he said jovially. "I have been making my calculations while we chatted."

"How much?" she asked fearfully.

"Not to worry. Your order will be filled within ten days. Your credit here is outstanding."

"But I can't accept a gift!"

"No, my dear," he said soothingly. "I would never put you under such an obligation. You will pay for what you buy, but there is no rush. I am simply offering you a loan to pay back at your convenience in whatever amounts you choose. We are quite solvent here. The matter is a trifle we shall not dignify with further discussion." Offering his arm to Vie, he invited her to inspect the oils and fixatives she had just acquired.

She walked with a dazed smile, holding her breath to make sure this wasn't a dream. As they passed the brilliant colors, Vie thought of a rainbow and had a sense that this strange, wonderful man was leading her to its golden end.

As they strolled into the storeroom, he talked to her about perfume. "An ancient, honorable, and also erotic art. Your father no doubt has explained that the word comes from the Latin, *per fume:* through smoke. In the East, we scented the air long before we scented fabrics or bodies. Our gods have always been inordinately fond of fragrance. Here," he said, stopping to take down a bottle of buttercup color, "is jasmine oil." He opened it for her to smell. It was extremely sweet and heady.

Chandra smiled. "Good, you close your eyes to sniff it. Very romantic, don't you find? Our god of love, Kama, holds an arrow tipped by jasmine blossom. When Kama shoots this through his bow of sugarcane, the blossom passes through the senses before it pierces the heart. A wise god," he said, replacing the lid. "He knew where the source of love abides."

"Now here we have oil of vetiver," he said, holding out the brownish-red oil.

"It smells like fresh-cut grass," said Vie, inhaling again, deeply.

"Very good. You have an excellent nose. The vetiver is derived from an aromatic grass that grows in India, particularly in the south. Formerly it was used to scent linens, and in the tropics it is still being made into mats." He returned the vetiver to its place on the shelf. "Try this," he told her, holding out something that was a grayer brown than the other.

Vie stepped back after the whiff, wrinkling her nose. "What's this awful stuff?"

"Perfect. You have the gift, my dear, no doubt about it. What you just smelled is not an oil. It is a powder held in suspension, used as a fixative. It's musk, probably the most powerful substance in perfumery. Never use more than a trace. Musk is the same as our Hindi word for testicle, and has been considered an aphrodisiac for centuries. It comes from a sac under the skin of the abdomen of the male musk deer. In the Koran, paradise is described as being made of musk. The nymphs who inhabit it also are formed of musk."

"In that case, I don't think I'd like to go to paradise," Vie told him, the harsh smell still offending her nostrils.

Chandra laughed. He brought other substances for her to sample, and Vie floated from fragrance to fragrance as though borne on currents, dipping from mood to mood through new sensations, each releasing in her another soft wave of emotion.

Then she could smell nothing. Chandra was holding something under her nose and she had no sensation at all. "What's happened to me?" she asked in alarm.

He chuckled. "Nothing whatever, my dear. You are splendid. Your nose has held out for longer than any I've had the pleasure to tour with. You are surfeited, that's all. Even you, with your magnificent ability, are mortal in the end."

"Will I ever be able to smell again?"

Chandra placed a hand gently on her arm. "In a few minutes your powers shall be restored." It was as though he had a magic wand at his fingertips, Vie thought. And it was true: her sense of smell came back before they'd reached the showroom.

"It is enough for an introduction," Chandra said, again bowing slightly to her. "When you return to pick up your order, I shall be most honored if you would permit me to continue exposing you to my pedantic trivia."

"Oh please! I can't wait. Please, tell me *everything*!"

"That would never do," he said. "For then I should have nothing more to offer."

Vie looked at him incredulously. He must know more than anyone in the world, she thought. He was an old, wise, beautiful man who possessed the key to knowledge and the senses. "Thank you," she said. "Thank you very, very much." She said the words fervently, but they couldn't express what she felt. He'd opened a new world to her, and she knew already that she would enter that world and inhabit it for the rest of her life.

Vie decided to say nothing to Armand until she had the supplies in hand and could present him with them.

On Wednesday, exactly ten days after her first visit, she went back to Chandra's store. He greeted her like an old friend and said her order was ready, but "a spot of tea first, my dear, don't you think?"

She laughed delightedly; she'd been looking forward to all of it: the place itself, the tea, the wonderful instruction she'd been given, and most of all, dominating everything, Chandra himself. Vie hadn't told anyone any of it; and her secret became more and more enchanted every time she looked back on that afternoon. Returning now was for her like reentering a spell or coming back again to a place she'd dreamed about.

Instead of seedcakes they had scones, delicious little warm biscuits that you first buttered, then covered with raspberry jam, finally adding cream on top. The Earl Grey tea, with its touch of bitterness, was a perfect foil for the scones, and Vie gobbled up one after the other, to her host's undisguised pleasure. "How you compliment me, my dear, in displaying such relish for my modest tea!"

"It's the most delicious thing I've eaten in my whole life," she said, like a little girl. "Am I eating too fast?" She couldn't remember ever enjoying a meal so much. The room was like a large dollhouse, everything in it perfect and shining. The by now familiar melody of Chandra's voice and the bottomless warmth in his eyes gave Vie a sense of having finally come home, to the snug, safe haven she'd always missed.

After tea they looked through the box of what she'd ordered for Armand. "Your father will tell you about these scents," Chandra said. "He will teach you the notes and play them for you."

"You tell me, please," she begged.

"If you insist—though I warn you I am not a singing master. Each perfume has a base and a topnote. It must have more besides; however, we shall let that be for the moment, and not muck about with the jargon generally referred to as 'technical language.' The topnote is the main impression a scent gives out. A person's topnote is generally his face, or perhaps his eyes. Your impression on first meeting someone will be, in all likelihood, a simple one: intelligent, kind, cunning, humorous, shy, lonely, whatever—the point being that you single out one overriding characteristic. Your eyes select it and report back to your brain.

"Just so with perfumes, though the messenger is your nose. But because scents merely arouse emotions and have none of their own, we characterize them by terms that do not carry the same weight of meaning as those we use for people. Each perfumer has a private vocabulary to help him recognize or memorize a scent, but common terms allow perfumers to talk to each other. There are basically seven divisions, the 'notes,' as in a seven-tone scale. These are: green, floral, aldehydic, chypre, oriental, tobacco/leather, and fougère notes. They are approximations, gross classifications, even metaphors if you will, and most of the seven standard notes are then further subdivided and qualified."

"I'm not sure I follow," Vie admitted, feeling distressed.

Last week everything had been so clear; she could understand what Chandra was saying with her mind and through her feelings. But today it all sounded abstract and difficult.

"Not to worry. It simply means that perfumers have stolen from music certain concepts that help them describe how a fragrance is made. We use the words *harmony* and *accord;* we are even arrogant enough to refer to our compositions as *symphonies.* But my dear Vie, forget the twaddle and trust your instincts. If ever you do decide to become a perfumer, you will learn all this with no greater difficulty than you had in learning the alphabet as a child."

"You really think so?" she asked dubiously. In the moment that Chandra suggested she *might* become a perfumer, Vie decided she definitely would. "Are you sure?" she pressed. "Will I really be able to learn *everything* about perfumes?"

He nodded. "You have my word."

She felt enormously pleased, buoyed with hope. "Do you think my father knows about all this, about the things you've been telling me?"

"Quite definitely. Take these to him now," Chandra said, putting the box in her hands. "But before you go, you must promise me something."

She waited expectantly.

"You must promise to take tea with me regularly once a fortnight."

"Oh, can I?" Vie wanted to hug him, but with the heavy box in her hands she could only stand beaming at him. He made dreams come true; she thought Chandra was the most wonderful person in the world.

"Has he seduced you?" Armand shouted. "Is that how you paid the Indian for this?"

Vie felt pure hatred for her father as she looked at him with disgust.

Armand knew he was behaving badly, even abominably, toward his daughter. But he couldn't help it. The sight of all the extracts in their bottles filled him with terror. He'd never actually intended to try making perfumes again—when he'd told Vie he'd do it if he had the ingredients, he had merely been pacifying her. But this box of oils and fixatives frightened him so deeply that he lashed out, unable to control his words, desperately thrashing for some excuse to return these liquids that were poisoning him; to make them vanish completely, as though they'd never been.

"If you say another word about him, I'll never see you again," Vie told her father.

The complete determination in her voice sobered him. She'd done something amazing. She'd done it for him, and now she stood at the other side of the room while he berated her.

Armand went back to the box and began unpacking its precious contents, reading out the name on each label: "Sandalwood . . . Patchouli . . . Lemongrass . . . Civet . . . Otto of Rose."

Not looking at her, his voice breaking, Armand said, "Forgive me, Vie." He turned. "Please forgive me. You are an angel. I have done you great injustice."

"Not only to me," she said in a low tone. Though she somehow understood that her father's fury had little to do with her, Vie couldn't forgive him yet. What he'd said had thrown filth on the happiest hours she'd spent, with a man she worshiped.

But here were the ingredients, which she would never return, for fear of losing Chandra's respect. She knew they represented many hundreds of dollars' worth. When Armand had unpacked them all, Vie said, "And now, get the book."

He brought it out. They sat together at the kitchen table, poring over the yellowed, sometimes cracked, pages. The writing was often faded. "Here," said Armand, pointing to a blank part, "I left out some of the formula on purpose, so that no one finding the book could reproduce it."

"Can you remember what it was?" She saw his blank, fearful look and heard him confess; "It is cloudy, Vie."

"Please try, Papa."

His answer was a humbled silence.

*   *   *

But over the next weeks Armand applied himself to the work, his moods ricocheting between confidence and despair. He worked only when Martine was out of the house. Vie noticed this and knew he had shut Marty out of his life, closing the door on her and taking Vie inside. Yet Vie felt her father had locked himself away from her, too. He'd placed a seal on his former life. There was much she didn't understand about him. She could imagine the loneliness and frustration Nina must have felt when she lived with him.

Marty stayed away, as before. Since the confrontation a few weeks earlier, she didn't bother to speak to her father at all; with Vie she was coolly hostile.

Afternoons she was always out. Vie usually worked with Armand at the makeshift organ he kept in his bedroom. Sometimes he spoke to her as to an apprentice, repeating or elaborating lessons she'd learned from Chandra, which she'd never tell him about.

"To describe odors," he said, measuring the sandalwood with an eyedropper, "it is necessary to classify them. These days we talk of *profiles*—we profile a fragrance by stating its chief qualities. Before the turn of this century a Dutch chemist by the name of Zwaardemaker developed a system with thirty-nine categories. I think I can still remember some of them: fruity, waxy, camphorish. Let's see, what else? Fecal was one, also fishy . . . " He looked up, shaking his head. "That's all. I can't remember more."

"Not to worry," said Vie.

He smiled. "You are right, little one. We perfumers must each invent our own system, words that are emotionally important, to fix the scent in the mind. Your mother was lavender and new grass; that's Anne. My mother is lilac. Chanel to me will always be her *No. 5*, and my father is a smell I cannot put into words. Maurice: his name brings it back. The smell I associate with him is not pleasant. It is early morning in our Paris home, tobacco is on his breath already, and I smell remnants of last night's supper when he talks to me. He has not yet made his toilette, the odor of his body comes through the dressing gown. Ah! So many years, and still the name is enough to resurrect the smell as though he were standing here." He looked at her helplessly, drawn by his senses back into childhood.

"To me you smell like an old book in leather binding."

"The pages, are they falling out?" he asked.

"No. The glue's strong. I can smell that, too."

He held up the beaker to inspect its color. "You give me strength, little one. Maybe I will find the old formula again."

But there was more trial and error ahead. The supply of Otto of Rose, their most expensive ingredient, was nearly depleted. When that happened, Armand told Vie, he would have to stop.

"Use something else in its place," she suggested.

"What! Do you understand nothing at all? Do you not listen when I teach you?"

"I'm trying," she answered.

"Then don't bother me with stupidities."

Offended, she left his room. When he didn't come out for dinner, she made a sandwich and brought it in to him, but he neither looked up nor thanked her.

A few hours after she'd fallen asleep, Vie was awakened by an urgent whisper. She struggled to consciousness and in the dim light made out her father's form, bending over her. "Come—right away, please," he was saying in her ear. She got out of bed and followed him. In his room, he held out a piece of impregnated blotting paper. "I think," he said shyly, "it may be I have found my old _Âme_."

She smelled it and all her senses came awake as she gave herself to the wonderful fragrance. She looked at him with sparkling eyes. "Papa, you've done it!" she told him and began to laugh in pleasure and relief.

He joined her laughter, but after a few minutes he told her, "There will not be much of this to sell. With what is left of the ingredients, I can make up twenty, maybe twenty-four one-ounce bottles, no more."

She calculated. At $30 each, if she sold them all, there would be enough money to settle the rent and pay back much of what she owed to Chandra. He would permit her to buy more on credit, and this time she could choose only

the particular extracts they needed for the formulation of
Âme.

"We'll get more supplies very soon," she said. "How
many ingredients went into the compound?"

"Seventy-one."

"That many?"

He nodded apologetically.

"Never mind, we'll get them." She would not allow
their elation to fade. "We have it, mon gros!" she told
him. "You've made the magic potion you promised me
when I was little."

On Saturday, she dabbed *Âme* behind her ears, on her
breasts, at the back of her knees. Her customers noticed.
"What you got on, honey? It's a great smell."

She took out a bottle from her handbag. "It's called
Âme."

"How much?"

"Thirty dollars for a full ounce."

"Thirty bucks for an ounce?" Mrs. MacCauley nearly
shouted. "You must be crazy, girl."

"It lasts a long time. It's romantic . . ."

Mrs. MacCauley, her head covered in her habitual chartreuse rollers, chuckled. "My old man's idea of romance is
going on a bender and sticking his hand down the waitress's
cleavage. And the only time he gets 'romantic' with me is
just before his mother's coming to visit and he wants to
make sure I'll treat her right—the old witch."

"It makes you feel happier"—Vie tried another tack—
"you feel good about yourself."

"Look, honey, for thirty bucks I could get me into
Manhattan and go dancing on the Starlight Roof." She
laughed at the absurd thought. "Now, you got any more
of that night cream? I'm running low."

Vie made out the order for $1.89 plus tax and continued
her rounds.

Other reactions, if not as colorful as Mrs. MacCauley's,
all turned out to be the same: there was not a woman who
would pay $30 for perfume.

By three in the afternoon Vie couldn't bear it any longer.

She abandoned her route and took the subway into town. If anyone in the world could help, it was Chandra.

He was busy with customers, but asked her to wait for him in their tearoom. After a few minutes he joined her there. "Your scent, my dear, is quite marvelous. A bit of the old grandeur: classical, elegant. Simply stunning, dear Vie."

"But what can I do?" she wailed, and told him about the events of the past few days: her father's success with the formula; her hopes; the rejections of today.

He put on the kettle, listening without interruption. When she finished, he brought the brewing tea to the table and sat down beside her. "This shop is called In Essence—a pun, of course, but think, my dear: what is a perfume in essence? Is it a few drops of liquid? Of course not. It is a product like no other, not even among the cosmetics. It is intangible, invisible: the air of promise, an aura of hope. You cannot sell the thing itself, la chose; you must sell l'essence." In French, Vie discerned, the word had a lingering, dreamy quality.

"Let me tell you a story from my childhood," Chandra said, pouring the tea tentatively first in his own cup to see if it was dark enough. Satisfied, he filled Vie's cup and then his own.

"My uncle was planning to take me into the mountains, but I didn't want to go. I was terrified of meeting tigers! I clung to my mother and wept, begging her not to send me off where I would surely be eaten alive.

"She tried to reassure me, but I was adamant in my terror. She pushed me aside and stood up. I still remember the pale-orange-and-gray sari she wore. She left the room, and I waited miserably for her to return, thinking it might be better to kill myself now than face the certain bloody death that awaited me in the mountains.

"Drink your tea, my dear Vie, it's getting cold." She sat enthralled as a child, but now she hastily picked up her cup.

"Good. When my mother came back, she was carrying a small golden vial. 'In here,' she told me, 'I have an elixir that makes tigers run to the other side of the world. One drop on your forehead, one on each wrist, and every tiger that ever was will tremble and hide itself. Tomorrow morning, Chandi, I shall anoint you with this and you will have nothing to fear.'

"I slept peacefully that night and next morning set out with my uncle in a happy and confident state of mind. We saw no tiger throughout the day. It was a splendid outing.

"Years later, when I was about eleven, I asked my mother if she still had the golden elixir. She laughed heartily. 'That was some leftover tea,' she told me."

Chandra chuckled at the memory. Turning to Vie, he said seriously, "For that magic, people would give up fortunes—a small price for courage. And thirty dollars is a minuscule price for beauty, or love."

She understood. What she needed, to sell *Âme*, was a golden vial and a sprinkling of magic words.

Through the night the problem kept tugging at her, never allowing her to fall into deep sleep. A golden vial would cost twice as much as the perfume itself. She tried to think of some other container, one they could afford, that would still seem to come out of mythology or the realm of magic. But drowsiness overcame her, and she dozed, waking with a start, feeling she almost had it, she was sure she'd dreamed a solution to the problem, but nothing presented itself.

By morning she was exhausted. She couldn't face going from door to door again and decided that, for once, she'd sleep late on Sunday.

When Vie woke again, it was midmorning. Through the long crack in the window shade she saw sun rays beaming in. She followed the shafts of light with her eyes to where they struck the old cut-glass knob on her bedroom door, splintering light into a brilliant shower of color, reflected up to the ceiling, where a rainbow danced.

Vie jumped up and ran to the door. She pried off the handle and held it in the cup of her hand. It was like a crystal ball, containing mysteries of the past and future. Its hollow core, she realized, would hold about an ounce of perfume.

2

1962

In her black gown, the mortarboard atop her head, Vie waited stiffly to receive her diploma. She felt like an outsider looking in on a local ritual: to her, a meaningless ceremony. The speaker was talking about beginnings, the "commencement" of life with responsibility. But for Vie this was merely a dress-up affair to get a functional piece of paper. Beginnings belonged to the past; last weekend she'd sold twelve one-ounce bottles of *Âme*.

"As you set foot upon the path of life as young men and women, remember that the obstacles. . . ."

Droning on; the words held no reference to her. In its heavy crystal, with a new name and a translucent plastic cork, the perfume was beginning to bring in profits—$360 in a day and a half. Though most of the money wasn't in her hands yet, she could count on getting it when she delivered the order in a few days. Three women had paid cash in advance, and Vie kept the money in a sock. She'd taken out the bills a few times, like a child digging into a Christmas stocking, to count them again, making separate piles for the tens (five of them), the fives (four), and the singles (twenty). By next weekend she'd have the additional $270 in hand, and new orders.

The glass balls holding the perfume provided most of the magic, though she bought them at thirty cents apiece from a hardware supplier. As Vie poured the golden potion into them, they became prismatic orbs to irradiate a bedroom or bathroom with dancing aureoles of color. Vie herself, who knew this was just an old doorknob, felt a thrill when she unstoppered the plastic cork: it was like releasing the secrets of a crystal ball.

A mysterious aura was captured in the cut glass, but the perfume's name didn't evoke the essence of romance or beauty, at least not for Vie's customers, who pronounced it *Aim* or *Am* and had no associations with the French word. She needed a word that could stir fantasies and evoke dreams of love. A word that sounded like a charm

First she'd thought of conjurers' phrases: Hocus-pocus; Open, Sesame; Aladdin; Genie. None of these was right— all were too fanciful, they held no promise of a dream fulfilled. Then she let her thoughts drift back to Chandra, as she'd done many times since she'd met him. A beautiful stately man, with an exotic music in his speech that called up faraway places, the spices of India. Within moments she had her new name for the perfume: *Taj*. Who hadn't heard of the Taj Mahal, the dream palace built as a sturdy monument to love?

The women who wouldn't touch *Âme* in its simple vial clamored for *Taj* in crystal. The plastic corks had been Chandra's idea. He ordered them to be made and gave them to Vie as "an early graduation present." They fitted smoothly with the design. In its new package, rebaptized, the perfume had become priceless.

". . . in the spirit of America. As you forge ahead to conquer new frontiers, may God be with you. Thank you, thank you all."

Applause. The handing out of paper scrolls. For what? For whom? The other graduates had families and friends in the audience, grandparents, younger brothers and sisters, neighbors, uncles. She'd been given six tickets to the ceremony, like the others, but her only guest was her father. She'd desperately wanted to invite Chandra, her mentor, guide, and dearest friend, but she couldn't forget or forgive Armand's comments about him the day she had brought home the essences. The two men had never met, and she didn't dare risk their meeting today.

"Jordan Neal . . . Stacy Nizer . . . Viveanne Nouvel. . . ."

She moved toward the podium. Marty hadn't even congratulated her. Not a single word. Nina's telegram this morning, sent from Colorado, was a lovely surprise. Frances Murphy had given her a corsage of carnations. But from Marty, nothing.

"Congratulations." Handshake from the principal.

She was an official graduate, diploma in hand, as she walked off the platform to find Armand. He took her out to lunch, but they had little to say. Each of them felt ill at ease in celebrating, as a couple, an event that should be shared by a family.

When they came home, Vie went to her room to change. On the pillow of her bed she saw a small white box, with the word "Congrats" written in Marty's still-childish handwriting.

Vie felt a rush of love for her sister. She'd not only remembered, she'd saved up to buy her something. Vie wished she were here now, so they could hug. They hadn't done that, hadn't even touched, for years. The little white box with its single word was an offering of peace. They'd start again, Vie fantasized: leave the bickering and harshness behind, become true sisters. This day was turning out to mean a new beginning after all, she thought.

She removed the lid carefully. Inside the box, on a bed of cotton, lay a gleaming oval. It was a bracelet of gold. Real gold.

Vie gasped, and for a moment she was overcome. Then she ran to her drawer and opened it. The sock was still there, but as she lifted it out Vie knew it was empty. Yet she turned it inside out before she was willing to acknowledge to herself that the money was gone.

The golden bracelet turned into a ring of ashes. She hid it, still in the box, under her mattress.

She couldn't go to anyone for advice, not wanting to reveal something so shameful. Not even to her father—especially not him, she thought. His anger might explode like a bomb to force Marty out of the house permanently.

What to do? Impossible to act as though nothing had happened. She would have to thank her sister for the bracelet in any case—and then what? Confront her, accuse her, or try, in some subtle manner, to get Marty to confess the crime on her own? But even as Vie went over the possibilities, she knew she'd be unable to use psychology on her, and she was sure, dreading it, that Marty would deny any knowledge of the missing money.

When Marty came home late that night, Vie pretended to be asleep. But the following morning she forced herself to go through with it. "Thanks, Marty," she said, trying to keep her voice light. "It's a beautiful bracelet. Where did you get it?"

"Picked it up in a jewelry store someplace."

"Must've cost a fortune."

"Don't worry," said Marty. "I only got one sister, and you don't graduate every day of the week."

Vie longed for it to be different, clean; so they could hug each other and not have this tension between them from the tainted gift. "I think you should give it back," Vie blurted out.

Marty's eyes narrowed. "You hate it," she said flatly.

"No. It's beautiful, really. But you took the money!"

"What money?" she asked in a cold voice.

"The money in my sock. The ninety dollars I got from selling *Taj*. We need it terribly. We have to pay back debts, the rent, the money we owe for ingredients. . . ."

"Don't tell me about your problems, I got my own." Marty started walking out of the room, but Vie ran over and grabbed her by the arm.

"Let go, you bitch," Marty shouted, pulling away and hitting Vie on the shoulder.

"Marty! You've got to help. I know you wanted to get me something, and I was really happy when I saw it. But we need the money!"

"I don't have it."

"Then help me get it."

"What for? You don't need me. You can do it on your own. Or go to your daddy, he'll do anything for you."

Vie wanted to scream, but she forced herself to regain control over her voice. She took hold of Marty again, gently this time, and told her, "I wouldn't go to him. He doesn't know anything about this." Marty's look of surprise encouraged her. "Just help me get it back, that's all. *Please*," she added softly.

Marty stood looking at her sister for a long moment. She felt angry at Vie for rejecting her gift, but she also

heard something in Vie's voice she'd never heard before.
It sounded as though she really needed her. Marty was
torn. She wanted to do what she usually did—just get out
of there and not be bothered by her dumb family. But she
also felt something like pity for Vie as the victim of a
robbery. If she got the money, Marty calculated, Vie would
love her. "OK," she said, "I'll do it," and gave her sister a
fleeting smile. But as Vie came over to touch her, Marty
took a step back. Then she turned and left the room, as
she always did when she was troubled by an emotion.

The jewelry on Magdahl-Hoffman's ground floor was
displayed in locked glass cabinets. Only the fake pieces—
costume jewelry made of glass, wood, woven fabric, or
fired ceramic—were placed on the counter, where customers would finger them, try them on in front of a mirror,
and usually lay them down again.

This was Vie's first visit to New York's most elegant
and expensive department store, but she hadn't come to
browse. Inside her handbag she carried two bottles of *Taj*,
and she was here to see Philippa Wright, head buyer for
the store.

She didn't have an interview, hadn't even phoned to ask
for one. Armand had dissuaded her. The memory of Margaret Pearson still rankled—and he'd convinced his daughter
that, without proper credentials, she'd never be given an
appointment.

"OK. I'll just go there."

"You are not being realistic, mon enfant," he told her.
"At such a place they have no time for little girls. In any
case, it would be better if *I* would go. Since your Indian has
told you that the buyer is a woman, she would be more
responsive to my charms than yours. I still *do* have a way
with women, you know."

"Maybe," Vie said coldly. "But we're not selling personal charm. We have something that people will buy."

"Stubborn. Once I was like you. Go, then, if you won't
listen. You'll wait there like a little mouse in the cold. No
one will speak to you or have any pity on you."

"I don't need pity. And if you're right, if Miss Wright
won't see me, then I'll come back the next day and the

day after that, for as many days as it takes, until I can talk to her."

"You are a little fool," he said, but tenderly, remembering the way he had defied his father when he left Chanel. Vie had inherited his stubbornness, his ambition, and, Armand thought, possibly the golden nose. Remembering Maurice's anger, Armand softened toward his child. "I wish you luck," he said, and then, as an afterthought, "If you *do* get to see the buyer and you are telling her about me, say that I learned my art from Jolaunay."

"What's that?"

"A man," he said sadly. "He used to be a man who made remarkable perfumes."

Vie looked at him quizzically, hearing in his voice an intimation of something she couldn't make out.

"You won't forget, will you? Jolaunay."

"No," she said, puzzled.

Now, in the great hall of Magdahl-Hoffman, she looked for the perfume counter. The ground floor belonged to accessories: gloves, scarves, handbags, cosmetics, jewelry, hosiery, and fragrances. It was a place of wealth and taste, purposely understated, with a touch of dowdiness.

Vie hadn't been exposed to it before, but she instantly recognized the power and wealth behind the deceptively simple decor. She didn't know the adage about old money and new, but Vie could sense, as she walked past the decorous displays, the unquestioning self-assurance of this store. The customers, she noticed, all looked as though they somehow belonged here, as though they shopped here regularly, in complete confidence that they were buying the best that the country had to offer.

They intimidated her. She wondered if the black linen-look sleeveless sheath she was wearing, bought at the thrift shop for two dollars, and the twenty-five-cent out-size rope of pearls were appropriate. It was her most elegant, most grown-up outfit. She'd bought it on impulse several months ago, feeling slightly guilty, and had never had a chance to wear it since.

At the perfume counter, flanked simply by an oversize bottle of *Joy* and another of *Arpège*, the saleswoman was bringing out bottle after bottle of scent for her customer to sample. None satisfied her. The customer was nearly six feet tall, in a dark-green silk dress with matching jacket, her dark hair pulled smoothly back from her face, showing a heart-shaped hairline with a widow's peak.

"Something new, Abigail," she softly entreated the saleswoman. "You know I have stayed with *L'Heure Bleue* for more than twenty years. It's still divine, of course, but I'm feeling reckless. My eldest son got married last month, and somehow I'd like to be frisky for once."

"I understand, madame," said Abigail, bringing out yet another sample. "This one picks up from the oriental undertones of *L'Heure Bleue.*"

The woman sniffed. "Nice, very warm, but I don't think it's for me. What is it?"

"*Réplique.*"

She sniffed again. "Too—what shall I say? Sultry. It's true I want to be reckless. But"—she laughed—"I can't have people thinking I'm a loose woman!"

While the customer was explaining this, Vie surreptitiously reached into her bag and undid a bottle of *Taj*. Quickly she put a drop or two behind each ear, closed the bottle, and moved up to the counter.

The tall woman turned, gave Vie the vague smile that people give who are accustomed to having met everyone before, and then suddenly leaned toward her. "What is that divine scent you have on, my dear?" she asked.

"*Taj.*"

"Bring out some of that," the woman told Abigail. "It's just what I'm after."

"What did you say the name was?" the saleswoman asked Vie.

"*Taj.*"

She wrinkled her forehead. "I've never heard of it before. I'm sorry, madame, we don't carry it."

"Order some. I'll come back next week."

"Yes, madame." The saleswoman looked at Vie with perplexity; Vie smiled at her and walked toward the elevator that would take her up to the top floor, to the executive offices.

*   *   *

Philippa Wright was a very busy woman—both of her secretaries told Vie when she came in.

"I'll wait," she said.

"You say you don't have an appointment?"

Vie nodded.

"And you are not personally acquainted with Miss Wright?"

"No."

"It'll be a long wait, I'm afraid. And I can't guarantee that Miss Wright will see you at all," said the older woman. But Vie's youth and determination must have impressed her, because she added, "There's no harm in waiting, if you don't mind. Give me your name again, and take a seat on the sofa. Would you like some coffee?"

"No, thank you," Vie answered and spelled out her name.

She felt chilly in the air conditioning and now understood why most women wore jackets on this hot June day. She sat on the plush charcoal-gray sofa and looked across at the geometric pattern on the wall behind the secretaries' desks. The wall covering of pale-gray shot silk was interrupted by large diamonds of diagonal pinstriping in deeper shades of gray and brown. Like an abstract painting, thought Vie, who'd never seen one in the original. The style of this room contrasted with the shopping floor. Downstairs the interior design aimed for assurance and familiarity. Here Vie could sense the presence of someone who was adventurous and uninhibited, with a strong personal sense of taste.

She knew nothing about Philippa Wright then, not even that her reputation was of being the boldest, most innovative trendsetter in the business. But Vie's sensitivity, and her lifelong habit of paying close attention to everything around her, enabled her to sense the force and individuality of the woman almost as soon as she entered the office.

She waited from late morning into the afternoon. The secretaries went in and out of the head buyer's private office, sometimes apologizing to Vie. "Miss Wright is still very busy. Looks like she'll be tied up all day. Maybe you'd like to come back later?"

"I'll wait," Vie replied each time. She saw other people

enter the office—people who had appointments and carried large leather portfolios or heavy briefcases. None of them stayed inside for longer than fifteen or twenty minutes. It seemed like a procession of worshipers, the continuing parade of men and women who had business to conduct with Miss Wright.

Once, as a willowy, beautiful woman came out, Vie thought she saw Miss Wright at the side of the door peering at her. Another time she heard a strong voice, which she took to be Miss Wright's, call out, "Is that girl still there?"

She waited into the late afternoon. By then she'd learned a little about Philippa Wright. About her reputation and also that she was, in addition to head buyer, a vice president of Magdahl-Hoffman. That meant, Vie translated for herself, her decision, either way, would be final.

It was nearly five thirty when the older secretary told Vie with a happy smile, "She'll see you after all, darling," and led her into the executive presence.

A dark woman with small, sharp features examined Vie from behind a massive antique desk. The top of it was thickly covered in papers and photographs lying layers deep. "What are you here for?" she asked abruptly.

The voice was the same she'd heard before, strong and gruff, surprisingly deep for a woman, especially one so small.

"To talk to you about a perfume," she said simply.

"Perfume?" Miss Wright frowned and touched the tips of her fingers together, forming a small cage. She waited for Vie to volunteer more, observing her steadily. When Vie said nothing, but matched her gaze, Miss Wright drew her hands apart, signaling to a chair. "You may sit down."

"Thank you." She took her seat and folded her hands in her lap.

"You're not here to talk, I assume. You're here to sell me something."

"Yes," Vie admitted.

"I don't know you, your name means nothing to me, and you've come here without an appointment. Why should I listen to you?"

"Because," said Vie, reaching into her bag, "I have something that your customers want."

The busy executive smiled. She liked brashness; she liked people who could hold their own without sniveling and could stand up under her fire. Also, the girl was amazingly pretty.

Vie came up with the open bottle in her outstretched hand. Miss Wright sniffed, looked surprised, and nodded. "Not bad at all. Let me smell it again. Yes, it's definitely got personality, but why haven't I met it before? Who makes it?"

"My father."

"What?" She bounded out of the chair, all four foot eleven and a half inches of her, and stared at Vie incredulously. "I've had people come in here to sell me everything, anything. I even had the moon offered to me once. But this! A strange girl walking in here to sell me a bottle of perfume her *father* made! I suppose if he were a baker, you'd be here trying to sell me a loaf of bread!"

"He's a perfumer," Vie said softly. "He made many great perfumes in France."

"His name?"

"Armand Nouvel."

"Never heard of him," she said and turned back to her chair.

Something tugged at Vie's memory. She got it out. "Jolaunay."

Miss Wright stopped. "The House of Jolaunay?"

Vie took a chance. "Yes."

Miss Wright came over again and stood at the arm of Vie's chair. "The perfumes are legendary. They're known as among the greatest ever produced. Your father was a perfumer at Jolaunay?"

"Yes."

"And is this an old Jolaunay formula?" she asked, pointing to *Taj.*

"It could be." Vie felt nervous and uncomfortable under the woman's questioning. She knew nothing at all about Jolaunay or her father's connection with him, but she'd seen the impact of the name on Miss Wright and sensed it might be the magic word that would lead her to buy. But more questions would destroy the potency of the name, since Vie had nothing else to tell her. It would have been better after all, she thought, if Armand had come himself. He could have explained everything.

"Let's suppose it is, or even a derivation from one of the classics. What makes you think anyone would buy it? Our perfume counter does well if it breaks even. We have it there to make our customers secure. That means we stock the traditional fragrances, those that women have been wearing for decades. Why do you think we should bother with this? Our customers remain loyal to their own brand. They don't switch."

Briefly Vie told her about the scene of this morning, ending with the customer's asking the saleswoman to order *Taj*.

A broad smile spread over Miss Wright's face. Her features were softened by the smile, and Vie realized she was attractive. The face was intelligent, unusual—striking.

The smile was followed by a laugh. "You're quite something! Sampling your product on my customers before you come in to see me—*without* an appointment. How refreshing you are, darling! You're the first pleasant thing that's come into my office all day, and"—she looked at her watch—"it's after closing time. Tell you what. Why don't we continue this charming conversation over dinner? It's early, we don't need a reservation. We'll go as we are. What do you say?"

"Thank you very much," she said humbly, overjoyed and very surprised at the invitation. "I'd love to, Miss Wright."

"It's Philippa, now the office is closed. And please remove that rope you have hanging over your chest."

Vie blushed as she took it off hastily. She'd *known* it was all wrong; she felt like a clumsy boor, with no sense of style at all.

"Here we are," said Philippa, holding out a silk square she'd taken from her top drawer. It had triangles of orange and yellow, intersected by bold black lines. "Let me put it on you."

Vie bent down. Her five foot eight made her feel like a giant next to the diminutive woman. Expertly, Philippa tied the scarf around Vie's neck, making a thick drape. "There. All you need for panache. The rope belongs in your handbag. You may wear it, if you're attached to it, with a long, oversize sweater. But you must push up the sleeves to your elbows."

She directed Vie to the mirror, where Vie could only marvel at the transformation. This was style! This was, she understood immediately, what fashion was all about. A simple touch, adding color and a different texture at the neck, changed the dress from ordinary to classic. "You're wonderful," she said in awe.

Philippa gave a low laugh. "It's a pleasure to be dining with such a lovely companion." Her eyes ran down Vie's slender body.

"Such pleasure, Meezright, to see you again!" said the headwaiter, bowing. "Always a pleasure. And the young lady too, une belle!"

"I didn't reserve, Henri. . . ."

"Ah, Meezright," he said reproachfully, "you know that for you we are always free. Your usual table is waiting, madame. Please."

They followed him to a corner table, where silver plates gleamed against a sparkling white tablecloth and a tiny vase held three roses: red, yellow, and mauve.

When they were seated, Henri bowed again. "Drinks, ladies. Your usual, Meezright?"

Philippa nodded and turned questioningly to Vie.

"A pink lady?" Vie ventured.

"Just how old are you, darling?" Philippa asked, laughing.

"I don't drink much," Vie explained, feeling embarrassed and very young. "Don't bother, I'll take whatever you're having."

"A gibson? No—takes years of practice. I didn't start drinking them until I was nearly thirty-five. Henri, bring the lady a gin and tonic, please."

She chuckled. "Pink lady! I'd forgotten them. Takes me back to high school."

"A good friend of mine used to drink them," said Vie, defending herself and feeling a need to stand up for Nina.

"Was she your age?"

"No—she was much older, like you." Vie blushed and, to make up for her rudeness, added, "I was closer to her than anybody. You remind me of her." She didn't know why, exactly. It wasn't through physical appearance, though both had dark eyes and hair. The similarity was more in the way Vie felt. Being with Philippa now reminded her of the excited, happy feeling she'd had when she first met Nina.

"Thank you," said Philippa, smiling. "I hope we will be very close." The drinks arrived. "Cheers. To us."

"Cheers." Vie lifted her tall, frosty glass with a piece of lime attached to the rim. She sipped and grinned. "I love it!" She looked around the room, at the beautifully set tables waiting for customers, at the glistening chandelier above them, at the trolleys laden with appetizers and desserts. "It's great. Everything is unbelievable!"

"Including you, darling." Philippa rested her small hand gently on Vie's for a moment, then took it away and leaned back. "Now tell me all about it, everything that led to my finding you on my doorstep."

"How should I begin?"

"Plunge right in, the way a good storyteller does it."

Vie began with Chandra's store, describing the bottles of colored liquid, the tiny tearoom at the back where they ate scones, the things Chandra had taught her and how he looked, the music of his words. She glowed, talking about all the things she hadn't dared mention before. And when Philippa said, "He sounds quite remarkable," Vie felt a rush of gratitude and affection.

Henri brought the menus. "You may be interested, mesdames, in our specials for today. They are coulibiac de saumon; the rack of baby lamb; and les cailles—the quails—Véronique."

"Good," said Philippa, "I'll have the coulibiac. And you, darling?" A glance at Vie informed her practiced eye that the girl was too inexperienced in restaurant dining to be able to make a selection, either from the specials or from the standard menu. "How about a steak?" she suggested.

When Vie nodded gratefully, Philippa ordered. "The filet mignon, please, Henri. Medium rare? Yes? À point. And, since I'm having the salmon and my companion has beef, we'll need a half-bottle each of red and white. For mademoiselle, a burgundy—let the wine steward select either a Beaune or a Pommard, whichever has the better vintage. For me, a Pouilly-Fuissé."

Vie listened, taking mental notes. Someday—soon, she felt—she'd need to know how to order in places like this and how to conduct herself. She observed how Philippa talked with Henri, differently from the way she spoke to the other waiters. She noticed that Philippa didn't butter her entire roll but broke off a small piece at a time and put butter on that. Vie quickly followed the example.

The filet mignon was so tender it didn't feel like meat at all. And with it, the thick sauce called béarnaise was amazingly delicate, with a taste of tarragon that mingled with other herbs.

As Vie ate and drank, she told Philippa more about herself. She talked about her father, her sister, Mrs. Murphy's house—even about the cats she'd played with years ago, Tiger and Jewel. Philippa often interrupted to ask for greater detail. What does Martine look like? What's your favorite color? How far did you have to walk to school? Vie answered each question, feeling proud and thrilled by Philippa's interest. She told her everything. About the only thing Vie took care not to reveal was her age. She knew that the black dress, her upswept hair, and the touch of makeup made her look at least twenty-one, the youngest she could appear if she wanted to be taken seriously as a business person.

After she'd ordered crepes suzette for their dessert, Philippa led Vie into the present and to business. "If I would decide to place an order, how soon could I expect delivery?"

The headiness Vie had been feeling from the rich food, the wine, and the exhilaration of talking freely cleared instantly. She was alert to the proposition. "That would depend on the size of the order."

"Say two hundred one-ounce bottles as an initial consignment."

Vie whistled, and Philippa laughed. "That's my girl! Nothing like a nice low-keyed, blasé reaction."

"Two hundred bottles! Thirty dollars each, that's six thousand dollars!"

"Your arithmetic is faultless, darling, but you're leaving

out a few factors. Thirty dollars is what you've been selling it for?"

Vie nodded. She'd told Philippa about her Windsor sales.

"OK, but you're selling directly. No middleman. If you want to wholesale through the store, you've got to allow for our commission. We've got to make a profit too, remember. Now, what's the cost to you per ounce?"

"I'm not sure. It gets less, you see, the more batches we make. At the beginning it costs about fifteen dollars. We charged double so we could get back what we'd spent on other ingredients." She worried that Philippa would think her too greedy.

"In that case, we'll sell for seventy-five dollars an ounce, which would be forty dollars the half-ounce, twenty-five the quarter." Vie stared as Philippa continued. "Markup on perfume can be as much as eight hundred percent over cost. Of course, that includes packaging, merchandising, promotion. Magdahl-Hoffman customers would turn their noses up at a perfume for thirty dollars—if you'll pardon the pun. Why is *Joy* our best seller? Because it is, as it frankly states, the costliest perfume in the world."

Vie was leaning forward, her head close to Philippa's. The scent of her was rich and worldly—perhaps that was *Joy*? "I can see," Philippa said, looking intently at Vie's face, "there's a lot I'll have to teach you, little darling." Softly, with her eyes fastened on Vie's lips, she asked, "Would you like that?"

Vie mumbled, "Yes," feeling herself blush for a reason she didn't understand.

"Do you have a boyfriend?" she went on in the same husky voice.

"No."

Philippa's eyes moved up until they held Vie's. "You are very lovely," she murmured. "Do you like me?"

Vie was feeling uncomfortable. She nodded in answer to the strange question. Like? Philippa was an amazing person, belonging to a higher sphere. Her knowledge seemed infinite, her taste infallible—and Vie was thrilled by Philippa's attentions. She was ready to worship her—but like? It seemed a peculiar word for her to use.

Their conversation was interrupted by the spectacle of

dessert. The trolley wheeled to their table held liqueurs, oranges, thin pancakes, and a small pan. Henri was accompanied by two waiters, who squeezed the juice, lit the flame under the pan, heated the butter until it was a melted amber, then added sugar and juice. The smells were mouth-watering. At a crucial moment Henri took command. With a slight movement of his hands he indicated to the waiter at his right to pour the curaçao and Armagnac. Deftly Henri tilted the pan, caught the flame, and shook it briskly as the fire leaped up. After it died, he placed the triangles of pancakes on two plates, spooned the sauce over them, and let the waiters each carry a plate to Philippa and Vie.

When they finished, Vie said, "I didn't know *anything* could taste this good." The smells, tastes, textures, sight of the whole meal were like a symphony playing on all the senses. It was money, she thought, that brought this. Money brought style, taste, a world of glamour and pleasure. It was a world she'd just entered, but Vie knew she never wanted to leave. She would become part of it and make it her own.

As though reading her thoughts, Philippa picked up their conversation. "If we sell for seventy-five dollars and take forty percent, that leaves you with forty-five dollars a bottle—nine thousand dollars."

Vie laughed, hardly able to believe what she was hearing.

Philippa went on. "We'll see how it does, starting with that small stock. We can't flood the store with it, but I'll put a few bottles in the windows, samples in the third-floor dressing rooms, in the bridal salon, the hair salon. Yes, I'm going to *insinuate* it through the store." She smiled, pleased with her strategy. She put her hand on Vie's, and this time didn't draw it away. "You'll see, darling, I'll bring you success." Her voice fell into a deeper register as she asked, "You'll be nice to me, won't you?"

"Yes." Again Vie thought the question strange. How could she not be? Philippa was doing everything for her.

"Good," she said, half closing her eyes. "Let's go to my place." Seeing a question on Vie's face, she added, "To toast our new business agreement. Don't you want to, darling? Don't you want to come home with me?"

"Yes," she answered fervently, thinking that this was the most incredible day she'd ever had. Walking out with Philippa, whose head came to just above Vie's shoulder, she remembered the transformation Philippa had wrought by tying the silk scarf around her neck, and she felt that in this woman's hands anything could happen.

Philippa Wright's apartment was elegant, far more subdued and warmer than her office. Japanese grass cloth of different types gave the walls a tactile quality. Throughout the rooms Philippa had arranged textures to contrast with and complement each other: rough with smooth, cool silk with warm velvet, metal with fur. The muted color scheme of grays and beiges served as a backdrop for bright touches of orange, purple, shocking pink.

Philippa poured Armagnac into two snifters and brought them over to the sofa. "Sit here, darling," she murmured, patting the cushion beside her.

After a few sips Vie felt the effect. She was unused to alcohol, she'd been in a state of excitement for the last few hours, and now, in this warm, dimly lighted room, on the soft couch, she became very sleepy. Philippa put an arm around her, and Vie slumped against her shoulder, feeling comfortable, drowsy, and happy. "Is it really true? You're ordering two hundred bottles of *Taj*?" she asked dreamily.

"Yes, darling, it's true. Now just relax, that's right—let yourself go." Her hand was unzipping Vie's dress in the back and unhooking her bra. "There, that's better, isn't it, darling?"

"Mmm." It was much better, more comfortable. "Am I drunk?"

"Just a wee bit tipsy. It's fine, little love. Don't fight it. Leave everything to me."

"Thank you," murmured Vie, letting her head fall on Philippa's shoulder. Philippa put a hand under Vie's chin, lifting up her face. She kissed her lightly on the lips.

Vie didn't respond. Strange, she was thinking; everything's been strange today. Philippa's lips were delicate as paper wings.

Philippa was taking off Vie's clothes, and Vie didn't resist. She felt like a little girl in the hands of this woman, being taken care of. It was cooler, more comfortable. She was wearing only her underpants.

The quick wings fluttered over her neck down to her breasts, circling them. Her nipples hardened, and Philippa's lips began sucking one of them, her fingers squeezing the other. Vie gasped in a mixture of pain and pleasure as heat rushed up her body from between her thighs. Philippa moved her mouth to the other breast, her tongue massaging the areola upward to the nipple, biting gently, while her hand reached down to the smooth, trembling flesh of Vie's inner thighs.

"Please stop!" Vie cried.

"Gorgeous breasts. Let me. Let me kiss them, little love. Let me suck on them." She went back to what she'd been doing.

"You shouldn't . . ." Vie began again.

"Hush now, darling, just give in to it. Let me do this to you." Her hands were under each breast, cupping them, and then moved out to the sides, massaging up into her armpits, feeling the sweat as Vie breathed heavily, her mouth open. Philippa moved down along the ribs, her hands coming together on the elastic at Vie's waist. With one quick movement, she pulled down the panties. "Beautiful," she said huskily, gazing at the pale-blond cluster of hair. She pulled off the panties, tossed them aside. Then she threw off her own clothes. Her body was younger than her face, with small firm breasts, broad shoulders, narrow hips. A boyish body on short legs, which made her torso nearly as long as Vie's.

She reached out and touched Vie's stomach, moving down to the wonderfully fair bush, tracing the horizontal line of the triangle, then the crease where hip meets thigh, down on either side of the hair. Suddenly her fingers moved up, separating the lips, sliding between them.

"Oh!" Vie cried out, trying to wriggle away. But her movements brought the fingers deeper, rubbing against her hard clitoris. "Oh, oh!" she cried again, writhing against the hand, feeling that she was drowning in heat, in electric currents flashing through her.

"Come on," Philippa ordered, pulling her up by the arms and kissing her with ferocity. She brought Vie's hand to between her own legs. "Feel that? Feel how wet I am."

Vie jerked her hand away, but Philippa had a strong hold on the other and pulled Vie with her into the bedroom. She pushed her down on the bed and threw herself on top of her.

"Please don't," Vie pleaded in a whisper, trying to cover her pubic hair. Philippa pulled her hands away roughly and bent to kiss her there, gently. Her tongue entered with slow licks, then thrusts as Vie began to moan. Hot, urgent feelings made her press down against Philippa's mouth, her awakened desire now urging the mouth to go on, do it harder, swallow her alive. Philippa took the erect little knob between her lips and sucked hard. Vie cried out in pain. The sucking became more gentle but insistent. Vie pulled herself up to see the dark head between her thighs. While sucking, Philippa was masturbating herself wildly.

"Stop!"

Philippa raised her head. From her nose down, her face was covered with thick moisture. "Am I hurting you?" she asked, not gently.

"Please. I've never. . . ."

"Never what?" she asked impatiently.

"Never done . . . this."

"With a woman?"

"With anyone."

That seemed to inflame Philippa. Her hand continued its ferocious strokings, and her mouth returned to Vie's clitoris. Her left hand slid under Vie's thigh, and her thumb began massaging around the unpenetrated opening, pressing gently, entering, thrusting in and out.

Vie felt the intense heat and the pleasure invading her. Her body stiffened, she pressed, straining for the urgent tongue. She felt she was going to urinate in Philippa's mouth; she tried to stop—and then she was throbbing, spasms overtook her, and she let go, coming, riding on waves into Philippa's mouth.

When she opened her eyes, Philippa was looking at her with pride. "Beautiful, my darling. You were wonderful. And it'll get even better next time—you'll see."

Vie shuddered and closed her eyes again.

3

1962–1966

The rush on *Taj* was unprecedented. Though Philippa had gambled on it, she was astonished by the success. Two weeks after delivery of the perfume to Magdahl-Hoffman, it had sold out. Women who sampled *Taj* in upstairs dressing rooms told their salesladies they'd take a bottle and had it put on their charge. Later they returned to buy it directly from the perfume counter on the main floor.

The fragrance sold itself, and when only a dozen bottles remained, Philippa decided the new order would be two and a half times the original one. Though *Taj* was the best-selling item in the store, Philippa was too seasoned a gambler to risk more than five hundred bottles as her second order. Similar fads had flared up in her experience; there was always a strong chance that sales like this only indicated a quick rally ending in sudden death.

She'd sent Vic a second check for $4,500 and included a note asking to see her again. They hadn't seen each other since the first time. And now Philippa was nervous as a teenager before a blind date, jumping up every few minutes, rearranging the perfectly placed cushions, checking on herself in the mirror.

In the wake of their lovemaking, Philippa had come to feel regret, even remorse, for her seduction of Vie. She'd taken the girl for twenty-two or twenty-three. Despite her inexperience, Vie had command over herself, and her natural grace gave no hint that she was still a teenager. Only seventeen, for Christ's sake!

"Why didn't you tell me?" Philippa kept asking, hoping to exonerate herself. But as she looked at Vie's lovely, very young face, fear entered, tiny slivers of ice. A minor, damn her! Suppose she told; made accusations?

Vie had refused Philippa's offer to spend the rest of the night there, and only after insistent urging did she agree to accept money for a taxi. She'd dressed with calm dignity, and when Philippa handed her a check for $4,500 as advance on the order, she'd put it in her bag without looking at it and had said only, "Thank you."

Of course the check was a personal one, for which Philippa later reimbursed herself. She couldn't write out a company check at four in the morning to a little girl of seventeen. But in giving her a check immediately, Philippa hoped to insure her silence through the business commitment.

Since then they'd spoken a few times, formally, on the phone. When one of her secretaries asked Philippa if "that beautiful blond girl" was coming to take part in *Taj*'s promotion, Philippa had answered brusquely, "No need for that."

Now she was coming to the apartment to discuss the new order. They could have met in the office, but Vie had simply said, "I'll be at your place at four."

Could that mean, Philippa wondered, pacing the room, that she wanted to continue their relationship? She was the loveliest creature in years, someone easy to get attached to. Even love, maybe—though that feeling lay far back in the past. But why was she so nervous now? Look at you, Philippa said to her trembling hands, anyone would think you'd never seen a girl before.

Vie arrived in a dress of butter-colored silk and matching jacket. She seemed at once younger and older than Philippa remembered, and almost painfully beautiful. Her vulnerability wasn't hidden, but neither was her strength as she smiled and walked into the room with an erect but unaffected bearing.

Philippa didn't dare touch her until after she poured the coffee and spilled it onto the tray because her hands wouldn't stop shaking. Then she gave a little laugh and went over to put her arms around Vie.

"No," Vie said quietly. "I can't do that."

"I disgust you?" She grimaced saying it.

"No. How could you? You're attractive, and you have more style than anyone I've ever seen. Besides"—she gave a little smile—"you have confidence in me. You took a chance on *Taj*."

"And it's worked brilliantly," Philippa said, feeling less apprehensive. "When I gave you the advance, I didn't know if I'd end up with a lemon or a rose."

Vie laughed and then became serious. "You gave it to me *then*. I've been thinking about it a lot, and that's why I wanted to talk to you here, not at the office. What I want to say is . . . well. What I mean. . . ." Her embarrassment made her look like a child.

"You want to say it's no good."

Vie nodded, and met Philippa's eyes. "I'm young. I never had . . . sex, before."

"And it revolted you."

"I liked it. I mean, it felt good. But I was scared. I don't even know why I was scared—maybe because it was the first time, or because it was with a woman, or maybe even I was scared *because* I liked it." She looked bewildered, struggling to find words that would explain her confusion. "But anyway, I realized it's not for me. Then I wondered if you gave me the commission so that . . . I mean. . . ."

"You mean, if I was paying you to come to bed with me?"

She lowered her eyes. "Yes. And I decided that even if you cancel the order, I won't do it again." She looked up, trying to smile at Philippa. "It's really not that I'm disgusted or anything. I mean, it's none of my business if you like to go to bed with men or with women, is it? But I'm not ready for—well, sex, yet."

Philippa thought she'd never seen anyone more enchanting. The faint blush, the silk of her hair matching the sheen of her dress, the serious eyes and the small lips barely touched with color all made her ache for the girl. It wasn't simply lust, though that was a part of it. But Philippa also felt tender, proud of her, protective. She was embarrassed by the gentleness she felt, almost a maternal feeling. "We want to order five hundred bottles," she said briskly, "to be delivered as soon as possible. And with this shipment, I think you can leave the old doorknobs where they belong."

Vie looked at her in amazement. "You knew . . . ?"

"Sure." Philippa laughed, and a second later Vie joined in. They laughed infectiously, as though a truly funny joke had been made, and went on laughing until they were exhausted and deeply relieved.

"Hell with coffee," said Philippa, who recovered first. "Let's have some drinks. Don't worry," she added, "I'll make you a very weak one, and I'll sit on the other side of the room with my hands behind my back."

"It's hard to drink that way, don't you think?" Vie asked mischievously.

"Hold on, darling, I'll get our gin and tonics."

When she returned, she said, "Now let's get back to what we both love most: business. I think you should start playing around with ideas for a company name. If the demand for *Taj* continues, you might start thinking of expansion. Other fragrance items, new scents. *Taj* is fine, but you need something behind it, the way Lanvin stands behind *Arpège*."

As Philippa talked, Vie completely forgot their personal involvement. She listened attentively, flattered by the advice and thrilled as she'd been on the first day by the interest and attentions of Philippa Wright.

"A French name would be best. Perfume has one nationality, throughout the world. French means status, luxury—something that's out of reach for others."

She remembered when Philippa first showed interest in the perfume, and suggested, "Jolaunay—couldn't we use that?"

Philippa shook her head. "Plagiarism. Stealing. And even if the name's out of copyright, it doesn't mean anything except to a few people in the trade. It's French, but too French. We need something shorter, easier to pronounce."

"But Jolaunay has a long tradition." Armand had told her about the generations of perfumers, extending over centuries. "It's part of history."

"That may be, but you can't sell history in America. Nobody wants it, trusts it, or even believes in it. We need a name that's short, memorable. Think of Chanel, Lanvin, Revlon. . . ."

"Helena Rubinstein?" Vie teased.

Philippa laughed. "Proves my point, doesn't it? Who thinks of perfume in connection with that name? It's face cream or lipstick. No, we're selling perfume. What about streamlining Jolaunay? Make it Jolay."

"Jo . . . lay," she repeated slowly.

"Emphasis belongs on the first syllable," said Philippa, grinning. "We don't want to make too much out of a lay, do we?" Vie's blush, thought Philippa, was adorable.

"The name sounds good," Vie agreed.

"Think about it for a few days. Then call me at my office and we'll talk to lawyers about incorporation. Also, I've set up an appointment for you with a firm that does damn decent work in packaging design. There's just a chance they'll come up with something less bulky than doorknobs."

"Will you go with me?" Vie asked.

Philippa looked at her, and the feeling she'd had before returned, warm and loving. "Wherever you want," she said with certainty.

Sales mushroomed. Piper & Strauss, Inc., designed new bottles for *Taj*, retaining the theme of gold caught in a rainbow, but the new containers were elongated almost to tear shape, made of a finely ground thin glass that meant they could be carried in large handbags by women who were on the go all day and into the evening. The bottles were packed in shimmering green-and-purple boxes. Smaller replicas, with the same taffeta iridescence, contained atomizers, ideal for the evening bag, holding only an eighth of an ounce of perfume and selling for $15. Perfect hostess gifts, unique stocking stuffers, the atomizers glistened like large tears and became an instant sellout.

Jolay Perfumes was incorporated, with Philippa, Chandra, and Armand on the board.

Chandra and Philippa had met before, and though they'd never developed a friendship, they felt instantly at ease with each other: peers who could respect each other's professional ability and recognize the hard work behind it. Armand was not relaxed with either of them, partly through jealousy of their influence over his daughter, and partly because he felt miscast in the almost technical role of chemist, when he could have been director of the whole enterprise.

Nevertheless there were no major disagreements among the three. Philippa suggested they call themselves the godparents of Jolay, and Vie was delighted by the sense of family the word evoked, by the security it gave her. She felt they were her actual godparents, present at the christening of herself as Vie Jolay, the name she'd decided to use for business. She was too young to be on the board herself but would be admitted when she reached the age of eighteen—though even then, the lawyers would have to rely on special provisions.

Chandra found a large space for rent near his store; this became Armand's lab. Formerly a speakeasy, it contained unending surprises in hidden cabinets, secret drawers, trompe l'oeil doors. Here Armand worked with an assistant perfumer and a girl who filled bottles from morning to night. Within a month and a half, a second assistant was brought in, and two more filling girls.

A week before Vie turned eighteen, she and Armand went to see the bank official Philippa had recommended. Donald Garrison was young, the bank's pet, an up-and-comer who gave out loans on the basis of hunches and had been wrong only once.

Vie told him why they needed a loan. *Taj* had been selling to stores in Boston, Philadelphia, and Los Angeles. They'd had persistent inquiries from the most exclusive store of the south, Neiman-Marcus.

He was impressed by the young woman's determination. He felt the slight tingle he got at the sides of his neck whenever something had the right touch, the glow that beamed out: I'll make it. "You the head of the company?" he asked.

"No," she said, and her father explained. "Vie is too young. When she is eighteen, she will be on the board."

Don Garrison grabbed hold of the table to make sure things were still in their place. *When* she was eighteen! He stared at her. He knew about people being precocious, he'd always been that himself, but this was a child prodigy! Maybe Mozart in disguise, he thought. Why not?

"How old is she?" he asked Armand, not willing to trust whatever might come from the mouth of a babe.

"Eighteen next Thursday."

"Well I'll be!" Garrison laughed, shook his head, and said, "You're getting the loan." He got up and gave Armand his hand on it, but his eyes were on Vie, and she could read that they were saying: *It's yours.*

On November 22, 1963, President Kennedy was shot while riding through Dallas in an open car. The news hit New York's lunch hour, and work was abandoned for the rest of the day. On Park Avenue pneumatic drills were silenced, and some of the roadworkers cried openly. Restaurants emptied, leaving plates of unfinished steak or half-eaten burgers for waiters to clear when they returned to work. Subway cars and commuter trains held silent passengers returning to mourn the death of the president with their families at home.

Vie was in the lab with Armand when one of the assistants came to tell them. He switched on the radio to confirm his story, and the three of them listened in shock as the dreadful bulletins were repeated over and over again.

They closed the lab and went back to their apartment on the upper West Side. "Death comes to everyone," said Armand.

"Quiet," said Vie, who felt that her grief was special. She turned on the television and remained glued to it. By midafternoon Armand joined her.

They didn't feel like making supper. Marty hadn't come home, and Vie felt a resentment toward her. This was a time to come together, forget grievances, and join in the grief that covered the nation.

Marty didn't show up that night or the next day. Lee Harvey Oswald, the reported assassin of the president, was shot by Jack Ruby, who claimed to have acted out of ardent love and patriotism. Marty didn't appear and didn't call. She hadn't been seen in school.

"Let her go," said Armand wearily. "She'll be back when she's hungry."

"She's not an animal," said Vie angrily and went to the police precinct by herself, carrying a photograph of Marty to show what her missing sister looked like. Marty was a month and a half away from sixteen.

She was lost for a week. Vie called the precinct every day to speak with Sergeant McBrien, in charge of this case. Every day his answer was the same. His voice sounded weary. He told her he had children of his own, one of them about Marty's age.

On November 30, Vie got a call in her office adjoining the lab. "We found her," said Sergeant McBrien. "I played a hunch and called our fellows down in Washington. That's where she is. They're bringing her back right now."

Vie's relief made her speechless. "You there, Miss Nouvel?" she heard, and nodded into the phone. Then she managed a soft "Yes."

The voice at the other end sounded pleased, with a note of pride. "I figured she might be there. Two of my own, you see, went down for the funeral. It's natural; the kids feel he was a kind of father to them, God bless his soul."

"Is she all right?"

"Fine, from what I hear. She'll be coming in around two, three this afternoon."

By one o'clock, Vie was too nervous to stay in the office. She was getting her coat to go down to the precinct when the phone rang. It was Sergeant McBrien again. "Got some bad news for you, I'm afraid, Miss."

Terror grabbed hold of her. "She's not . . . hurt, is she?" Vie stammered out, imagining the worst.

"No," he said slowly, "nothing wrong with her that way. But the boys found jewels on her, sapphires and diamonds. We're sure they're hot. We have suspicions of where they may come from. You have any reason to think the jewels could be hers?"

"No," Vie said, feeling her throat constricting.

"Afraid we can't let her go. We're booking her on larceny."

*   *   *

The Park Avenue lawyer took advantage of her age, the financial strength of her family, and her older sister's remarkable position in the business community. The sapphires and diamonds were returned, the case never went to court, and Marty was given probation in the judge's chambers.

Coached by Vie, Armand promised the judge that he'd send her to a girls' boarding school in Westchester, where she could be properly supervised at all times. Vie had spoken to the headmistress and gotten her to agree to see Marty, who was released for the day in the custody of Vie and the lawyer.

Though Marty was uncommunicative during the interview, her tests showed she had exceptional aptitude in most subjects, and the Sanford-Binet placed her IQ at 150, near or in the genius range. She was accepted by the school, where tuition was $3500 a year.

During the ride up and back Vie continued to question Marty, who remained silent. She wouldn't even reveal how she'd gone to Washington and simply stared ahead when Vie asked about the jewels.

Later, when Vie tried to find out something from the lawyer she had engaged, he shook his head. "Sorry, but my client has the right to absolute confidentiality." If Marty had confessed to anything, he wasn't telling. And the prosecutor had no more success than Vie. Though he'd hoped Marty would be forced by court order to reveal how she'd gotten the stolen gems, and from whom, she was protected by her age and the arguments of her lawyer.

She went up to the school and stayed there until graduation, a year and a half later. She didn't come home for vacations, and Vie sent money for her to spend the summer with three of her schoolmates, on a trip through the United States organized by a wildlife association. Reports from the school said that Martine was doing well generally and was outstanding in social studies.

Marty had never done badly in school, despite her disdain for it. Her quick intelligence had always kept her grades well above average. Now, isolated from distractions on the street, her natural aptitude for learning blossomed, and she became competitive. Academic success was easy, and as Marty came to realize she was smarter than the other girls, she grew determined to get to the top of the class. By showing the others she'd show Vie, too, who—Marty knew—had never done particularly well in school.

Her college-entrance exams placed Marty in the top 10 percent and she was accepted by every college she applied for.

When Vie received her first letter from Marty, it was written on scented notepaper. She held the offending page as far from her as she could and read that Marty had decided on Radcliffe.

She wrote back immediately with her congratulations, and reaffirmed her commitment to pay all Marty's tuition and living expenses. As she licked the glue of the envelope, Vie felt a sudden depression overcome her. She would never go to college, never be able to lead a life where she was responsible for nothing except the stimulation of her own mind. She could never escape her responsibility for making the money that would allow Marty to go on being free.

The odor of Marty's letter rankled in Vie's nostrils. What a vulgar thing to do, she thought angrily, and then realized Marty was intentionally mocking her.

In Dallas the launching party for *Zazou* was in full swing. The ground floor of Neiman-Marcus had been converted into a discotheque, with strobe lights that caught the black designs on the silver balloons, making them appear as though they'd been cut out.

Paper streamers arched from a central rosette, converting the large room into a carousel. The theme for *Zazou* was carefree youth, burbling and spontaneous. The Jolay salesgirls were dressed in crisp, crinkling paper dresses, in pastels of pink, yellow, blue, and violet. Paper dresses had just come on the market, and Vie saw instantly that they'd provide the perfect costume to convey a bright, airy, devil-may-care message. As catchword for the new line Vie had chosen: Irrepressible. From the walls, the letters flashed in the strobe beams: *Zazou*—Irrepressible—*Zazou*.

She herself had chosen to wear a paper gown, ankle-length and falling in a straight column of bronze. Though paper, it had cost $150. Philippa had encouraged her to have it specially designed, a gown that picked up the evening's emphasis on spontaneity, since it was made of paper and would last only a few hours, but which also gave Vie the necessary maturity to distinguish her from the girls who would be selling *Zazou*. The classic, gleaming line of her dress contrasted with the girlish flounces of the puckered pastels, their full skirts riding over half a dozen stiff white paper petticoats.

"Queen Vie!" exclaimed Neiman-Marcus's manager, going on bended knee before her. He was the first to give her the title, though it would soon echo out from Dallas and reverberate through the perfume industry.

Candy-striped vendors offered cotton candy in the four pastel colors. The band played Beatles songs, Elvis. Everywhere faces were flushed with dancing, and the manager whispered to Vie over their champagne that this was the best party they'd ever thrown at the store.

At eleven o'clock Vie finally sat down for a moment's rest. She'd been going since she'd left New York yesterday morning, on only four hours' sleep. Gratefully she lowered herself into the white rattan armchair, barely nodding to the man at her right, who introduced himself as Dick Lewis from San Francisco. She recognized the name, of course; he was the owner of a fabulously successful chain of luxury boutiques in California and Florida. I should talk to him, she told herself, what a client he'd make! But she felt so utterly and completely exhausted that even the prospect of such a plum couldn't rouse her professional charm. She smiled wanly and let her head rest against the back of the chair.

A moment later she was on fire. Sparks from his cigarette landed on the front of her dress, just above her breasts, and ignited the paper immediately.

It was all over in seconds. Dick Lewis threw his drink over the flames, then quickly smothered what remained of the fire by grabbing her in his arms and pulling her tightly against him.

She felt a slight soreness on her chest, nothing more.

The gauzelike lining of her dress was made of a flame-
retardant fabric. Vie knew she hadn't been seriously burned
but, pressed against the broad, fair-haired man, she was
suddenly afraid of being exposed, nearly naked, when he
released her.

He seemed to understand. Maintaining a tight hold on
Vie with one arm, he removed his jacket and put it around
her. She pulled it closed when he released her, anxiously
asking if she was all right.

"Thanks," she told him. "I just got a bit heated up,
that's all."

Others were running toward them. Dick Lewis put his
arm around her again and began steering her toward the
door, waving off and pushing aside the people in their
way.

"I'm taking you home," he told her.

She couldn't protest, since she was wearing his jacket
and could return it only after she'd changed. All she wanted
was sleep, but as they got out of the taxi and walked to
the entrance of her hotel, Vie agreed to meet him in the
bar in fifteen minutes, have a drink, and give back his
jacket.

When she came down half an hour later, Vie felt almost
refreshed. The cool shower, followed by latherings of rich
lotion, drew out all soreness from her skin. She'd splashed
cold water on her face, deftly repaired her makeup and
brushed her hair, sprayed *Taj* lightly all over her body,
and put on a loose black sweater over a straight beige
skirt.

Dick Lewis came over to escort her to the table. "I'm
almost grateful for the fire," he said. "Since it did no real
harm. You're even more stunning than before." Her hair,
piled high on her head at the party, now hung loose below
her shoulders like a fine veil of hammered gold. She looked
younger, more vulnerable—a delicate princess instead of
a commanding queen.

She smiled and handed him his jacket. "Thanks for the
protection. I don't usually need it."

"Anytime." His eyes drank her in. "Just send up a flare."

Vie laughed and accepted a cognac. She was feeling
restored enough to think of business. Though she didn't

much care for after-dinner drinks, she knew that an unspoken protocol required having a drink with a prospective client.

He was anxious to do business with her, he said. In fact, that was what had brought him to Dallas.

She told him about the "doors" Jolay had—entrance to thirty of the most prestigious stores in the country—and how they usually handled promotion. But his eyes looked glazed, and she could feel he wasn't really paying attention. "Why don't we go upstairs and talk about it in private?" he suggested. "Away from all this smoke and noise."

The bar was not particularly noisy. Vie understood his intentions; it had happened often before. She stood up. "If you'd like to discuss it further, why don't we meet for lunch tomorrow? I have to be at Neiman-Marcus in the morning, but you could pick me up there at twelve thirty. I can take an hour off."

He looked up at her dully, his desire so evident that she felt slightly sick. "Let me come up, baby," he said in a thick voice. "I'll make it good. And I promise you the biggest deal you've had yet. I'll give you twenty new doors by breakfast."

"Thank you for the drink, Mr. Lewis. I don't think you should bother coming around for me tomorrow." She walked quickly out of the bar.

Next day, as lunchtime approached, she felt a slight curiosity about whether he'd come, after all. If he did, it meant that he'd accepted the terms on which she'd do business. Getting the Lewis chain would mean she could stop worrying about debts, the constant pressure of rents, salaries, tuition, and the mountain of bills that always managed to exceed their income. It would be a coup that would free her from financial worry.

Twelve thirty passed, and she refused the manager's offer to go out for a bite. At one o'clock she suspected; at one thirty she knew: she'd lost the Lewis commission because of one catch. But after the night at Philippa's apartment nearly five years earlier, Vie had made a vow never again to sell anything through her body.

4

September 1968

Vie's frequent travels meant she couldn't maintain control over the lab. She left that to Armand and concentrated on the work that always awaited her at the office. Elaine Smollett was a paradigm of efficiency, who took care of small matters herself, answered all inquiries, and prepared for her boss only what she called hard core. "Without you," Vie told her affectionately, "I'd drown in paper."

"Without you," answered Elaine, welcoming Vie in a warm hug, "there'd be no papers to drown in." Elaine was the rare kind of employee who took almost equal pleasure in running the show during her boss's absence and in retreating to the sidelines when Vie was there. She was secure in her abilities and neither sought the limelight nor shunned it. Vie never worried about the office when she was away. Elaine always had her phone number in case of urgency, but basically everything was under control.

When Vie visited the lab for the first time in months, the two chief assistants rushed up to complain that Armand was driving them too hard. "Your father's a perfectionist," said Peter Thwaite, whose permanent suntan made him look more like a lifeguard than the aspiring chemist he was.

"What's wrong with that?" asked Vie.

"He treats us like mules, not like people," answered Willy Gumpert, the other assistant.

"He drives himself, too," Vie pointed out.

"Yes," said Peter, "but he's *obsessed* with his work. It's not healthy."

Vie frowned. Peter Thwaite was a Californian, competent in his work but easygoing and unhurried. In comparison to Armand, he was undisciplined, his casualness almost an affront to the European sense of form, her father's traditionalism. For a moment she thought of replacing Peter, then realized that Armand himself had hired the young man after interviewing dozens of others. Vie sighed. "I'll talk to him," she promised unhappily.

As she walked along the polished corridor to Armand's private lab, Vie was grateful for the air conditioning. Every year September's heat came as a surprise. It dragged out the summer, like dinner guests who took forever in their good-byes. But when she knocked on Armand's door and heard his muffled, annoyed reply, Vie realized that the discomfort she was feeling had little to do with the weather.

Armand looked harried, and his hair was in need of washing. "Talk?" he said. "I have no time to talk. There is work to be done. I am not flying off to California or wherever. I am making the fragrances."

She felt the unfairness of his accusation. "Fine," Vie replied angrily, "and I am making the money."

He turned away from the organ to stare at her. "Money," he repeated sarcastically. "And what is it, you think, that you are making the money from?"

She looked at him blankly.

"When you were little, I told you I could make gold. But you—look at you now!—all you can think of is dollars."

Vie took a deep breath before speaking. She touched his shoulder. "Papa. All of this is due to you. I know that. There would be no money, no Jolay without you. We're working *together,* you and I."

"Are you sure?"

She started again. "Before the war, in France, the world was different. I know that your life was glamorous, people lived in a high style"—for an instant Vie envied them, the faceless parade of women in evening gowns, all of them secure in their wealth, dedicated to their own amusements—"but this is America. We have other rules. The most magnificent fragrance ever created won't sell an ounce without promotion. Business is the life of any idea."

"Yes," he said tonelessly, turning back to his vials. "This is another country. For the young."

They were both silent. When Armånd began speaking again, his voice was low. He looked out into space, addressing Vie but keeping his face turned away. "As a young man, I had faith in myself. I followed my talent. Nothing could turn me aside. I defied my parents, and lost their home and my father's love.

"That was the hardest. But I had the faith. La foi, Vie!" He sighed. "But you have forgotten your French. Now I am here in this new country—an old man—unsure. . . ."

Vie began to protest.

"No, do not interrupt. Hear me, and perhaps you may understand why I work as I do. I am obsessed with my work, but not in the way I once was. Now I am obsessed because I am afraid. Every day I think this is a mirage, it will vanish, and then everyone will see that I am incompetent."

Moved by his words, Vie wanted to go up to her father, embrace him. She stopped herself so he wouldn't think she was pitying him. "Your talent's intact," she said. "Everyone recognizes your exceptional ability."

Armand shook his head slowly. "You're too young to understand what it means to doubt yourself. Enough of this. I must get on with my work."

Vie kissed the top of his head and let herself out quietly.

Six years after its official founding in 1962, Jolay, Inc., was doing roughly $6.5 million in gross sales annually. Their clients remained loyal to Jolay for high-status, high-quality products.

Recently, however, a disturbing pattern had begun to emerge: an increasing number of shipments was being returned, and a few outlets were not reordering. Vie pored over the figures and consulted with her sales manager, who told her what she was dreading to hear. At the board meeting, two days after she had spoken to Armand in the lab, Vie heard more unhappy news. She went to see Armand again, bringing the figures with her.

"It's me," he said, looking haunted. "All my mistakes."

He stayed in the lab until midnight and returned next day at dawn, after a breakfast of nothing but black coffee. He was looking ten years older than his age, Vie noticed in alarm, and walked with the stoop of an elderly man. She begged him to relax, take time off—but he was deaf to anything but his own compulsion.

The following Sunday, Vie heard Armand moving about in their apartment and rushed from her bedroom. He was dressed to go out, and she ran ahead of him to block the door. "I won't let you go, Papa! You're making yourself ill."

"Who will do the work if not me? All of the others are lazy."

Vie shook her head. "It's no good. You become too tired. Your work suffers." His self-condemnation had been accurate, unfortunately. Most mistakes—inconsistency of quality—could be traced directly to Armand and to his fatigue.

"No!" he argued. "Not *my* work. It's those lazy young people. They want their money, yes, but not to work for it. I'll get rid of them all, the good-for-nothing assistants, the secretaries, the. . . ."

"What are you talking about?" Vie asked, still barricading the door.

"Yes, and then I will sell this worm of a company to people who know how to run things." Armand looked at her accusingly.

Vie was incredulous. "Are you blaming *me* for the mistakes?"

He shrugged. "What do you know of business? A girl. . . ."

She exploded. "You'd be out begging if it weren't for me! You weren't willing even to try doing anything to support us. You depended on Nina, then on me!"

"I am so grateful, madame," he answered with hatred. "But permit me to remind you that Jolay is *mine*. The perfumes are all my own invention."

"I sold them. I took care of packaging, marketing, promotion. It was I who brought you the ingredients in the first place. And the company is *ours*," she blazed.

"You, you—it is to vomit. Where is *my* name? Where is

a photograph of me in the papers? Always it is you, the beautiful blond girl. Your mother," he said, using all his force to thrust her away from the door, "was much more beautiful than you."

Vie leaned against the door after he'd gone, her eyes closed. She felt exhausted; it was only seven in the morning. Thank God, she thought, that Don Garrison had advised her as he had in dividing out the shares of Jolay among the family. It meant Armand was powerless to realize his threat of selling. When Vie had become president of the company, at twenty-one, she'd arranged that she and Armand each receive 40 percent of the shares, the remaining 20 percent to be placed in escrow for Marty until such time as she joined the company or reached the age of twenty-five, whichever came first.

He couldn't sell without her approval, but Vie felt no satisfaction in that. The anger they'd released on each other was terrifying to her, both as a daughter and as a businesswoman. Armand could bring down the whole edifice of Jolay, either through carelessness or by intent.

She walked slowly to the kitchen and went through the automatic motions of making coffee. Armand, she noticed, had made just enough for himself.

Something had to be done. His fear was making Armand dangerous. His pride had to be salvaged. Vie groaned. It was up to her now, and only her, to dream up something, and she had to do it fast.

Another crisis. She put a piece of bread in the toaster and poured herself a wineglassful of orange juice. It seemed that her life was strung up of crises, with barely enough thread to make it from one end to the other. She hadn't had time for herself in years, and none for her friends, either, or for a social life. She saw her closest friends, Chandra and Philippa, only when there was business to discuss. No time to live, she thought. She'd forgotten to press down the toaster. No time to grow or develop normally.

She let the toast go. All she needed was the coffee to fuel her into the day. She'd meant to go through the accounts this Sunday, but now she had to try devising a project for Armand. It had to challenge him, satisfy his need for independence, and restore his self-confidence, so he would stop blaming others.

What about my own self-confidence? Vie thought as she took her seat at the desk in her study. She was still in her nightgown, but she'd wash and dress later; she didn't have the energy now.

How little Armand knew when he said she was too young to doubt herself! Maybe she'd be able to find the project she was looking for in the course of the day. But then what? Vie realized it made no difference if she dressed or not. At the end of her workday she'd only have to get into her nightgown again and go to sleep, alone.

She knew doubt well, particularly in terms of being a woman. Nearly twenty-four, and a virgin. There was never enough time to get to know a man, for desire to ripen naturally on her part. She stared bleakly at the photograph of her mother on the desk. Vie felt that youth and sex were rushing past her like a train going in the opposite direction.

Who was at fault? Her mother, for dying? Marty? Vie grimaced. She couldn't blame her sexual immaturity on a younger sister, no matter how many years of experience Marty probably had. Armand?

Vie finished her coffee and pushed her seat away from the desk. Though they had little physical contact with each other now, she and Armand, Vie could remember his being very affectionate with her. He hadn't been the perfect parent, certainly, but he'd been loving. He'd retained abiding love for her mother, and Vie knew he'd loved Nina—at the beginning, anyway. And she could remember feeling his love like a bright ring of light around her, though sometimes she felt she was at the center, in darkness. But he'd hugged and kissed her often when she was a little girl, Vie was sure.

She'd *had* physical warmth from him and later from Nina. Yet men accused her of being frigid. Maybe, Vie worried anxiously, I'm not normal.

Her only sexual experience had been with Philippa. Though she'd never wanted to repeat it, she hadn't been repelled at the time. Is that it? she wondered. Is something wrong with me that way?

Vie knew she attracted men; why, then, didn't they attract her? Sometimes she'd fight them off in panic, as though they were wild animals.

It must be something in me, she told herself. She thought of Nina, with her husband Carlos—how they'd met romantically, both seeking shelter from a downpour under the canopy of a San Francisco hotel. He'd invited her for a warming drink, then dinner, and six weeks later they were married. Vie had flown out to the wedding alone, without Armand. When she met Carlos, Vie didn't know what would upset her father most: Carlos's enormous success in business as a self-made man, or the happiness dancing on Nina's face whenever she looked at her husband or said his name.

Nina's ebullient love for him hadn't dimmed in the two years they'd been married, and he was obviously in love with her. Carlos showered Nina with gifts, praise, and most of all, his adoration.

Why can't I find someone like that? Vie wondered. But she didn't mean Carlos. The girl in her was yearning romantically for *him*—whoever he was—to come along.

She sighed, stood up, and went back to refill her cup. No more of this, Vie told herself sternly. There was work to be done.

When Vie wrote to ask if she could come up for a visit, Marty's first reaction was disbelief. It was a joke in bad taste, she felt, and she'd write back no.

This was the beginning of Marty's last year in Cambridge. The first two years she'd lived on campus. As an upper classman, she'd moved to an apartment of her own, a single-room loft with a bathroom so tiny she could wash her hands while sitting on the toilet and a kitchenette so narrow that she stood with her back against the wall while cooking. But she loved it. This was the first place she felt at home in; it was *hers*, hers alone, and she'd chosen it over much larger, more luxurious places she would have had to share with at least one roommate. Her loft held a bed, which doubled as a couch when she took the trouble to throw a spread over it; a large desk, straight-backed chair, wastebasket, armchair, beanbag, and a table she'd constructed from an iron stand rescued from a garbage truck and a piece of slate she'd gotten for a dollar at a mason's yard.

Here she slept, had her meals, did her work, and entertained whomever she liked. Occasionally they were classmates, and she'd had two assistant professors and one lecturer spend the night, but usually she invited guys she knew from one of her three hangouts—two of them bars, the third a pizza parlor. This loft was her world, and she wasn't going to have it desecrated by her sister's blond ass walking in and taking over.

If the letter wasn't a joke, what the hell did Vie want? Did she intend to gather bouquets of thanks, the "heartfelt gratitude of a younger sister who owed her everything"? Marty grinned to herself. Whenever she thought of Vie, clichés would gush forth like the messages on greeting cards, blanketing true sentiment and thoughts in a blizzard of gibberish.

Or was Vie's purpose in coming up to place Marty "firmly on the path of the future"?

Whatever lay behind it, a visit from Vie sure as hell wouldn't be fun. They'd seen each other in New York a few times, when Marty came down for a semester break, but there was always an edge of tension. She could feel it from the first moment. Vie would be too polite, acting out some Hollywood screenwriter's version of The Reunion of Two Sisters. And Marty would hold back, for honesty's sake, and also because she couldn't think of a thing to say. Vie's world seemed unreal. Her father barely acknowledged Marty's presence in the apartment. At least *he* was honest, she thought grimly.

But she had to admit she felt disappointed each time. Why she should expect anything at all from him after all these years, she didn't know. But nevertheless she did, as though she still believed in magic and would someday come home to her father's warm embrace.

Though she felt tense in Vie's apartment, Marty had learned to handle herself. They didn't have the big fights they used to when they were kids and still wanted the other to be a friend or at least to understand. The two sisters lived in different worlds now, barely touching, acknowledging each other only by a soft flurry of vibrations whenever they came close to each other. Vie was a businesswoman, cool and detached from the murk of emotion and private lives; Marty was a fighter and lover, who had learned to use her brains with the same gusto as her body. She had plunged into her studies, roughed them up, got to the meat, and done very well. She wasn't a scholar; she grasped for ideas as she did for affection, impelled by an old hunger.

She was beautiful at almost the opposite pole of Vie, and very sexy. She never expected love, but in its place took desire and gloried in her ability to ignite it in the eyes and hearts of most men. The brainy side of her was OK, but Marty didn't completely trust it. Her true sense of life came only through her body.

She and Vie had little to talk about. But when Marty sat down to answer Vie's letter, she realized she was too curious about her sister's motives to tell her not to come. Also, though she'd often rationalized her way out of it, she couldn't completely get rid of the sense that she *was* obligated to Vie, and was somehow not *entitled* to refuse her anything.

But still, that didn't mean Vie had to come up here and invade her sanctum. Marty got up and paced. She left the letter for the next day, then the next. But by the end of the week Marty had found a solution.

Clyde, a Yale senior she'd met last spring on the train coming up from New York, called up to invite her for the weekend of the first home football game. She asked if he could get a date for her sister, somebody a few years older, and Clyde said he had the perfect guy: Jeff Wilkins, a third-year law student with a great personality.

Marty wrote back to Vie inviting her for a college weekend, not in Cambridge, but in New Haven. As she dropped the letter in the mail slot, she realized she'd never seen Vie with a man. It would be an interesting experiment.

"If it puts you into such jitters, my dear, why not simply cancel?" Chandra asked over a bowl of shark fin soup in a Chinese restaurant on Pell Street. It was their first dinner together since early spring.

"Because I feel I must see her in her own element, where she's comfortable," explained Vie. Armand's antagonism and near-defection had led Vie to serious thinking about Marty's joining the company. She wanted to propose sending her to business school after her BA and suspected Marty would be more willing to consider the proposal if Vie came to her instead of summoning her down. It meant a loss of time, but Vie decided that was a necessary investment. She also had vague hopes that her visit to Cambridge could lead to more than just a business agreement. With Marty taking her around to places *she* knew, Vie could enter her life for a while on an equal footing, and they might be able to talk as sisters.

"But New Haven," she went on, as the waitress brought the sweet-and-sour fish and moo shu pork while they were only halfway through the soup, "isn't her home." She felt, but wouldn't admit even to Chandra, that Marty was rejecting her again by not permitting Vie to come where she lived. "We won't have a chance to be alone together. It's some sort of big weekend at Yale. Marty writes that there'll be loads of parties, and she even has a date for me! Can you imagine! Somebody I've never seen before, whom I'm expected to spend the entire time with!"

"It may be quite amusing." Chandra encouraged her. Vie needed to be with people her own age, he felt.

She looked doubtful. "What will I talk to him about? I've never been to college, they'll think I'm stupid."

Chandra smiled. His little Vie, who had marched into his shop with such assurance, who had started a business when she was seventeen, who had never been intimidated by anything, was now frightened to death by the prospect of being among students! "Dear one," he told her, tapping the back of her hand lightly with his long fingers, "you must be brave as a little boy going into the mountains."

She looked at him questioningly.

"Tiger potion," he reminded her.

She smiled. "Yes, that's what I need."

Chandra dipped two fingers into his cup of tea and

anointed her with a drop behind each ear and one on the forehead.

"Thank you. I'll be brave," she promised.

But when she stepped off the train in New Haven's Union Station, Vie was nervous again. Marty stood on the platform with two men, both of them looking impossibly young. What can I say that would interest them, Vie worried—forgetting that she usually regarded people from the other point of view, assessing whether they would be of interest to *her*.

Marty introduced them as if they were inanimate. "This is your date," she said, "and this is my date." Names were secondary, it seemed.

When they came into the residence, the same anonymity prevailed. People were identified not by what they did or who they were, but chiefly by whom they were leased to for the evening, making them sound like private property instead of human beings. When Vie heard herself being presented to someone as "Jeff's date," she flushed angrily and turned away. But she didn't dare lash out yet, conscious that she was an outsider who didn't know the rules.

The weekend started badly, and got progressively worse. Her clothes, Vie discovered, were all wrong, out of place. They were too well-designed, too expensive, and their quiet elegance came across as dowdy in contrast to the bright garments of the other girls at the dance.

She danced badly with her date, who insisted on holding her so close that she nearly suffocated in beer fumes. She resisted his hold, and he became more insistent, pressing his body against hers, his sweating cheek against her cheek. "Loosen up, baby. You're here to have a good time."

When he started nibbling her earlobe, she pushed him away firmly and walked off the dance floor. She passed Marty, glued to her young man, her arms around his neck, her pelvis grinding against him. Marty gave her a look of amusement as she passed, and Vie felt a wave of disgust, almost panic. She had to get out of here.

On the street the air was fresher, but the temperature

had dropped considerably during the last few hours, and she felt cold without her jacket. But she couldn't go back in there, not yet. She had to regain her composure, figure out a way to get through this terrible evening without losing control. It had been a mistake to come. She hadn't been able to spend even a moment alone with Marty, and Vie strongly suspected that her sister had planned it that way. She could leave in the morning, Vie promised herself, back to the city where people knew how to behave. Where she could handle them.

"Hello," said a friendly voice behind her. "You look chilly."

She realized she was hugging herself to keep warm. The owner of the voice stepped up to her. He was tall and heavyset, with an open, smiling face. He looked as though he belonged on a football field or logging in a wilderness camp. "Had too much of the dance?" he asked, beginning to remove his jacket.

"No, I'm all right," she said hastily.

He shrugged and slipped it back on. She wondered why she'd said that; she really *was* cold.

But he wasn't offended. He walked along, keeping pace with her, and his voice was reassuring, kind. "You been to Yale before? No? Good. That means I can give you a knowledgeable lecture on your surroundings, pointing out the different influences on the architecture, and you won't call my bluff. Now, to your right is a fine example of English Gothic, modeled after the house where an ancestor of Shakespeare's once delivered the immortal line, 'Bubble, bubble, toil and trouble.' "

Vie laughed. Under the streetlamp she could see the intelligence in his eyes. His face looked more mature than those she'd seen tonight. "The building beyond it represents a feeble attempt by an overpaid architect to capture the spirit of Henry the Eighth upon rising from a breakfast of cow stuffed with goat stuffed with pig stuffed with goose stuffed with pheasant. And a little further on. . . ." He stopped to enjoy Vie's laughter. "My name's Mike Parnell. I'm studying law here."

They shook hands. "Vie Nouvel."

"You don't know Yale, so you must be going to grad school somewhere else."

"No," she said, tickled by his assumption, "I'm in business."

He nodded approvingly and asked her about it. She was reluctant at first, but Mike's easy manner, the sense of goodwill that radiated from him, put her at ease. When she finished telling him about Jolay, he whistled. "You look younger than I am, and you're out in the big world while I'm still a schoolboy. Something tells me I'm in the presence of a genius, and I've been making a fool of myself."

"Could I borrow your jacket?" Vie asked smiling. "You were right before—I'm feeling chilly."

He put it around her and lightly squeezed her shoulders. "I have to get back," she told him. "My sister invited me up, and I don't want to be rude."

They crossed the street and returned on the other side. Vie told him about the discomfort she felt here, that she was out of place.

"Not place, Vie, *time.* You've moved way ahead of these kids; they need time to catch up with you."

"I'd like to move back," she said, "even for a day. Sometimes I feel I've never been young."

"One day you will be," he assured her, holding the door open.

When they came toward the table, Jeff Wilkins was looking at them belligerently. He tried to stand up but was too drunk to manage it. Mike patted him on the back. "It's OK, buddy. Vie and I are old friends." Turning to her, he whispered, "Good luck. Maybe I'll see you later on?"

She thanked him as she handed him his jacket, and he walked away with a little wave, making Vie feel stranded in a world of strangers.

Marty and Clyde came up from the dance floor. "Party! We're going to party!"

"I can't . . ." Vie began.

"Spoilsport! Don't be a spoilsport, Big Sister. We're having *fun!*"

Vie went along reluctantly. The party was taking place on the second floor of a brownstone. As centerpiece on the shellacked wooden table stood a large silver-plated bowl containing a punch that smelled dreadful. It tasted worse, and overpoweringly alcoholic. Vie learned it was made of rum, champagne, and maple syrup.

Around her, people were shouting. Small fights sprang up that ended almost immediately with at least one of the contestants sprawled on the floor in a stupor. Hanging on to the bookcase, a young man who'd come alone was vomiting copiously. The smell spread out from him, but no one except Vie seemed to notice. Propped against the wall, couples were mauling each other. Hands on breasts, bra straps showing, girls half-undressed, the front of their dresses completely unbuttoned. Marty and Clyde walked into the bedroom and shut the door behind them.

Vie looked at the closed door and knew she wouldn't be able to reach her sister. She was leaving the party without a word of good-bye when a hand on her arm stopped her gently. Instinctively she recoiled, but a man's voice was asking anxiously, "Are you all right, Vie?"

She looked up into the concerned face of Mike Parnell and felt sudden relief. Then she tightened with suspicion. "Were you following me?"

"Not really." His hand dropped away and she felt curiously unprotected. "Just had the thought that a small-town girl from New York might need a bodyguard in a place like this."

Vie laughed and slipped her arm through his. "Thanks."

"It's nothing," he said and, with a boy's shyness, asked, "Can I take you home?"

"Please." His kindness touched her, and she noticed that his eyes, in the smokey light, were navy blue.

They walked along the street as they had earlier in the evening, but this time Mike offered no tour. He was pensive, as though saddened by what the evening had done to her.

Mike spoke about his childhood in Missouri, mainly about his father, a family doctor who went to the far north every summer at his own expense, to treat Eskimos isolated from medical care. He traveled the last hundred and fifty miles by dog sled, his supplies bundled in a large knapsack.

"How wonderful!" Vie said, her arm still linked with his.

"Yes," Mike agreed. "Dad's sixty-three now, but he

goes every summer. When we were growing up, my brothers and sister and I, none of us ever felt he was leaving us when he went north. That had a lot to do with my mother, I think. She made us feel we were part of it, helping him to do his work.

"I wanted to be a lawyer since I was nine. To help set things right, you know?" he said with embarrassment.

"Yes." Vie tightened her hold on his arm for a moment. "I know you will. I wish you all the luck in the world," she said passionately, and found herself crying.

"Hey—what?"

She recovered immediately. "Sorry." She sniffed.

He brought out a large handkerchief from his trouser pocket and handed it to her. Vie wiped her eyes, blew her nose heartily, and returned it to him. To have parents like that! she was thinking, but what she told him was, "I've never really talked to anyone my own age."

At the door of her hotel he kissed her lightly on the lips. "Guess you'll be leaving tomorrow?"

She nodded. Mike asked if he could call her when he came to New York, and Vie told him she'd be looking forward to it. She waved and walked in.

Next morning, after only four hours' sleep, Vie checked out of the hotel and took a taxi to the railroad station. On the platform she glanced around, vaguely hoping Mike would be there. Then she boarded the first train back to New York.

5

October–November 1968

April is the month for Paris, but October belongs to New York. The bright, crisp days are so vibrant that anyone who didn't already know this is the most vital city in the world would feel it in every breath, see it in bursts of color embroidering the trees, hear it in the wingbeats of thousands of migrating birds, taste it in the hot pretzels vying with the season's last Good Humors, and smell it in the autumn air.

On a clear Wednesday, Vie decided to walk all the way to her office. She went from their apartment, overlooking the coppery Hudson, east to Central Park and followed its walks through foliage so deep-toned and brilliant that the leaves could almost be taken for gems: amethyst, ruby, topaz, and her own birthstone, opal, with its iridescent play of colors.

When she arrived at work, Vie felt exhilarated. The walk had rustled up many new ideas, and she'd simply jotted down a lead word or two. Entering her office, she asked Elaine not to disturb her as she expanded the notes. She knew from experience that no matter how sure or fully fleshed an idea seemed, it had to be caught on paper or it would evaporate.

Years ago, before she learned this lesson, she'd sit in puzzlement, trying to reconstruct an inspiration. If she couldn't, she figured it hadn't been valid in the first place. Anything important would simply grab hold of the mind and not let go.

Philippa had disagreed. "Never take anything for granted. That's the first rule of business," she said. "And don't expect inspiration to be any stronger than dreams. You know how *they* are: you wake up feeling something very important has happened to you. You reach out to it, and maybe grab hold of an image. By noon it's hazy, by evening it's gone. Never let that happen with your ideas, darling. The people you're competing with know how to salvage everything. Keep a notebook."

Vie had taken her advice. Simple, but it worked. Now she had a stack of little black books. Flipping through them, she'd come upon notes, words, concepts she hadn't been able to make use of before, which provided the key to a present dilemma.

This morning she wrote down a few things that might help Armand later. She didn't want to interfere yet, when his enthusiasm was newly awakened. Her suggestion of a separate line under his own label hadn't had any visible effect at first. But a few days later he initiated the subject, and days after that he began working with renewed commitment. The Armand (for Jolay) line was to be exclusively his; he had complete backing for anything he wanted to do with it. Armand decided to call it "A," in honor of Anne as well as himself, and because A was the first letter of the alphabet, the top of the line. This meant, for a company producing only luxury products, that the A line would produce limited quantities, each bottle numbered, like rare wine; each personally signed by Armand.

Vie wrote down, "Beyond compare." She'd offer it as a possible motto if and when Armand asked for her advice.

When the phone rang, she frowned at it, wondering why Elaine hadn't put the caller off. But her watch said nearly eleven. The luxury of walking to work meant she'd lost well over an hour of office time, and she couldn't go on scribbling notes all day. Sighing, she picked up the phone.

"Mademoiselle Jolay? Here is Hubert Montalmont."

The name rang a bell, though she couldn't place it yet. The voice was rich.

"I have a matter to discuss with you. . . ."

Vie hit her forehead with her hand, wondering how anyone could be as forgetful as she. Montalmont was the leading perfume house of France, a name as familiar as Chanel. Of course Elaine let the call through; she, at least, hadn't become absentminded. Montalmont! The head of the company was Henri, an old man. This must be his son and heir, vice president of the company his father still controlled, though many years, perhaps decades, past the age of retirement.

It all came back in a flash. Armand had told her the history of Jolaunay, with whom he'd worked in Paris. The Montalmonts had been the traditional rivals of the Jolaunays for centuries. A Montalmont had set fire to the shop of Claude Jolaunay, interrupting the line of perfumers in that family. After that, Montalmont had ascended to the throne formerly occupied by Jolaunay. Her father's employer was a new generation, hoping to start again. His shop, too, Armand had told her, was burned to the ground.

"Yes?" she said intently, holding the receiver tight in her hand. "You want to talk business with me?"

"Ma chère mademoiselle. . . ." The voice on the phone vibrated like a string instrument, bass or cello. "You will do me the honor of dining with me tonight?"

"The honor, sir, would be mine," Vie answered gaily, surprising herself with her own flirtatiousness, "but I cannot accept." She'd agreed to go to Philippa's to meet Murray Schwartzman, someone Philippa was pushing as a candidate for sales manager, a job that would become vacant in a month.

"Then would you consider luncheon tomorrow? Perhaps we could take it out of doors?"

"A charming offer, but again I must refuse." Vie was enjoying this old-style repartee; a welcome and delightful relief from usual business conversations. "May I expect you in my office later in the day? At three o'clock?"

"Alas! It is not possible. In the evening. . . ."

"At four, then?"

He sighed. "For you, dearest Mademoiselle Jolay, I shall move mountains."

I wonder why, Vie thought—and was immediately answered by his saying, "If you look as you do on your photographs, there is not a man in the world who would not rearrange the world for you."

"Then you *will* come at three?" She was being naughty and loved it.

"That would mean rearranging not only the world but the sun and moon. I shall be there at four."

"Till tomorrow, then," she said.

"I shall count the hours. Au revoir."

She hung up smiling. The exhilaration of early morning was still with her, though now it was even more bubbly. What a fabulous voice, she thought. If he looks anything like he sounds, he'll be the most attractive man I've ever done business with.

But, though she was already looking forward to tomorrow's meeting, she wondered: What does Montalmont want?

At home that evening Vie told Armand she'd had a call from Hubert Montalmont, who said he had business to discuss.

Armand grasped the ends of the dining table. Vie didn't understand; she'd thought he would be amused by the call. But her father's face had gone white, like a ghost's.

The next day, at four o'clock precisely, Vie was looking at a man who took her breath away. His features were perfect and rugged at the same time, athletic and elegant. She read in the strength of his face something wild and adventurous; an old-world James Bond or a young Errol Flynn. Swashbuckling, intense, Hubert Montalmont seemed to have stepped out of the pages of a storybook.

Vie gave a little cough and invited him to sit down. He hadn't said a word since entering, had only gazed at her fixedly with his dark eyes.

Her voice seemed to pull him from a dream. Raising the back flap of his English-cut jacket, he took a seat. "Pardon," he said, in his deep baritone. "I have been staring so because it is a shock to see you."

"Not a fright, I hope?" she teased, her eyes never leaving his face.

"It is as if I have always known you."

They looked at each other in silence, not knowing how to go on. Vie wanted to cry out, "Me too! I recognized you the moment you came through the door!" But instead she lowered her eyes to her cluttered, busy desk, and softly reminded them both, "You've come on business."

He shook his head as if to clear it. A shiny black lock of hair fell forward and she wanted to reach out and touch it. "Yes," he agreed, almost sadly, "business. We have been noticing the success of Jolay and are impressed by the quality of your perfumes and the artistry of your packaging."

"We?"

"I speak for the company, though the proposition I intend to make is entirely my idea."

She blushed.

"The House of Montalmont," he went on, "as perhaps you know, is one of the oldest in France. We have been making perfume for centuries. . . ."

"Yes, and your rival was Jolaunay."

"You know that?"

"I learned it from my father. He used to work for Jolaunay."

Hubert frowned. "He was a collaborator, they say. My father has mentioned him."

"I never heard that. Maybe you're just keeping up the feud, as in *Romeo and Juliet*. What were they called?"

"Capulets and Montagues. Montague is close enough to my own name; I shall be Romeo and you, fair Juliet."

She smiled. "They came to an unhappy end."

"But before that they were the world's greatest lovers!" He looked at her significantly.

"You're here to make a proposition?"

"Yes. I shall speak to the point. Montalmont is interested in acquiring Jolay as its American subsidiary."

"I see." She tilted her head to one side, as if considering what he said. His long, curled lips were slightly parted. No reason, Vie told herself, to let him know your answer immediately. "How long will you be staying in New York?"

"For another week, at least, depending. . . ." Again he gave her a look full of significance.

"Then we will have time to go into it more fully."

"I intend to, beginning tonight. You will dine with me at La Folie? It is home away from home for me."

"And if I refuse?"

"I shall be forced to take stern measures."

"Will you burn down my shop?"

He looked at her intently. "I shall set a fire somewhere else."

Vie shuddered in delicious anticipation. "Then I am forced to accept?"

"Yes. You must pick up my challenge."

"I will."

"At eight o'clock, then." He stood up. "En garde! We are ready to begin." He kissed her hand, and again Vie blushed.

Hubert was a fencing master. His skill at one of the oldest, most intricate sports in the world had earned him a title and the respect of avid fencers in France and America.

"The lunge must be timed exactly; otherwise you are exposed to attack," he was telling Vie over their escargots, the rich, garlicky smells of the snail butter nearly numbing their nostrils. She was in a silk Yves Saint Laurent original, that looked to be made of silver leaf, with a choker of opals and tiny diamonds at the base of her long, slender neck.

"You must teach me," she said.

"Yes," he said, his eyes moving up to her lips, "I will teach you to parry when I thrust."

"Will you do that for business or pleasure?"

"I will do it for us, Vie." He raised his glass in salute, and she brought hers to his, clinking softly. Their eyes locked, and she couldn't draw hers away. "Fencing is the greatest of the martial arts," he explained in his smooth, resonating voice. "It belongs to Mars, god of war, but Mars himself belongs to Venus, goddess of love. To fence with you is to engage in combat that may pierce the heart."

She pouted charmingly. "But if we duel with words, no one can get hurt."

"We start with them, and go on to more dangerous weapons."

"Dangerous for whom?"

"For us both, I hope. We may forget the world."

"And business too?" she challenged.

"Who knows?" He gave a slight shrug, a gesture she recognized from her father—typically French. "Maybe even that. Romeo and Juliet forgot their warring houses."

"Not for long." Whatever happened between them, Vie knew she would keep Jolay. But for now she wanted to forget everything except this man sitting across the table, whose masterful strokes, she hoped, would conquer her.

He had ordered for both of them, and now the saddle of veal appeared, with pommes noisettes and asparagus tips, accompanied by pale, crunchy leaves of endive salad. The wine steward poured a 1959 Pommard, full-bodied, with an aroma of forest beds. The tastes, textures and smells of the meal were intense—so overpowering to Vie, whose senses had become as vulnerable as a snail out of its shell, that she couldn't eat.

She apologized to Hubert, not wanting to offend him, but she was brimming over, satiated by looking at him, feeling the butterfly kiss of the hairs on his skin brushing against hers. He picked up her fingers one by one, fondling them as if each were slim columns of rare, polished ivory. "You are determined to live only on l'amour et l'air fraîche?" he asked.

"I'm not sure."

"Pardon," he said laughing. "I forget you do not speak my language. It is a saying we have: to live on love and fresh air alone."

"That's not a bad idea," she told him, weaving her fingers through his. "Does it work?"

"We will make the experiment."

He called over the waiter, who asked Vie if she would like an eau-de-vie. When she looked puzzled, Hubert explained that this meant water of life and insisted she try one.

The liquid was clear and icy, and tasted like a distillation of raspberries. He smiled at her look of astonishment when she sipped. She finished quickly, and Hubert paid the check.

"Now," he whispered behind her as they walked toward the door, "the first part of the experiment: fresh air."

"Wonderful," she told him when they stepped out.

The doorman was ready to escort them to a waiting

taxi. Hubert looked at Vie inquiringly. "Would you prefer to walk? Where would you like to go?"

"With you. Anywhere," she blurted out. She had no ready phrases to express what she meant. She didn't know what a woman said to a man she wanted to seduce, or even how to show him she was willing. All she knew was that she'd never wanted anything so badly in her life.

He gave an astonished laugh, put his arm around her, and guided her firmly up the street. On the corner of Third Avenue he took her in his arms, and she clung to him. "You are the most beautiful woman I've ever seen," he said softly.

"Please be quiet." She turned up her face to his and brought his head down until their lips met.

Their lips fastened together, opened, and their tongues slowly explored the other's mouth. She released him a moment to catch her breath and then pulled him toward her again. This time they didn't stop. She forgot who she was and where, abandoning herself to his searching, insistent tongue as she opened her mouth wider. She was drowning, riding a crest; they were in a secret garden, on the banks of the Seine, gliding through the sky on a kite, lost in deep chambers of the sea. They were nowhere in the world, they were simply together, twin beings fired by a single passion. They formed an island on Third Avenue, as passersby circled around them, some smiling, others annoyed by the presence of lovers in their midst to remind them of what they'd lost or never had.

Eventually they drew their lips apart. "I must have you, Vie," he whispered harshly.

"Yes," she answered and turned to hail a taxi.

"I can't believe it." They were in the bedroom of his suite at the Pierre, naked on the gold satin spread, his hand delicately outlining the circle of her breast. "I did not know virgins were still to be found in the world. In Paris they have been extinct for years."

"Quiet," she ordered softly, looking up at his face. She arched her back, bringing her breasts up to him, and he lowered his lips to a nipple, sucking it slowly, gently pulling it into the cavity of his mouth. Her breathing was quick and shallow; she trembled as his hand traveled down the smooth skin of her abdomen.

Again he had to speak. "Unbelievable, you are. A businesswoman, a woman of the world—and so untouched!"

"I was waiting for you," she said simply.

He gazed at her in amazement. His hands moved over her long, silky body as though they caressed the most fragile object in the world. Her skin responded to his touch, came to life under his fingers, and he followed with his lips. He wanted to make love to her for years, taking days for her shoulders, ears, neck; weeks for each breast, months for her belly and the long thighs.

She was trembling and moaning softly. Tiny pearls of perspiration stood out on her forehead and her upper lip. Her pubic hair glistened in the light like a nest of fine gold threads. He wanted to bury his face there. She smelled of lilies and fresh-plowed earth, of wild rosemary, heather, and early thyme. He breathed in her skin, he tasted the light film of sweat in her armpits, the dewy moisture between her breasts.

"Oh, God," she begged, pulling his head to her face, moving dry lips against his ear. "Please. Please."

"You want me to?" he heard himself ask, but his hand was already between her thighs, spreading them gently, firmly, as he ached to get into her.

"Yes, yes. Please. Now."

He eased in slowly, guiding himself with his hand, trying to be gentle, to penetrate only with his tip, but she was pulling at him, crying, urging him in, and he thrust deeper, his rhythm grew faster, and he was aware of her crying, her moans as he moved blindly, unable to stop or control himself now, going deeper and deeper into her until he heard her scream, looked at her flushed, tear-stained face caught in a mask of pain and intense pleasure; he thrust once more and, screaming himself, flooded into her.

The next morning, inhaling the smell of her that rose from the pillows, he still couldn't believe it. He saw the dark stain on the satin cover where her blood had rushed out when he withdrew.

Never in my life, he thought, jamais de ma vie. He

smiled: Vie, ma vie. She was as exotic as a flower that bloomed once in a thousand years. She was full of contradictions. She was a miracle.

He had met thousands of women, made love to hundreds. Hubert Montalmont had a reputation as a Don Juan which seemed to increase his desirability. He was sought after by beautiful women, rich women; by parents of debutantes and young heiresses. In his own circle he'd let himself be seduced by the pretty wives of men he associated with. He loved women; each was as mysterious as an unopened flower until he touched her and she disclosed herself. He adored the feel and smell of women's skin, he liked listening to their voices, watching them move.

But in the past twenty-three years, since he'd donated his virginity at fourteen to a cast-off mistress of his father's, Hubert had never been so totally swept away by a woman.

Before leaving Paris ten days ago, he had almost decided to marry the woman his father was urging on him. He'd become bored with conquests and listened with more than usual attention to his father's arguments in favor of producing heirs.

Henri Montalmont, Hubert's father, shared certain similarities with his son. He was a womanizer, a lover of food and drink, and a brilliant businessman. He wasn't as sensitive to smell as Hubert, but his success in whatever he did had no reference to sensitivity. He had bullied and wheedled the House of Montalmont from a position of established respectability to a corporation worth tens of millions. At seventy-four he had no intention of stepping down in favor of his son for at least a decade. After that, he told Hubert, they could discuss it. His pragmatism, however, dictated that his son should learn as much of the business as possible and be given practice in autonomy. Henri gave Hubert America.

Starting a franchise would mean spending an inordinate amount of time in America, Hubert had thought. Certainly at the beginning he would have to spend many months in setting things up, hiring the people, learning about doors and markets. It would be tedious work, away from the pleasures of Paris that were, to Hubert's mind, the only civilized enjoyments left in the world. When he read of Jolay's high reputation, and learned that its president was not only very young but a woman, Hubert decided instantly that he would buy the company as Montalmont's subsidiary and leave the work to it.

He'd expected to seduce the young Jolay woman as a matter of course and even of politeness. When he'd first asked her, on the phone, to meet him for dinner, he was deliberately planning to sweep her off her feet. Once in bed, he figured, she would find his offer difficult to refuse.

The photographs of Vie Jolay showed her to be an exceptionally pretty woman. But Hubert had often learned that photographs lie. Some of the most photogenic women he'd met were gawky and almost plain in real life, while a number of enchantresses turned flat or flaccid when caught on camera. He'd expected a good-looking but basically uninteresting woman when he entered Vie's office. Seeing her in the flesh had made him lose his composure. She was a beauty, whose attraction owed as much to strength as to fragility. The moment he laid eyes on her, he knew that his life was about to change.

This morning, in the aftermath of their lovemaking, Hubert was totally and gloriously mystified. He'd been the first man ever to have her, and yet he thought of himself as the male in one of those insect species where the female makes use of her mate for procreation and discards or devours him afterward. She hadn't maltreated him, of course, but in some way he felt that, despite her innocence, Vie was so fiercely independent and so adamantly herself that he'd been simply a vehicle for her pleasure. It was a rare feeling, and it excited him. He could hardly wait until evening.

They had dinner in the Village, at Rocco's on Thompson Street. They drank Campari before ordering, and Vie reproached him playfully. "You mustn't phone so often. It makes my secretary very curious."

"Only three times. . . ."

"Four."

"Four, then. Once every two hours—that is not excessive. You wouldn't speak to me more than a few moments each time," he reproached her.

"I must work, Hubert. I always have more than I can finish in a day."

"What is work?" he asked, staring at the strip of cleavage in her beige cotton jersey. The simple costume suited her even better than last night's elegant gown, he thought. It was looser, more féminine, sexier. "Love is the answer."

"That depends on the question," she said crisply. Twenty-four hours ago I was still a virgin, she realized with shock. But everything had flowed naturally, as though it were inevitable. All day she'd been thinking about him. Each time he'd called, she'd wanted to set aside the papers, the queries, the mess of business she'd mistaken for life. Feeling the weight of Hubert's body upon hers, Vie had understood for the first time that passivity could be strength. By totally giving herself, she'd found herself, as a more passionate and aware person than she'd ever suspected. But she had to remain cautious, and she'd tried to go on working today as though nothing out of the ordinary had happened. "You can't pay bills on love and fresh air alone."

She regretted it the moment she said it. He looked crestfallen. "The roses," she acknowledged. "The white roses you sent—they're magnificent!" She touched his hand and added teasingly, "Though when the boy brought them to my office, I thought he'd made a mistake, that they were intended to blanket the winning horse at Belmont."

"Darling woman," he said, "most adorable Vie. I cannot yet believe that I have really found you."

"Was I lost?"

"You must stop this sparring, my beauty, or I shall take you fencing."

"Yes! Oh please, Hubert."

"Tomorrow? Or would your *work*"—he said with ironic emphasis—"interfere?"

"At lunch. Instead of eating," she said.

He blew her a kiss. "Let the duel begin!"

"But it already has," she told him.

He picked up her fingers and tasted the tip of each. "In you," he said, "I have found my match."

She trembled with excitement as his tongue swept lightly over her skin. She realized they would make love again later tonight. "And you are matchless," she said, smiling.

"Yes, I need a partner."

She withdrew her hand from him gently. "But our houses are unmatched. Jolay would be the daughter annex to Montalmont, the parent company."

"Forget business," he groaned.

It was easy to do. When Philippa had called Vie at the office this afternoon, she'd begun the conversation in her usual brisk tone. "What did you make of Murray Schwartzman?"

"Who?" Vie asked.

"Baby." She sounded genuinely shocked. "Murray Schwartzman—your new sales manager, I hope."

"Oh him. Yes," she said vaguely. "I think he'll do."

Philippa knew something was drastically wrong for Vie Jolay to be so unconcerned about a matter of business. "Are you sick?" she asked, worried.

"No." And then, like a lovesick girl whose secret has become unbearable, she confessed. "Philippa, I've fallen in love!"

There was silence at the other end. When the voice returned, it sounded much older than before, and tired. "A man?"

"Yes. The most wonderful man in the world!" She wouldn't tell Philippa his name, knowing she'd recognize it and suspect a business angle. "No, I'm not trying to tease you," she insisted. "I can't tell you who he is, but—oh Phil! I've never felt so *alive* before!"

"Then give yourself to it," was Philippa's advice. "God knows you deserve it. You've waited long enough."

"Thank you," Vie said softly, feeling her friend's generosity.

When she hung up, Vie laughed out loud. All the clichés about love were true. You did fall into it—suddenly, headlong, with no hope of stopping. And "making" love was accurate too: the act of love was the most astonishingly creative act in the world. Business had been her life until yesterday; now it faded beside this stronger force.

Hubert extended his stay in New York by one week, then by two. He and Vie were together every evening and on weekends. The nights were clear, the days golden and sweet as honeycomb. "Private-label weather," he told her. "I had it specially formulated for us."

They sailed off the coast of Long Island's north shore in a rented sailboat and, when the wind fell, made love on the boat's deck, cradled by the Sound as they rocked in each other's arms.

Hubert took her to his fencing club and began teaching her rudimentary skills. She took to the sport with such immediacy that he was flabbergasted. "The en garde position usually takes months to learn, and you have it in five minutes! A miracle. You are a genius of many dimensions. There is no woman like you in the world."

"Show me more," she begged. "Teach me to lunge and parry. What do you call that maneuver?" she asked, indicating fencers on the other side of a glass wall.

"That's the flèche, a number of quick running steps beginning with the rear foot. You need much speed for this—if the attacker misses, he is extremely vulnerable."

Vie was fascinated. She listened carefully, observed every gesture, and immediately tried it out herself. Her lifelong talent for taking in details and committing them to memory enabled her, after only two hour-long sessions with Hubert, to speak accurately of quarte and sixte, to distinguish between parries and counterparries, ripostes and counterripostes. She was fixing in her mind the movements that went into a composed attack.

"Amazing," said Hubert, after he'd kissed her for the twentieth time. "You take to fencing as you do to love."

"It's a matter of involvement," she told him sweetly. "And then all you have to do is pay attention."

"Is that the secret of your success in business, too?"

"I think so. Except that at the beginning my involvement came out of need, not passion."

"They are often the same."

"No," she said carefully, gazing at his face for an answer to the question that floated disturbingly to her consciousness from time to time: Was Hubert simply in love with her, or did his interest in her arise—in part, at least—from his desire to buy up her company? But his eyes, deep and loving, gave nothing away. "No," she repeated, "one springs from strength, the other from weakness."

"But you, my darling beauty, are never weak."

Except about you, she thought; sometimes I think I'd let everything else go if I could stay with you.

They'd brought suitcases to the club and, after showering and changing, they rode up to Ridgefield, Connecticut, in a chauffeured car, to the splendid, sprawling estate which was the American "cottage" of France's most successful dress designer.

Eighteen guests had been invited to stay for the weekend, and dozens more came for the party on Friday night. Vie noticed that everyone seemed to know Hubert. The women, almost without exception, flirted outrageously with him, and Vie felt nauseated with jealousy. A new cliché coming to life: Never before had she experienced this sick feeling, being afraid to talk because she was sure she'd cry.

They rode back to New York on Saturday before lunch. "You were the hit of the party," Hubert told her proudly.

"Me? You are completely crazy, Hubert," she said, snuggling against him.

"Crazy in love, yes. But not crazy in seeing how everyone took to you. Particularly our host, he spoke of nothing else but your beauty and charm."

"Nuts." She lifted her face for a kiss.

On Monday morning the designer called Vie's office at ten minutes after nine to invite her for lunch so they could discuss using Jolay perfumes on his mannequins when he showed his collection at the Metropolitan Museum of Art.

At the same time that Vie was speaking to him, Hubert was trying to placate his father, whose bellowings from Paris assaulted his eardrums while he picked at a croissant left on the breakfast tray.

"You should have been back here weeks ago, you good-for-nothing! You leave everything to me!" shouted the vigorous patriarch. "It's a woman, isn't it, you rascal?"

"Partly," Hubert answered with evasion.

"I know which part! But no woman is worth the price. Business up front, the woman behind." Henri Montalmont chuckled at the joke he'd made hundreds of times before.

"Can you still remember that you went to New York to buy a company?"

"The status remains uncertain," said Hubert unhappily, brushing the crumbs off his stomach.

"Your ass is uncertain. Get it moving. Must I do everything? America is yours—I have left it to you completely. Why can't you settle this business in a few days? A little American company—pouf! We are *Montalmont*— they should be pissing in their pants at the offer. You can take it up to fifteen million, but no more. Is she French, your new cocotte?"

"American."

"Slumming, my boy. They are ignorant in the ways of love. I've had a number of them—they think their pussies are made of sugar and will melt with the heat."

"Stop that!" Hubert shouted back, his hand tightening on the receiver to strangle it. "This is serious."

A long, pregnant pause. Then Henri's voice came back again, cutting as a razor. "I must be losing my hearing. Did you say 'serious'? About an *American*? The most eligible bachelor in Paris becomes 'serious' about a Yankee-Doodle? No, that is straining credulity too far. My moronic son, did no one tell you that Americans don't have *family*? Even the wealthiest—they are all butchers' heiresses: all money and no blood."

Hubert was too angry to speak. He slammed down the phone, and when it rang again a few minutes later, he ignored it and threw the breakfast tray viciously across the room.

Vie hoarded her secret from Armand. He'd asked her, two days after she'd received Hubert's first phone call, on the day that had begun for her in Hubert's arms, if she had seen "that Montalmont." When she said yes, he looked at her angrily and muttered, "Pimp."

She didn't know why Armand was still carrying on the ancient feud of his former employer, but she didn't mention Hubert to him again. She secreted her love away, protecting the most precious thing she'd ever known. To Martine she couldn't talk at all; hadn't phoned or written to her since the Yale fiasco.

Philippa knew, and Chandra shrewdly guessed, but Vie's family never suspected that she could do something so out of character as fall hopelessly and totally in love.

On their last night before Hubert's return, Vie had delicately scented the sheets with *Taj* and came to him scrubbed and naked, perfumed only by her natural odors.

It was a time for reckoning, she knew. By midnight she would have to give him her answer about Jolay. And then? Would he fly off above the clouds and leave New York like a mist under him, their honeyed days turned to amber? Would he return to the arranged marriage he'd told her about, with Danielle of the dimpled elbows, who held out to him the keys to her ancestral château? Vie knew he didn't love the woman, and she could feel, in the answering fires of her own body, that the love the two of them were making was deep and abiding. But on what would it survive when he returned to France? Was his courtship for the prize of Jolay? And denied that, would he simply place a lid on the episode?

"Marry me, Vie." He was naked, too, holding her at arm's length on the scented sheets, inhaling her with his eyes.

Tears of joy ran softly across her nose.

"You will, my darling!" he said in a choked whisper, pulling her toward him.

"Wait," she murmured, holding him off. "Maybe this is a dream. We've known each other such a short time. . . ."

"Centuries. Since the world began. Since the moment I walked into your office."

She propped herself up on an elbow, looking down at him through her tears. "I love you, Hubert. So much it frightens me. I feel there's nothing left of Vie, only her love for Hubert."

He reached up, but still she resisted. "If I marry you, we would live in France. Montalmont would own Jolay."

"Partners, darling."

"I parry when you thrust. You would have the power and control. Vie Montalmont . . ." she let the name hang in the air, suspended like a rare essence. "My darling. I would have to bury Vie Jolay under a different name in another country. It would mean giving up my independence, leaving behind everything I've done up to now."

"The answer is no?" he asked bitterly.

She leaned down and kissed his eyelids. "I want you more than anything I've known."

"Then what holds you back?"

"Everything I've been."

"I will help you. We will be very happy. We love each other," he said.

"Yes." She was weeping in joy. "We do. And maybe that is the only important thing in the world. Give me a little time, let me be alone so that it can all settle and I can be sure, whatever the decision is, that it's the right one."

"And I?" he asked, almost angrily. "I cannot live in a limbo while things are 'settling' for you."

"Will you come back?"

Her intense fragility aroused him so that he, too, began to cry. "Yes, my Vie, my life. I shall come back in exactly a month's time," Hubert said, and she lowered her lips to his.

"But until then," he told her at the end of the kiss, "we will not speak or write to each other. Time will be held in suspension. That is the only way. I shall continue as usual with my life while you are doing the same with yours. If this *is* only a dream, as you fear, each of us may awaken. Or," he said, feeling her body tremble against his, "we may discover that the dream is life."

"Yes." She tried to press even closer, as if to forge their bodies into one. "That's the best way. In one month we'll know. And now, silence."

That night was more voluptuous than any, filled with longing that continued after their bodies were satisfied. Through the soft hours they took each other again and again, almost savagely. She begged him to penetrate her where he never had before, and though the pain made her scream, she ordered him to go on, loving the pain that gave her to him, that seared her with his passion and would brand her as his.

When she woke in his hotel bedroom, Hubert had gone. True to their agreement, he left no note behind.

6

December 1968

As winter entered the city, knocking leaves off trees and shooing away the last half-hardy birds of summer, the A line was nearing completion. Armand had accepted Vie's suggestion, and "Beyond Compare" emblazoned every layout design for the discreet, limited, but potent promotion they planned.

Father and daughter were embarked on something like a second honeymoon together as Armand's pride in his work restored his confidence. He called her "ma p'tite" again, and she answered, "mon gros." They had dinner together two or three times a week, at a little French restaurant near home or in their apartment. For Vie, this was possibly the last time they would have together. She still hadn't made a decision about Hubert, but she missed him achingly. She longed to talk about him, to feel the sweetness of his name on her tongue, but Armand's mistrust of Montalmont was becoming more and more evident.

"Why did he call you that day?" he'd asked Vie. "What could that snake have wanted?"

"Why do you dislike him so? Have you ever met him?"

"No, and I hope I never will. He's dangerous to me. Not the boy, I mean; the father. Henri Montalmont, he's the Grand Inquisitor."

"What *do* you mean?"

"Better that you know nothing," he answered mysteriously, but she could read the fear in his face and knew that something in the past was still hounding him. She half-hoped he was suffering from some kind of delusion, that his fears rose from paranoia and not from actual events. Why should he hate Hubert's father?

Armand refused to discuss it, but he kept returning to the subject like a dog scratching at an old buried bone. As the time approached for Hubert's return, the name of Montalmont came to Armand's lips a few times a day.

On Sunday it would be exactly one month. Vie decided definitely to marry Hubert. Two hours later she decided that love, however great, couldn't take the place of everything else. An hour after that, she was doodling the initials V.M. She vacillated so often, she was sure she'd drive herself out of her mind. On Sunday, Vie promised herself, you'll see him and *know*.

Tuesday she had a call at the office from Mike Parnell. He was phoning from New Haven but would be down for the weekend. Was there a possibility they could meet? He sounded nervous.

Vie hadn't thought about him in weeks, she realized, though on the train back to New York she'd reconstructed their conversations of the night before and had felt a schoolgirl's flutter at the prospect of seeing him again. How long ago that was! Back in the ice age, before the liberating thaw brought by fire.

She was sorry, Vie said, but she wouldn't be able to see him. "I didn't really think you would," he answered sadly. "I know you're very busy."

Vie pictured him, remembered his kindness and how entertaining he'd been. She felt actually sorry, now, not to see him again, but before she could say anything else, Elaine broke in on the line to tell Vie she had a long-distance call waiting. She hung up quickly, her heart pounding in her ears. But the call wasn't from overseas, just Texas.

On Wednesday, Vie went to the lab to invite Armand for dinner to celebrate the A line. He smiled broadly, looked younger and more charming than in years. "I accept only if it is my invitation. You will do me the honor of permitting me to escort such a beautiful woman," he said with his old gallantry, "even if people will say she's young enough to be my daughter. I will make arrangements, and you will be surprised."

She returned to her office. At six in the evening she transformed her business suit into a dinner outfit by removing the jacket and adding two thin gold chains, gold earrings, a brightly colored scarf around her waist. While she waited for her father, she worked, but by seven she was restless. Sunday was drawing closer, ebbing her powers of concentration. Perhaps Armand was waiting for her to pick him up? She dialed the lab, but got no answer. The switchboard was probably turned off.

Vie pushed her papers neatly to the side of her desk, put on her black fur blazer, and took a taxi over to the lab. The door was unlocked, the lights were still on, but the lab seemed deserted. Vie walked down to Armand's room, saw that light came from under his door. She knocked loudly enough for him to be able to hear if he was alone inside. No answer, so she knocked again. Then she turned the handle and went in.

He was slumped over his workbench. "Papa," she called, but he didn't move. Oh God, she thought in terror: a stroke. A heart attack.

She went up to him, and she saw the blood. It spread from the lower part of his face over his clothes, over the vials and bottles, over the countertop. Everything was saturated with blood, deep red with a hot smell. His arm was stretched across the bloody counter; in his hand was a pistol. His jaw was missing, shot away. Vie reached out to the hand. It was cold; there was no pulse. Under it lay a piece of paper. Two words were written on it, in block letters: ARMAND JOLAUNAY.

On Saturday morning, the day before Hubert was due back from Paris, Armand's funeral was held in the small chapel of a funeral home on Manhattan's West side. Marty didn't come to it, or to the burial afterward, at noon, though Vie had called her, as she had Nina.

Vie rode in the car between Philippa and Chandra. No one spoke, each pondering the mystery of his suicide at a time when Armand had achieved success. Vie told no one of the strange note. Robot-like in her terror, she'd pocketed it before calling an ambulance. She didn't think about it now, sitting erect between her "godparents," feeling herself, at twenty-four, an orphan.

The other car held Don Garrison, Frances Murphy, and Elaine Smollett. When they arrived at the cemetery, Vie noticed a gray-haired man standing on a knoll, watching her. He seemed to be gesturing, trying to tell her something, but she didn't recognize him and turned away, walking slowly toward the grave.

As Armand's coffin was being lowered into it, a gun-metal chauffered limousine brought Nina to the cemetery gates. She ran toward Vie in a long chinchilla coat and floppy hat, her face distraught. "Plane was late," she whispered, kissing Vie, who nodded silently. "Where's Marty?" Nina added. Vie's eyes filled with tears. The two women held hands.

It was over. Vie took a deep breath and raised her eyes. The stranger had gone from the knoll.

The small wake at Vie's apartment ended quickly. She refused Nina's and Philippa's invitations to stay with them for the night. They respected her wish to be alone.

In the morning Vie woke, bathed, and dressed. She waited. The day crept by in slow minutes, but no word came from Hubert. She heard nothing from him on Monday, and knew she never would again.

The dream had come to an end.

V

MARTY'S
JOURNEY

1969–1970

1

"Place your bets, ladies and gentlemen. Faites vos jeux."
The players, most of them squinting through the aromatic smoke of their French, American, Turkish, and English cigarettes, lazily nudged their chips forward on the green baize of the blackjack table. The dealer barely moved her dark, curly head as her eyes swept the stakes. She sensed the men taking in her opulent body, copping mental feels. Good, she thought, setting her lips in the faintly amused smile required of the dealer, that'll keep their minds off their cards.

Marty had the quickest hand of the dealers on the S.S. *Nordica*, a Scandinavian cruise ship plying the southern Atlantic route via Gibraltar. She'd learned the arts and skills of the casino from Johnny Lisbon, who'd gotten her the job. He was a former ship's captain who'd become alcoholic and had recently retired to his house in Provincetown on Cape Cod. She'd met him there a few months after her father's death, when Marty skipped Cambridge, forfeiting her lease and the bachelor's degree she would have been given in June.

After Vie called, on that cold December night, Marty hadn't been able to stop crying. "You bastard," she kept cursing him while she cried helplessly. "You bastard had to go and fucking kill yourself."

A relief to be rid of him, she told herself, but she cried through Sunday. At the end of the weekend she stopped crying, washed her face, and began to pack. On Monday she hitched to the Cape, feeling a need for the salt air and high dunes, where she could run barefoot in the cold sand, propelled downward toward the sea.

Only a few places stayed open through the winter. The flashiness of summer was buried under bulky fisherman's sweaters; the rouged and feathered drag queens had returned to the city; gaping tourists were back home showing slides of their vacation to neighbors. The writers, psychoanalysts, lawyers, and politicians had long ago left their summer houses, and the lower Cape now belonged to its year-round residents: a few shopkeepers, fishermen, artists, and retired people. The Portuguese bakery continued to provide fresh loaves every morning, the laundromat and supermarket at the edge of town, off Route 6, stayed open, and the long beach lining the town was busy with gulls, a few cats and dogs, and fishing boats.

Marty talked with the fishermen and met them again in the evening at Porky's on Commercial Street, where she ordered hearty fish stew or the highly spiced linguica, a Portuguese sausage usually served with spaghetti.

Most of the sailors had grown old quickly on the decks. Their faded eyes reflected long hours of vigil over the sea for schools of fish that never appeared. They were short, wizened men who spoke to her kindly, but none of them offered Marty what she was looking for.

She didn't know what that was, except a way of getting out, to go beyond even this easternmost tip of America, and escape into another existence, where nothing would remind her of the past.

Johnny Lisbon wore a large diamond on his forefinger. He pointed it at Marty and said, "You could make a bundle at sea."

She was interested, particularly since her funds were nearly exhausted. He told her about the transatlantic liners, where you got a stateroom and meals in addition to a salary; you could spend your days on deck watching the sea stretch toward its sometimes indistinguishable border with the sky, and you spent your nights with first-class passengers who had money to burn and, sometimes, interesting propositions to offer.

It sounded perfect: to be in no particular place ever, but always sailing toward adventure. Johnny taught her what there was to know, made a few phone calls to old mates in New York, and told Marty to be at the Scandinavian pier for her interview on Tuesday morning.

She was hired on looks. Her dark, voluptuous beauty would stand out against the statuesque pallor of the mainly Nordic girls who worked in the casino. The personnel director of the *Nordica* knew that customers liked contrast, and a sexy little dark thing like Marty would attract the Anglo-Saxon types.

Her table was always filled. This was her fifth crossing, and she brought in more for the house than any other dealer.

"All right. No more players, the game is about to begin. On commence le vingt-et-un." She dealt the cards quickly, her vigorous movements lightly jiggling the large breasts sheathed in gleaming scarlet. She often wore red, to bring out more emphatically the whiteness of her skin and her nearly black hair. She wore red as a signal, and the passengers, mostly men, flocked to her green table, feeling her with their eyes as she dealt their hands.

The first wanted to be hit. She dealt a nine. Bust.

The second stuck. So did the third. The fourth player, a woman whose smooth face was held up by a heavily wrinkled neck, giving her the fantastic appearance of a melon set on the head of a turkey, decided to split her cards, playing one line at a time. She stuck with sixteen on the first, nineteen on the second.

The man at her left held Marty's eyes. "I'll take what you got," he said flippantly, smiling. She placed a two next to his cards. He nodded. "OK, baby, give me more."

The next was a three. He stared openly at her breasts, half-uncovered, straining against the tight satin. "I like what I see. Keep it coming, doll."

An ace. That meant a definite five or under. He grinned at her. "Good girl. I'm satisfied—for now."

She moved to the next, who went over with an eight, and then to the last. Dealer flipped over her two cards: a natural—ace and queen.

The player with the five cards whistled. As he passed over his chips, his hand deliberately brushed against Marty's, over her wrist, starting up the smooth firmness of her arm. She drew away quickly. Cardinal rule on the floor was: Don't fraternize with passengers. She'd seen a few girls fired for breaking it, and Marty was too smart to take unnecessary risks. She was willing to gamble only when she had a strong chance of winning; when the cards were stacked in her favor.

He gave a lazy smile and ran the tip of his tongue slowly across his lower lip, never taking his eyes off Marty. Looking up, she felt a sudden arousal as she met the veiled green eyes. They reminded her of Casey's.

It wasn't just the color of the eyes, either; there was the same defiance in both of them, a mocking look, as though nothing could ever intimidate them.

Two more rounds until closing time. The man stayed, earning back what he'd lost earlier when the dealer paid nineteen, and again when she paid twenty-one. "Nice work," she complimented him, smiling, as she packed up.

He was the last to remain, rocking on the back legs of his chair and looking at her with open sexual interest. He pitched forward suddenly and took hold of her wrist. "*You're* a nice piece of work," he said. "Who put you together?"

She laughed. "I did, I guess."

"Terrific job." He let his eyes run appreciatively over her body. "I can see the parts are all of superior quality. One of a kind. No, sorry, my mistake"—he stared frankly at her breasts—"*two* of a kind."

She laughed, throwing her head back, flaunting the firmness of her neck.

"Miss Nouvel," came a disapproving voice as the supervisor of the casino took Marty by the other arm and pulled her away from the table. The man she'd been flirting with stood up, but she made a gesture at him indicating he wasn't to interfere. Anything he'd say would simply exaggerate the incident. She could handle herself by now, God knew.

A few minutes later the pit boss had a silly smile on his face and the promise that Marty would have a drink with him that afternoon. She knew he'd try to get her in his cabin, but it wasn't worth thinking about. She would or she wouldn't—what the hell difference did it make? She'd do what she felt like doing when the time came. Sex was never a problem, and it was the easiest way she knew of paying for whatever she wanted.

She walked out on the Promenade Deck and took the stairs up to Boat Deck. It was three in the morning under a full moon, with cool breezes that didn't disturb the calm surface of the sea softly rising and falling like the belly of a pregnant woman. Marty pulled her shawl closer around her, breathing in the air that cleansed her every night after many hours in the smoke-filled room. This was the best time, the only time of day she felt was truly hers, with the sea spray against her face, the boundless quiet and gentle rocking motion. At such times she'd imagine she was the only human being alive and the sea, sky, and stars existed only because she was perceiving them.

A sound behind her made her start. She turned in annoyance at being interrupted. "I was hoping you'd still be up and that I'd find you. I want to apologize." He was standing close to her, without touching, his lips inches away from her ear. She realized his presence didn't disturb her; that she was happy to see him and had somehow been expecting to.

"Apologize for what?" she said gaily. "For making me laugh? I enjoyed it. I don't get to laugh often enough."

"Happy to oblige." He bent down and kissed her lightly on the lips. "The name's Jean-Luc Delbeau, and you don't have to tell me yours, Marty. I've been watching you from afar."

"How intriguing!" She smiled up, hoping he'd kiss her again—a real kiss this time.

"And I'm here to give you warning: I'm going to make you fall in love with me."

"Romantic too! When do I start?"

"Soon." He held her face between his hands and looked at her in the palely gleaming light as though he were reading something there. Then he took his hands away. "I know you, Marty."

"You do?" She felt a touch of alarm. "From where?"

"Not that way. We haven't met before, but I know who you are, what drives you. I know because I'm very much

the same. And I'm going to have you. But not yet. I'll wait
until you know that you want me, until you work to get
me."

"But why?" she asked, thrilled by his determination
and arrogance.

"Because a woman like you can have any man. They
don't mean anything. You take them and drop them immediately afterward, like a newspaper you've glanced through.
But I'm not going to be one of those. You're going to come
to me. I'll wait until you're ready to give me more than
you give to any other man." He was smiling at her.

"You're pretty sure of yourself, aren't you?"

"Sure of *you*." He bent to give her a chaste kiss on the
forehead, hardly rougher than the sea spume, and then
walked quickly away.

Marty stood at the railing, following him with her eyes.
His style of dressing, the sound of his voice—even the way
he moved had class. When she couldn't see him anymore,
she turned back and looked out to sea. She remembered
the shore she'd come from, the busy land where her sister
stalked her like a ghost. She saw Vie's face smiling from a
photograph on the perfume display counter at Bloomingdale's. Marty had gone to the store to pick up some gold
stockings the day before they shipped out. On the ground
floor the picture, sleek and regal, jumped out at her. Vie's
smile shocked her, coming so soon after Armand's death.
But of course, Marty had realized, the company was now
hers alone; Vie *was* Jolay.

And she, Martine Nouvel, was here buying stockings to
complete her outfit as a croupier. Marty cried out silently
to her sister's image: I'm going to erase that superior
expression from your face—just wait until all the chips
are in! Then she'd gone to the pay phone and dialed.
Perversity, Marty told herself, remembering; it couldn't
have been anything but that.

The last good-bye? Final leave-taking? The impulse that
propelled her to call Vie was controlled by cliché, a giving
in to the bourgeois world of her sister. Never again, Marty
vowed. The meeting had been as painful as touching burned
skin. What do I need it for? What has that bitch ever done

but pay the bills? No sweat for her—she's rolling in money. Uses it to wipe herself clean of guilt, of me.

The image sank and reappeared on the heaving water. They'd met at the small bar of the St. Regis, next to the King Cole room, a place of discretion for the powerful, where money whispered in many languages. Vie was seated when Marty arrived, and the waiter, whose disapproval of Marty stiffened him into a marionette on her entrance, melted into his natural putty when he saw whose guest she was. Vie, in cream silk and gold chains, smiled nervously as she offered the side of her cheek for Marty's imprint of affection. Marty ignored the offer.

Her superciliousness! Her words, served to Marty at just the right temperature, proffered in the crystal of her tone. "The college wrote this . . ."; "I'm sorry you felt it necessary to do that . . ."; "endangering your future . . ."; until Marty could think of nothing but the desire to hit her, knowing that if she did, the sound would be of splintering glass.

"You don't know me, Vie," she'd said. "You never did, and don't try to understand me now. Our worlds, our values are diametrically opposite. . . ."

"Values?"

"Yes. Or don't you think I have any?"

Marty had seen that Vie was afraid to answer and became inflamed. "You don't, do you? You think values belong in the paraphernalia of the rich, something you acquire like designer clothes, the right label that tells the world you're right. But let me tell you something. It's *you* who has none—no values, and no vision either. All you can see is a narrow strip of convention and conformity. Your only cause is making money, your only belief is in business."

"Wait a minute," Vie had flashed angrily. "You've never been anything but selfish. Expecting everything to be handed to you. No responsibility to anyone, especially not to my—to our father." When she stopped, Marty knew Vie was waiting for her to say something about Armand. She didn't.

Then Vie had asked, "Why were you suspended from Radcliffe?"

"What do you mean? I quit."

"Yes," she'd said in her long-suffering way. "They called and told me you'd left on your own. But they also said you were on probation."

"For what?" Marty had been curious to hear how they'd put it.

"Creating disturbances, threatening violence. . . ."

Marty had just laughed. You could depend on the establishment every time, she'd thought—they kept their scare phrases in stacks with the outgoing mail. To them, any commitment to life or liberty was a violent threat. The same thing everywhere, she knew, even in France, where the student protest movement had started and then spread to American campuses including her own.

Laughing, Marty had offered no defense, no explanation. She'd had a clear image of the two of them, sisters facing each other on opposite sides of the barricades, ready to shoot. A few minutes later, they'd parted. To Vie's last question—"What are your plans now?"—Marty had answered, "I'm shipping out in the morning."

Vie's face blurred on the silver surface and disappeared into the quiet depths of the sea. The image of Jean-Luc rose, and Marty stared with her mind's eye at the reflection of the man who would, she felt, change the direction of her life.

He was there every night, at the casino, but he didn't sit at her table. She could feel his eyes on her, though, holding her like an invisible net from across the room, and whenever she looked up, she met his gaze.

He didn't speak to her, didn't approach her again. Every day Marty felt more drawn to him, felt the net pulling her, but she couldn't go to him. On the casino floor it could cost her her job. She waited on the Boat Deck every night after closing, but he never came.

She felt impatient and frustrated. She flirted with the pit boss when she met him for drinks, but he made no overtures, and she didn't try to provoke them. He was paunchy and balding, his remaining hairs resting in greasy stripes across his scalp. He wasn't a trophy; his power was minor. Marty decided she'd try for the captain. That would help to get her mind off Jean-Luc, she thought. Damn him; she'd teach that arrogant bastard a lesson.

Sexual tension made her restless, spoiling for action. She loved the exhilaration of conquest. That, and comfort, were all a man could give, she knew from experience. At twenty-one, she'd come to the conclusion that lovemaking was a vigorous, thrilling sport, usually without bad aftereffects, providing moments or hours of feeling safe, and almost happy, in a stranger's arms.

Sverre Lindblöm, the tall, blond captain, responded to Marty's obvious interest by inviting her to his cabin in the afternoon. They drank a clear Riesling and then tumbled into bed, each taking the other for his own sport. To the captain it was a compliment: the dark, pretty girl was younger than his eldest daughter. To Marty it meant another notch in her belt: the most important figure in the ship's hierarchy.

When she went to her own cabin to get ready for work, Marty thought of what Jean-Luc had said—"You use men and discard them," something like that. As she spread pale foundation over her skin, she could feel the glow of sexual aftermath, though she realized it had nothing to do with the man, and she didn't care if she made love with Sverre Lindblöm ever again.

But Jean-Luc and his mocking green eyes wouldn't let go of her fantasies. She couldn't stop thinking about him even now, still dewy from another man's embrace.

Why? All men were basically the same, she knew. You used them before they could use you. Why, then, did this one keep filling her thoughts?

Marty frowned at herself in the mirror as she applied translucent blusher below her cheekbones. She'd asked the other croupiers about him and discovered only that he was wealthy, unmarried, and rumored to spend a lot of time on the yacht of Sophocles Menarchos, whose fortune rivaled those of Queen Elizabeth and J. Paul Getty.

Whatever his purpose on the yacht, it was clear that Jean-Luc belonged with the Beautiful People, in a world Marty longed to enter. But first she had to conquer him.

The silver eye shadow glistened on her lids as Marty began the intricate painting of her lashes. They were naturally long and curled, but she emphasized them by many coats of mascara, above and below. Deep navy first, then powder to hold it; another layer of navy, then forest green, topped by black. She'd wrestle him down with her eyes, she thought, inspecting the final effect.

But he didn't come to her table until the last night before the ship's arrival in Casablanca, first stop on the way to Genoa.

He sat at the end, his chips a neat pile in front of him, wearing a white silk dinner jacket with a yellow rose in his buttonhole. Marty wondered if he'd gotten it from a woman.

She sucked in her stomach, making her breasts more prominent in the black crepe, sequined at the low neckline and again at the hem. Her upper arms were encircled with gold slave bracelets, and a wide gold choker was at her throat.

"Incredible," he said softly, looking down at his cards. She knew he was talking to her. When he accepted another card, he didn't bother to glance at it. "I'm in your hands," he whispered.

He was winning nearly every round. By midnight he'd won $80,000. People had drifted to the blackjack table from all around the casino to watch.

Jean-Luc dropped $30,000 on the next two rounds, but quickly made them up. By one thirty he had more than $100,000 in chips. The passengers looked over his shoulder, but no one was willing to sit at the table with him. He was the only player left.

"Double the stakes," he said, watching her carefully.

Marty knew the house rules. "I'm sorry, sir," she told him, not looking up. "You've exceeded our limits. I can't accept that bet."

"All right. I'll change the stakes."

She raised her head. He was pushing his entire pile of chips forward. "If I lose," he said, "you take all the money. If I win, I get *you*."

There was a gasp from the bystanders, and then silence as Marty held the cards in her hands for a long moment while holding him with her eyes.

The man and woman seemed caught in a spell. No one

said anything. The casino was hushed. And then Marty's voice rang out, clear and determined: "No more players. The game is about to begin."

She dealt the cards quickly as the onlookers, in one body, moved closer to the green baize.

His eyes stayed locked with hers; when he glanced at his hand, a slow smile spread over his face as he saw what she'd done for him.

2

Apollo, at 120 feet in overall length and with a cruising speed of fifty-eight knots, was bigger and faster than Stavros Niarchos' *Mercury*, the first yacht built with exclusively jet engines. Vospers of England were the builders of *Mercury*, and Sophocles Menarchos went to them to order a ship more powerful, larger, and heavier than his rival's.

Technical problems slowed them down; the increase in size and weight required new calculations. The Italian designer Menarchos had insisted on was so high-strung and temperamental that the British engineers walked out on the project five separate times.

It was three years after he'd placed his order that Sophocles Menarchos first set sail on his *Apollo*, the most lavishly appointed yacht in the world. In the past five years he'd increased its opulence and added a fourth deck. The pink Carrara marble walls were kept gleaming. The floors were covered with Persian carpets. The dozens of sets of dishes included one each of gold and silver. Paintings by old masters—among them Correggios, Titians, a rare Giorgione—hung in the staterooms. In the library and Menarchos' private study priceless Gobelins muted the walls, contrasting with the gaiety of the ballroom, dominated by a large mural painted on commission by Joan Miró.

Everything on the ship, down to the delicate tracery of the silverware and the bathroom sinks of English bone china, was designed with artistry and fashioned of the finest materials in the world. Wines that would sell wholesale at $200 a bottle lined the shelves of the ship's cellar. Sides of venison hung with Scottish lamb and Argentine beef on hooks in the meat cooler. Tiny strawberries from France and wild mushrooms from Bavaria were kept in the enormous pantry, divided into compartments that housed luscious chocolates from Lindt-Sprüngli in Zurich, exotic fruits from the southern hemisphere, cheeses from around the world. Even among the globe-trotting guests, there was hardly one who could think of a delicacy not available from *Apollo*'s kitchens.

When Marty boarded the ship with Jean-Luc, she was stunned. Despite the weeks of training in Paris, she gave a loud whistle. "This is some bathtub!" she told Jean-Luc.

He laughed. "It's just home to me. Modest and unassuming, of course, but comfy."

"You crazy." She flung a pair of lace underpants at him as she unpacked, and the matching bra after that.

He threw them back at her. "You'll get used to it," he predicted. "The way you got used to Paris. Remember how you were at the beginning? A little mouse."

"Me? Never! I've always been the big cheese."

"Ah, good," he said. "I feel like a nibble."

He advanced on her, and Marty stood stock-still, waiting for his touch. When she felt it, she trembled. She'd learned to take love slowly, to be quiet and listen to her body responding in its own time. He'd taught her that, in Paris.

He'd taught her many things, subjecting her to intense weeks of basic training to become someone who'd pass as one of Menarchos' usual guests. He'd promised her, in their first hours alone, after she'd jumped ship and they'd taken the next flight out of Casablanca, "I'm going to teach you what I know. I'll make you a star of the international set."

"Why?" she'd asked, thrilled.

"You've got the ability, and I want to do it. And because of Menarchos."

Jean-Luc Delbeau was born in Casablanca in 1930. At the age of fifteen, the year the war ended, he left home to seek his fortune. He'd reached his full height and looked older than his years. His greatest ability, a natural one he'd discovered in school, was for languages, and within two months he was employed by the American occupation forces in France as a translator. All the English he had was from the classroom, but he told the commanding officer that his father had been a corporal in the American army, and no one bothered to check. His determination and the need of a translator got Jean-Luc the job on the spot. Within two months, he told Marty, he was talking "like a Yank."

She asked if he'd been on his way home when he boarded the *Nordica*. "Yes," he said, "my first trip back in more than twenty years."

"What happened?"

"You. I could feel the same energy running through you that I used to have. I knew you were on the run, just like me, and you made me realize there was no point going back. You've got to cut your losses at each step of the way and keep moving."

"Yes," she agreed. They were on their way to Paris, strapped in their seats, drinking brandies. He hadn't touched her yet, except for another light kiss when he complimented her sleight of hand, stacking the deck so she would lose to him. He said he was proud of her finesse: dealing him a natural with the queen of hearts, like a bold Valentine.

She'd acted out of instinct and need. Until that moment Marty hadn't known what task she could perform to win him. When he stated his bet, it became clear she could win only by losing. Her hands obeyed almost before the thought took hold.

They'd gone straight to the airport from the harbor, and now, like fugitives, they were escaping to Paris to begin a new life together. They'd both entered into the pact, without time for more than a brush of the lips and a squeeze of the hand.

Strapped into their seats in the sky, they began exploring each other. Marty had expected him to grab her after takeoff, but she'd forgotten that he wasn't like any man she'd known. Instead of hands, he used words, telling her about himself and asking about her.

She told him some of it: That her mother had died when she was a baby; she'd lived with her father and sister in Brooklyn but never got on with them. "I made my own life," she said defiantly.

"Where?"

"On the street. At least until my sister sent me up the river to a girls' school. I went to college after that, but it wasn't for me. I skipped out and went to sea."

"Your father and sister are still in Brooklyn?"

"The old man's dead. *She's* in business, making money hand over fist."

The tone of her voice, the bitterness Marty put into the pronoun *she*, made Jean-Luc refrain from asking more. "You're like me," he mused again. "We go our own way. We don't bother with other people."

"Except to use them," Marty said, wondering what it was about this man that made her feel she could tell him anything.

"Except to use them," he repeated, nodding, and wondered which of them was using the other.

Jean-Luc needed her to get back a sense of his own power. He'd been Menarchos' boy for too long, getting everything he'd dreamed about in wealth, women, life at the top, but in return having to lick Menarchos' ass whenever he showed it. Jean-Luc needed to master someone else in the same way. Marty attracted him. She had a fire in her that he was going to bring under his own control and then unleash on Menarchos. God, how he hated the man! How he worshiped him!

They checked in at the Hotel Crillon on the Place de la Concorde, dropped their bags in the rooms, and went out to shop. "We're starting at the outside, working our way in," he told her. "First come the clothes."

He began literally at her skin, choosing underwear and garter belts, fingering each item and discussing it with the saleslady while Marty stood by, her high-school knowledge of French catching only an occasional word of the fast dialogue. When he was satisfied, he ordered her to try them on and then came to inspect her in the dressing room.

She felt shy, exposing herself to him like this. The lacy underthings seemed more intimate than nakedness, and the saleslady stood next to him, both of them examining her as though she were on display. Marty turned her head to disassociate it from her body. She was conscious of his stare, wanting to hide from him and yet feeling aroused by his indifference. She felt degraded, and it excited her.

"Bien," he said to the saleslady, abruptly ceasing the examination. "On les prend. Tous." To Marty, he said, "You can put your clothes back on now."

Humbled, feeling a mixture of excitement and resentment, Marty silently followed Jean-Luc from store to store, into boutiques for handbags, scarves, gloves, to designers' salons for evening dresses and a tailored suit, out to pret-à-porter shops for ready-made sports clothes. The shopping spree took three days, until they reached the final outerwear, a shimmering leopard-look silk raincoat from Dior. Then they stopped. Jean-Luc told her the furs would come later, after the summer, when she'd have grown into the style of her clothes.

Each night they returned to the hotel exhausted. They ate in the restaurant downstairs and retired to sleep in their separate bedrooms. Marty couldn't understand what she'd done wrong, why he wouldn't come to her. She feared he might be homosexual, but then she couldn't puzzle out why he had wanted her and staked his claim on the ship.

The morning of the fourth day he came into her bedroom while she was eating the breakfast she'd ordered by phone in English. "Today," he said, "we begin the French lessons."

They started at nine thirty sharp, broke at one for sandwiches and a glass of wine, and resumed again at one thirty. They continued until five, when Jean-Luc slammed the book shut, stood up, and told her, "Now go and bathe. Then wait for me on your bed."

She was naked when he came in. He stopped at the door and looked at her, sweeping her body slowly with his eyes as though this was the first time he was seeing even a part of her.

Marty forced herself not to move. He came toward her slowly, saying nothing, staring at her. When he reached the bed, he remained standing for a few minutes, his eyes fixed on her breasts, then on her pubis. "Open your legs," he ordered softly, loosening his tie.

She lay with her legs apart, her most secret place opened up to him as he removed his clothes, staring at her parted inner lips until she felt such shame and desire that she brought her legs together.

"No!" he said. "I want to look at you."

Almost painfully, she forced her legs to open up again to reveal the hot flush of red.

When his clothes were all off, he moved toward her face. His body was long, lean, almost hairless. He was fully erect, and he brought his erection to her mouth, cupping one hand under his testicles. With the other he touched the top of her head. "Take it now," he demanded.

She obeyed him and then lay against the pillow while he held her thighs wide apart with his hands and took the wet lips into his mouth. When she made loud noises, he stopped. "Quiet," he told her. "Just lie there and concentrate."

When he mounted her, she ground her hips up toward him, thrashing and moaning. He took firm hold and held her down, not moving himself until she subsided. "Don't act," he said. "Don't think. Give yourself over to me. I am the man. Be quiet and let yourself be the woman."

She did what he told her, and when he finally came to climax, she held her arms tightly around him and whispered, "You were wonderful, you were the best I ever. . . ."

He placed a finger on her lips. "Quiet, Marty, love. Don't lie. I'll make you come, in time. Don't pretend, to me."

"How could you tell?" she asked in amazement. Every

man before had told her she was a great lay. Not one had noticed that she never came.

"Any man can tell, if he pays attention. Have you ever had an orgasm?"

"No," she admitted, feeling a burden she hadn't known she was carrying suddenly lifted off her. "Never with a man. Only when I masturbate."

His fingers moved down and began gently to coax her. After ten minutes, when she felt herself straining, nearly there, then falling away, she took hold of his hand. "No more," she pleaded.

He let her direct him and kissed her face gently. "It'll work," he promised. "Soon. Don't be afraid anymore, little Marty. Put yourself in my hands. I'll make you into a lady *and* a woman. Please trust me."

She put her arms around his neck and cried softly against his cheek.

Five weeks later, in the bedroom on Menarchos' yacht, Marty stood trembling while Jean-Luc's hands ran over her body. When he lifted her skirt to penetrate her, she was ready, and they made love standing up, coming together in the strong new rhythm she'd learned from him.

She was a woman, and taken for a lady. Her French, though limited, was flawless in accent. He'd drilled her every day, from breakfast until lovemaking, forcing her to repeat a sound over and over until she had it perfectly. She repeated the word *rue* 107 times—she counted—before he was satisfied, and then came his only form of praise— "pas mal," not bad. He himself spoke English like a native-born American, and he demanded from Marty the same perfection he demanded from himself.

She understood, even when she complained about his bullying, that Jean-Luc believed in her more than anyone ever had. She could feel his respect for her intelligence in his conviction that nothing lay outside her grasp. And he didn't separate her mind from her body once they started making love. No one had ever respected her body so deeply. He met it with his own, as an equal, his maleness dema[nd]-ing the full force of her femaleness, not permitting [the] sex to be anything less than the coming together of bo[th] fully conscious of themselves, wrenching their demands from the other; egotistical, proud, and free.

Her clothing now lightly suggested what was underneath instead of flaunting it. She'd thought the soft tops conservative and unsexy when he first ordered her clothes. But when she came to understand what real sex was about, Marty saw that her veiled breasts were far more exciting than the hard tits she'd carried out in front of her as though they didn't belong to her body.

At dinner, the first night on the *Apollo*, they were seated with three other couples at a round table. Menarchos himself wasn't on board yet. No one was sure when he'd actually arrive, but the anchored ship was kept in a condition of readiness to sail at whatever moment he gave the signal.

He'd be the supreme test for Marty's transformation, but right now Jean-Luc watched her with pride as she lifted the fish knife and delicately inserted it at the backbone of her baby salmon, revealing no concern on her face as she answered questions in English and French, careful not to say more than necessary, in case her accent in either language gave her away.

Brooklyn still lingered in her speech, and it was much harder for Marty to break sound patterns in her native tongue than to acquire new ones from scratch. In French her acute ear would tell her, almost as infallibly as Jean-Luc's, when she was even slightly off. But in English she'd often not hear it, and her broad, drawn-out diphthongs gave her away. Until she was sure her vowels would come out with the sound of money resonating in them, like the speech of the woman sitting opposite her, Marty told herself to bring her lips together as quickly as possible after a word and obey Jean-Luc's dictum, "Silence is golden when your vowels are Brooklyn."

He introduced her as Martine de Nouvel. If anyone asked about her background, she brought out the history she and Jean-Luc made up: her father, youngest son of an impoverished aristocratic French family, had gone to America in the early nineteen thirties and amassed a fortune in textiles. His wife, née Rousel, came from an important family in Savannah. She had died of diphtheria—"Isn't that straining it?" Marty had asked, and he agreed to change it to pneumonia—when her daughter was three. Martine de Nouvel had no siblings; she'd insisted that Jean-Luc make her an only child.

She grew up in New York and Greenwich and was now simply traveling around the world, as so many of her fellow debutantes were doing, diverting herself while looking for an appropriate husband. She and Jean-Luc were "just friends," she would say with a slight pause of embarrassment. Having a foreign lover was an excellent and approved manner for young women of her class to get "broken in," so they could later offer their American husbands the pleasures of Old World experience. It wasn't done, however, to confront anyone with the fact; the discreet phrase, with perhaps a little cough or catch in the voice, would both titillate and reassure: no scandal, nothing messy, simply the next step in a proper education.

The golden-voiced woman opposite smiled knowledgeably, letting her gaze sweep both Marty and Jean-Luc to indicate that she was in on their secret but wouldn't tell. "Have you been on *Apollo* before?" she asked.

"No," Marty answered sweetly. "I've been all booked up with safaris."

Jean-Luc choked on his creamed spinach. That's my girl, he thought happily—tough as a rhino.

"How fascinating. What do you think of Kruger Park?"

But Marty wasn't listening. She was staring at the huge man who had just entered, filling the room with his presence. Jean-Luc followed her stare and jumped up to greet Sophocles Mcnarchos.

His name had been given him by a sister at the orphanage, who was reading *Oedipus Rex* when he was carried in. Of all the dramatists, she loved Sophocles most, and she bestowed the name on the little bastard like a fairy godmother bringing the gift of posterity.

He ran away at twelve and lived like an urchin, sometimes stealing but usually scavenging for food, until a priest found him sleeping in a doorway and brought him home. He gave the boy a bed and proper meals, but return demanded his labor. Sophocles cleaned the chur did the gardening, and took care of Father Dominikos' personal quarters. He did everything but cook, a task left to plump Yaya, who doted on her master.

After a few months Father Dominikos began to institute a daily routine of reading. Taking young Sophocles into his study, he read aloud first, then taught the boy ancient Greek and coaxed him through the Epistles of St. Paul. The priest could see the boy had a quick mind, and after a year of good food, hard work and hard sleep, he was starting to fill out like a man. At thirteen, Sophocles was already taller than the father.

In the drawer hidden behind fake paneling Father Dominikos kept his collection of erotica. It consisted mainly of reproductions of paintings by European artists and photographs of Indian relief sculptures depicting the act of love in different positions. When Sophocles was nearly fourteen and his voice had begun to break, Father Dominikos locked the door of his study behind them and pulled out his hidden drawer.

He watched the boy's face as he held out one picture after another, noticing the light sweat on his skin, the heavy breathing. Then he came to the picture that made Sophocles cry.

It was by a Dutch master and showed an eagle raping a woman. Its talons were tearing her flesh, her face was in a swoon, and her soft, luminous body was naked under the predator's open wings. The eagle's beak was hard, its eyes in profile like a gleaming stone. The young woman was abandoned to ecstasy, her thighs parted, her breasts bleeding from deep wounds the bird had inflicted.

Sophocles gaped at the picture, and blood rushed to his head. He felt himself grow hard, so hard that his flesh screamed against his trousers.

The priest smiled as he saw the boy's throbbing excitement. "You like what you see?"

"It's wonderful!"

"Yes," said the priest slowly, putting the pictures back in the drawer. "I shall leave you to think about what I have shown you until tomorrow. Then we begin with new lessons."

Sophocles could hardly sleep that night. Every time he

thought of the pictures he'd seen in the priest's study, particularly that one, he would feel himself getting so hard that he thought he'd explode. Near dawn he reached down and grasped his enormous erection. It was enough; the touch alone brought out a hot stream, spurting over his hand onto the sheets.

That afternoon Father Dominikos asked if he had anything to confess. Sophocles blushed but wouldn't answer. "The pictures I showed you," the priest urged gently, "didn't they warm your bed at night?"

He nodded, looking down at the floor.

"And would you like to see them again?"

"Oh yes! Please!" he blurted, his face crimson.

The father brought out his collection again, and this time he sat very close to the boy, his hand resting gently on his thigh. As Sophocles' arousal mounted, the priest moved his hand down, to the inner thigh. Sophocles fidgeted in his seat, and his movement made him harder, bigger. Father Dominikos was breathing heavily. Quickly he undid the buttons of the boy's fly and slipped his hand inside.

"Wonderful," he breathed. "Go on looking at the pictures. What I am doing to you will give you ease, my son." He bent his head to the rearing member and took it between his lips to the hilt as Sophocles groaned and released his hot semen into the priest's mouth.

That evening he ran away, with a small bundle of clothes, the money he'd taken from the collection box, and the picture of the eagle raping a woman.

From that evening on Sophocles became a man. He took work where he could find it, and when he couldn't, he stole. But most of the time his large build and unusual height brought him jobs along the waterfront. He was given most of the heavy labor of carrying and transporting material for shipbuilders, and then he became an apprentice.

He learned everything about ships and soon was a builder himself. He became more successful than his master. By the age of twenty he was leasing a small fleet. After that, he entered into the birthright given him by the sister at the orphanage as he started carving out his posterity in shrewd acquisitions and manipulation. By twenty-five his investments had spread from shipping to steel, oil, and copper. At thirty he was one of the richest men in the world.

Ten years later, when he met Jean-Luc Delbeau, Menarchos was a legend. The stories that spread about him were fanciful, often scurrilous, and usually true.

He'd been married four times, each time to a woman of voluptuous beauty who was titled or at least wellborn. His background made Menarchos crave legitimacy, and his often shady dealings made him need the protection offered by the acknowledged respectability of his wives' families.

Each of his wives left him under mysterious circumstances. The first was found dead, her body washed up on the shore of Mykonos. The second entered an asylum. The third simply disappeared after having last been seen at a Canadian homestead. And the last died in a hospital, of unspecified causes. He had no known children.

Sophocles Menarchos was certainly not a "nice" man, everyone agreed who'd met him, but he was fascinating, almost mesmerizing and, despite suspicions that people might have about him, nothing had ever been proved against him, either in business or in his personal life. Only Jean-Luc, who'd been with him now for seven years, knew the perverse forces that drove this man.

"Welcome, sire," Jean-Luc greeted him ironically, with a deep bow.

Menarchos glared, then gave a wide grin and took Jean-Luc in a gorilla's embrace, pounding him heartily on the back. "Little brother, you have forsaken me," he said; and then, suspiciously, "Were you trying to run away?"

"Never," declared Jean-Luc. "Besides, how could I? The world isn't big enough to escape from your sharp sight."

"That's right, isn't it?" he answered happily. "My eye is like God's. I see everything. Who is that?"

Jean-Luc didn't have to turn to know who Menarchos was looking at, or to know that she was returning his stare. "Martine de Nouvel."

"Hmmm. We'll have some fun with that one." He winked.

Jean-Luc felt a flash of white anger. But he'd felt it so

often with this man that he could compose himself in an instant. "Perhaps," he said.

Menarchos gave him a keen look. "I see. The poor boy's in love and means to keep her for himself. Selfish of you, my child. But never mind. The lady will decide." He walked into the room with a flourish.

Jean-Luc prayed that she'd hold him off. He reminded himself that he was the first real man in her life and she'd told him, on their last night in Paris, that she loved him. Certainly she'd come to depend on him and need him.

But did she have the strength to resist Menarchos? If he saw her begin to weaken, Jean-Luc told himself, he would tell her what he knew.

After their last meeting at the St. Regis, Vie was too angry and disappointed in Marty to care what happened to her. Since childhood she'd tried to do right by her sister, to make up for their father's indifference to Marty and his favoritism to herself. For years she'd felt she owed her sister a deep debt, contracted before Marty was born. No more. Since Armand's death, followed immediately by the loss of Hubert, the struggle just to survive took up all her energies. She couldn't handle the problem of Marty and didn't care if she never heard from her again.

But as the months passed, bringing their slow, inexorable healing, Vie sometimes felt uneasy about Marty's disappearance. What if she were in trouble, or ill? Deeply depressed? Vie was still confused about her father's death, unable to understand why a man who had been so on top of the world could shoot himself a few hours later. What if Marty were suicidal, too?

When Mike Parnell phoned in June, saying he'd taken his degree and was now living in New York, Vie was eager to see him. Because she'd met Mike through Marty in a way, she associated him with her. But when he invited her to dinner on Saturday, Vie said she was busy. Since Hubert, she'd not dined with a man. Though she remembered the young lawyer as someone who made her laugh and allowed her to be herself, herself was not someone Vie was comfortable with just yet. One man had killed himself because she didn't recognize his needs; another had

simply decided he didn't want her. Twice abandoned, by
the two men she'd loved most, Vie didn't dare risk herself,
even for dinner. "Sunday afternoon?" she suggested. "Tea
at the Plaza?"

"Well. . . ." His voice sounded disappointed.

"They have strolling violins and trays of pastry," she
cajoled.

Mike laughed. "Right, tea it is. But swear to me it'll
never get around that I'm taking tea and cakes. A rumor
like that could destroy the reputation of a hearty Irish lad
trying to make a living in the Big Apple."

"Not a word. I swear it."

"Four o'clock, then. You'll recognize me by the glint in
my eye and the flush on my cheeks."

After tea they took a stroll through Central Park and
went on to dinner. For the first time since the events in
December, Vie was able to relax completely. She told
Mike of her worries about Marty. He suggested hiring a
private detective to find her.

Vie's first reaction was no. There was something squalid
about looking for your sister through a detective. But next
day at the bank Don Garrison asked her almost immediately, "Do you know where Marty is?"

"No. Why?"

"She's about to turn twenty-one. She's not entitled to
her shares held in escrow yet, but she could reasonably
demand fifty percent of Armand's former shares as her
legitimate inheritance. It might be a good idea to locate
her."

When she returned from the meeting, Vie phoned Mike.
He assured her he'd go through a friend and could
guarantee complete confidentiality. He asked how much
Vie was willing to pay.

"I don't know." She thought a moment. "Anything they
ask, I guess."

"Why? It didn't seem that the two of you are on particularly good terms."

"She's my sister," Vie said flatly.

"I know about that," Mike answered. "Thanks for
yesterday, Vie."

"Thank *you*, Mike. You dragged me out of my shell for

the first time in many months. It was lovely. I felt—well, like a girl, almost."

"You know what I wish, Vie?"

She waited.

"I wish I could have kept you with me all night."

Vie was grateful he couldn't see her blush. "No you don't," she said flippantly. "I'm sure I snore. 'Bye, and thanks."

Ron Dryden, recommended by Mike's friend, came to see Vie at the office on Wednesday. He was young, well-mannered and matter-of-fact. He asked for data only, showing no curiosity about why Marty was to be located or trailed. Vie hired him immediately and wrote out a check for $1000 to cover preliminary expenses.

The trail was faint. All there was to go on was the probability that she'd left New York by ship. When Dryden finally got to Provincetown, she'd been gone so long that most of the fishermen who'd known her were at sea, and only the owners of Porky's could remember something about her going down to New York to see if she could get a job that Johnny Lisbon had lined up for her.

Johnny Lisbon wasn't talking to a cop, he said, and it didn't make a speck of difference to him if the dick was private or not. All that the detective could discover was that the man had known Marty for a brief time.

Dryden tried the New York harbor itself. He went to the passenger lines for lists of their employees. He also went back to the old neighborhood in Brooklyn and, because the photographs showed a girl who'd be a natural for hustling, he sent out word through some of his contacts that he was looking for her.

Vie received monthly reports, none of them particularly encouraging. When she finally learned that her sister had taken a job as a dealer on the S. S. *Nordica,* she was also supplied with the information that Marty had abandoned ship in Casablanca.

Vie shook her head, reading a pattern in Marty's behavior. She'd run away from school only months before graduation. She'd run away from her job on the ship. Always running, escaping whatever she couldn't handle. Vie saw Marty at ten, running out of the kitchen. At fifteen she'd run further, brought back by the police with stolen jewels. The threat of arrest stopped her for a while. With school, then college, it had looked as though Marty was quieting down.

But the pattern must have been etched too deeply, thought Vie. An acid in Marty's brain, telling her to break away, escape confrontation by running out the nearest door. She'd jumped ship.

Wearily Vie drafted an answer to Ron Dryden's telegram, authorizing him to continue abroad and promising another large check. But Vie was sure that by the time he discovered her whereabouts in Casablanca, Marty would have pulled up anchor again and sailed away.

Menarchos was courteous to Marty. More than that. He had the cabin she shared with Jean-Luc filled with fresh roses every day. Beside her plate at dinner each night she found a present from him: first, a gold rose on its stalk, with tiny pearls nestled among the petals; then white coral earrings in the form of water lilies, sparkling with dewdrops of diamonds. Tonight a bracelet of black pearls with a clasp of blood-red rubies.

Jean-Luc sat next to her grimly when she opened the gifts, but he told her to do what she liked with them, adding that she'd be insane to give them back, since they were each worth a bundle. In their cabin, among the roses, he asked, "What would you do if Menarchos wanted you?"

"That's not possible. He has his mistress on board." The stormy affair between Menarchos and Mila, Yugoslavia's most famous actress, was common knowledge. No one had seen Mila yet; she refused to come out of her cabin; but everyone knew she was on the ship.

"Never mind that. Answer my question," Jean-Luc told her firmly.

Marty shook her head. "Don't ask that. You're the only man in my life. You *gave* me my life."

"And you're grateful," he said harshly. "But what if I decided to give you to him? Suppose I made a gift of you to Menarchos. Would you go?"

She shook her head in bewilderment. Did he think so

little of her? Or so much of Menarchos that their own love affair meant nothing? She looked at Jean-Luc, leaning against the doorframe in his white silk dinner jacket, and tried to understand what he was attempting to do to her, to them. Just looking at his eyes could make her wild with wanting him.

"No," she answered, letting her heart speak.

In one long stride he was beside her, holding her tightly against him. "Darling," he murmured. "Marty, love. Stay with me."

"As long as you want," she answered, understanding now that he'd been testing her because he was frightened.

She was comforting him with caresses when a knock came at their cabin door, and he went to answer. "For you," he said, holding out a written invitation for Marty to come have a drink in Menarchos' suite. She was expected immediately, it said.

Marty and Jean-Luc exchanged a long glance. Finally it was he who turned away. "Go," he said in a low voice. "Isn't that what you want?"

They looked at each other again, and this time Marty saw that he was relying on her for the strength to do what he couldn't do himself: oppose Menarchos.

Her bare shoulders gleamed in the candlelight, pale against the jet-black of her taffeta sleeves. Her mouth was scarlet; to Menarchos, it looked like a bleeding wound set in her face.

"Have more calvados, my dear. It's older than you, and just as smooth down the gullet."

He watched her lips while she sipped, then moved his eyes down to her full bosom. He pictured the white skin, the dark nipples. He'd order her to rouge them in deep purple, covering the areolas. Her naked breasts would appear tipped with heavy bruises from where he sat when he told her to strip.

Marty sipped the rich apple brandy, feeling his eyes undress her. She was used to that and had always taken it as a compliment. But her habitual ease with men deserted her in the presence of Menarchos. She'd never met anyone, anything, like him. She could think of nothing to say, and she wanted to hide from this man who was like a hurricane, whose force flattened everything he found in his way.

During the past three days she'd seen him turn with fury on anyone who displeased him, even by a single word. She'd seen the look on his face, the glint in his eyes that made her shudder. It was her first encounter with pure evil.

"Show me your breasts," Menarchos said in a voice that was low and threatening.

Marty remained in her chair, powerless as Menarchos came toward her. Taking hold of her shoulders, he pulled her to her feet. His hands were on the front of her dress, his eyes fixed on her face when he called out, "Enter."

Marty was aware that someone had been knocking. Jean-Luc came into the room through a side door. She tried to turn toward him, but she was as though hypnotized, unable to control her movements.

Jean-Luc looked at her, then at Menarchos. He nodded to his employer and said, "Excuse me." He turned stiffly and walked out, again through the private door.

Menarchos released Marty and gave her a lazy smile. "You can leave your dress on for now," he told her as he went back to his seat. "Sit down and finish your drink."

She obeyed him, shaking.

Going back to his stateroom, Jean-Luc felt anger, disappointment, fear. Fear most of all. It had all happened too quickly for him to use the final weapon he'd been saving up: the weapon of revelation.

He'd primed Marty for him, knew that Menarchos would fall for the full-breasted young woman if he could make her seem plausible as a member of the upper class. It worked, obviously—but not the way Jean-Luc had planned. He'd meant it to backfire in Menarchos' face, not in his own.

Why hadn't he told her before what he knew about Menarchos' sexual appetites?

Jean-Luc had learned about his employer's predilections when he visited Menarchos' second wife in the asylum. He'd gone out of curiosity, hoping to understand why all the women had fallen away from so powerful a man. Rosemary, a delicate English rose with wrists narrow as a

chicken's leg, her enormous breasts impaled on a scare-
crow's body, had no sense of who Jean-Luc was. But she
told him her former husband's secret—both of his secrets.

"The children, don't you see?" she'd said in a dreadful
whisper. "He kept ordering up more of them. They were
driven away, after he'd finished with them, in a large
black motorcar. They'd never speak when they left the
house. Pale as paper moths, bless them, with their blood
sucked out and their staring eyes." She grabbed hold of
Jean-Luc's arm. "And then there was me. The other side
of the emperor's coin. Adult women, large breasts. That's
what he chose for his hatred. To put out his cigarettes,
take a razor and cut them up."

Jean-Luc had extricated himself from her bony hand
and run out of the asylum. He knew she was mad, she'd
been certified as a madwoman and her family had left her
there to her disgraceful fantasies. But in the following
years Rosemary's words had come back to him as he saw
schoolchildren brought into Menarchos' study. He was
never sure that all of those who went in came out again.

Jean-Luc had never let on, and he'd never told what he
knew to anyone else. Menarchos had made him a rich
man, treated him like a younger brother, had become his
family and shield against the law. Jean-Luc was now so
implicated in several of Menarchos' deals, transactions he
accomplished through extortion or blackmail, that he knew
Menarchos would sacrifice him in an instant if he tried to
reveal anything.

It was none of his business, Jean-Luc told himself. A
man's sex life was private. He didn't believe that the
deaths of Menarchos' first and last wives were accidental,
or even self-inflicted, but he recognized that the man he
worked for was a figure larger than justice, who would
never be brought to account but who could easily send a
meddler to his death. He was trapped and had been for
many years. Marty represented Jean-Luc's hope to become his own man, which meant to him a person who
could control another. He'd hoped, and half-believed, that
she'd be able to reject Menarchos, thereby freeing them
both, himself and her, to escape from the dark realm and

start a life together. He'd felt more affection for Marty than for any woman he could remember.

But she was just one more in Menarchos' net, he saw, another trinket Menarchos could buy and use any way he wished. Jean-Luc couldn't protect her; he told himself she'd made her own decision.

Trouble was, he couldn't believe it.

He didn't go back to their cabin. Instead he went straight to the bar and downed one drink after another until he could barely stand upright. Then he weaved his way to the deck and sank into a chair.

He woke with a sense of imbalance, as though the world had tilted on its axis. There was consternation around him, people running and talking excitedly. When his mind finally cleared enough for the sounds to be heard as speech, he understood that Marty had jumped into the sea.

3

"A mermaid!" exclaimed George Barclay, second son of Lord and Lady Exeter, as he ran to help Marty out of the lapping waves.

"Please shut up," she said and sank into his arms.

He dragged her to a high, dry part of the beach, removed the life jacket she was wearing, and held her in a sitting position while he struggled to fit his sweater over her. She murmured alternately, "Thank you" and "Go away," so that he knew she hadn't fainted, she was simply exhausted from her time in the water.

Lovely girl, he thought, who really did resemble a mermaid. The long black skirt of her dress molded her legs together into what looked like a tail. She was breathing very rapidly. He took her pulse; it was rapid.

Her lashes, long and thick, rested against her lower lids. He sat down on the sand beside her, content to watch her sleeping. She must have come off the *Apollo*, he decided, the splendid yacht just anchored offshore. George Barclay had noticed it when he took his early morning jog along the beach, and later, at breakfast, the waiter had told him it was the Menarchos yacht.

"Welcome to Torremolinos," he told her when she opened her eyes. "I hope you had a pleasant swim."

Marty grinned. The cool, clipped accent made everything sound rational, as though escaping through the water in an evening dress were the most natural thing in the world. "Not bad," she told him, "but next time I'm going to take swimming lessons before I set out."

"Yes," he agreed, "that's helpful. And you might buy yourself a bathing costume. I believe that's what they're wearing for the sport this year. Name's George Barclay," he said, extending his hand.

"Martine de Nouvel." She regretted it the moment she said it, but Jean-Luc's drilling had branded the name into her, and it came out spontaneously. Jean-Luc. Would he come after her? "Please," she said to the young Englishman, "do you know where I can get some dry clothes?"

"Follow me," he said, pulling her up. "Or would you prefer to be carried?"

"I'll walk." But she was unsteady on her bare feet and had to lean against George for support as they started into town.

He took her to a villa, his parents' "escape hatch" in the south, and there servants ran her bath, brought her hot tea and whiskey, prepared her bed, and laid out an assortment of clothes.

When she awoke, it was late afternoon and she was ravenous. Marty dressed in a pair of wool knickers with long stockings, a man's silk shirt, and a brown cardigan. She guided her feet into leather slippers and made her way downstairs.

"You look spiffy, my dear," said George, approvingly.

"I've had Cook prepare us a high tea. Will you have a sherry before?"

She relaxed over the delicious meal of scones and jam, tiny sandwiches of cucumber, watercress, radishes, and cheese. She ate the warm pork pie and the Scotch eggs, ending her feast with a large slice of rhubarb pie and cream. "Is this what Old England tastes like?" she asked the flaxen-haired man who looked to be about the same age as herself.

"Have you never been? No? How super! Then you must join me, as my guest, when I return day after next. Father and Mummy will be thrilled. Do come."

She smiled. "I'd love to but I don't have my passport."

"Not to worry. I'm known at the American consulate in Madrid. You'll have what you need tomorrow."

She nodded in relief. If Jean-Luc—or worse, Menarchos—came to look for her, she'd have flown away. No one could possibly think of searching for her in England. At the thought of Menarchos' rage Marty trembled. He'd kill her if he found her, she was sure of that. But if she escaped, he'd probably let her go. She knew he had nothing to fear from her. Even if she told about the razors strapped to his fingers, no one would believe it. And *if* they believed, Marty realized, there was no one in the world who would be able to do anything about it. If he saw her in his path, he'd kill her in momentary annoyance. But if she kept out of sight, Marty was sure she'd be safe. Where in the world, she wondered, were all the other women Menarchos had taken, or tried to take? Terrified and lacerated, most of them must still be alive, hiding their dreadful secret in shame and horror.

At least she'd escaped without a cut. But Jean-Luc must have known, and still he'd made no move to protect her. However sick she felt at the thought of Menarchos, she hated Jean-Luc more. Jean-Luc was the man she'd loved! She'd obeyed him as she had no one else, she had given him all of herself; and yet he'd been willing to sacrifice her to a moment of Menarchos' pleasure.

"I'd love to go to England," she told George Barclay. "I'm just in the mood for a change of scene."

How amusing she was! thought George. Cast up on the

shore like a beached mermaid only hours ago, and bored already at teatime. "Marvelous spirit," he said approvingly. "You're rather like my old mother."

Marty couldn't have had a more ideal rescuer. Rich, English-speaking, George Barclay regarded the world as a place of continuing entertainment. His tolerance for anything at all was so great that it never occurred to him to ask Marty why she'd been in the water in an evening gown without knowing how to swim. If he'd thought about it at all, he would have concluded that she'd become bored on the ship and had simply decided to strike out for somewhere more entertaining.

She was amazed that he asked no questions, and at first she suspected that he might know about her, perhaps even be an acquaintance of Menarchos himself. But his smiling pale-blue eyes, his perpetual agreeableness, soon convinced Marty that life was a kind of joke to him, and if he missed the point sometimes, he preferred to let it go rather than having the joke explained to him.

She went to bed after their high tea, slept sixteen hours, and when she woke, they went shopping for clothes and luggage. In the evening they packed and next morning took a flight to Madrid, from where they caught the plane to London.

No sign of her in Casablanca, came the report, and it didn't seem worthwhile to fan out into the country or to other cities of Morocco. She'd been seen leaving the ship in the company of a man Interpol had down as Jean el-Dhouni, a racketeer operating under the protection of Sophocles Menarchos, and going by different aliases.

Martine probably knew him as Jean-Luc Delbeau, the report went on, since that was the name on the *Nordica*'s passenger list, a name el-Dhouni used for his more or less legitimate business.

To save Vie's wallet from depletion, Dryden had suggested that his agency contact its man in the south of France to locate Menarchos, in hopes that el-Dhouni and Martine were with him. It could be that they were all on his yacht *Apollo*, now cruising the Mediterranean.

Even without sending a man overseas, the costs of the

investigation were becoming considerable. Vie had sent
three checks of $1000 each during the past ten days, and
she didn't know when it would stop. She looked so distressed when Murray Schwartzman, the sales manager,
walked into her office that he chucked her under the chin
and said, "Bossbaby, you look like you lost your best
friend, or your last nickel."

"Close," she said. "Actually, it's my sister and my bank
account."

"Tell Papa."

"A dreary business, Murray. My younger sister is running loose somewhere in Europe, probably with a bunch
of crooks, and I'm shelling out a fortune to private investigators who can't catch up with her."

"Wow," he said, opening his eyes wide. "You could
write a book!"

"It wouldn't bring me in enough to pay those detectives,"
she answered with a sad smile.

"What do you want to get hold of her for? Outside the
obvious fact that she's family, of course."

"There's a problem with the transfer of my father's
shares, now that Martine's not a minor anymore. I've let
it ride, but the lawyers and accountants are pressuring
me, and I need her signature on a few documents."

"I'll forge it, sweetheart. Let me be your little sister."

"Nobody'd believe it," she said, shaking her head.

"OK, then adopt me. I'll get the papers ready. But
seriously, bossbaby, I tell you what you should do: go
after her."

"What? When experienced bloodhounds can't find her?
Where would I look?"

"There's instinct in families, like them sticks to find
water. You get near where she is, you start feeling it in
your bones."

"You're crazy, Murray! Besides, we're not even true
sisters, just half."

"Then you feel it in half your bones."

"Murray," she said, looking at him seriously, "I sometimes think I was out of my mind when I hired you."

"Better believe it. All the women go nuts when I'm
around."

"Out of my office!" she ordered, laughing helplessly.

But later she thought: Why not give it a try? What's to lose? She could combine the trip with business, visit suppliers in the south of France, and go back via Paris and London, to renew contacts with Jolay distributors. On her former trip Vie had left out Paris. She couldn't bear to go to the city she might have lived in as Hubert's wife. But she couldn't keep avoiding it, she told herself; it was too important for business, and her agent had reported that Paris Jolay was feeling slighted by her.

A good time to make amends and hold out her stick to see if she could locate Marty. Murray and Elaine could hold the fort between them for two weeks. She'd settle all urgent pending business and fly off. "Elaine," she said into the intercom, "could you book me a flight to Marseilles a week from Monday? And start setting up appointments in Paris and London for the week after that?"

"My dear George," said his mother, holding out her cheek for him to brush with his. "How divine that you've come! Just too kind that you took the time to break away from all that jogging! Ah, you've brought somebody. How clever of you, darling, just when we needed another woman! Never enough of them, don't you know, for the hunting season."

"This is Martine de Nouvel, Mummy. I found her on the beach in a drenched evening gown that she'd worn to swim away from Menarchos' yacht."

"Did you really? How do you do? Are the two of you sleeping together, or would you prefer a separate room?"

"Separate, please," answered Marty.

Lady Exeter sighed. "Oh dear, I was afraid you'd say that. My darling George is so timid about that sort of thing. Can't imagine where he gets it from. I suppose we'll put you in the Camellia Room. Needs airing, though. Hasn't been used since poor Blakey Spofford suffocated under her bedclothes."

"Is she for real?" Marty asked when his mother had left the room.

"Oh yes," George answered, "Mummy's very real. In fact, she's the realest person I know."

But Marty couldn't believe it. And when she met the other house guests, she felt they were acting out parts in a play. Everyone was saying clever things all the time, no one ever took anything seriously, and their accents were so clipped that she had a hard time following. She could think of nothing to say, and though she knew the chatter was regarded as witty, she felt she couldn't stomach any more of it. Everyone was so damned superior; they all had their noses in the air, and no one paid the slightest attention to her. Not even George, who now seemed to regard her as dull among all these glittering wits.

She wouldn't join them on the hunt because she didn't know how to ride. Lady Exeter looked at her in amazement. "Just where did you grow up, my dear?"

"New York—and Greenwich," she said, hating her trained response.

"They have horses, don't they?"

"No. I mean, yes, but I never learned to ride."

"How perfectly extraordinary!" she said, looking at Marty as though she'd dropped from another planet.

Lord Exeter turned to her. "Who is your family?"

She stared at him and found herself unable to answer. The invented history of Jean-Luc rose to her lips, but she wouldn't let it out. Lord Exeter was waiting. Lady Exeter looked at her expectantly.

"I don't know!" she shouted and ran out of the room.

When the party returned from hunting, they discovered that the American girl had driven off in one of the family cars. "Good Lord!" said George's father, shocked.

"She seems to have taken the household money from the piggy in the kitchen, sir," said the maid with a little curtsy.

"And the two gold plates from the side table," said another maid.

"As well as the Queen Anne dinner service," added the butler.

"A disgrace!" Lord Exeter cast a baleful look at his son. "That girl you brought—she's a common thief!"

"Really?" said Lady Exeter. "How divine!"

*   *   *

Following the signs to London, Marty drove the dark gray Rover through Gloucestershire. If George's parents alerted the police, she'd be stopped any moment. She hadn't even bothered to do anything about the license plates. She didn't own a license, but she'd learned to drive in Cambridge and had used Johnny Lisbon's car in Provincetown. Luckily that had been a shift car too, also with four forward gears.

She drove quickly, her eyes glued to the road. If she got caught, she wouldn't even bother to resist. But right now she was concentrating on escaping, getting away from those terrible, superior people who made her feel like nothing. She didn't feel any obligation to George. He'd rescued her in Torremolinos and given her a way to get beyond the reach of Menarchos and Jean-Luc. Fine, great—but she meant nothing to him, Marty knew. An amusement, that was all.

It was the same thing with Jean-Luc. He'd picked her up, won her in a card game, and then used her for his own purposes. She was his property until she got away.

Who the fuck am I? she thought fiercely, her tears beginning to blur the road. She ordered herself to stop crying, and obeyed instantly. George belongs in that awful world with his crazy mother. Jean-Luc belongs to Menarchos. And me?

When Lord Exeter had asked her about her family, Marty felt something in her give. Now, running away again as she'd done so often, Marty realized she'd never stop running until she found out who or what she really belonged to. Armand was dead, Vie was only her half-sister. She'd had a mother too, once—a person about whom she knew nothing.

Gripping the steering wheel with force, Marty realized that Armand had never talked about her mother—only Vie's—and for the first time she realized that she had never, in all her life, asked him anything about her own mother.

"Jesus Christ!" she said aloud. The road was clear. She was dry-eyed and alert as a hawk ready to swoop. She saw her objective plainly: Before she moved any further, Marty had to go back into the past. There she would search for her mother.

When she got to the city, Marty abandoned the car, congratulating herself on her good luck at not being caught. She didn't know it wasn't luck; she didn't understand people like Lord and Lady Exeter, to whom the messy business of pressing charges and being made to appear in court was as unthinkable as drinking coffee at teatime. They preferred to do nothing, trusting the car would somehow be restored to them, and perhaps the smaller objects as well. Marty was unwittingly playing their game when she left the Rover in Knightsbridge. She kept the gold and silver, however, and the cash. One hundred twenty pounds—worth about $200.

She stepped into the large department store—Harrods—hoping to find a locker where she could leave the heavy bag. Harrods reminded her of Bloomingdale's combined with Magdahl-Hoffman. It was vast and rich; you could feel the wealth, like invisible curtains draping each counter. She walked past the perfumes and stopped dead when she saw the smiling face framed by pale gold hair. "Miss Vie Jolay will be present at Harrods on March 29," read the caption underneath, "to introduce her newest fragrance, *Cabal*."

"Can I help you, madame?" came a voice from behind.

She whirled around so quickly that she nearly knocked the man off his feet with her suitcase. "Yeah," she said in flat Brooklyn, "I need to get out of this place."

"The travel agency is on the third floor, madame," he answered in his upper-class accent.

Marty gaped at him and then let out a great happy laugh of astonishment. "You betcha, kid," she told him and began lugging her haul over to the elevator, while the nonplussed salesman shook his head at the never-ending comedy provided by Americans abroad.

The plan was to end her tour in England with a presentation at Harrods. Despite Murray's assurance that family instinct would guide the way, Vie hadn't come any closer to Marty's whereabouts than the detectives. In fact, her latest information—that Marty was aboard the *Apollo* and that the ship was now cruising along the coast of North Africa, after a few days' holdover on Spain's Costa del Sol—had come from the agent's report. It also said that Menarchos would permit no one to board his ship, which was heavily guarded at all times and which carried guns. Further progress in the investigation would have to wait until *Apollo* docked, and that would be at a place and time determined only by Menarchos' whim.

With Marty on the high seas, Vie resigned herself to following her business itinerary. She flew to Paris and checked in at the Georges V, where she found her room ablaze with flowers. From my admirers, she thought sardonically, all of whom are wooing me for my business.

She directed the bellboy where to put her luggage and hung up the raincoat she was wearing over her suit, its fur lining packed because of the mild weather. When she'd tipped the boy and he'd gone, Vie went over to the bouquets to read the cards. The prettiest was a loose arrangement of field flowers and the card she lifted out read, "To our bossbaby, the best in the field. Success, love, Murray and Elaine." She smiled as she bent down to smell the wonderful blend of wild perfumes. The traditional long-stemmed roses came from Jolay Paris.

The most extraordinary of the bouquets consisted of many varieties of orchid, speckled and smooth, colors ranging from deep brown to white, but no gaudy purple. She picked up the card, gasped, and let it fall to the floor. It landed with the written side up: "En garde! Hubert."

She held on to the table's edge. Why was he doing this? Oh God, she prayed, looking down at the handwriting, don't make me have to go through that again.

She'd seen Montalmont perfumes dominate a counter that Jolay was meant to rule and had felt, going to the manager to rearrange the display, that fencing was all that remained of what they'd had together. Their houses had not laid down the challenge; but the love match was long since dead.

He'd married the one he'd mentioned to her, the wealthy Danielle with a châteauful of ancestors. Vie knew it from gossip columns; she'd had no word from him since their last night in his bedroom at the Pierre.

Vie sat down on the bed, feeling she didn't have the strength to go through with her Paris visit. Would he follow his card with a call? What was it he wanted? Could he possibly be so callous as to be still running after her business? And was this all he'd wanted from her, throughout their affair?

She couldn't believe that. No one could be such a consummate actor. But why, then, had it ended so abruptly, in such brutal silence? She felt again, as she often had, looking back on those five worst days in her life, that Armand's suicide was obscurely connected with Hubert's decision. She had no real reason to think so, but an instinct, persistent and sure, told her he would have returned to her if her father hadn't died.

Despite the horror she had felt at the moment of discovering his bloody body, Vie had removed the paper with "Armand Jolaunay" written on it before she called the ambulance. She recognized the name, of course, but why was that her father's stark, final message?

Vie never mentioned what she'd found to anyone. In the agitation and depression of the days following, she could think only one step at a time: arrange the funeral, call Marty, call friends, select something black to wear. But the name kept hammering at the back of her brain until, without effort, she had an explanation: her father hadn't merely worked *at* Jolaunay, he *was* Jolaunay.

The pieces began to fit together. The magic book from which he'd developed his "classical" fragrances contained formulas from one of the greatest perfumers of the century. Armand's arrogance combined with his fear of trying again: these traits would suit the man who had once stood at the acme of French perfumery. His sense of pride when he talked about the Jolaunay family history, his seemingly senseless hatred of Montalmont—all these were explained.

A Montalmont had set fire to the shop of Claude Jolaunay. Did the roots of Armand's hatred extend back over generations? Or had the feud continued in his lifetime? The rumors about Armand Jolaunay said he was dead and that he'd been a collaborator during the war. But if

Jolaunay was her father, Vie thought, that meant the first rumor was false. Perhaps the second also. She'd never know for sure, and Vie realized she wouldn't try to dig up the past. She'd leave it sealed, as he had done.

She sat on her bed, looking down at the floor where Hubert's card still lay. Her father had left the single message of his true name for her alone to read. He was telling her why he had chosen that time to die. Armand must have seen Hubert's visit as a repetition of the past, Montalmont coming to Jolaunay. This triggered old memories, too unbearable for her father to live with.

The phone rang. Vie jerked her head up and stared at it. It rang again, and went on ringing.

Hubert had ordered the most beautiful flowers he could find to be sent to Vie Jolay at the Georges V. He hoped she would understand; it was the most he could do without exposing any of them.

Since the last time he'd seen her, Hubert had tried to forget Vie. But he carried the imprint of her face in his thoughts. His marriage the following spring had done nothing to erase her image; his mind was a trap from which memories of Vie would never escape. Conversations came back; he remembered every meal they'd eaten together, her brilliance in fencing, and most of all, her body with its wonderful aroma.

The orchids were meant as a tribute to her rare beauty, and for that reason he had rejected the conventional purple. But the card was a warning.

Henri Montalmont was still the head of the company, though he had celebrated his seventy-fifth birthday in May. Hubert refused to see him except on professional matters. He'd closed his father off from his private life—but business was something he couldn't escape.

The break between son and father had come a few days before Hubert was to return to New York to hear Vie's decision. They'd had angry words on the subject of the American girl Hubert hoped to marry and had traveled separately to Grasse for the annual inspection of the harvest.

It was a dark, wet afternoon when they had begun

walking across the fields together. Without preamble, Henri jumped into the subject of Vie. "The girl is Jolay, right?"

"Yes."

"And the sample of perfume you brought back, the one called *Taj*, that's made by Jolay?"

"Yes. It's very successful."

"No doubt—so it was when it first came out in the thirties."

"What do you mean?" Hubert asked, stopping still in the cold rain to look at his father. A rumble of thunder sounded in the distance.

"I mean that it's nothing more than a remake of *Âme*, by Armand Jolaunay. You remember him, don't you? The Nazi traitor. He's the father of your intended." Henri gave his son a look of triumph.

"I knew I'd smelled that scent before," Henri went on. "At first I didn't know where. Then I identified it, and I had a nice little investigation made over there in your America. That's when I learned the traitor still lives. He, who supplied les Boches while the great House of Montalmont was closed in patriotic duty and I labored in the Resistance for the glory of France! If you so much as look at that daughter of his again," said Henri menacingly, "I will expose her and her father to the world and destroy them!"

"You wouldn't."

Henri merely smiled. Hubert raised his hands to plant them firmly around his father's throat when a crash of thunder unnerved him. He let his hands fall; the old man was still looking at him with an unchanged smile on his wet, wrinkled face.

Two days after that, on the Friday before his departure for New York, Hubert received a note delivered by hand in his Paris office. The handwriting was his father's. "Justice is done," it said. "The traitor is no more."

In that moment Hubert knew that Vie was forever dead to him.

She kept staring at the phone until it stopped ringing. Then she stood up and retrieved the card from the floor. En garde! meant the beginning of a duel. How could he be so cruel as to ask her to pick up her sword again, after he'd thrown it down?

But when the phone rang again, she answered. It wasn't the voice she feared and hoped for, however. M. Sauveterre, her business agent, was calling to welcome Vie to Paris and remind her of the soiree she was expected to attend later that evening.

He picked her up at eight, and they drove to a small château outside Paris, where the Marquis de St.-Denis was giving one of the parties he was celebrated for, attended by cabinet ministers, financiers, actresses, and successful novelists. The Marquis enjoyed mixing people from different milieus, and at his parties newspaper editors chatted with jockeys, labor leaders with duchesses, artists with politicians. He provided the setting in his enchanting sixteenth-century small castle, reached by drawbridge over a moat, and made sure the wine was of admirable vintage and the food both delicate and unusual.

Vie's heart wasn't in it, but she put on the beige-and-gold tapestried gown by Oscar de la Renta, a small tiara of white gold with seed pearls and opals, and the Roger Vivier pumps with their single accent of gold leather.

When she entered the château's mirrored ballroom, the crowd parted to make way as M. Sauveterre led her to greet their host. The Marquis bowed low over her hand. "You do me honor, madame," he said in English. "It is a privilege to be able to welcome a queen."

She smiled at his extravagance and moved on, with her agent, to get a glass of champagne. Before she had time to drink it, a burly man with angry eyebrows asked her to dance. "France's most eminent physicist," whispered M. Sauveterre.

She could never get back to her glass. Whenever the music stopped, another man came up to tap her partner's back and to ask, "Permettez?" She was caught up in dance after dance, her shoes tightening as the evening wore on, but she didn't want to stop, feeling young and carefree, her thoughts banished by movement and music.

Despite the formality of the château and the clothing of the guests, the band was playing a twist, a Gallic version of a song that had come out of New York's Peppermint

Lounge ten years earlier. Vie let herself go, not bothering whether she had it right, letting the rhythm work through her body, forcing her to gyrate to the beat. She was nearly out of breath but went on twisting until the number ended. Panting, she looked up and met his gaze.

Hubert's face was drained of blood, his lips dry. Her own lips parted, but her gasp was almost soundless. Neither of them said anything as they stared across the dancers, seeing only each other. Neither moved until the music started again and he disappeared in the swirl of moving bodies.

Her agent came up to Vie. "Hubert Montalmont is here, with his wife. I just saw him. Perhaps you would like me to introduce you? He is an important person for you to meet."

"Thank you," she said, collecting herself with great effort. "We've already run into each other. And now, could you take me back, please? I'm tired, it's been a long evening."

"Of course, Miss Jolay. And you have a full day ahead of you tomorrow."

But next morning Vie checked out of the hotel. She left all her flowers behind and rode out to the airport, where she booked a seat on the next shuttle to London.

She'd canceled her appointments, claiming an emergency. Seeing Hubert last night showed her she wasn't strong enough to remain in Paris and risk meeting him again: her rival, the man she still loved deeply.

4

By air shuttle the two greatest cities on either side of the Channel are within fifty minutes of each other. Marty sat looking out the window as she strapped her belt for landing. She recognized many landmarks of Paris below. Sacré-Coeur, the Étoile with its Arch of Triumph, Notre Dame. She'd visited these with Jean-Luc, speaking only French because it was during their "school" hours.

She'd make him pay, she told herself. The bastard owes me.

Not now, though, she reminded herself. Revenge would have to wait. He probably wasn't in France in any case, and she'd flown here to start her search, to see if she could discover roots or even branches of a family she belonged to and knew nothing about.

She took the metro from the airport and went directly to the Gare de Lyons, where she boarded a train destined for Marseilles. She was working on the slimmest of clues, the only one she possessed.

"Could be in the south," Jean-Luc had said, handing the picture back to her. "But who can tell? It's a terrible photograph."

Marty didn't know why she'd been keeping it with her all these years, wherever she went, from the girls' school to college and then across the ocean on the *Nordica* to Paris. She always kept it in her wallet with the bills. It was probably destroyed by now, she guessed. Menarchos wouldn't have held on to it as a souvenir. Probably he didn't bother to check what was in her bag before he threw it away or hurled it overboard.

Riding through the ripening valleys and orchards, her only lead resting in the memory of a faded photograph—image of an image—she told herself: sure ain't much. She reconstructed the snapshot in her mind's eye. Not difficult. She'd looked at it so often, she knew it by heart.

It was a black-and-white print, turned gray through the years and imperfectly focused, showing Armand in the foreground, standing at a tilt with a baby—herself—in his arms and Vie standing next to him. She must have been three or four.

Marty had never been able to make out her own features—just a blur of baby—but Armand's were clear. He looked young, with a neat mustache. Handsome, but with a fearful look on his face, as though something was about to spring on him from behind and he knew it. At his side, Vie looked more like a doll than a real child.

The angle distorted them. They were posed in front of a crenellated stone wall, between two turrets. It could have been a movie set, with unpracticed actors posing for an incompetent photographer. But Marty knew it must have been taken in the town where she was born and that the photographer must have been her mother.

Mother. Odile.

Her first name, a stone wall in France, and the information that she'd worked in, or owned, a pharmacy: that was all Marty had to go by. And the tools she had for her detective work were a good enough command of French to be taken as a native, a small cache of gold and silver to take care of her expenses, and an urgent need to uncover the past.

Farms and terraced villages were framed a moment by the train window and then slid back. With each village they passed, Marty wondered if this could be the one, if that was where she was born.

"You are very interested in the landscape," commented the stout man who was sitting in the compartment with her, puffing sweet smoke from his Gauloise.

What the hell, she thought, and told him what she was looking for: a town or village with an old stone wall and turrets.

"But of course I know!" he said importantly. "You are

describing Fougères. An old fortified town, with a great wall and the castle rising up—as a child I looked at it in wonder!" He smiled tenderly at the memory of himself as a boy.

"Where is it, what part of France?"

"In Brittany, the northern part. My parents took me there when I was—"

"How do I get there?" she asked impatiently.

"But, mademoiselle, you are going in the wrong direction!" He laughed heartily. "Fougères is in the north, and you are traveling south!" He seemed to find it the most marvelous joke in the world.

She got off the train twelve minutes later, at the next stop, Clermont-Ferrand. It appeared to be a junction, but the stationmaster told her they had no trains going to Brittany. She must return to Paris, take the train headed for Brest, and get off at Rennes. The next train to Paris would be leaving in exactly six hours and fifteen minutes.

She was cold and restless. The coat they'd bought in London on the way to George's parents offered more style than protection. She ordered an onion soup and a half-liter of red wine in the station restaurant and decided she'd stay in Paris long enough to unload the family silver and maybe the gold plates as well. No point carting the stuff around with her, and besides, she needed money.

When she arrived in the city the following morning, Marty went over to where the boat train came in. An hour's work, using her skills in French and in flirting, combined with her street knowledge, got Marty to a dealer who took all the hardware off her hands for a price far beyond her fantasies. Since nobody could be that honest, she figured the stuff was worth at least four or five times what he paid her: $6000 worth in a mixture of currencies, and she believed him when he said the money was clean.

She bought herself two heavy sweaters, a large bar of chocolate, and a bottle of whiskey. Then, with a suitcase that seemed filled with air compared to what she'd been dragging along, Marty boarded the train for Rennes and on to Fougères.

It was a walled town with turrets, though Marty couldn't

find a stretch of wall framed by two towers as shown on the photograph. The shops were already closing; it was late afternoon, time for an apéritif before dinner. But first she took a room at the Hotel de Commerce, with a large brass bed, washstand, and heavy armoire. She went down for a meal, returned at eight, and taking off only her coat, fell on the bed and slept until dawn.

When she stepped out for breakfast, the air was teeming with birds. Swallows and house martins dived in front of her; blue tits bustled in the awakening branches. March had only a week to go before it died into April, when full rebirth would bring blossoms to the trees.

After a café complet with a basketful of petit pain and a pot of marmalade, Marty set out feeling as sunny as the morning. But before noon she'd been to every pharmacy in town, and to the three other shops that carried fragrances. No one knew the name Nouvel, Odile or Armand. No one recognized the description she offered of her father. Whoever she asked gave her a blank look, or a suspicious one. They could see by her speech and movements that she didn't come from around these parts. Her French was too smooth, her gestures too fast—probably a Parisian. No, they answered to all her questions.

She made a circuit of the wall, but nowhere could she find the exact setting of the picture.

What next? She'd already paid for tonight's lodging in the Hotel de Commerce—the concierge had demanded to know if she was staying the night before Marty went to breakfast—and now, with hours to kill before nightfall, she went up to visit the château.

The priest who greeted her retained only a few wisps of ashy hair on his narrow scalp, and when he smiled, which was almost constantly, he displayed the four remaining yellow teeth in his mouth. He was very friendly, eager for company, and insisted on taking mademoiselle for a tour of the castle. She agreed only because she had nothing else to do, but hardly paid attention to his tedious historical lecture. It was almost over when they stepped into the room containing the last duke's hunting trophies: stuffed birds, antlers, the tusks of a boar. On one wall hung an etching of a walled town. "Is that Fougères?" she asked the little man.

His lips curled away from his gums to display the yellow teeth. "But no, mademoiselle! Do you not recognize Carcassonne? It is une merveille, a marvel of France since the time of the Romans and the Visigoths. It is, I am forced to admit, even more splendid than our beautiful Fougères, which is known, however, as the Carcassonne of Brittany."

"Where is the town?" she asked, stepping up to study the picture carefully. The crenellated walls around the château were sentried by turrets close enough to each other to frame a snapshot.

"In the south, not far from Toulouse, near the Spanish border."

She thanked her guide, made a contribution toward further restoration of the château, and ran out, her hopes swirling ahead. She'd forfeit the advance on her room, she decided, and set out immediately. To the south!

On the train again, its final destination Marseilles, she realized how dumb she'd been to attempt the north. As a little girl Marty had known they sailed to America from "Ma Say" in France, and she used to picture plump Ma, waving good-bye with a large red handkerchief as their sailboat drifted out to sea. Ma Say, of course! How could she have taken so long to recognize it as Marseilles? The south, that's where she came from.

Slate streaks across silver gave Carcassonne the backdrop of a Gothic fairytale. At the top of the hill, the château rose up from the fortified cité in charcoal-gray silhouette, its coned roofs appearing as spikes to hold up the ash-and-silver sky. It was a wintry day for the south, unusual at this time of year.

The river Aude, like a pewter ribbon, ran below the cité, under the old bridge into the bustling low town, Carcassonne Ville Basse.

Marty turned in at the first pharmacy she came to, on the rue de Verdun. The old woman behind the counter wiped her glasses. "Odile?" she repeated. "Ah yes, I remember Odile." Marty strained forward eagerly as the woman continued. "Bright red hair, like a carrot. Oh she was a terror, that one! Such a tragic death!"

"What happened?" Marty breathed.

"She was run over by a train. They *say* she fell, but I know better." The old woman paused significantly. "And I know who pushed her. Her own husband! He was having a liaison with the butcher's daughter. Everyone knew. They married a month after Odile's death, and the child was born six months later!"

"When was that?"

"Let me think. It was before we moved to the rue de Verdun. 1940? No, wait, it was before the war, 1939."

Marty felt the eddies of disappointment. That was long before she was born, even before Vie was born. "Thank you," she said.

"Wait! I will tell you what happened to the child of the butcher's. . . ."

But Marty was already out the door.

She continued her search. Carcassonne was twice as large as Fougères, with three times as many pharmacies. But the answers were the same as in the other town.

Toward closing hour, Marty came to the main square, where an old well stood at the center. On one side of the square Marty saw a pharmacy and hurried toward it. The bells tinkled as she walked in, and the middle-aged couple behind the counter looked up in annoyance. She could see they were starting to put things away for the night. Behind them, bottles with brightly colored liquids lined the shelves, looking like something from a children's book.

"Pardon," Marty said. "Do you know the name of Odile Nouvel, or her husband, Armand Nouvel? They worked in a pharmacy in Carcassonne during the war."

"Nouvel?" said the man, whose features were taffy in the sagging flesh of his face. "Armand Nouvel? No, never heard of him."

She turned to leave when his birdlike wife chirped, "Don't you remember, mon vieux? Someone used to make perfumes here, a stranger. Was not his name Armand?" She said to Marty, now standing directly in front of her, "But that was *after* the war. I remember exactly."

"Yes," Marty agreed. "It's possible. Please tell me more."

The woman ignored Marty and addressed herself to her husband. "The one who ran away—you must remember, Lucien. Le grand scandale. How shocked we were to discover he was a German!"

"You are speaking of the one who came into the Benoit family, mon chou? Benoit the war hero. . . ."

"Yes of course, Lucien, my pet. The old man in the wheelchair. His daughter was running the store when the Suarez family bought it."

"And sold it four months later," he said with a sneer.

"To us," she reminded him. "The Benoit daughter—Odile, that was her name."

"Odile Nouvel? Was her husband's name Armand Nouvel?" Marty pressed.

The woman shrugged. "He was a German, disguised as a Frenchman. Terrible impostor."

"But his name was Armand," her husband said.

"No doubt it was false. But the daughter, I remember clearly that she was Odile, as in Sainte Odile, the patroness of Alsace," she said, flaunting her knowledge.

"What about her? Tell me!" said Marty impatiently.

"I have just told you, if you would listen. She ran this store before the Suarez family bought it."

"And the name? What was her name?"

Lucien leaned forward to protect his wife from the girl's noisy insistence and spoke loudly, enunciating each syllable as though she were deaf. "Mademoiselle, my wife has been telling you! Benoit. The Benoits owned this store for decades."

"And her husband, what was he called?"

"Who knows? I remember now, Lilette," he said, smiling at his wife. "There were all the bottles in the cellar when we came here, with green labels saying *Zazou*. Perfumes—they told us the German made them."

"Where's the perfume now?" Marty asked, feeling herself tense.

The man continued speaking to his wife. "What did we do with them?"

"Nothing, I believe."

"Then they're still in the cellar?" Marty was almost

shouting. They looked at her with disapproval, and she lowered her voice. "Please, you must take me there."

"We are closing, mademoiselle," said Lilette. She glanced at her wristwatch. "No, we *are* closed." She looked toward the door significantly.

Marty reached into her handbag and pulled out her wallet. The woman's eyes dived down to it. "If you want to *buy*—in that case, Lucien, bring up a bottle. Fifty francs each."

Extortionist, thought Marty, taking out a bill of 100 francs. "I'll have two." Maybe the scent had evaporated in this time; with one bottle she wouldn't be able to tell.

"It's a pleasure to be of assistance, my dear," said Lilette sweetly.

When the bottles were brought up, Marty unstoppered one and was instantly, dizzily, transported back to Brooklyn. "I recognize it," she murmured. Imploringly, she asked, "Where can I find out more about Odile Benoit?"

A 100-franc note turned out to have restorative powers on the memory. "She went mad after her husband ran away," said Lilette.

"Crazy," affirmed Lucien, anxious to show that he, too, could provide information. "She was in shock."

"She didn't die?" asked Marty.

"Die? A Frenchwoman doesn't die because she has a bad husband," Lilette informed her sternly.

"The child. Odile had a child, didn't she?" Marty could hardly get her words together. That's me, she thought, Odile's daughter, granddaughter of a hero.

Lucien gave her a perplexed look.

"I'm not sure," admitted Lilette. "But perhaps you could find out at the registry office."

"Thank you, thank you very much." She grabbed the bottles and ran out of the pharmacy.

Marty was at the door when the office opened next day. The town clerk brought her the book and she carried it in trembling hands to a table. She read down the *B*s to Benoit, Charles. My grandfather? she wondered. Below him was Benoit, Claude. Or was it he? Then Benoit, Marguerite; Benoit, Odile.

"Born July 3, 1909, daughter of Claude Benoit and Jeanne (Darrès) Benoit. Married Armand Delarue November 6, 1946. Died, December 17, 1969."

Marty stared at the date. Three months? Little more than three months ago her mother was *alive*? She kept staring, almost willing the numbers to change in front of her eyes. All her life Marty had believed her mother was dead. Her mother and Vie's mother were both dead; that's why they lived with their father.

She put the book down and went outside for air. But she needed to fill her lungs with something stronger. She walked down to the tabac, bought a pack of Gauloises, and lit one, dragging on it heavily, holding the smoke in for as long as she could, as though it were a joint of marijuana.

When she finished the cigarette, she returned to the registry office, to the book still lying on the table. She turned the pages to *D*. Darrès—no time for that now. She flipped to Delarue. Only one entry under that name: "Delarue, Martine. Born January 7, 1948, to Armand Delarue and Odile (Benoit) Delarue."

Birth. Death. Marty felt a suspension of time, as though the tobacco she'd smoked really had been pot. She sat for so long, staring at nothing, that the clerk finally came over and asked, "You are finished with the book, mademoiselle?"

"No!" She looked up at him, her hand on the book to prevent him from taking it away. "Do you have certificates, birth certificates? Death?"

"Not the originals, but we usually have copies. At least of those made out since the war. We lost most of the others."

"Please." Marty wrote out the two names, requesting a birth certificate for one, a death certificate for the other. The clerk picked them up, frowned, said he'd see what he could do, she could call back in a few days.

"No, it's urgent. Please, you must try to get them now!"

"Impossible."

She didn't know whether to try bribing him. It might work; on the other hand, it might make him refuse absolutely if he decided to take it as an affront to his honor or to the glory of France, or whatever it was that minor civil servants like him put next to God. She smiled flirtatiously, wetting her lips. She lowered her lashes and brought them up in a slow sweep until she met his eyes. "What is your name?" she asked softly.

"A-Albert," he stammered.

He'd had a bad case of acne, she saw, which had left behind a webbing of scars over his face. "Albert," she murmured, "it is so very important for me to see those papers. Is there nothing I can do to help you find them quickly?"

His mouth dropped open as she took his hand and brought it to within a millimeter of her breasts. She held it, looking in his eyes, a smile flickering over her face. "Will you do it for me?"

"Th-th-this afternoon. Come back at four."

She let go. "You are so good to me, Albert," she cooed. "I'll never forget you."

Marty picked up her bag and left the office. By the time she crossed the threshold of the outer door, his name was obliterated from her memory.

Her birth was registered by her mother and a Dr. Stefan Mallaquin, identified as the godfather. Why not her real father, she wondered? Had he tried to disown her from the moment she was born?

The death certificate for Odile Benoit hadn't been sent to the Carcassonne office yet. She had died in a village about sixty kilometers away, in the mental hospital of Ste. Anne. He'd had a lot of work finding that out, the clerk said, gazing at Marty as if she were the moon and he a new-born calf. He waited for her to compliment him, but all she said was, "Thanks," and left him mooning with his arduously collected information. She walked out briskly, calling back, "Good-bye, Alfred."

"Albert," he murmured disconsolately.

The fifth driver she asked agreed to take her out there, provided she paid in advance. She handed him the bills ungraciously and jumped into the back of the cab, not bothering to look out the window as they drove.

Forty minutes later the taxi stopped in front of a massive nineteenth-century monstrosity with stone walls and turrets. Marty stared at this gray prison for the mentally ill, designed in a grotesque parody of Carcassonne, until the driver called out to her, "You going in or what? This is Ste. Anne's, what you asked for."

She got out. "Wait here for me."

"How long? Anything over an hour is extra."

"Con," she cursed softly in French, bringing a look of surprise, then admiration, to the driver's face. "You'll wait until I'm finished in there."

"Yes, ma*dame*," he agreed, recognizing a commanding officer.

Marty walked up to the main entrance, into a gray hall only a touch less forbidding than the exterior. She told the guard—no, it was a nurse—that she was here to get a death certificate and followed the stiff, uniformed matron into the funereal office of Mme. Fouquet, keeper of records.

Mme. Fouquet had eyes like stakes, impaling her visitor on the stained green armchair. Marty concentrated on looking at the woman's earlobe while she spoke. She told her quickly why she'd come.

Mme. Fouquet sniffed the air. The expression on her face said she found it malodorous. "You are telling me, mademoiselle, that your mother was a guest in our institution for more than twenty years, and you never once came to see her?"

"I thought she was dead."

"Oh? A convenient notion, no doubt."

Marty wanted to strangle her. She spoke through the closed cage of her teeth. "I'm not here to discuss family relationships. Just give me the death certificate."

"You will not speak to me in that manner!"

"No? Don't bet on it. That document is in the public domain. Besides, I'm her next of kin. You have it or don't you?"

"What do you take us for? Sainte Anne's is efficient and well organized."

"Then why haven't you sent it down to the registry office in Carcassonne yet? It's over three months."

"If you have come here to tell us how to run our affairs,

then I suggest"—Mme. Fouquet stood up—"that you leave this instant!" She screamed the last five words.

Marty walked out, strode back to the guard nurse and demanded to see the director, or directress, of the institution.

"You have an appointment?"

Marty was spitting angry by now, angry enough to break down in tears or to run out of the place. Instead, surprising herself, she held firm. "I don't need one. I'm from the press, and if I don't get to see the head of this godforsaken hellhole within ten minutes, I'm doing a piece about malpractice here that will make you swallow your teeth!"

The woman scuttled away and returned eight minutes later to escort Marty into the director's office.

He was a florid man, Eugène Grandneuf, who was trying to stub out his cigar and simultaneously rearrange his tie when she entered.

"Bon soir," she said cordially. "Sorry to have come so late in the day and without warning. I've just arrived from Washington," Marty improvised, enjoying herself now despite the lugubrious surroundings. She'd been so emotionally charged all day that her only refuge was a sharp gallows humor, played to an audience of herself. "My chauffeur's waiting; I have little time. I need to see the death certificate of Odile Benoit Delarue."

"But of course." He motioned the nurse to get it.

"While you're at it," Marty called to the woman, "bring in her entire file." She turned to the director. "That's so I can vindicate you. We've heard rumors she was poisoned here."

She almost laughed aloud to see the red-faced man turn purple at the accusation. "But how is that possible, mademoiselle? I myself eat here."

Marty shrugged, enjoying herself grimly. "That's not the first report we've had," she told him.

The nurse returned with the papers. The official document recorded her death, at sixty, as being caused by massive cerebral hemorrhage. The file on Odile Delarue contained notes and observations by nurses, a listing of prescriptions, and doctors' reports of diagnoses, treatment, and progress. She was paranoid, with delusions of grandeur.

She had extreme depression, manic phases. She'd received volts of electric shock, pills to calm her or make her more awake.

Marty read the reports, the Latin phrases, the generic and brand names of prescribed medicines. It's my *mother* they're writing about, she thought: a real, living woman, whom they manipulated by chemistry and electric charges so she wouldn't be the way she was. The woman who gave birth to me. Who lived in their maneuvering hands throughout my life.

"She died peacefully," Grandneuf assured her.

Marty couldn't understand what he was saying. She looked down at the file again, handwritten, with all its prescriptions, the detailed notes of her final hemorrhage. After she died, the body had been claimed by Dr. Stefan Mallaquin.

The same man, or his son? My godfather or his descendant? His address was given as Poste Restante, Aille-sur-Bois. That meant general delivery, in a town she'd never heard of.

But the cabdriver knew it well. His niece lived there, with her husband and twin sons. He didn't recognize the name of Mallaquin but suggested they drive to the village tonight, where Marty could stay with his niece and begin the search tomorrow.

His offer was the first kindness Marty had received in a long time, and she accepted immediately. Alain Brieux sped on through the darkness, proud of his passenger who had cowed that monster, Grandneuf, head keeper of Ste. Anne's, where his brother had been incarcerated when he was sent back from the war.

She sat in front on the way to Aille-sur-Bois. When Alain Brieux discovered she was American, he reached over to offer his hand. "We are friends," he told her firmly. "I was there when your countrymen liberated Paris."

They stopped at a brasserie for a quick meal while he called ahead. "My niece is very happy," he told Marty on his return. "Anyone who makes Grandneuf cringe is welcome to her house."

"Good, but why?"

"Her father died in Ste. Anne's," Alain said.

"Maybe he was a friend of my mother's," Marty thought aloud, accepting the firm squeeze of his hand. It was so simple to become related, she thought. You didn't have to know a person to feel kinship.

She found him through the help of Brieux's niece. Stefan Mallaquin lived in rented quarters on the second floor of a tatterdemalion house isolated in a field eight hundred meters from the village. Marty climbed the stairs and knocked. She heard shuffling from within, like rats running over the floor. When he opened, a strong reek of decay came out from the apartment, and Marty took a step back.

He peered at her with one eye, the other fixed on something behind her. She couldn't tell which of them was glass. He wore a soiled navy dressing gown speckled with greasy stains and encrusted in several places with remnants of food that had dropped from his mouth or spoon. From the gray and white bristles on his cheeks hung tiny particles of a recent meal.

"Dr. Mallaquin? Martine Nouvel. Could I speak to you for a few minutes?"

The eye shifted focus and the other one glinted at her. "You want my recipes? You've come to hear about my love affairs? Well, well, enter."

She held her breath and stepped into the hall while he closed and bolted the door behind her. Then, leering at her, he led the way into his sitting room, where soiled plates and utensils lay on the floor and on the furniture while ants crawled over them. "Would you like some tea?" he invited her.

"No, thank you," she said, shuddering, trying to find the least revolting place to sit. She selected a straight-backed wooden chair and removed a cup from it. "Dr. Mallaquin . . ." she began.

"What do you want from me?" he shot at her.

"I am the daughter of Odile Benoit."

"You?" He stepped up to peer into her face. "The one from America?"

"Yes."

"Your mother is dead," he announced.

"I know. I never met her. That's why I'm here—I was hoping you could tell me about her."

He clasped his hands behind his back as he paced, looking down at the floor and then up at her, one eye focused. "She looked like a dish mop after she went mad."

"When was that?"

"Don't try to fool me!" he threatened. "*You* know. She became crazy when the collaborator ran away, that husband of hers, Armand Jolaunay."

"No," Marty corrected him. "She married Armand Nouvel, who called himself Delarue."

"It was the traitor Jolaunay." He stopped and looked at Marty as though trying to recover something, and she realized he'd forgotten who she was. "That bastard," he went on, resuming his pacing. "We found out all about him, me and my men. Ah, the days of the Maquis! Those were the great days, young woman. Their like shall never come again.

"Armand Jolaunay, I'll never forget him. Good-looking he was, but a Nazi all the same. He bottled his stink to please the Boches. Married a German woman and had a child with her before he came down here."

Marty sat mesmerized, fearing he was senile and yet sensing that he was telling the truth. "Young lady," he said, glaring down at her, "why have you come?"

"Please—the Maquis. Tell me more."

"Yes." He smiled and walked toward the kitchen. "I'll make you tea."

"Don't! I mean, please don't bother."

He came back. "Yes, you've heard that I was a leader in the Maquis. We had to keep hidden, but now I can admit it. Yes, Stefan Mallaquin was the leader for the Carcassonne region. We hid, with the ears of foxes and the sharp eyes of ferrets. A man came to the town with a little blond daughter. He called himself Delarue. In an hour, maybe it was a year, we knew he was the one who'd murdered one of our brothers."

"Murder?" she breathed.

"Come, come, you remember. He shot him through the heart, or maybe it was the head. After the burial." He stopped, and seemed to have finished his story.

"Burial," Marty prompted. "Who was being buried?"

"The German wife. She died the night before, giving birth. Our men planned to take the traitor in the cemetery. But he was a vicious one, he wrestled the gun out of our comrade's hands and shot him."

"Did you catch him?" she asked, as though she were listening to a story about someone else. She couldn't fix it in her mind that this man was her father.

"Odile, when will you talk sense? You know you are dead, that is why your memory fails you. I told you what I knew about him, and you begged me to wait until you gave the signal. You, you were a terrible woman. Worse than a black widow."

"I'm sorry," she said involuntarily.

"That's my girl, yes, smile for me. As sweet a smile as you always had for your Uncle Stefan. When you ran into the room with an armful of cornflowers, I thought I would marry you later. The child would have been ours."

"What child?"

"Are you dumb as well as dead?" He turned to the kitchen again, stopped before its entrance, and came back. "The child Martine, my godchild. If she had been ours, you wouldn't have tried to kill her."

"What!"

"Your poisonings. All your schemes. Burning the house, tearing her limbs like a chicken. You went too far. You were truly evil. I would have had the collaborator killed for you, maybe even his little girl. But our child, Odile! Not her! I think," he said, placing the tips of his fingers together, "that you were insane."

Neither said anything. The old man shuttled back and forth to the entrance of the kitchen, always forgetting, when he reached it, what he meant to do there.

"He was a bad man, your husband, but better than you. He saved the child."

"Which one?"

He stared at her. "*You* are the child, Martine. Why do you torture me? Take off your clothes."

"No!"

"Just like your mother. You want the wedding band

first. I will find one for you another day. In the meantime, undress."

She stood up, terrified and feeling she would be sick if she stayed in this rancid room any longer.

He looked at her mildly. "Why leave? You came to hear about your mother, and I'll tell you. I'm the only one alive who knows all about her.

"She is dead. She died in December of cerebral hemorrhage. Before that she was manic-depressive with overtones of paranoia. Otherwise her health was good. We used to take long walks together every Sunday. She hated the food there."

"You saw her every week?"

"She was the daughter of my closest friend. I felt a responsibility for her—I'd known her since she was born, when I held her at the baptismal font, just as I held you. Now, I insist we have tea." This time he entered the kitchen, as if he had finally come into reality. His movements back and forth across the floor were like travels in time, crossings over a gap between dimensions.

When he returned, he was angry. "You are the cause of my exile, Odile. It's thanks to you that I live in this filthy hole. They never believed me, my comrades thought I was protecting Jolaunay for your sake. But it wasn't true. I told you I would wait for your signal only because we were not fully prepared. But on the day you came running to me, so wild, so crazy, we were armed and ready to go in any case.

"But he'd fled with the children. They thought I'd helped him. They accused me of arranging his escape!" Tears ran slowly as drops of glue down his cheeks. "Me! A son of France! Me they accused of helping the collaborator! I became the hare, and they were foxes."

"They caught you?"

"What do you think, slut? Stefan Mallaquin is a match for anyone! Except," he modified, "that Jolaunay. Perhaps he collaborated, perhaps he was just a businessman, naïve but not disloyal. He killed our comrade only to save his own life, not out of spite—the way you intended to kill our child, Odile. He saved her life. You should be grateful to him. I heard that he went to America, where our little girl is growing up."

Marty couldn't bear anymore. "I must leave. Open the door for me, please," she instructed firmly.

He obeyed her tone, walking like an automaton to the door. He opened and held out his hand. "Such a pleasant visit. I don't get many visitors these days. You must come again, and I'll make us some tea."

She had both feet on the other side of the threshold. "Thank you," she said in a thin, shaking voice, and began running down the stairs.

"When you next see your father," he called after her, "tell him I have forgiven him."

Outside, running across the field, Marty let out a long wail like the moaning of an injured animal. She heard the sound she was making and stopped abruptly. No point in running anymore. Her search was over. It was time to head back home.

VI

THE
JOLAY
SISTERS

1973–1982

1

Marty received her MBA from the Harvard Business School with the third-highest average among the graduates. Watching the dean of the school award the degree, Vie's grip tightened on the bag in her lap, and her face tensed in the conflict between her sparring emotions, pride and regret.

Her own graduation, twelve years earlier, had brought only a high school diploma. Up on the podium in her black gown, Marty was accepting her master's with the assurance of someone who'd worked through the system and reached the top.

Marty held her head high as she walked down the stairs toward Vie. When she was abreast of her, she grinned at her sister and gave a broad wink.

Vie frowned. How had she managed to do it on her own, without asking for funds? Vie remembered the gold bracelet, Marty's graduation gift to her, the empty sock—and knew she'd never dare ask, not even conjecture, where the money for her education and living expenses had come from.

She knew almost nothing about Marty's life during the past five—no, it was closer to six—years. When the private investigators lost track of her in early 1970, Vie pulled them off the scent and reconciled herself to Marty's disappearance. Inquiries aboard the *Apollo* had resulted in nothing. Jean el-Dhouni, alias Jean-Luc Delbeau, admitted that he'd been with her in Paris but said he had no notion of her whereabouts after that. He'd last seen her seven weeks ago, he said, when he left Paris to join

Menarchos. The other passengers of the *Apollo* claimed
never to have heard of her.

The last report said she'd checked out of the Crillon on
the same day as Dhouni—Delbeau; investigators had been
unable to find any leads. She might still be in the city—or
she might be anywhere. Vie wrote back that they should
stop looking.

She had provisional papers drawn up for the transfer of
Armand's shares. His 40 percent was divided so that Vie
and Marty each received 15 percent. The remaining 10
percent was divided equally between Chandra and Philippa,
who became the executors of Marty's additional trust.

January 7, 1973, was Marty's twenty-fifth birthday and
Vie had vaguely expected or hoped to hear something
from her then. But no word came until May, five days ago,
when suddenly Marty's voice was on the other end of
the phone and she was asking Vie to come to Cambridge.

She didn't say where she'd been or why she was calling
now. She sounded as calm and matter-of-fact as if she'd
last called a week or two earlier. To Vie's excited, half-
hysterical questions she answered coolly, "We'll talk when
you get here."

Frustrated, Vie begged her to say *something* about herself,
anything at all.

"I've changed my name," Marty replied.

"To what?" Vie pressed.

"Martine Jolaunay."

Vie stared at the receiver, too alarmed to answer. What
could have happened to her since Armand's death?

After Alain Brieux drove her back to Carcassonne, Marty
took a train to Marseilles, where she knew she'd be able to
get news of the *Apollo*. She asked around the harbor and
discovered her luck: it was headed back, due to dock here
in three days.

Marty took a room in a sailors' hotel and waited, while
her resolve hardened. She saw that the path ahead was
clearly marked for her. She'd return to her own country
and begin again. That meant finishing college first, getting the BA, and then on to business school, to cram what
she needed before joining the company, Vie's firm. She'd

match Vie and overtake her, becoming head of Jolay and dedicating her success to Armand's memory. Whatever he'd done during the war, she knew one thing for sure: he'd saved her life. Her dead father would learn what kind of person she was; his ghost would see that Marty could do everything he'd hoped for, more than Vie had done. *She* would be the daughter he was proudest of; his favorite. She'd restore his name and make it the biggest in perfumes.

Marty waited in Marseilles for the ship to come in. She needed money, and she'd get it legitimately, for services already rendered.

On the third afternoon it landed, and its crew and passengers disembarked. She saw Jean-Luc coming down the gangplank, stepping onto the dock. In front of him was Menarchos. Marty hid in a doorway until Jean-Luc was by himself. Then she walked out and gave a low whistle. Jean-Luc spotted her immediately. She gestured to him with her shoulder that he was to follow, and he did—alone.

"Thank God you're alive," he said when they were in her hotel room, attempting to take her in his arms. He'd known that she'd escaped, but her living flesh reminded Jean-Luc of how close it had been.

"Shove it," she said, pushing him away. "I didn't ask you here to renew sentimental ties. You're a rotten bastard, and that's it. But I'm not letting you off scot-free."

He was standing on the bare floor in the center of the small room, looking at her apprehensively. Marty stood facing him, arms crossed over her chest, a look of concentrated determination on her face. "I fell for you, for the whole setup and the send-off. You told me I was so bright, I could learn anything. . . ."

"That was true. It still is."

"You don't say?"

"Marty, my darling woman, I'm sorry—"

"Stay right where you are! Don't you dare come any closer to me! I wanted to kill you when I first got away from that ship. But not anymore—it's over. I'm not even angry. All I want is to say good-bye in a clean way." She stood her ground and looked at him as though he were already in the past.

"You know? You actually did teach me a lot. After all

the playacting you had me do, I ran off to find out who I really was. I found out more than you planned for.

"And another thing: you made me learn so fast that you convinced me I have the equipment to do whatever I set out to do. So I'm going back home, and I'm going to become a business executive. An extraordinarily success-ful one. And you're going to foot the bill for it." She paused, enjoying the perplexity on his face. "I need thirty thousand dollars, and I want it by the day after tomorrow, when I'm sailing home on the S.S. *Genoa*." She didn't have a booking, but that wasn't any of his business. The sailing date had come as an inspiration, to set a deadline for the cash. But she liked the idea as soon as she thought of it: returning by ship, the way she'd come, had a nice round feel to it, a kind of justness.

"That's a lot of money. . . ."

"Education ain't cheap."

He looked at her helplessly, knowing that he'd have to do what she asked of him. Standing opposite him so fiercely, her anger glistening on her, Marty was more desirable than he'd ever seen her. She was strong! He saw her as a young Amazon, a woman warrior. He longed to touch her, grab her, have that dominant woman under him. But he knew, looking at her now, that he would never have her again. He'd let her go that night on the *Apollo*, down into dark waters from which she might never have surfaced.

In Torremolinos he'd questioned everyone. People as-sured him that no body had washed up on the shore. He'd been frantic for news of her, but no one had any informa-tion to give until he interrogated a waiter at the terrace cafe overlooking the sea. The waiter told Jean-Luc he'd seen a drenched young woman wearing an evening dress come up from the beach late in the morning. She was with the young English milord, George Barclay. "Always eccentric, the English," he said with a shrug.

Jean-Luc handed him a $20 bill and asked for a descrip-tion of the woman. Smallish, with short, dark hair; black dress; pale skin, the waiter reported. Jean-Luc grinned and returned to the *Apollo* without saying a word to Menarchos.

After he knew she was safe, Jean-Luc kept going over in

his mind what he should have done, how he'd failed both her and himself. He wanted to find her again, make it up to her somehow—but his thoughts floundered and came to a dead end. He knew her well enough to realize she'd never forgive him. The single moral code she lived by was personal loyalty. She'd told him about her gang in Brooklyn, about Casey—and Jean-Luc knew that his own betrayal was unforgivable in her eyes. She had loved him, he was sure of that. But he was also sure she'd jettisoned that love when she jumped overboard from Menarchos' advances. All she would ever want from him again was revenge.

He'd begun speculating how she'd go about it, had become afraid of her. Now, in this bare room with a single lightbulb hanging from the ceiling and a tattered blanket on the iron bed, Jean-Luc felt relieved, almost, to hear her demand. It was a lot of money and wouldn't be easy to get hold of in such short order, but that's all it was, and he knew he could trust her to abide by the contract once it was made. The deal would be final: $30,000 from him, and he'd never hear from her again. She wouldn't talk, she'd never accuse him, and she'd take no more revenge. He understood that, but still he wanted to reach out, hold on to her so she couldn't sail out of his life forever. She was the woman he wanted, the only woman he could look up to, the female body he desired most in the world.

"Get out now. Come back here day after tomorrow at seven thirty in the morning with all of the money in hand."

"If I do bring it, how'll you get it into the States? You'll have to smuggle—"

She cut him short. "Don't worry. I'll manage. I can look after myself, remember?"

She held the door open until he went through. Then she locked it. She had no doubt at all that he'd come at precisely seven thirty the morning after next with the full $30,000. And that money would buy her a college degree, and then the most prestigious education in America. She'd hurl herself up to the top of the heap.

*   *   *   *

I don't know anything about Marty at all, Vie realized, waiting in her seat until the entire ceremony was over. The dean was handing out more degrees, to people she didn't know, and Vie stopped bothering to pay attention. I don't know what she's done with these four and a half years, or what kind of person she's become.

And what about me? Vie thought. Am I the same person I was then?

In many ways, she was forced to acknowledge, nothing had changed. Jolay was bigger now, much bigger than it had been when Armand died. Murray Schwartzman had built up a sales staff as dependable as an elite army corps and as tough as the Green Berets. They had many new products now and their own advertising department. *Fortune* gave her the highest profile of any businesswoman under forty. At twenty-eight, president of an expanding company, she was hot copy. She appeared on the cover of *Business Week*.

She had a new apartment on Central Park South, and her wardrobe was filled with sumptuous designer clothes, new furs. But basically nothing had changed. Increase, expansion—these were simply predictable developments as the company snowballed. But her own life remained unmoving. Her closest friends were the people she'd known at seventeen. Her daily routine was the same. No shattering event had caught her up since her father's death, and no man had captured her since Hubert.

Marty's life was flash and fire. Her own, Vie thought, missed even a spark. The few men she'd gone to bed with ignited no flames in her. Afterward she'd feel as though the actions had been part of a dance: pleasant enough, but never touching her emotions.

The men in her life were all friends, all connected to her through business—Chandra, Murray Schwartzman, Don Garrison. And Mike Parnell. Mike had become a partner in a Wall Street firm three years after his bar exam, and now he handled Vie's private legal matters. She'd trusted him from the first time they'd met, and over the years she'd become closer to him. Good-looking, attentive, someone who could always make her laugh, Mike was the perfect escort for the elaborate or formal events Vie was often forced to attend. They had fun together despite the crushingly boring people, tedious speeches, cardboard food. Sometimes, after an elegant but tasteless dinner, Vie and Mike went for pizza at Ray's or Gino's, looking like refugees from an invaded kingdom in their incongruous evening clothes.

"*Not* like a penguin—you're a great black-backed gull," Vie would insist when he'd grumble about the tuxedo. Though big, Mike was muscular and athletic. "You don't waddle," she assured him. "You soar."

He'd asked her to soar with him a few times over the years. He was very dear to her, she loved his looks, his intelligence, his wonderful restorative powers that never failed to raise her spirits. But there was no sexual fire. Vie apologized, kissed his cheek, told him that she loved him dearly—but no. Mike was her good friend. With him she felt no risk, none of the danger she'd felt with Hubert.

Her life was flat, Vie thought, as the Dean came down to the Ws. Even in business she rarely now felt a thrill of accomplishment. Jolay was growing, her staff was loyal, and Vie was generally recognized as a leader in her field. But she didn't have the verve of Philippa, she felt, who threw herself into each new project as though it were a love affair. "You're taking care of too much drudgery," Philippa had said. "You need a partner who'll handle the business end and free you to take care of the creative aspects." That might release her, Vie agreed, but Jolay was too intimately *hers* to think of someone else's stepping in. It had to be family-run.

Since this morning, since her discovery of Marty's achievement, Vie had allowed herself to imagine working with her sister. The thought ignited small flickers of hope.

At the beginning Marty would have to be trained. But maybe in time, if she showed aptitude and willingness . . . then Vie would stop herself, giving her fantasies warning that Marty might have other plans, might even have accepted another offer already.

The ceremony was over. Vie went to find Marty and shake her hand. Fellow graduates and professors milled around on the smooth lawn, congratulating her and praising her high academic standing. A bearded man was drumming heartily on Marty's shoulder. Marty smiled over at Vie and introduced her. "Professor Glick, who taught me Creative Marketing Strategy—my sister, Vie Nouvel, founder of Jolay Perfumes."

Professor Glick abandoned Marty's shoulder for Vie's hand, which he pumped vigorously while beaming through his bifocals. "A pleasure to meet you. Your sister is the best student I've had in years. The kind of person who makes teaching worthwhile."

She smiled back and over at Marty, telling her, "I'm proud of you. This is quite an accomplishment."

"Ain't it," Marty agreed, grinning. "Now come on, I'm taking you to lunch."

Vie started to protest, to say that *she* was inviting—but Marty had taken hold of her arm and was already propelling her out, with the firm walk of one who's in charge.

Marty's ease in the expensive restaurant, her perfect pronunciation as she ordered in French, her knowledge-ability as she studied the wine list—all these amazed Vie and made her puzzle even more over the missing years. From street urchin to cosmopolitan woman of the world. She was relaxed enough in her sophistication to make fun of it, to let Brooklyn enter her speech for comic effect, to raise the glass of Beaune to her ear, deliberate a moment as if undecided about whether or not to accept it, and then slowly nod to the waiter, telling him, "Sounds good." But her humor only emphasized her self-possession, high-lighted her unmistakable air of command.

Vie was burning with questions about Marty's past and her future plans. Marty herself volunteered no information, and Vie pondered ways of broaching the different subjects without seeming to pry. She started with what she hoped would be innocuous. "How did you learn such good French?"

"Just picked it up," Marty answered, shrugging it off.

"Did you spend a lot of time in France?"

"Not long—I had a crash course." She let 'it drop. Vie tried other questions to open up Marty's reserve, but nothing worked. Finally, she asked bluntly, "Did you meet Sophocles Menarchos?"

Marty put down her fork and didn't answer. Vie held

her breath, waiting for Marty to ask how she knew. She'd have to admit hiring detectives, snooping on her sister. It was too late to retract the question; she tried to prepare for Marty's attack.

Instead, Marty picked up her fork again. "I met him," she said tonelessly. "A maniac."

Vie watched her eat the duck and wild rice in silence. Marty would offer nothing unless forced, she realized. She'd have to take the chance and make a lunge. "Do you have any plans yet? Job plans? I hope not, because I'd like you to come work for me."

She registered no surprise, looking up. "Under what conditions?"

"The same as anyone else entering the firm."

"Not *anyone*, Vie; an executive."

"Of course, that's what I meant. I'm sure you'd be able to advance quickly. You could learn the ropes in maybe half a year."

She tilted her head. "I'm fast, Vie. I might surprise you. I'm ambitious, I like to get where I'm going quickly."

"And that's . . . ?"

"To the top." She grinned. "Where you are."

"You're aiming for *my* job?" Vie asked mildly, smiling. "Good. I like your initiative. You can try, but I've had nearly twelve years of experience, and that takes a long time to catch up with. You haven't seen me work, Marty. I'm good at what I do."

"So you won't have to worry, will you, that I'll take your place?"

"Maybe someday in the future we can be partners," Vie offered placatingly.

"Who knows?" Marty answered. "Stranger things have happened."

They shook hands like equal parties to a contract, each knowing she'd take the lead. Marty's resolution in Marseilles had grown stronger since her return to America. Graduate school was difficult and had been a real challenge at the beginning. But she'd persisted. It was a tough world—she knew that well enough—and the only way to make it was through power.

2

Marty entered Jolay like an armored tank. Fresh from business school and its accolades, wearing the security of Harvard like an invisible mantle, Martine Jolaunay came to conquer.

Vie took her around the office, through the departments, showing her the "library" of scents, where new aroma chemicals were stored on shelves, along with traditional substances and fragrance compounds made by Jolay or its competitors. There was also a bookshelf with articles from perfumers' and chemists' journals, reporting on the latest developments in the field, from formulations of new scents to recent ideas on the launching and promotion of new products.

She introduced Marty to the people working there in private offices, at desks, in the storeroom. "So you're the boss's sister," said Murray Schwartzman. "Nice piece of cake."

"I'll be giving orders around here pretty soon," Marty snapped and turned away.

Murray shrugged and whispered to Vie, "So how was I to know she doesn't want me to call her your sister? She is, isn't she?"

"Half-sister," Vie reminded him, troubled by the vehemence of Marty's reaction.

"Where's my office going to be?" Marty demanded when Vie caught up with her again.

She'd thought about it but, because Vie couldn't predict how Marty would eventually be placed at Jolay, had decided to wait a few months, until Marty had worked through various departments and begun to settle in. "You'll have a desk for now, while you look us over and get to know how we do things here. You'll need three months at least for your apprenticeship. After that, we can set up an office for you."

"Now," Marty said with a touch of menace, walking past Elaine, without greeting her, into Vie's office. She closed the door behind them. "I want an office next to yours. I'm not some kid apprentice, and I don't need to be patronized. I control more than a third of the company, remember?"

Vie nodded unhappily. When Armand's shares had been divided Marty's original bequest of 20 percent of Jolay had been increased to 35 percent. "There's no room for an office next to mine, as you can see," Vie answered, avoiding the issue of shares. Vie's office emphasized privacy.

She kept her door closed during meetings and even when she was alone at her desk. Visitors entered her secretary's office through a heavy oak door. Elaine's office itself was roomy, though the nine-by-fifteen-foot space was diminished by filing cabinets and lockers.

Vie's large room had a wall of windows with a view onto lower Fifth Avenue. Most of the furniture was Brazilian, the smooth reddish-tan of the leather blending with the teak or walnut frames. Walls and carpets took up the theme of earth colors, the walls pale, the carpet dark and muted. Potted trees—citrus, fig, and a small eucalyptus—stood in a random pattern, freshening the air, and brightly colored art—a Miró lithograph, a Rothko painting, a photographic enlargement of bottles in Chandra's store, a Calder mobile—livened up the office, made it cheerful without being frivolous. Above all, it had style. Vie and Philippa had designed it between them, substituting taste and personality for the services of an interior decorator.

"I'll *make* room, then," Marty answered. "I'm not sitting behind some desk in an open pool. I won't be patronized, and you don't have to bother showing me around anymore either. I'll do it myself."

"But you don't know the first thing about perfume!" Vie said in desperation.

"I don't have to know about perfume. I know business!" Marty challenged from the other side of the long desk.

"That's nonsense!"

"Oh?" Marty said, smiling crookedly. "Why?"

Vie groped for an analogy, her usual way of fixing thoughts in the mind. She hadn't known she habitually did this until Elaine first, then Mike, had commented on this trait in her. Mike had diagnosed her use of analogy as a result of her lifetime involvement with scents, the need to translate an olfactory impression into a concrete image. "Because it's, well, like being a general who knows military theory or even tactics but doesn't know anything about the country where the fighting's taking place," she said.

Marty kept her wry smile. "*We* know where it's taking place," she said softly. "Don't worry, I know the tactics. And my groundwork won't take much time. See you."

Vie didn't try to stop her walking out of the office. Let her try. Her cocksureness would disappear in a few days as she came to recognize that there was no business without the product. And that the product was elusive, unlike any other, and required a special sensitivity. A hard head for business was fine, but success in perfumery required a nose.

For the next weeks Marty threw herself into work. She observed, she read, she interviewed people, working eighteen hours a day without taking a break or needing one. Her thoroughness, which had earned her the respect of her professors, reached over into every aspect of perfumery. She studied reports going back to the founding of the company, including sales figures, operating expenses, advertising and promotion budgets. She visited the lab in the East Twenties, made a tour of it, and returned three more times until she was satisfied that she knew what was being done in each area of the place. She repeated her exacting inspection at the factory in New Jersey, taking notes on how the original fragrance formula was revised for quantity, adjusted for either the 20–25 percent strength of perfume or the maximum 6 percent strength of cologne. She watched the compounder at work, traveling on an electric trolley along rows of pipes to weigh out the ingredients, which were then passed into a mixing vessel and finally poured into large drums. These drums were then sent to the annex, which housed the distillery.

Bottling, sealing, labeling—these were done in yet another factory, four miles away. The finished bottles were placed in boxes, usually cardboard cylinders with a metallic finish.

After a day "in the field," as Marty referred to her tours, she spent her evenings memorizing charts and lists of fragrance materials, natural and synthetic, until she could describe the odor of each as though she'd actually experienced it.

She spoke with salespeople, account executives, market analysts, chemists. Within a very short time she had learned to categorize scents, using the ten to twelve customary classifications—floral, green, oriental, fruity, and others—based on the dominant note, or smell impression, that a fragrance gave out. She knew a few chemical formulas for the more common substances and the scientific or brand names for many NFMs (New Fragrance Materials).

She was driven, and whenever Marty channeled her monumental energies and her quickness of mind, she outstripped all possible competition. It had taken her only five weeks to learn French; making up her last year of college and then completing her MBA had taken less than three years, from September 1970 to May 1973. She'd worked without break, carrying the heaviest curriculum allowed, and getting credit for some of her first-semester, senior-year Radcliffe courses by taking, and passing brilliantly, the final exams.

Within two months of receiving her degree from Harvard Business School, Marty's ability to digest and assimilate information brought her to a more detailed, intimate knowledge of Jolay than anyone else in the company possessed. Including—she was sure of it—Vie.

The two sisters hadn't seen much of each other during that time. Marty had determined to learn everything from the sources themselves, not through Vie. She felt there was nothing she had to ask her older sister about, and though she made no point of avoiding Vie, Marty was too busy to seek her out.

Vie was willing to wait and see. She rationalized the first day's friction as having little significance. Marty was used to doing things on her own, was edgy in new surroundings where she appeared as the stranger, and so had become defensive, touchy. But Vie was optimistic that once Marty felt more at home in her new enterprise, the two of them would be able to find an accord, a way of working together, in different functions, that would benefit each and, most of all, the company. By all the reports Vie had heard, Marty was doing a tremendous job of educating herself.

"Watch out she doesn't try to bury you," Mike Parnell said. It was the eve of Vie's twenty-ninth birthday, and they were having a late dinner at the base of the Brooklyn Bridge, with the skyline of lower Manhattan spread before them across the water.

"You've never trusted Marty," Vie answered.

"Right, and I don't now. She's power hungry."

"Maybe," Vie said, unconvinced. She didn't want to tarnish the image of herself and Marty working together in the family business, each in her own sphere, autonomous but dependent. "She's ambitious, I'm aware of that. But so am I."

"More than that," Mike insisted. "She won't be satisfied until she beats you out."

"You're overdramatizing," Vie said crossly.

"I hope so, honey. I don't want to upset you, particularly not tonight. It's your birthday! To you," he said, lifting his glass. "To the incomparable Vie! Light of my life."

Vie smiled, clinking her glass against his. "See? Always exaggerating. It's the Irish in you, lad."

He grinned back, shrugging his shoulders like a schoolboy who's been reprimanded for telling a truth that the grown-ups didn't want to hear. Vie was the loveliest woman he'd ever met. Her champagne hair, her topaz eyes: always out of reach, the princess whose knight he'd become willingly, waiting for her signal to be rescued.

"Marty's tough, but she's good. We're very different, even though we're sisters, but I think we respect each other. You don't know her, Mike," Vie pleaded. "She had a very rough time of it in her childhood. I wasn't a good mother to her, I was too young myself, and sometimes I resented her."

"Are you going to be making it up to her for the rest of your life?" Mike asked in a cutting tone. He too had a sister and had taken on responsibility for her care since he'd left law school.

"I don't think I'm doing anything out of the ordinary. People in families help each other, that's all," she said flatly. Then, her anger suddenly flaring, she blurted out, "Besides, I don't see that it's any of your business!"

He looked away from her to control his own anger. If Vie was determined to be a bloody saint and martyr, let her. The hell with her. "Yes, madame," he mumbled. "I should know my place."

She saw that she'd hurt him and instantly repented. Reaching to touch his hand, she said softly, "Forgive me. You're a good friend. I know that you're trying to protect me. But you're reading things that aren't there. Trust me. I know my sister."

Mike downed his glass of wine in one swallow and took a deep breath. "All right," he said. "We'll declare Marty off limits. Not another word. How about us going dancing after dinner?"

She thought of the work awaiting her tomorrow, of her alarm set as always at six o'clock. He'd asked her in a casual way, as though it didn't matter. He was waiting for her answer. "That would be lovely," she said, and he slowly let out his breath.

By the end of Marty's first year at Jolay, sales figures were up, and the volume of business had increased by nearly 14 percent. Marty's title of production manager was replaced by vice president in charge of production. "You're doing a wonderful job," Vie commended her.

"Right," agreed Marty happily. "What about that office?"

"Find the space, and it's yours. We'll have to check the budget. . . ."

"I've already done that."

"You have?" Vie asked in surprise. "Well, then—fine. You know the limit on expenditures."

Marty nodded. "But nothing says I can't add my own money to it."

How peculiar, Vie thought. "I'm sure there's an ample allowance—and after all, it's just an office, not the Taj Mahal. Any advice or suggestions I can give. . . ."

"I'm doing it on my own," Marty informed her.

Two months later Philippa phoned Vie late in the afternoon. Philippa had left Magdahl-Hoffman in 1970 to become an independent consultant for the fashion industry. Her ties to Jolay were closer than ever. "What do you think of Marty's new office, love?" she asked.

"I didn't realize it was finished," Vie said. "I haven't seen it yet."

"It's larger than yours, and everything in it is more expensive," Philippa revealed. She was fascinated and amused by The Whirlwind, as she sometimes called Marty. The girl's determination and drive reminded her of her own younger self.

"How do you know that, Phil?"

"Because"—Vie heard a low chuckle—"I designed it for her, of course."

"*You?*"

"Don't underestimate your sister, love. She has the knack of getting the best people for the job."

"And in this case that person was you?" Vie asked frostily. She was annoyed, even jealous.

"But naturally, darling. In matters of taste I have no equal."

Vie couldn't help laughing. She felt reassured. Why shouldn't Philippa, a professional consultant, advise Marty? Business was one thing, their friendship another. "I hope Marty paid you?"

Philippa's deep laughter rippled through the receiver. "You bet, sweetheart. Through the nose."

When she hung up, Vie went to see for herself. The office was stunning and reflected Marty's bold personality. Large zebra stripes on the wall, furniture upholstered with antelope pelts, a large black standing lamp with arms of varying lengths, like branches of a tree. "Wonderful!" she said enthusiastically.

Marty was almost shy with pleasure. "Really? You really like it? I was waiting for the last of the cushions to come in before showing you—I wanted it to be a real surprise."

"It certainly is," Vie said. "But I might have expected it—Philippa's taste is infallible."

The pleasure dropped from Marty's face, as though she'd been struck. "Fuck you," she said.

Vie was too startled to answer. Marty went on. "You're so damn superior to everything. You look down your nose at me. Your nose"—she laughed harshly—"you should get it insured at Lloyd's of London. It's the most precious thing in the world to you."

"I don't know what you're talking about," Vic said hotly. They were standing in the middle of Marty's office, facing each other like pugilists.

"No? You wander around in a world of 'bouquets' and 'harmonies' and 'aromatic' I don't know what. If you didn't have someone to do the books, you would've fallen flat on your face."

"We got along fine before you came in," Vie reminded her. "This is our twelfth year, and we managed without Harvard degrees."

"You're lucky. Philippa's been helping you, and she's a smart businesswoman. Murray knows what he's doing. You lucked on a good staff, and they've kept you afloat in your dreamworld. But you can bet Jolay wouldn't be expanding now if I hadn't come in. The old bottles were gathering dust in the stores. If I hadn't replaced them with the new designs, all those nice black figures would've been red."

"The figures reflect the excellence of our perfumes, not the containers they're put into. You're not coming in here and telling me about the perfume industry. I started out in it while you were still playing your war games on the streets. Perfume has been my *life*. I've loved it since I was a child, since Papa first introduced me to it."

Marty winced. "Yeah," she said harshly. "Your own true love—yours and Armand's."

"That's right," Vie said. "He was an artist, too. Perfume is more than just business. It requires creativity, subtlety. . . ."

Marty cut her short. "It's a business, just like any other. You get people to buy what they don't need by convincing them that the product you're pushing will do something good for them. In the food industry you play up health, fitness, long life. With cars it's power first, then status. Status is our main pitch—and it wouldn't matter if it's perfume, designer clothes, or French champagne. Nobody needs any of them, but they pour out their millions because they've been conditioned to believe this stuff will give them class, make them better than their neighbors. Superior." She walked away from Vie and stared out the window, not seeing the city below, hearing the loud drumming of her own heart. I'll show her, Marty thought with childish rage. I'll show them both.

She was determined to prove herself beyond anything she'd done. In the last few years she'd had testimony enough to her brains, beauty, talents of every kind—from bed to business. But she needed a lot more. Position and money—to be fabulously rich, to control everyone around her. Menarchos' billions let him do whatever he liked, outside law and conscience, not even bound to respect life itself. Money was power. Marty vowed to become rich enough to be able to buy up all those streets she'd littered with her childhood.

"You're getting carried away," Vie said angrily behind her. "Because we had a good year, you think it's all your doing and you have all the answers. I've given you every opportunity and the freedom you asked for. It seems that was too much. You just pour out the things you learned in school, but you haven't grasped the most basic thing about perfume. And that is, always was, and always will be: fragrance. You can't understand it without a nose, and you don't have the gift."

Marty spun around and advanced on Vie, her arm raised. Vie took a step back as an image flashed through her mind: in the kitchen, in Brooklyn, Marty punching her in the chest, screaming, "I hate you, I hate you both."

Marty's arm fell to her side. "I've never been as good as

you, have I? You thought I was scum, and you convinced Armand to do the same."

"That's a lie! I was the one who always took care of you. I was the one to bail you out of trouble. If it weren't for me, you would've gone to prison. *He* didn't do anything. I made the money to pay for your private school, and I put you through college."

"Guilt money," spat Marty. "You always wanted to be rid of me. The money meant you were in charge of everything. Why do you think Armand killed himself? I bet I know: you took away his pride in himself. You treated him the way you've treated me, as a hanger-on."

Vie was trembling. She felt nauseated. "Please stop."

Marty looked at her a long time. "OK," she said at last. "I'll stop. But I know things about him you don't. About your mother, too."

"What do you mean?"

"Before I came back to America, I made a trip. By myself, to the south of France. I came on a lot of interesting information about the past. I learned that our father was a Nazi collaborator—along with your mother."

"No! You're crazy!"

A hard, tired smile came on Marty's face. "Someday I'll tell you stories about our family. They're not pretty, but they're true."

"If you have any facts, I want to hear them," said Vie, struggling for control.

"Some other time maybe. I worked hard to get those facts, and I'm not going to throw them at your feet. They're mine, and I might want to save them for future use. Besides, if you're so curious about the past, why didn't *you* ever try to find out about it? You're your father's daughter, aren't you?"

She waited a moment for her words to sink in. Then Marty walked briskly to her desk. "I've got a lot of work to finish, so if you'll excuse me . . . ?"

Vie marched out, holding her head as high as she could manage.

Over the next two years, Jolay kept growing. Despite their personal antagonism, the two sisters had made a weave of their different but equally extraordinary talents and were often cited in magazines and newspapers as the perfect example of how a family business should be run. To the increasing numbers of young women entering business, in corporations or on their own, the Jolay sisters were synonymous with the success they aimed for.

Though their private lives diverged sharply, Vie and Marty were almost equally admired by people who worked with them. Chandra was the exception. Despite his acknowledgment of Marty's quicksilver brightness, he'd taken an immediate dislike to her. She lacked fantasy, the quality Chandra most admired. She was tough, indifferent to nuance, and because Chandra had taken Vie into his heart as though she were his own child, he wanted to protect her against the callousness and manipulations of her sister.

A few others—Elaine, Mike—felt no great affection for Marty, though they'd come to respect her abilities and even, at times, fall in awe of them. "If Marty ever decides to auction off any of her extra brainpower, let me know," Mike told Vie in a rare reference to the subject that usually remained off limits. "I want to be sure to make my bid."

Philippa usually began her meetings with Vie by asking what The Whirlwind had stirred up lately. She hadn't meant to like Marty particularly, out of loyalty to Vie and because of the competition between the two. But almost in spite of herself, Philippa found Marty adorable. She held back from friendship, knowing this could lead to complications in her relations with Vie, whom Philippa considered her closest friend, but she was fascinated, intrigued, and enormously entertained by the younger woman. The few times they'd been alone together, Philippa had felt the beginnings of a dangerous attraction, and she tried to avoid such encounters from then on. Yet she was able to mediate between the sisters, pointing out to each the strengths of the other. Vie had been quicker to accept Marty's qualities, but eventually Marty had come to recognize that starting a company before the age of eighteen took courage and faith. Vie possessed both of those, and a resilience that Marty lacked. "A classic example of experience versus educat'on," Philippa had pointed out. "Vie's been forced to make hundreds of adaptations as she's gone along, feeling her way by instinct and an unswerving belief in what she was doing. You, on the other hand, come armed with a blueprint; you've done the design and engineering ahead of time, then you set about implementing it."

Marty gave Philippa one of her slow, wonderful smiles. "Thanks, hon, you've just made me into Michelangelo."

Philippa felt hot and uncomfortable. It was a marvelous sensation. Marty in her red wool dress, full-bosomed, glowing with vitality, was a feast for the eyes. Philippa was annoyed and grateful when her secretary came in, interrupting them.

Marty's blueprint was designed for expansion and annexation. Stevens John was an advertising agency known for its aggressive and unusual campaigns, characterized by saturation of local markets through all available media. When Marty called them in, she was aware also of their reputation for demanding the highest fees in the city. She met Burt Sillcoe and knew, by the end of their first meeting, that he was the man for the job. His fierce looks appealed to her: the overhang of black eyebrows, the thick cap of black hair, his height of six foot five. She saw him as a kind of bodyguard, the account executive who would lead them into the fray, scattering competitors as he went.

Vie didn't like him. "He's so unpleasant," she complained to Mike, who replied mildly, "You don't have to live with him."

Sillcoe was hired and set to work on a campaign that would "make Estée Lauder look like a discount brand." For television spots he used exotic settings—Kruger National Park in Africa, Nepal, Victoria Falls, Bali—showing a beautiful woman sleeping in the magnificent landscape. A handsome sheik or prince rides up on a white horse, dismounts, kisses the sleeping beauty. She wakes, smiles, goes into his arms. Soft music is playing and the slogan comes on: "JOLAY. Perfumes to make your dreams come true."

When she saw the rushes, Marty wanted to veto. "Trust

me," Sillcoe told her in the viewing room. "Let it run for a month, and if you still don't like it, we'll take it off."

"It's tacky," Marty said.

"Maybe." Burt Sillcoe was immune to criticism. "But my research shows a strong trend toward romance. Maybe the women's movement led to it as a backlash, maybe it's a reflection of general boredom, no sense of national purpose or individual goals. Perhaps it reflects pessimism about the future. Who knows?"

"Be serious, Burt."

"I'm very serious," he answered, scowling. "Romance is in. You'll see—flounces and lace will come back, champagne consumption will increase."

"OK, but even if you're right in that, what about the dialogue?"

"What dialogue?" asked Burt.

"Exactly. Or didn't you notice you've gone back to the silent screen?"

"Sure. Part of it," he explained tersely. "Lets the viewer write her own scenario."

"I don't think it'll work," Marty persisted.

"Trust me," he repeated. "If you don't like to think of do-it-yourself scenario, just keep in mind that a large percentage of TV viewers turns the sound down or off during commercials. I like to think of my audience as deaf."

"One month," Marty said. "Thirty days and no more."

Burt nodded gloomily.

His gambit worked, and the silent, romantic commercial became an instant classic, winning prizes for Sillcoe and the agency. Marty held back her skepticism when he devised his print campaign, intended mainly for *Vogue*, *Harper's Bazaar*, and a few others. It was aimed at an educated, cultured audience, the classiest campaign Stevens John had ever undertaken. "Great Moments" was the theme, featuring Newton, Leonardo da Vinci, Einstein, Beethoven, Voltaire. The copy described the great discovery or accomplishment of each "giant," in a tone implying the reader was familiar with it, and then asked, "Isn't it time for your great moment?"

Jolay was established as the most exclusive, elite line of

fragrances in the world. Marty sent a memorandum to Vie: "We've done it in your image, as far as we can take it. Now it's time for a change."

Vie called a board meeting and asked Marty to explain. "We've got the superrich," she said, "and those who want to be. Now we've got to aim for the middle class." Marty's plan was to expand the line into bath products, dusting powder, maybe even deodorants and hair sprays. She also thought this was the time to go public, offer stock on the big board.

"Absolutely not," said Vie flatly.

Don Garrison, Vie's original backer, looked thoughtful. "Don't be hasty," he advised. "Marty's radar is pretty reliable."

"I started this company," said Vie, "and it's always going to stand for the highest quality, top-of-the-line fragrances. Deodorants! The women who buy Jolay don't sweat."

"But perhaps they perspire," suggested Philippa.

"No." Vie answered angrily. "And my company isn't going public. Not ever." She adjourned the meeting.

In the spring of 1978, Jolay, Inc., was offering shares on the New York Stock Exchange. As a public company, its direction altered. Responsibility to shareholders implied more than financial matters. It also came to mean responsibility for serving more of the public with a larger range of products.

Vie had no way of stopping the trend. Her advisers, all of them people she had trusted over the years, assured her that holding back from expansion could only lead to the disintegration of the company. Her only alternative for maintaining the elite image, they said, was to offer Jolay for sale to a larger company.

The alternative was no alternative. She had to agree to go on building, even though she no longer felt at home. Murray Schwartzman sympathized with Vie, but he assured her that Marty's direction was the only one they could take. "This company's a jewel," he told Vie, "a perfect jewel. But we have to take it out of the vault and let people see." He patted her arm.

"Murray," she said, "we've been together a long time. I always felt that Jolay was an extension of myself. But since Marty joined, it's different. It feels more like an artificial limb."

"Don't be frightened, bossbaby," he said, giving her a large kiss on the forehead. "You'll see. It'll come up roses, I promise you."

3

Nicolo Benedetti applied for the position, recently opened, of chemist in charge of Jolay's lab. When he first met Vie, at the interview, he thought she was the classiest woman he'd ever come across, a real lady of the kind that didn't exist anymore except in the imagination.

The test she gave him was old-fashioned, too, but original and challenging. She held out to him fifteen pieces of blotting paper, one at a time, each dipped into a beaker holding a different scent. Vie identified each for him as he sniffed it. Then she placed a blindfold over his eyes and held out the samples in random order. "If you get two or three correct, that's nothing," she told him, "it could even be chance. Half of them means you know your business."

When she removed the blindfold, her eyes were sparkling. "You got all fifteen! All of them! You have the golden nose."

Nick grinned. He could have told her that, of course, but he'd discovered years ago that nobody would believe him. His olfactory genius, his ability to distinguish as many as twelve thousand distinct odors was a rare, inherited trait possessed by no more than fifty men and women in the perfume industry throughout the world. Recently he'd learned that the extra factor in his olfactory system was known as Jacobson's Organ. But he didn't need a name to know he had the gift. As a kid in Queens, he'd earned the nickname Sniff because he could lead his pals to food by sniffing the air. His prowess brought them to many free meals—bags of groceries left on door stoops or fire escapes, a box of warm pizza in a baby carriage, and once, a roast-beef dinner for twelve waiting for them in a caterer's open truck.

"So I get the job?" he asked her, still grinning.

"It's not for me to decide," she said tersely. "I'll write my recommendations, we'll go over your file, and then we'll set up an interview for you with Ms. Jolaunay."

"Who's that?"

"My sister. We both adopt the name of Jolay for business purposes, but her name is Jolaunay and mine is Nouvel." Seeing his puzzled look, she explained. "We're half-sisters. We run this company jointly, and staff are hired by both of us. I was the first to see you because I'm able to filter out those who don't have the real gift. God-given or genetic, whichever you prefer."

"That means *you* have it, right?"

A smile flickered over Vie's face. The young man was rough but intuitive. As far as she was concerned, he was the perfect choice. She'd note that down for Marty. "I worked with my father, devising formulas," she told him. "My sister is really the business end. It'll be up to her if you get the job or not, because"—she paused to let him get the full impact of her words—"because I've decided to recommend you without reservations."

He jumped up and pumped her hand. "Thanks, Ms. Nouvel. You're wonderful."

She enjoyed his spontaneous gratitude. An attractive, open young man, without the pretensions or guardedness of other prospective candidates.

She returned the chemist's handshake, smiling. "No thanks are due, yet. You'll have to convince my sister the way you did me."

Marty agreed to see him the following week. When he walked into her office, she felt she'd found him—and she didn't mean the man for the job. His gait with its slight swagger, his strong build, square jaw, and black eyes sent out instant magnetism. It had been years since she'd met anyone so attractive. He radiated sexual energy, animal appeal. Marty took a deep breath and looked down at her desk, trying to regain composure. She hated those men who hired secretaries on the basis of their figures or their baby blues. The businesswoman in her was contemptuous of the decision her feelings had already made.

"Please sit down, Mr. Benedetti."

He took his seat, staring openly. Vie Nouvel had been lovely, but her sister was stunning. Probably older than himself, he figured, but what a fox! Could a woman who looked like that know anything about business?

He had to command all his will power to be able to concentrate on her questions. For the next thirty minutes he answered what she asked, forcing his eyes not to wander below her neck. But when she stood up and paced a few steps, he looked at her. Fantastic breasts, round hips— man, is she built! he thought. When she turned, he instantly began studying his fingernails.

At the end of the interview, Marty said, "You sound as though you know what's going on out in the industry. Seems you snowed my sister, too"—she grinned at him—"at least, her report recommends you as an outstanding chemist."

"So I get the job?" he asked, grinning back.

"You bet." She let her eyes sweep over him. "You'll be in charge of the whole lab, testing and developing. We'll start you in right away on a men's line. You'll be making sixty thousand a year, all right?"

"Make that ninety, and you've got your man."

"I've already got him," she said with a smile that made him swallow hard. "It's just the price we're haggling about. I'll give you seventy."

"Eighty-five." She reminded Nick of the first woman he'd ever had, when he was fourteen, strong for his age and already shaving. A waitress in the coffee shop, auburn-haired, with huge breasts, fat pink nipples. His eyes ran down Martine's body.

"Seventy-five, and that's final." She put a hand on one hip, teasing him.

"Just one more push, little lady, and it'll all be over. Eighty thousand dollars a year, and I'll let you have your way with me."

She gave a loud laugh. "You're funny. I like you. Eighty thousand, but you better be worth it."

"I promise—I'll make sure you're completely satisfied."

She shuddered delightedly at the double meaning. He was only twenty-nine, but Martine felt that Nick Benedetti was a match for her. Sharp, talented, ambitious—he was like herself; they were the same kind of people.

Nick came to work the following Monday, reorganized the lab to suit his taste, pinned up a *Playboy* calendar, and brought out an ashtray shaped like a vulva. When others in the lab gaped, Nick smiled. He liked to shock people, particularly in the big phony world he'd entered eight years before. Most of the fat cats running the perfume business couldn't even smell a rat—much less the delicate notes he balanced to produce a fragrance that went into bottles and was sold for larcenous prices to dupes willing to believe that a few chemicals mixed with alcohol would make them more desirable. To Nick it was all a crock, but he didn't care so long as it could make him rich. He rarely used any scent himself, unless he thought it was free advertising for something he'd formulated. Otherwise he preferred the smell of his own body. And he didn't like the woman he was with to use perfume, either. Each body had its own odors; each was distinct. He could remember a woman by the way she smelled long after the image of her face or even her body had evaporated from his mind.

Into the vulva-shaped ashtray Nick placed a burning cigarette. Cries of protest sounded through the lab. He picked it up and took a deep drag, letting the smoke out slowly. Mediocre noses were threatened by cigarette smoke, he knew. They made up a whole fetish about it, claiming it destroyed their sensitivity.

Another crock. When Nick reached a satiation point after inhaling dozens of different odors, he'd light a cigarette and let the smoke anesthetize his nostrils a few moments before he turned back to work on the organ. Other perfumers took a saline solution into their nose to clear it, but Nick had tried that only once. The cold salted water sucked in by the nostrils, made him feel he was drowning. Cigarettes were a lot more pleasant. Besides, he could rely on them to provoke shouts of outrage all around.

Let them shout. He was in charge here, and Martine Jolaunay was practically eating out of his hands already. In a couple of months all of Jolay would be virtually his.

Martine came into the lab. Some of the workers didn't recognize their boss—she'd been in only twice during the past three years. "Put that cigarette out!" she ordered in a voice of steel.

Surprised, but still in control, Nick gave her a slow, welcoming smile. "I need it to clear the nose. Too much...." He stopped in mid-sentence as she marched over and stubbed it out.

"I don't care what you need it for. Other people here don't like it, they say it obstructs their ability to work. And I will not have you interfere with productivity, no matter who you are or what you're worth. You're worth *nothing* to me if you antagonize my other employees. We're running a business here, not an opera, and I won't have any prima donnas."

"Look, lady," he retorted. "You hired me to be in charge of the lab. That's what I'll do, and I promised you satisfaction. If you don't get it, you can fire me. But as long as I'm taking over in here, this is *my* territory, and you're not telling me what to do." His face was close to hers, his anger white-hot.

Martine stepped back, uncertain how to reestablish her dominance. His rage held something magnificent, hard and forceful against the power that she commanded. She bridled against the force of this man, resolving not to let him win. "If you want to smoke, you have an office to do it in."

"Yeah," he agreed. "Or I could always sneak into the little boys' room."

She gave him a smile, he returned it, and the technicians watching them recognized that a truce was being made, though they couldn't understand what battle had been fought.

He watched her hips as she moved out of the room.

That woman's for me, he decided. She's dynamite, and I'll be the one who sets her off.

At the door Martine turned, caught the look in his eyes, and gasped as she realized this was fire and might rage out of her control.

Marty kept away from the lab, though she was unable to banish Nick Benedetti from her thoughts, sometimes even her dreams. He couldn't forget her either, but made no attempt to get in touch. The office was her territory, his the lab. Someday they'd collide like moving particles, he was sure, but until the explosion came, it was safest to stay out of her path. She had the power to kick him out whenever she chose—and he wasn't going to give her the chance. His ambition, like Marty's, was to move to the top, clearing the space until it was his alone.

With Vie he felt at ease. Vie visited the lab regularly and showed her deep understanding of the work done there. Usually she'd ask to consult with Nick privately, and then her questions would be direct, interested; her suggestions invaluable. Nick relied on her opinions of a new fragrance, and her knowledge of the old ways often gave him fresh ideas on how to tone down an overly dominant note or how to remedy the rate of fatigue in a compound. If the scent disintegrated too quickly—the fatigue factor—it meant that customers wouldn't come back for a second bottle.

Vie admired Nick, both for his innovative skills and his sensitivity to suggestions. He never held on to an idea or a technique out of pride. Show him a better way, a more economical solution, and he jumped at it. Vie thought of him as a true scientist whose ego was subordinated to discovery. She wondered how he and Marty got along— such different people, with almost opposite sets of values. But when she asked him, Nick said abruptly, "I never see her."

4

The twenty-first birthday party for Jolay would be held on the first Sunday in June, at Tavern on the Green in Central Park. It was meant more as a sentimental occasion than as a promotion party. There'd be no particular product to sell; it would be a reunion for all those who had stood behind Jolay during the past two decades.

To Marty the planned event seemed a perfect opportunity for sending out feelers to get a reading of where people stood, or would stand, on the subject of expansion.

Jolay was doing all right as a small-to-medium company. All right, but not spectacularly. Its growth was predictable, secure, and just enough to maintain its status quo. But Marty had set her sights on greater rewards. If Jolay changed its image, opened out to a larger market, it could vastly increase its sales. A broad-based Jolay would also mean a shift of command, from Vie to Marty.

In fact, Marty thought, only by a change of direction could she unseat her sister and become the undisputed head of the company. There was nothing she wanted more. She knew, however, that a contest of wills between the two of them would never result in a clear victory for herself. She had to get Vie out—and with this fixed goal Marty had gone to Motek and begun negotiating in secret.

She took nobody into her confidence, fearing the project would be sabotaged if Vie heard even a rumor of it. Getting the giant conglomerate interested in acquiring Jolay had been hard and discouraging work at the beginning. But now Marty was starting to feel hopeful. If she played her cards right, the takeover might be accomplished within six months—a year at most.

The Motek officials, already faced with a monopoly violation suit in their children's furniture division, were as anxious as Marty to keep the proceedings secret and their name out of public view. Her requirements were a great deal of money and a position of uncontested power; they in turn demanded exclusive use of the name Jolay and a cadre of highly competent people to come in with her.

Vie would be offered a place, but whether or not she accepted, the new Jolay would be essentially Marty's company. And Marty was almost sure Vie wouldn't accept. She'd mentioned that possibility to Motek a few weeks earlier, but quickly retracted when she saw their alarm. An independent Vie Jolay meant competition, and if that were to be the case, the negotiating executives told her, Motek wasn't interested in buying.

Marty didn't bring up the subject of Vie again. Not to Motek, anyway. She quickly sought legal advice on her own and was assured by the lawyers that Vie could be forced out of competition when the time came.

"I'm bringing in the best chemist in the business," she assured the executives. She knew she could count on Nick, but she couldn't rely on any of the old guard if Vie refused to join.

Philippa was someone any company would want as an ally. If Marty could promise Motek the consultancy services of Philippa Wright, the deal would receive higher priority. Philippa's reputation had been firm as granite ever since she'd started out, a wunderkind in business, who'd become the first woman vice president of Magdahl-Hoffman when she was twenty-eight. From there, she had carved her own territory, innovating and directing fashion throughout America. In 1959 she'd traveled to the American exhibition in Moscow, bringing along twenty models, nine of whom were black. Her fashion show was a sensation; she'd lunched with the Nixons, who'd come for the opening, and had had a private meeting with Soviet Premier Khrushchev. Two years later, she'd brought the styles of swinging London to New York and the rest of the country. She was the acknowledged power behind many thrones of fashion.

"You coming to the birthday party, Phil?" Marty asked casually over the phone.

"Wouldn't miss it for the world. Canceled two weddings and a memorial service. Twenty-one years!" She chuckled. "I can hardly believe my baby's come of age. I'm the godmother, you know darling. I was there at the christening."

"Right," said Marty, feeling pessimistic. But Philippa was never a person to act out of sentimentality. "Have you been noticing that our yearly rate of increase is slowing down? It's barely above the national growth median."

"Frankly, no. Hadn't taken that in. But you still have every reason to celebrate. Jolay is the only successful independent perfume company in America."

"What price independence?" Marty mumbled.

"What's that, darling? Independence? You can take it from me—that's the most important thing there is."

Marty sighed. Of course. Philippa's background of independence made her a natural foe of takeovers.

"What were you calling about, Marty love?" Philippa asked.

"Nothing. Just a friendly call. See you at the party." She hung up, discouraged.

The others who'd been present at Jolay's founding were Chandra Ghannikar and Don Garrison. Chandra was as good as dead, Marty reflected. His massive heart attack a year earlier had left him too enfeebled to do any work, and his business had been taken over by his son, a man of about forty, who'd suddenly arrived in America looking for his father. The younger Ghannikar showed no particular acumen, and In Essence was now just a small-time supplier. Vie's weekly visits to Chandra annoyed Marty.

Don Garrison, the last of the three, might see things Marty's way. He cared about money, and he'd recognize the obvious advantages of going over to Motek. Marty decided to wait for the party itself to talk to Don, sounding him out under the guise of casual conversation.

On that Sunday evening, the weather was mild. Champagne bubbled, reflections of light sparkled over smooth hairdos and bare skin. The soft air was perfect for outdoor dining and dancing.

Seated at another table, Marty hadn't had the chance to get Don alone when he stood up and called for silence. He wanted to be the first to offer his tribute on this occasion, he said.

"Looking back over all my years at the bank, nothing has given me greater pride than my decision to back Jolay, at a time when its founder was still a minor. . . ." Marty looked down at her plate and knew she had to count him out too.

Other tributes followed. When the speeches ended, the band started again. Music rose up to the blooming trees and trailed out over the fragrant fields and bushes of Central Park. At the side of the dance floor Vie stood next to Nina, who had flown in from California for the celebration. Mike was at Vie's other side, his arm resting lightly around her waist. She felt happy and secure.

"Dance?"

Marty looked up at Nick Benedetti. Her lips parted, but she stood and went into his arms silently. His mouth brushed the side of her face. "I've been waiting," he said in an urgent voice.

Marty closed her eyes. I've got him, she thought.

Many guests turned to watch them as they danced: the two dark heads, the two bodies moving as one slowly across the floor.

"Who's that with Marty?" Mike asked Vie.

"My head chemist. Brilliant. He's the rock on which Jolay stands."

Mike frowned. There was a darkness about the pair. They seemed locked together in their own sphere, bound as tightly as twin magnets, the force between them powerful enough to destroy an empire.

Marty's intensity over the next few months reached the level of obsession. Though she had to continue working at Jolay, she thought and breathed Motek: the takeover was her fixed, exclusive goal.

She set up breakfast meetings, lunch meetings, dinner meetings. She consulted her team of lawyers almost daily to make sure that the moves she planned were legally safe.

Over the summer, Marty didn't let vacations interfere with her progress. Though no board meetings were planned, she turned this to her advantage by approaching Motek executives individually. Whoever met with her was intrigued by the combination of strong business sense and dramatic beauty. Marty included these attributes in her calculations but didn't rely on them. Over the months she carefully rounded up qualified and ambitious people who would come in with her.

She had researched Motek's many interests and holdings, and in meetings could come up with figures that even the executives were unaware of. In negotiating she stressed the mutual advantage—expansion on both sides—if Motek would acquire Jolay.

Only four months after Jolay's birthday celebration, Marty had lined up the deal. When she heard that Motek was buying up Jolay shares in blocks, Marty knew she was secure. And in October, on the day of Vie's launching party for *O! de Vie*, Marty was ready to move in and take over.

VII

THE

FORMULA

1984

1

The crystal in the palm of Vie's hand refracted light from the pale winter sun. She looked at the brilliant colors dancing on her skin: purple, yellow, emerald, orange. For a moment she forgot everything, engrossed in the dazzling display. Then she heard a voice calling, "Ma'am?" and looked up from the rainbow in her hand to the drab light from the window that was its source. She remembered who she was, and that she'd just lost her domain.

"We're through now, I guess." The moving man spoke gently, as though apologizing for the work he and his men had done. People have often been kind, she thought fleetingly.

Vie smiled at him. "Thanks, Chris. You did a fine job. Wait—let me pay you now."

Her eyes searched the room, empty of everything except the fixtures. Her handbag on the marble mantelpiece was the only remaining sign that these rooms had been occupied. The furniture that used to stand here would be going into storage, for a time at least, with the paintings, sculptures, most of the china, silver, linens. Vie's maid, Ludmilla, had left yesterday, in tears, but Vie had placed her with the Garrisons, whose youngest was still only eleven, and she knew Ludmilla would be happy.

The trees and bushes of the greenhouse were donated to the New York Botanical Gardens in the Bronx; smaller plants went to friends. In the outside closet hung Vie's mink-lined raincoat. In her hand, the crystal; over there, her bag.

She shrugged, aware that the men were waiting, went

over and took out her checkbook-wallet, placing the crystal ball inside her bag. She wrote out a check for the moving expenses and handed it to Chris along with a large tip in cash. She turned away while he thanked her. Keeping face had always been important to Vie, and she didn't want him to see that she couldn't hold her smile any longer.

Vie walked to the window while the men let themselves out and stood there a long time, as though in quiet mourning. She didn't notice Mike Parnell come in. He stood watching her: a fair, somehow reverent figure in soft beige, her golden hair muted by strands of premature silver. Motionless in the gutted room, she reminded him of a beautiful carved wooden statue he'd once seen in a royal tomb in France.

"Vie?" he called quietly, but her name exploded in the silence and she jumped. He crossed the room and took both her hands. "Marie Antoinette?" he asked. "Or is it Mary, Queen of Scots?" Immediately embarrassed by his analogies, he bent to kiss her hands.

Despite herself, Vie giggled. For a big man, his gesture was awkward, ridiculous—and touching. "Mike, you old bear—I mean, dear," she said affectionately, touching his hair lightly with her free hand.

He straightened up. "That's better, a bit of twinkle in the old peepers." He reached into the inside pocket of his overcoat. "Here. I got us some bubbly." He brought out a bottle of vintage Moët & Chandon, her favorite champagne.

Putting it on the window ledge, Mike conjured two delicately stemmed, miraculously unbroken glasses from his outside pockets. He gave one to her, expertly loosened the champagne cork with one hand, and let it rocket into the air while his glass under the bubbling neck of the bottle caught the first froth.

Vie watched him in stupefaction. When he'd poured her glass, she gave a wail of protest. "You crazy! What're we celebrating? I've lost my company, my home; I'm being dispossessed of everything, and you're pouring champagne! Didn't anyone ever tell you, Mike? You don't celebrate losses, you grieve over them."

"Same as with death," he answered, undaunted. "We're

having a wake." He clinked glasses with her, and raised his. "To Vie! To life! To the road ahead, a new beginning!" He grinned and sipped, but he was noticing the tension around her eyes, a delicate etching that told him she was getting older. Usually she looked younger than her age.

When he'd met her, at the Yale weekend, she'd stood out like a diamond among the coal. Out of place there, out of sync, she'd emanated an intelligence and sophistication he'd never met in a woman before. And beauty. He'd wanted simply to take her in his arms and keep her there, but he'd felt inept, boyish, intimidated by her worldliness—or, as it had appeared to him strolling through the campus, her otherworldliness. Instead of talking about her loveliness, he'd forced himself to chatter about architecture.

And now, nearly twenty years later, she remained as distant as a cathedral he didn't dare enter.

There had been a few times when he'd allowed himself to hope they could be more than friends. Once they'd even planned a weekend together. But Vie had canceled because of business—a trip to the Southwest, he seemed to remember—and Mike had gone alone to the cabin in Vermont. A pretty girl he met up there—Rosalie? Roseann? Rosalind?—gave him the comfort he'd needed, but Mike was too hurt and angry after the weekend to call Vie for several months.

She'd been the one to call first, and when they met again, she asked if he would be her personal lawyer. He accepted, feeling doomed to a working relationship that would make him even more invisible to her as a man. He could feel her affection for him; it had always been there. That was all he had from her, and he couldn't risk losing it. So he remained on the sidelines, a good friend, whose hopes for happiness she unwittingly held in her beautiful hands.

"I should have let you handle all my affairs," Vie said, reproaching herself. "Why didn't I let you represent my business interests years ago?"

"I wish you had," Mike said glumly. The twelve years as her private lawyer had allowed him to remain close to her and become her confidant. It had enabled him to do minor things—like insisting she hold out for a larger sum when the first offers came for her cooperative. Most of the money she received would have to go into paying up the company mortgage. Mike had seen to it that they sold high enough for Vie to retain an amount that could guarantee at least a modest income.

"From now on you will. Isn't it strange, Mike? Everything turns out the way it should have, but always too late. Chandra once said to me, 'Be careful what you wish for—you might get it.'" She tried to smile, but her expression was wan. "Now I have you as my business lawyer, but there's no more business to transact."

She looked out the window. "It's bleak," she said wearily, "and I'm tired of fighting. The past months have taken everything out of me. I did everything I could, and I lost. I suppose the best woman won. It's a world I can't handle anymore. I've become redundant. Maybe there's a cave somewhere I can crawl into and hibernate."

Placing a hand lightly on her shoulder, Mike gestured to the park below them. "It's the *end* of winter, lassie. You'll see. Soon the trees will be budding, the birds chirping, a smell of spring in the air. A new life opening up."

"A new Vie?" she teased sadly, playing on her name.

"I hope not, seeing as how I find the old one close to perfect. But believe me, new things *will* happen, sure as sap rises. You're not Queen Vie for nothing. You'll start over, the way this old earth of ours has to do every year after the ravages of winter."

"Maybe. Right now I'm feeling like the last child left after the party. The one whose mother forgot to come and pick her up."

Mike scrutinized the elegant profile. Self-pity wasn't part of Vie's character. But of course the road would be tough. Did she now regret her decision to resign? She could have stayed on as Jolay's co-president when the conglomerate took over, reaping wealth and security. But not this woman, he thought. She has to be proud of what she does. The art and tradition of perfumery mean more to her than a few millions.

"Maybe I acted too rashly." Her hazel eyes were questioning him.

"You think so?"

She didn't answer, and in Vie's steady gaze Mike understood she was testing him. "You made the only possible decision under the circumstances—for *you*."

"That's right, isn't it, Mike? How could I be part of that multinational Motek? *Cake* mixes they make. Puddings. Car parts. Even baby carriages. How could fragrance ever permeate such a network? I feel sure Jolay can't maintain its image there, or its identity."

"On the button," he said, smiling. He'd predicted, without letting her know, that the perfume company would become, to the corporate management, as elusive as fragrance itself; like an afterthought never fully expressed.

"So," she said matter-of-factly, "there wasn't any choice. That helps. Looks like I've got to start over whether I want to or not. But with what, Mike?" She stared at the bare walls. "I loved this place. It was *mine*. I designed it, I bought every piece that was in it. And my greenhouse—I was so proud of that! This place and the company were what I had. They were all I wanted. Other women have families, babies—but I made myself a *world*." She looked around the room again. "It's so terribly empty," she said in a low voice, close to tears.

He refilled their glasses, wishing they could sit down, that he could take her away from here, but he knew she wasn't ready to leave. "Vie, sweetheart, please try to look at the other side. See it as a challenge. You can meet it."

"Can I?" She looked more vulnerable than he'd ever seen her.

"Think of everything you've done in the past, your track record, your following, your wonderful talent. Then add the capital you'll get from the sale of the penthouse." He raised his hand to forestall the objection he knew was coming. "I know, there won't be much left after the company mortgage's taken care of, and then you have your legal fees. Still, we might retrieve two hundred thousand dollars.

"But I'm trying to paint the whole future for you. On the positive side of the balance we stack your ability, reputation, your not inconsiderable name, *some* money for investments and financing, your determination, brilliance, beauty. . . ."

She interrupted him, laughing. "Sure you're not leaving anything out?"

"And me, of course. One of your assets."

"The greatest," she said, putting her arm through his. "But now let's hear the other side."

He frowned and continued in a softer voice. "Well, there's that damn agreement you signed. Bastards, those lawyers. Particularly Duane Olcott—Martine couldn't have found better representation for herself if she'd gone straight to the devil." His Irish was up. "Vie, if you'd only let me tackle him—I would've stayed on his back until he cried uncle."

"I learned my lesson," she said sadly. But she didn't really believe he could have changed the outcome. He would have put up a better fight, but in the end. . . . "The fact is, Mike, my signature's on those papers."

"Yeah," he said, still glowering at his unseen adversary. "And that means you've legally agreed to stay out of competition for five years."

"So if I *do* start over again . . ."

"You'll have to fight the Motek octopus. And the money due you for the sale of your interests in Jolay will be tied up pending legal action."

"That's why I sold the apartment." Now she was the one trying to cheer him up. But she felt hopeless. To fall from the pinnacle, she thought, was much, much worse than never having reached it. At least then you had a fixed goal and could keep looking up. But scrambling *back* was something else.

"Mike. Do you mind? I'd like to be alone for a little while, think about things."

"You've always wanted to be alone," he said bitterly.

Vie looked up, startled. "Did I say something wrong?"

"No. That is. . . ." Now, he told himself. Now was the time to take her in his arms, lay claim to her, while she was vulnerable. "Vie, I . . ." he started again, taking a step toward her.

"Yes?"

He didn't advance further. He'd always known her as a

strong, proud woman, fiercely independent. It was that woman he'd loved from the start, and he'd been as proud of her as she was herself. At this moment, even if she'd give in, what would she be giving him? Her momentary weakness, her temporary vulnerability. Even if she gave him her affection, too, it wasn't right. He'd have to wait until her strength returned. If she ever came to him at all, it would have to be an independent Vie, sure of herself and sure of wanting him. "Nothing," he said. "I'll leave you to yourself. But, Vie?"

"Mike." She went over to give him a good-bye hug.

"Any time you want me . . . anything at all. . . ."

She held his face between her hands. "I know," she said softly. "You are very dear. And I love you very much." She kissed the tip of his nose. He didn't try to kiss her back and walked out without another word.

When he was gone, she went back to staring at the park below. Gusts of light snow blew up from time to time, blurring the landscape into an impressionist painting. I'm like my father, she thought, seeing the similarity of their fortunes. He, too, had started work as soon as he finished high school. He had a flourishing business in Paris then, before his downfall. Like father, like daughter—she'd inherited his rare gift of smell and his sense of enterprise. Had she also, she wondered, inherited an unseen weakness from him, a fatal flaw that threatened destruction by the age of forty?

The lights of Central Park went on suddenly, diffused spots of brightness behind the brushstrokes of snow. It was beautiful and hushed, like a darkening theater before the play begins. What can possibly be out there for me? she wondered. I'm an actress who's played her last starring role.

Vie thought of the clothes that she and Ludmilla had packed in large cartons, protecting them from wrinkles with tissue paper. She couldn't bear to part with them, the beautiful costumes of success. Not with the diamonds either, though she'd sold many of her jewels. The clothes went into storage with the furniture, except for two cartons she was keeping at Philippa's. Costumes and trinkets—

exactly. The paraphernalia of a has-been actress, Vie told
herself harshly. She'd always been tougher on herself than
on others. Maybe that was her mistake? No, it was some
kind of damned romanticism in her, an unwillingness to
compromise with standards. And why not? Vie argued
with Vie. Why not retain principles?

Because, answered the other Vie, you go broke.

But, countered the first, you know Mike was right. You
had no choice but to do just what you did.

Right, answered the adversary, there was no choice *at
that point*. But think back over the past ten years.

"Made a clean sweep of it, did you?" came Marty's
voice as the room flooded with light. "Guess they haven't
turned off the electricity yet."

Vie turned angrily. "Did you come here to gloat?"

"Why should I? I didn't know you were here."

"Then why did you come?"

"To check it out. Remember, the penthouse was a
company expense. But here are the keys," she said, giving
them to Vie. She got out of her sable, letting it fall to the
floor. "An extra set for the new owners."

Vie accepted them. "In a way, I'm glad you're here. I've
been wanting a chance to talk to you directly." Though
she'd seen her sister often in the last weeks, they were
never without lawyers, secretaries, reporters, accountants.

"Oh boy, a confrontation."

Vie sighed. What was the use? But the opportunity to
talk wouldn't come again soon. "I know you don't like
me," she began in a low voice.

"You're my family," Marty said tersely.

"Then why did you do this to me?"

"Do what? You mean Motek? I didn't do anything *to*
you, I did it for us, for the company. Your decision to keep
out of it is your own affair. I advised you to stay on. I
can't see any reason why we couldn't go on working
together. Our skills complement each other's. You're the
most innovative perfumer in the business. And I'm the
best executive director."

Two perfect halves, thought Vie, that can't maintain a
whole. "Then why didn't we continue as we were? Jolay

was doing fine. You made expansion part of our regular operations. Our sales volume was increasing every year."

"Right, and that's why we could command the highest price. You often look back, Vie. You've always done that, like Father did, and a lot of times it paid off. He went back to old formulas; you often restored old dreams of elegance. That's fine, as far as it goes.

"But I'm the one who looks ahead, always. You say Jolay was expanding? Yes, sure it was, but at a slow, regular pace. We were still basically confined to fragrances and to a luxury market, despite the cosmetics and the drugstores.

"We couldn't have gone on forever, Vie, not with the image we projected. We left out too much of middle America. We were still going to specialty stores instead of shopping centers. We were doing the same thing with our foreign franchises, too, forgetting that economies everywhere are being leveled, that the top is being squeezed out as much as the bottom, and people don't want to 'invest' in crystal bottles or silk-lined boxes. Sure, those things still have snob appeal, they're good for promotion. But you can get richer selling potatoes than caviar, and people want potatoes. Use the crystal for displays, maybe, but sell them products they see as honest: down-to-earth products in simple containers."

"And Motek will do that?"

"They sure will. They've given me the green light to develop a line of 'basics.' I'll even use recycled paper for the labels!" She laughed. "That should bring in the ecology freaks."

Her voice was clear and sharp as a trumpet's, ringing out to a hint of echo in the bare apartment. Her dress was fire-engine red. With her nearly black curls, her buttermilk skin still elastic as a girl's, and the ebony choker at her throat, Marty looked exciting, totally in command, and only slightly dangerous. Her mind, Vie thought, was as brilliant as her dress, sending out electric waves that prevented Vie from coming any closer.

"Why do you want to do it?" Vie asked.

"Why? It's pretty obvious, isn't it? For money."

"But you have lots already."

"And I want more! There was never enough when I was a kid."

Vie winced. "You went to college. . . ."

"Yes, on your money. Look, Vie, I understand poverty, I've seen it. I was on the streets for years, remember? It's no good, I know that. They say power corrupts, but that's bullshit. The opposite is true. Being powerless is what corrupts a person, and power means money. I'm determined to have it, as much as I can possibly get, for the rest of my life."

Vie drew in a deep breath. "I wanted to get away from poverty, too, you know. It scared me. It was destroying Papa. I had to get out of it, rise above it."

"And you did. A real achievement. But once you got to a certain level, you didn't care anymore."

"And you do?"

"My life is a war against it," she said grimly.

They were both silent, unused to exchanges of feelings.

Vie wanted to go over and put a hand on Marty's shoulders. Instead she said, in a tone that came out all wrong, "You think you and I could ever be partners again?"

The superiority in her voice made Marty freeze. The queen addressing a subject—damn her, damn the Ice Goddess, she said to herself, using an epithet that others had invented behind her sister's back. No matter what Marty did or what she accomplished, Vie could still make her feel like an unpolished kid, part of the retinue, never an equal. "Look, Vie," she said roughly, "I'm determined to make it on my own and to go on making it."

"Yes," Vie answered frostily. "You've made that quite clear." A few years ago, Marty had met Charles Revson at a party and told him, "I'm going to match you, Charlie— and then spring ahead. My company will be bigger than Revlon."

To Vie's amazement, Revson had hugged Marty and said, "If anyone can do it, you can. Good luck, honey, and come out fighting!"

Vie started toward the closet. "We come from different molds," she said, "even though we're sisters."

"*Half*-sisters," Martine corrected. "Genetically, we may not even be related."

Vie looked at her. "Are you trying to disown me?"

"How could I?" Martine gave a bitter laugh. "You've always been my fate. You and I, the Jolay sisters, so photogenic, a great promotional gimmick."

"I took you into the business," said Vie curtly.

"Right, and you would've fallen flat if you hadn't."

"I very much doubt that," Vie told her. "My success was due to a particular ability, not to circumstance. I had something you've never understood: a nose."

"Inherited from your father, right? But I'm the one who really knows him. I dug him up from the past he tried to bury."

"Look," Vie said, grabbing Marty by the shoulders. "Either you have something to say about the past or not. And if you have anything to tell me, you better let me hear it now."

Marty wrenched free from Vie's grip. "All right," she said, a gleam coming into her eyes. The two sisters stood opposite each other across the bare room as Marty told Vie everything she'd uncovered.

When Marty finished, Vie said quietly, "You better go now."

Marty picked up her coat from the floor and hugged it against herself a moment. "I'm sorry," she murmured, and walked out.

2

The saxophone wailed softly from the other side of the garden, complaining in rich notes about betrayals of lovers and partners. Or so Vie imagined, hearing it as she prepared to leave her brownstone apartment. The music

moaned over the heads of still-sleeping crocuses, through
naked branches tipped with hard pea-green buds. She
hadn't known she'd be getting these free concerts when
she'd decided to take this place.

It had taken her about three minutes to make up her
mind. The price of the three rooms was $720 a month—
"ground floor apartment, a real down-to-earth bargain"
the real estate man had told her, not realizing he was
being funny—but it wasn't the price that made her decide
immediately. It was the garden. After giving away her
plants, Vie had become lonely for them. She missed the
living things she'd tended every day and realized she'd
come to depend on them somehow, as though they were
companions. But when she started apartment hunting,
she soon gave up hopes of finding a place big enough to
keep even two trees inside. Most places were co-op, and
she could no longer afford to buy. The $180,000 she'd
realized from the sale of her apartment after paying off
the mortgage was carefully invested, providing a sure
income of between $20,000 and $30,000 a year—by no
means extravagant for anyone living in New York City,
and barely adequate for Vie's needs. Buying a co-op would
use up all her capital, and Vie was determined to hang on
to it until she could invest the money in her own business.

The few apartments listed for rent, not sale, were so
stingy in space and so extravagant in cost that she began
to despair of finding anything at all. In the midtown area
any set of rooms for less than $2500 a month reminded
her of Brooklyn—and nothing, she felt, could be worse
than going back to the cramped drabness of Mrs. Murphy's
house.

The agent had suggested other parts of the city, the
outskirts of Greenwich Village reaching across Hudson
Street toward the river. The area was lively, bustling with
young people whose apparel made her think they were
auditioning for revivals of 1920s or 1930s musicals. Vie
expressed doubt. "I think I'd feel like a den mother here,"
she told the agent, who didn't understand her remark and
insisted on showing her just one more place.

One look at the garden, and even though nothing was
yet in bloom, Vie reached for her checkbook. A miracle,

she still felt it was, adjusting her scarf in the mirror on her way out. She had only to open her kitchen window to smell the budding flowers, the dewy grass. And the savings over a midtown apartment were enough, she calculated, to cover newspaper advertising in the launching of a new product. If I have one—no, she told herself, when I have one.

Closing the door and silencing the saxophone, Vie walked down the stone steps, heading east. She hadn't made an appointment with Don Garrison, purposely waiting to arrange a formal meeting until she had something concrete to offer. But if she happened to drop in on him, Vie would be able to feel him out, get an idea of where he stood now in relation to his former "baby," Jolay Perfumes. She'd chat with him as a friend of twenty years and discover his attitude toward the takeover, the degree of his willingness to help her start again.

Entering through the marble doorway of Atlantic Mercantile's main branch on Park Avenue, Vie felt a momentary loss of composure. The gleaming marble, stately and regal, had never come into her consciousness before as anything more than an appropriate backdrop for her dealings. Madame Jolay, president of her own company, ruler of a small dominion, was a figure who belonged in an atmosphere of pomp and wealth. Even in her early twenties she'd felt at home here. But now, approaching forty, stripped of her rule, Vie felt out of place, an actress who'd stumbled into the wrong play and didn't have her lines. Lifting up her head, she briskly crossed the main hall toward the safe-deposit area, feeling vulnerable, exposed to eyes she sensed were on her. As she neared the vault, she noticed a tall, dark-haired man who was looking at her openly. He was extraordinarily attractive. The frank admiration on his face as he watched her made Vie turn her face away, unnerved by him. He made her feel like a girl—something she hadn't felt in a very long time.

Don Garrison came out of his office to greet her.

"Vie! Welcome, stranger. Haven't seen you in months."

At fifty-three Don was still good-looking, his face more suited to a midwestern farm than a Park Avenue bank.

"Don." She hugged him briefly, feeling the dark eyes at her back.

"How're things going? I heard through the grapevine that you've got yourself a place in the Village. You intending to become a modern-day hippie, by any chance?"

"Not if I can help it." She smiled. "It's really a terrific place, Don. I've got the whole ground floor of a brownstone, with a garden in back."

" 'Cultivate your own garden,' eh? Never knew what that meant. Step into my office."

The dark-haired man watched them enter the office of the vice president in charge of loans.

"So," said Don, closing the door behind them, "how're things with you? Lonely? You're looking wonderful—you always do. The most beautiful woman in business, I've always said."

"Not anymore. And you? Life as usual?" Vie picked up Don's staccato style of speech whenever she was with him.

He frowned. "Not too good at home."

"The children?"

"No, wife. We're having a rough time. Not too sure we'll make it. Painful stuff, better to leave it alone. At least that's something you don't have to go through."

"No," she answered thoughtfully.

"But tell me, honey, didn't you ever regret it? Not getting married?"

"I never had a chance, I was always too busy working." It was a half-truth. With Hubert, she'd wanted to very much, she'd been deeply in love—and yet, even then, she'd had doubts.

"And now?" he asked gently. An image of the dark man in the hall made her heart suddenly beat faster. She smiled at Don and shrugged. He reached for her hand and fondled it in his. "Have dinner with me, Vie," he entreated her.

She extricated her hand. "I'll be coming round to you in a short while to talk about business," she warned.

"So soon?" He sounded dubious. "All right, whenever you say. But have dinner with me anyway. Friday?"

She looked down at the hand he'd been holding a few minutes earlier. "I don't know. . . ."

"Please. You know you can rely on me," he said.

She gave a wide smile. "I always have, and I guess I won't stop now. OK, Friday. Come by for drinks before—I want you to see my new place."

"Good girl. Now back to business. What've you heard about Jolay? How's Marty handling it?"

"I was about to ask you the same thing."

"I'll find out what I can and run it to you Friday," Don Garrison promised.

"Thanks, but don't bother. I'll give Marty a buzz myself in the next day or two." Vie didn't want him or anyone to know how deep the rift went. Her sense of pride, her protectiveness toward the family made her rush to cover up. Though people knew that she'd strongly opposed the takeover and had then resigned from the company, only Philippa, Mike, and Elaine knew the whole story. A feeling of shame, for both Marty and herself, prevented Vie from revealing to others that her sister had betrayed her.

They shook hands, and Vie left Don's office dissatisfied. She'd learned nothing, and she was annoyed with herself for the careless slip that let him know she wasn't in touch with Marty.

Frowning, she made her way toward the vault but was stopped before she reached it by a man's voice close to her ear. "Don't I know you from somewhere? From our future maybe?"

His velvet eyes were the most beautiful she'd ever seen. "How can I answer a question like that?" she protested, smiling, and felt a warm flush rise to her face.

"Say yes, and we'll start making up for the years we've wasted."

She couldn't help laughing. His approach was ridiculous—but charming, totally charming. "That's it," he said, "that laughter. I know it from all my springtimes."

Romantic, she thought. Could he be making fun of her? As though reading her thoughts, he said, "Please, don't be annoyed. It's just that I don't know how to pick up a woman."

"Is that what you're trying to do?" she asked earnestly.

"You didn't notice? Good, that means my infinitely subtle ploy worked."

Vie was laughing again when a clerk from the bank came up to him and said something in a low voice. He nodded, turned back to Vie, and said, "Princess, I've got to go harness a few horses. Please don't leave, I'll be right back." As he walked away, she realized she didn't even know his name.

But that didn't affect the way she was feeling. How long had it been? She tingled as though she'd been swimming in a clear stream. Ridiculous, she said to herself as she went toward the security officer. Ridiculous, she repeated as she handed him her identification and the key to her safe. Ridiculous, she said again as she followed behind him and he brought out the strongbox. But totally charming, she added.

She took the box into a cubicle and closed the door. It contained no money or securities, no important papers, nothing of great commercial value. More like a child's secret treasure trove than an executive's coffer, the box held a cut-glass doorknob, the bottle of Windsor cologne Nina had given her at Jolay's twenty-first birthday party, a plain gold ring, a blue-white diamond, and a leatherbound book. The ring had been her mother's, whose fingers must have been as slender as her own. She had tried it on years ago and found it a perfect fit. The diamond, too, had belonged to her mother—it was the last remaining gem from a brooch that Armand had broken up and sold piecemeal.

After her father's death, Vie hadn't wanted to sell it. He'd told her the brooch was his gift to Anne when she agreed to marry him. At three carats, the diamond was less valuable than many that Vie had bought since then. She kept it in this, her special safe deposit box, and not in the one that held her appraised jewels, because she vaguely planned to have it reset one day into a ring.

The doorknob and the cologne symbolized the beginnings of Vie's empire.

But she'd come for neither of these items. It was the book she needed, her father's black "bible," whose pages had been the collateral on which he'd built his success and, later, hers. Vie reached out for it now as the source of inspiration for a new venture.

Carefully she picked up the book, fingering its soft, worn leather stained by sweat, chemicals, tears, and at the end, blood. A book with magic in it, and terrible pain. She glanced through the cracked, yellowing pages and then wrapped it in a silk scarf.

When she returned to the gleaming banking hall, she looked around but couldn't see him anywhere. A man out of a dream, she thought. She hugged the book closer. Armand had taught her when she was a small child in Brooklyn that dreams could be made to come true.

"So far down it looks like up to me," said Don Garrison coming into Vie's living room.

"Great line, but I think it's copyrighted." She held out her cheek for him to kiss.

"Didn't know there was anything but wasteland between midtown and the Street. But I got to admit, Vie, this squalor of yours is classy."

She made a face at him. "The usual?" When he nodded, she poured two and a half jiggers of J&B over two lumps of ice. She'd bought the bottle of scotch especially for him, remembering he was proud of steadfastly sticking to the same drink over the years, despite promotions and increases in salary. He was disdainful of more expensive brands. "Chivas Regal, Johnnie Walker Black—they're for the parvenus—rich peasants. Give me plain old J&B every time," he'd told her, as though making a claim for his old-fashioned virtues.

She poured herself a smaller drink and carried both glasses back to the sofa where he'd made himself comfortable by kicking off his shoes and sprawling in a corner. "Here's looking at you, honey," he said, raising his glass. "Which, I might add, is always a pleasure." He threw back most of it, and Vie realized that the moment of discomfort she'd felt when he kissed her cheek rose from the alcohol on his breath. He'd been drinking before he came here, and Vie worried that he'd go on all night, permitting his marital troubles to stand as justification for slowly submerging himself in a stream of scotch. If he got drunk tonight in honor of his collapsing marriage, Vie was sure he'd make a pass. Then he'd get insistent, and Vie's refusal would put a strain on their professional relationship. Even if Vie wanted to accept, she'd never allow a valuable business ally to become a lover. Sex had never been so important that she'd let it interfere with her work. Except once, a long time ago.

After he finished his third drink, she swallowed the remains of her first and went to get her coat. Though they'd agreed at the bank they'd just be going out to dinner as friends, enough had happened in the past three days to make Vie determined that the evening would be devoted to business. Maybe not overtly—and she wouldn't deny Don the chance to confide in her about personal matters—but the *purpose* of tonight's dinner had changed in Vie's mind from a date to a meeting.

Things had started happening after she left the bank with the book in her hand. When she got home, she went out into the garden, put a pillow on the seat of the cold wrought-iron chair, and reverently withdrew the "bible" from its silk wrapping. The chill in the air fanned her expectations; the aroma of young buds soothed her, and the saxophone started up again in a sad-happy blues. She sat like this for an hour, poring over the pages in her lap, trying to reconstruct in her nostrils the scents indicated by notes and numbers. There were secrets in the book that had remained hidden for all these years. A fragrance for men: Armand's formula for his private-label cologne, one he had made up only for himself to use. In the margin, in stronger ink—probably jotted down later, Vie thought— was written, "Remember Chanel 19."

At first she didn't know why. Chanel's scent was characterized by a green note, whereas Armand's formula called for a topnote of leather. She looked at the words in the margin again, and now realized they weren't in Armand's handwriting but in her own. Vie must have put down that reminder to herself ten or more years ago and then forgotten, while the book lay buried in its vault.

Now she remembered: Chanel's *No. 19* had been a private-label scent, used only by Mademoiselle Chanel herself and a few select friends. After her death it was released for public consumption, unlike other private labels—Balenciaga's, for instance, where the formula had been destroyed, according to instructions, after the originator's death.

In 1984 the men's fragrance market was growing as never before, Vie thought. The men's colognes of the 1960s and 1970s—*Aramis, Brut, Pub, Chaz*—had helped to break down the traditional resistance by American men to wearing scent. Now the men's designers were bringing out fragrances: Bill Blass, Ralph Lauren, Gucci. The women's designers too: *Halston for Men*, Yves Saint Laurent's *Kouros*, Dior's *Eau Sauvage*. Estée Lauder had come out with her high-status *J.H.L.*, and then of course there was Bijan's "virile" fragrance, selling at $1500 a bottle.

Men's fragrance, Vie realized, was now competing in sales with women's within the luxury price range.

That's how she'd launch her new business, Vie thought with excitement. A successor to Armand's *A* line. She'd call the first scent *Nouvel;* or maybe simply *N* would be better. In any case, the name could wait; she wouldn't even propose one to Don when she told him her ideas for a men's line.

If only he stays sober, she thought to herself as she glanced at the mirror for a final check of her makeup and a quick run of her pocket comb through her silvery gold hair. Her inspiration in the garden hadn't evaporated after that hour. On the contrary, it grew and solidified. She'd taken notes, made sketches for bottles and boxes, and by this evening had a fully elaborated project to offer Don.

"Let's go," she said, giving him her most charming smile to compensate for her abrupt ending of their cocktail hour. As he felt around for his shoes, the phone rang. "You have three minutes exactly," she told him, going back to her bedroom to answer.

The caller had a faint French accent and gave his name as Paul Mescaux. "I've spoken to you before, haven't I?" Vie asked, with only a dim recollection.

"Yes, madame. It was some months ago. I rang you in your office."

"Right. You said you had a business proposition for

me." Whoever he was, Mescaux had called while she was in the final throes of the takeover battle. She'd told him truthfully that she was in no position to hear his proposal then. Now she was in even less of one. "I'm sorry, but this is not the time. . . ."

"Madame, what I have to say will interest you, I am sure. We will meet in an hour, yes?"

"No. I was just on my way out. And I am not accepting business propositions now. . . ."

Again he cut her off. "It is not exactly business I mean to present to you. I knew your father in France, and there are things about which you should know."

"What things?" She was clutching the receiver so tightly that her knuckles were pale.

"When we meet."

"All right then, tomorrow? Sunday?"

"I am afraid that is not possible."

"Suggest a time then, tonight's out." What could he tell her? Was there a chance he could repudiate Marty's story?

He answered with the formality of his previous sentence. "I am afraid it is not possible. I shall ring again."

"Hello? Wait. . . ." But he had hung up. Puzzled and upset by the call, Vie replaced the receiver and went out to where Don was standing in his light overcoat, waiting for her. "Anything important?" he asked.

"I'm not sure," she told him, biting her lip. "But I have the feeling it probably is."

At Lutèce, Vie was greeted with all the attention given to a hometown girl returning at last. "We have not seen you for a very long time, Madame Jolay," the headwaiter fluttered, with a hint of reproach.

"Sorry." She dazzled him with a smile. "I've been dieting."

"You, madame? But you are perfect! And I am desolate, truly dé-so-lé. Your table is very unfortunately occupied. I had no idea, you see, when Mr. Garrison called, that he would be with you tonight, and. . . ."

"It's all right," she said soothingly. "It'll be an adventure to sit at a different table."

They were seated in the anteroom, where new customers, out-of-towners, and the insignificant were placed. Another demotion, Vie thought to herself, sitting down in the chair held out for her. Then she felt she'd been ridiculously spoiled for many years.

These days she was eating in little Greek, Italian, or Chinese places when she didn't cook at home. Suddenly she had a clear memory of her first meal in an elegant restaurant. She was seventeen, in a black dress from the old thrift shop, and didn't know what to order—couldn't, in fact, even read the menu. Philippa had done it for her.

"What's the smile for, honey? What're you drinking?"

"Nothing, Don. I'm remembering myself the first time I had dinner at a place like this. I was such a child!"

"Carried it off perfectly, I'll bet. Sure you won't join me?"

She shook her head. "I was green. I didn't know *anything*." She remembered the rest of the evening, shook her head again, and gave a little cluck with her tongue.

They ordered Veal Orsini, preceded by snails for her, pâté for him. Their wine was the regular house red, ordered almost belligerently by Don, who said, "It's drinkable. Why blow fifty or sixty bucks on a label?" In fact, Vie knew, the wine list included a number of bottles priced at over $500.

Don was eating, Vie saw with relief—he was taking in enough food to absorb the alcohol, partially at least, and that was sufficient to keep him alert.

He listened to her proposal, chewing thoughtfully. When he finally commented, it was not what Vie had hoped for, had even expected. "Sounds OK," he said in a tone that indicated the opposite, "but I don't see it somehow. Another line of fragrances—who needs it? Nothing new, hundreds on the market. And for every *Brut* that makes it to the top, you got a dozen *Cads* and *Cons* and *Punch* and *Wallop* that sink. Offer me a car that does seventy miles on a gallon, or a cigarette that tastes like Marlboro without any nicotine or tar, and I'll be first in line with the money. But you're asking me to invest in something you can't even put your hands on. A smell—a puff of smoke. How can I get my bank to go ahead with it?"

"You did before," she said angrily.

"Twenty years ago is ancient history, sweetheart." He

spoke more kindly now, but she realized he would remain
firm. "In those bygone days you could build slowly, gain a
reputation through word of mouth, quality excellence,
customer loyalty. Today we've got conglomerates control-
ling just about everything in the beauty business. They've
got bucketsful to invest in advertising and promotion, to
get the word out, create instant images and mass awareness of the product. Hell, Vie, every designer you've never
even heard of is putting out a fragrance line, selling name
and status—*not* the product itself."

"What about my name?" she asked in a low voice.

"You don't own it anymore," he reminded her.

"No," she said painfully. "But I still have my experience and my nose."

"One of the finest in the business," he agreed. "By
reputation. Hate to say this, but it's lost on me. Can't sniff
the difference between one woman and another."

She tried to smile but gave up. "I thought you believed
in me."

"I do, honey, I always did. You've got brains and talent.
But the bottom line is you're going to need something in
the neighborhood of five, ten, maybe twenty million bucks
to get your new venture going. And suppose it doesn't
make it? The bank's not going to be exactly thrilled at the
opportunity to invest that kind of money in something
intangible. We're going with oil, software, new microchips
in the area of home computers."

Vie looked down at her plate, feeling baffled and hurt.

"Look, sweetheart," Don said, "I'm not underestimating
you. I've seen you work. You set your mind to something,
you make it happen. But if you're going with a single
product or single line—it can't be old hat."

"But this is a new formula! It's never been tried on the
public."

"New wine in old bottles. Or old in new, never got it
straight. Won't go, honey—you're not going to find the
backing you need unless you come up with something
revolutionary!"

"Like what?" she asked listlessly, pushing her food around
her plate.

"How the hell do I know? Say, I'm sorry. Maybe you

shouldn't be listening to me. Tell you what, go see Josh Manning."

"Who?"

"Venture capitalist, about your age, a ladies' man. He comes into the bank a lot. Has some wild investment ideas but knows where to get the money to back them. I respect the guy."

She remembered the deep brown eyes. "Was he there last Tuesday? The day I came into your office?"

"Let's see. Tuesday. Yes, I think he was. Why? You know him?"

"We sort of met," she said, feeling a tinge of excitement despite herself.

"Terrific! Go see him, maybe you'll find out I'm all wet. Want me to set up an appointment?"

"No," she said slowly. "Not yet."

"Whenever you give the word."

"Thanks, Don." The smile came easily. He had a name, he could be reached; maybe he'd turn out to be Prince Charming, who'd find her the backing she needed to become a queen again. But she didn't know him, didn't know what kind of approach to use. She'd save him for later, as a last resort. Meanwhile she'd turn to friends and do some research of her own on Josh Manning.

She was home before eleven. After he'd told her to go see Manning, Don announced that they weren't going to let business spoil the fun of their evening out. Fun, Vie soon realized, was his synonym for drinking. They'd gone from Lutèce to the St. Regis where, forty-five minutes and five Rusty Nails later, Vie left him and hailed a taxi home.

Eleven o'clock in New York meant 8 P.M. in Los Angeles. She picked up the phone, remembering the strange, disquieting call she'd received before dinner. Why were so many parts of Armand's life blank to her? Had he confided in *anyone*? In Nina, perhaps? Probably not.

When Nina answered, Vie told her she had something important to discuss. She preferred not to do it by phone. Was there any chance they could meet?

"Tomorrow!" Nina answered happily. "I'll give my travel agent a buzz right now, and there'll be a ticket for you on

the TWA noon flight—from La Guardia, I think." Nina
rarely flew in anything but their private jet, larger and
more elegantly appointed than that of the President of the
United States. She gave enough business, however, to
commercial airlines in tickets for friends and acquain-
tances that she was free to ignore considerations of whether
a particular flight might be booked or not. For the visitors
of Nina Corazon, a seat was always found.

"I can't wait! I'm sure I won't get to sleep at all tonight.
Maybe you could come on an earlier plane?"

Vie laughed. "Noon is fine. Thanks, Nina."

"See you at the airport, baby. You'll be getting in around
two, our time. Toodle-oo till then. I love you, baby."

"Love you, too." She hung up, smiling. She'd show
drunk old Garrison. Nina was family. She'd support
Armand's new line, reformulated by Vie from out of the
past.

Next afternoon, as they sipped gin and tonics, dangling
their legs in the ninety-degree pool, Vie talked about the
project, to Nina's enthusiastic encouragement. "I'll need
backing for it, though," Vie said. She told her vaguely
about Garrison's reaction, emphasizing his lack of feel for
fragrances rather than his financial arguments. A sense of
pride, or good business intuition, made Vie present the
situation as though it was she who'd decided not to accept
the backing of someone who didn't understand and didn't
show enough interest in her product.

"How much will you need?" Nina asked.

"As seed money, I'm sure a million dollars would do it.
Once I've set up the lab and developed the fragrance, I
may need additional investment to push the line in stores.
I'll go the same route as before, starting with the top: a
luxury line for men sold in prestigious stores and specialty shops."

"A million's peanuts, these days. Too bad Carlos isn't
here now—but he'll be back from Frankfurt the day after
tomorrow. You can talk to him then."

"I have to be getting back, love."

"You mean tomorrow?" Vie nodded. "Hell!" said Nina.
"I don't want to be a one-night stand."

Vie laughed. "No, you're not the type. But anyway,

Nina, I feel it's better if *you* talk to Carlos. He's your husband and I—well, don't really know him that well."

"Sure thing," said Nina, resting her glass on the edge of the pool and diving under the water. She figured Vie was too proud to ask for money from anyone but family.

When Vie left, twenty hours after her arrival, Nina promised to call. But Vie heard nothing from her on Monday, when Carlos was due back, or on Tuesday or Wednesday. Thursday evening Nina called to say she'd be in town next day; could they meet for drinks at her hotel?

In the Carlyle's Bemelmans Bar, Vie waited nervously. Why hadn't Nina reassured her on the phone? Maybe she'd asked for too little. If a million was peanuts, Carlos might think she wasn't serious. On the other hand, Nina might have forgotten to mention it simply because she took for granted, and expected Vie did too, that such an amount was forthcoming.

Nina's face when she entered the bar told Vie that it wasn't a matter of forgetting; it was no. Carlos had full control over the money, Nina explained; whatever belonged to her was in trust, and Carlos thought scent too frivolous to invest in. He liked food as an investment, or buildings or machines, but not, as he put it, "a smelling gas that's sold as a liquid inside a solid."

"I'll sell my jewelry," Nina said, removing the large diamond bracelet from her wrist and handing it to Vie. "Take this as a start, baby."

"No!" Vie exclaimed, almost shoving it back at her. She was painfully reminded of the jewelry Armand had been forced to sell to keep them alive. "Sorry, Nina, but that's not how I want it. I still have jewels of my own I could sell, and the capital left from the apartment sale. I'm holding on to that, though, to support me in my old age—which will be upon me almost immediately if I can't start a new business," she joked sadly. "And if I *can*, that money will be essential for promotion, advertising—all the extras. But I can't afford to venture into business again on my own—I don't have the funds or resources for that. I need a backer, Nina, not diamonds. Thanks for your support, though." She smiled at Nina and pressed her hand warmly.

Not through jewels, not through sentiment; Vie vowed to start her new business only when she could find a firm foundation of capital, and belief in her venture.

The words she was thinking resonated and came together in "venture capital."

She turned to Nina and began comforting her. "Your husband knows what he's doing. He's as successful as he is because he plays his own hunches. He happens not to believe in the perfume industry. It's OK, Nina. I'm the same way. I've got to believe in what I do and play *my* hunches."

So far they'd led to rejections: two out of two. She'd go more slowly, figure things out, determine on a realistic amount for starting a new business, and then give it a markup. Price creates value—she'd learned that in her Windsor days and knew she was a fool to ever forget the maxim. When she had her figures down, her portfolio filled, she'd put on her most sensational outfit and go pay a call on Mr. Manning.

At Jolay's lab Nick was working on the men's line, to be launched in time for Christmas. This gave him less than a month before the products would have to be camera perfect.

Burt Sillcoe wanted a rough, masculine image for the line, an old-fashioned sex-appeal pitch to stand out against the status fragrances. No man in a gray-flannel suit, the collar of his pale-blue shirt showing in an elegant strip above the back of the jacket. That was a designer's ad, like others featuring expensive clothes, gold cuff links, polished brown leather. Jolay's man didn't care about the best-dressed list; he preferred girlie rags to men's fashion magazines, the *Daily News* to the *Times* or *The Wall Street Journal*. He liked beer with his football, stayed away from the opera and ballet, and regularly attended his weekly poker game. He was a traditional man's man, who sought out the company of other men and hoped to score with every attractive woman he met.

The line would be on sale in drugstores and supermarkets after a nationwide saturation campaign in all media.

There were only two problems: time and a name.

Marty had been the choice for a long time, finally rejected because it was too soft. The *y* at the end made it sound like a kid's name, and its echo was dangerously reminiscent of *Charlie*, the fragrance for young women. What they were looking for, Sillcoe told Marty, was a name with one syllable that packed a punch; a sound instantly perceived as macho. He favored *Duke* for a while, with its evocation of John Wayne, but after a few days rejected that also because of its inescapable aristocratic overtones. Until they had a name, they couldn't really go ahead with layouts or display ideas. The fact that the products weren't formulated yet hardly concerned the people at Stevens John. The packaging designs were in; the line comprised a total look, including hair as well as body, and would feature, in addition to the toiletries, a comb-and-brush set, a razor, and a tobacco pouch to be used as a carrying bag for travel. Brown was a predominant color in all the designs, emphasizing the masculine image.

Marty hadn't been in the lab since Nick had installed himself. Often she had her hand on the phone to call him and then stopped herself. Business and pleasure didn't mix; she wouldn't interfere with progress on the new line. She'd wait until the first of April.

When Nick walked into her office unannounced, as though he had every right, Marty was torn between anger at his impertinence and admiration for his bravado. Men were intimidated by her; it was rare to find one who could dominate, and in fact, those who did had all been men of great wealth and power. Nick, who was younger, not rich, and an employee of hers, was a first.

"What can I do for you?" she asked evenly, deciding not to show her anger lest she also reveal its flip side.

"You can get that asshole Sillcoe off my back for one, and you can finally give this stuff a name for another. All that sex-appeal bunk Sillcoe talks about isn't going to firm up the formula until there's a name attached."

She shifted in her chair, forcing her thighs to come together. "You mean to tell me you don't even have the compound yet?"

"Look. You know we've been working on it. We've got the bottles, boxes, the bases for soap, shampoo, aftershave, all of it. We could go with the damn stuff the way it is, but that's a cop-out. It needs a touch, a dab of something or other. The missing ingredient I can't find until this amorphous, long-lasting, stable whatsis has a name. Sillcoe gives me 'theme words,' as he calls it. 'Sweat' is one of them."

"What's wrong with that?" Her bra was made of a glistening, see-through fabric under her silk blouse. At certain angles to the light, her nipples were clearly marked. She shifted by inches until she saw his eyes fasten on the dark tips of her breasts, hardening under his gaze.

"You're a damned attractive woman, Martine," he said. "Sexy as hell."

Her erect nipples were begging for his touch. Her lips were parted, her eyes flashing at him.

"What's wrong," he went on, ignoring the invitation, "is that I can give him Sweat if he wants it. But he doesn't, and neither does Jolay. Because nobody would buy Sweat. The whole idea of fragrance is to get away from body smells."

"How about 'brig,' or 'jug'?" she improvised.

"Jail terms. The guy wants to be tough, but he doesn't want to get caught and be put in the slammer. No action there. He's tough, but he's buying this junk to get broads, not to make a hit."

"Hey, that's not bad," Marty said.

"What?"

" 'Hit'—being the hit of the party, making a hit with a woman."

The way she looked at him made her meaning plain. He walked over to her and stood so close that her head was five inches away from his belt. "Why not call it *Stud*?" he asked.

She shivered. He looked down at her, grinning, thrust his pelvis forward, and then abruptly walked away to the other side of her desk.

"Nick."

He turned. "That's it. That's our new line. Call up Sillcoe and tell him. I'll have it ready before the first." He strode out of the room without looking back at her.

"Bastard," she said softly. "Fucking arrogant bastard."

She picked up the phone and told her secretary to put her through to Sillcoe. She was shaking.

Later that afternoon, when Nick was back in the lab, he had a call from Marty. "You better think about looking for other employment," she said angrily. "I told you at the start that I'm not having prima donnas, and I meant it. Unless you can get it through your head that I'm the boss here, you better go elsewhere."

"Yes, ma'am," he said through clenched teeth and slammed down the receiver.

3

Manning & Associates had offices on the twelfth floor of 230 Park Avenue, the blockbuster building that rises from the lower depths of Grand Central Station to the whir of helicopters on Pan Am's roof. A modern colossus, it stands astride the avenue, cutting off the tail below Forty-second Street from the sleek body. Joshua Manning, president, was also founder of the entrepreneurial firm that was primarily committed to high-technology industries and health-care services.

Vie knew that Manning was born in 1941 in Pittsburgh, had gone to Yale and MIT, and had two children of college age by his former (and only) wife, Lacey Stanton, a socialite he'd divorced in 1969 after a marriage of six years.

"He likes fast cars and being out of doors. He also likes blondes," Philippa had told Vie over her martini at the Oak Bar. "But the man's greatest and most persistent love is making profits. Even your spectacular blond beauty,

still the same as when you seduced me into buying up
your father's baked goods. . . ."

"That's not fair! Philippa. . . ."

"Relax," she said, patting Vie's hand. "I'm not going to
hold it against you. Point I'm making, love, is that your
charm, beauty, and all the rest of it won't move the Rock of
Gibraltar or make Josh Manning part with his money. He
might want to whisk you away in his arms, but he won't
shell out for a perfume company."

Vie sipped her gin and tonic. "Don Garrison advised me
to go to him," she pointed out.

"Probably to get you off his back. *He* wasn't interested
in financing you, was he?"

"No," she admitted. "But I thought he was being conservative and that Manning is willing to take risks."

Philippa shook her head. "I hate discouraging you, baby,
but I don't want you to get your hopes up for the interview.
As I told you, I don't know Manning personally, but I've
heard a lot about him. He's done some wild things—and I
mean *wild*. Like underwriting Safari Park and arranging
insurance for the rhinos, elephants, and Bengal tigers they
brought in. I heard it's become a real success. In any case,
you've got to realize the man is out for high adventure.
He'll take crazy risks, but he won't stake investors' money
on fragrances, no matter how good they are. Give him an
explosion, and he'll be interested."

"Then what should I do, Phil?" she asked, like a little
girl. She trusted Philippa more than anyone else. In her
mid-sixties, Philippa was as far from retirement as she'd
been when they first met. Head of her own consulting
firm now, she was the acknowledged eminence of merchandising, remaining the power behind many thrones.

"All you can do," answered Philippa, "is get a job,
develop liquid dynamite, or perform a miracle with Josh
Manning."

Vie finished the remains of her drink and shook her
head to the offer of another round. "If it's a choice of
those, I'll start by working on the miracle."

But before Vie made an appointment to see Manning,
she arranged to meet Nick Benedetti. Vie knew it was

risky to see him, but the time had come when all she could afford was a risk. She knew two things about Nick: that he had the greatest nose of any working chemist in the business and that he wasn't happy with his job. The word had filtered in from a few former employees who, on Vie's urging, had followed Marty to Motek. She herself could offer them no work, she'd told them, and had encouraged them to they retain their jobs if Marty offered. But she couldn't stop their personal loyalty, and they reported to her that the chemist had had some kind of showdown with his boss.

Playing the hunch that he wouldn't inform Marty of her call, Vie had phoned him. When he called back, she asked for a meeting with him on a "confidential" matter. She stressed the word, and to her relief heard him acknowledge the need for secrecy by suggesting they meet at Pale Tulip, a jazz club near her apartment in the Village. "It's dark, noisy, and full of kids," he said. "Not the kind of place where fat cats are likely to prowl."

On the Friday night Vie put on designer jeans, a silk shirt, and a wide belt. Over these she wore a suede jacket. She let her hair hang loose around her shoulders and put on only a touch of makeup. In dim light she could still pass for a possible habitué of Pale Tulip.

He came up to her as she walked toward the back of the club. His hair was tousled and boyish, his shirt open nearly to his waist, his smile at once disarming and sexual. I don't trust him, Vie thought, and she had the impulse to tell him it was a mistake, she'd come to cancel their meeting.

"I've been looking forward to this," he said, leading her to his table. The hubbub in the room indicated a break in the music, the interval between sets that people rushed to fill with conversation. "You look young enough to be Marty's kid sister."

"Nick. . . ." She stopped. He charged the air around him with the force of his energy, and she felt as though she'd come here at his bidding, not he at hers.

"What can I do for you, Ms. Jolay?" he asked, suddenly switching tones. "Are you about to offer me a bribe, or is it just a routine assignment in spying?"

Vie stiffened, realizing how foolish she'd been to call him. She made a move to get up when Nick again changed his tone, this time to a gentle one. "Don't be offended, please. I knew you resisted the takeover, and that you and your sister had a falling out. So I made a little joke. In bad taste. I'm sorry. Please stay and have a drink with me." He looked as contrite as he sounded.

Vie decided to stay. "But the drink's on me," she insisted. "I'm the one who wanted to see you. It's to ask for advice. I'd like your opinion on a formula for a man's scent."

Now he was evaluating her again with hard eyes. Vie knew he was working on a men's fragrance line for Motek. He'd be able to tell her if Armand's private-label scent was revolutionary. Of course she was taking the chance that he'd steal the formula for Motek, but she thought his antagonism to Marty would provide her own protection. She was operating on a very delicate balance: what she needed was expert confirmation that she had a product to take to investors, and she was risking betrayal to get it.

"You like playing with fire, don't you?" Nick asked harshly. "Let's hear your proposition."

Members of the band were returning to the stage. In a few minutes they'd begin playing, and the possibility of talking would be drowned out. Vie took a deep breath and plunged her hand into her bag. She'd written out the formula on a piece of notepaper. If he possessed the extraordinary powers she suspected he had, he could read with his eyes and take it in through the nose. She handed him the slip.

He studied it, sniffing the air. After a few moments he nodded. "Interesting—subtle, masculine. Could go far."

"Is it *different*?" she asked eagerly. "Is it unlike any other product on the market?"

"Well, let me see, little lady," he drawled at her. "You couldn't be asking me to divulge information about the line *I've* developed, could you?"

She felt herself blush. The way he said it sounded as if she really was asking him to spy for her. She hadn't intended that—not consciously, at any rate. But now, seeing things from his point of view, what she was doing certainly appeared to be conspiracy. "No, it's not that," Vie told him, suddenly doubting her own motives.

The band was starting up, opening the new set with a rousing number that combined acoustic and electronic sounds. Vie sat back and tried to concentrate on the music, but even despite the volume of sound, she kept blocking it out as her feelings and thoughts overwhelmed her. She recognized her antagonism to Marty as it surfaced to her thinking. But why had she gone to Nick? Even if he was the best in the business, she could have consulted others. But she chose him, Vie now saw clearly, because he was a way to get at Marty. She wasn't even sure what that meant, whether she'd imagined persuading him to join her in a new venture or whether she just wanted his admiration, his acknowledgment that she was far superior to Marty as a perfumer.

It gave her a sick feeling, like discovering someone was cheating on her. That someone was herself.

"Are you all right?" Nick said into her ear.

She looked up at him with new respect. It was his question that had led her to doubt herself and bring her to honesty. He was bright, intuitive, and tough—a male counterpart of Marty, Vie thought. No wonder they had difficulty working together.

The band finished to applause, did an encore, and ended again as the tide of speech rose in the room. Vie turned to Nick. "Please don't mention our meeting to my sister. Let the whole thing drop; it would hurt her to know."

"But you're planning to establish a rival line, aren't you?"

"I don't know." She shook her head in true bewilderment. "Sometimes it seems I can't figure out what I'm up to."

Nick smiled. "I like you, Vie Nouvel. You're straight."

She opened her eyes wide. "How can you tell me that?" she protested, laughing. "You were telling me before that I was crooked."

"Yeah," he admitted, joining her laughter. "Crooked but straight."

From her first feeling of mistrust Vie had progressed, through the short evening, to affection. She liked the man; she could even see him as a potential friend. And she talked to him as though he already was, openly revealing to him that she hoped to revive the old Jolay in spite of the legal constrictions she was bound by. She would take the chance that by using the name "Nouvel" she could circumvent violation of the contract she'd unwittingly signed. "I was really angry at my sister for tricking me into it," she confessed. "And I guess it was that anger that made me want to get back at her."

"I guess so," he agreed.

"But right now, Nick, I don't have anything to get back at her with. I need to form a company, and nobody's willing to invest in me unless I have a product that's remarkable. Something that knocks people's eyes out. I'm not sure I've found it in this formula—are you?"

"Don't worry about it, honey, you've got it anyway."

"What do you mean?"

"You. Look at you—you'd knock anybody's eyes out."

Again she reverted to her first impression. It seemed clear that he was trying to make a pass. And yet, she felt that he was detached, not really interested at all, toying with her. She looked down at the table. "Let's not go on with this," she said, calling the waitress over. She paid the bill and stood up. "It's late. Thanks for meeting me tonight."

He remained sitting in his chair, looking up at her with what women had called his bedroom expression. He knew he was making her uncomfortable. That was part of the technique. Nick liked the game; he enjoyed priming a woman, as he put it: manipulating her until she lowered her defenses. It was most exciting with the proud, sophisticated ones. He'd break down that independence; he wouldn't offer to take her home until she asked. He'd let her fear of walking alone through dark streets make her beg him.

"Good-bye," she said, holding out her hand. "Sorry to have taken your time." She began walking toward the door.

"Hey!" he called, jumping up and following her. "How're you getting back?"

She looked genuinely surprised. "Walking, of course. I don't live far from here. Stay. Listen to more of the music."

She continued making her way out among the customers. Nick returned to the table, frowning. That rugged individualism—it reminded him of the other one, of *her*. Damn those Jolay sisters, he thought; why weren't they more like other women?

He'd told Vie she could knock anybody's eyes out, but he wasn't thinking of her. This morning, when Marty had come into the lab, striding like a general off her horse, he'd wanted to jump on her, pin her to the ground, make violent love to her right there. He wanted her so much he was trembling. But she just gave him a cool smile and marched farther back, to talk to a new assistant. Damn her, he'd thought then, he thought now. He had to have her and he didn't care how. He had to conquer her, bind her to him. He'd do anything, even hurt her, to be able to take that woman. She inspired him, filled his thoughts, and treated him like somebody beneath her. If he could contribute to her downfall, he thought wildly, maybe she'd weaken enough to give in.

Walking briskly along Hudson Street, Vie felt nervous. She *was* afraid of walking home alone in the dark. She wouldn't give someone like Nick Benedetti the satisfaction of knowing, any more than she'd let Don Garrison guess how difficult it had been for her to come back alone after their dinner. Men used such things as weapons, she knew. The same argument that made them protective also made them deny you loans. "The little woman," she thought angrily, but at the same time she was afraid of the dark streets.

Footsteps behind her. She increased her pace. What to do if he caught up with her, grabbed her, pulled her into a dark alley, and then. . . . You've got to stop this, she told herself. Think of something else, anything. Forget your fear, remember the tiger potion.

Chandra's face came back to her, and a deep sorrow engulfed her as she realized she'd never see it again. He had been nearly eighty when he died, but she'd still felt it was too soon. She missed her friend. She'd liked the person she became when she was with him: eager, trusting, honest.

Looking back on her last few hours at the club with Nick, Vie felt, for the first time since Jolay was bought by Motek that she might simply have to give in and accept her defeat. Did she really want to set up an attack on Marty and go through a vicious duel?

Fencing was one of the most beautiful of sports, but it wasn't life. She'd kept it up after Hubert left, become a master, and though women's competitive fencing is restricted to the foil, Vie was proficient enough with the heavier weapons also, the epée and saber, to match many men in her club.

The footsteps came closer. She tensed, trying to maintain her pace, and then they were on her. She took a deep breath as the person came up and overtook her—a young woman in an oversize army jacket, hands in her pockets, oblivious to Vie. She's younger than I am and not afraid, Vie registered; why should I be?

She'd grown more insecure over the past months. Did she really want a duel with her sister? she asked herself again. For most of their life Marty had been battling against *her*. Now she was the one spoiling for a fight. Yes, she realized, yes I want to do it—but only if I'm sure of winning. Against Motek?

If I don't fight, what's my choice? she thought, turning the corner onto her own street. Philippa said I need three things. If Armand's formula isn't liquid dynamite, that leaves only two: a miracle with Josh Manning or a job.

When she approached the house, she unzipped the side compartment of her handbag for the key. The street was deserted of people; only trees and the line of parked cars stood in the lamplight. She noticed a gleaming white Rolls-Royce near her house. Symbol of luxury, queen of cars, its pale elegant body gave her a moment's regret. The car reminded her of the white apartment she used to have, its tasteful design combining opulence and simplicity. The door of the car was opening. She walked quickly toward her door, the key in her hand.

"Vie . . . Vie."

She spun around toward the voice, its imprint on her mind after sixteen years making her body react before her brain identified it.

Hubert Montalmont stepped out of the shadow into the light of the streetlamp. Vie's breath caught. He was as attractive, as wildly romantic as on the day he first came into her office. The years had merely added a patina to his looks, emphasizing their elegance without detracting from their charm.

He came up to where she stood frozen and stopped a few feet away, groping for words. "Vie, you're looking. . . ."

"No, please," she begged, unable to take her eyes off his face.

"May I talk with you a moment?"

Why? she thought wildly. Has he come back to propose again? She thought of asking him into her apartment and rejected it. She was tongue-tied and rigid.

"Please. Will you come in the car? We can drive somewhere for a little supper if you wish. . . ."

She saw them dining together as they used to, with flowers and candlelight, a musky wine in their cupped goblets, their glances locked. Her eyes closed over the image, and she shook her head. "Not again. Darl—"

She stopped the endearment that came naturally to her lips, but he'd heard. He smiled and stepped closer to her, placing the tips of his fingers gingerly against her arm as though testing for fire. "A cup of coffee, a glass of wine?" he offered. "Anywhere you choose, chérie."

She wanted to come into his arms, feel his body against hers, take in again the smell of his skin, whose odor she'd never been able to forget.

"All right," she breathed. "Just down the street is an espresso place, open all night."

At first they simply looked at each other, devouring each other with their eyes. Vie wanted him to explain, to tell her something she could understand and forgive, so they could pick up the foils and start again. Then she remembered he was married, with children. She didn't know what to say and waited, her eyes on his face, for him to begin.

Hubert saw opposite him the beautiful woman he had deeply loved and had been forced to betray. He'd had no choice, had learned about the foul deed only after it was committed. Did she know about it, he wondered? Could she be looking at him this way if she did?

But he hadn't come to explain himself. It was business again, the same motive that first propelled him to her. In the past fifteen years Montalmont had dropped the thought of an American company and had been selling to the United States only through distributors. Hubert had refused to return, despite Henri's threats and bellowings. But now Henri held no authority anymore. Though still alive, he was nearly ninety and had been forced to give up his position at Montalmont. He was still rational but only in spurts, his memory thinning out like used elastic, his body functions out of his control.

As the new president, Hubert had vowed to compensate Vie for what his father had done. Hearing about the sale of Jolay, and Vie's resignation from it, he decided the moment was right to approach her with his offer.

Hubert shifted his gaze, breaking the spell of their eyes. He cleared his throat. "We're planning to set up an American branch of Montalmont, owned by us but with complete autonomy to produce and market its own fragrances. No one in the country is more suited than you, Vie, to head the business."

"Isn't there a strong degree of déjà vu about this?"

"It is a different time, a different proposition."

"Yes," she agreed sadly. Then, she had refused his offer out of her strength. Now, whether she refused or accepted, it would be out of weakness. She realized he was aware of her position and might be offering this job out of pity. "I don't need charity," she said in a strong voice. "Montalmont and Jolaunay are rivals. If one of them fails, the other doesn't insult him with a handout."

"You are proud, Vie, and more beautiful than you've ever been. But you must believe I am not trying to do you a favor. This is business, and you know that I am as hard in it as you. I want our American firm to flourish. I need someone at its head whom I admire and can trust to take over all operations. You are the perfect, and perhaps the only, choice."

She was still looking at him dubiously. "I admit," he said, "that when I heard of your present situation, I thought you might consider this offer seriously—and that there was a good chance you'd accept. And why not, Vie? At least think about it. We would both profit. I would not interfere in your work."

"Would you let me develop a new fragrance, perhaps a line of fragrances?"

"Yes. That is the idea. You would have ten million dollars to launch it. After that, the new products would be supported up to an additional fifteen million, to provide for the time lag before they catch on."

"That's a lot of money," she admitted. With that much backing almost any product could succeed, particularly one that had been a reliable winner in the past. Even Don Garrison had said that with heavy financing she didn't need something revolutionary. Take a job, she told herself; forget about dynamite and miracles.

But she parried. "I've never been employed by anyone. That's one reason I refused to go to Motek. If I ever did work *for* someone, I would have to be able to trust him entirely."

"We knew each other so well. . . ."

"Did we? If I remember, there was a breach of contract—though, of course, it was only verbal. But you see, it could happen again that something I consider binding isn't binding to you."

He reached for her hand, and she didn't have the will power to draw it away. It remained passive, enclosed by his. "If I had come back to you after that month, what answer would you have given me?"

"I don't know," she whispered.

"Yes," he said, painfully. "I knew you didn't love me enough."

She stared at him as she felt scabs being ripped from old wounds, making them fresh again. She couldn't bear to tell him that she'd loved him more than any man, that even the sight of him in Paris years ago had affected her so strongly that she couldn't function professionally.

That was true. But it was also true that she'd gone on after his silence, that her work had consumed her as she committed herself to it more and more, the rewards of her labor becoming her deepest satisfaction. Her father's death had made her more determined than before to go on with the work, to build her own small empire.

"I loved you," she said firmly, "but I wouldn't have married you."

The pain she felt was reflected in his expression. "Let's leave the old wounds," she suggested. "Our dueling time is over."

"I'm not sure of that," he answered in a low voice.

They walked back together, and at Vie's door Hubert pleaded again that she consider his offer. He said no more about love.

"I'll need time to think about it," she told him.

"Déjà vu." He smiled. "I must leave New York tomorrow, but I shall return in two weeks. Then I will come to you for your decision."

"No. This time we're changing the script. Leave me your number, and I'll call you when I've decided."

He wrote down a list of numbers for her, with dates. Handing it to her, he asked softly, "May I kiss you?"

She longed for his lips again, but she turned her head away. As she let herself into the apartment, she promised him, "You'll have my answer."

4

When the phone rang, Marty cursed it. Opening one eye, she read the luminous hands: two o'clock in the morning. Whatever the hell it was could wait, she decided, pulling the covers over her head to drown out the sound. It finally stopped, and Marty lay in the dark trying to figure out who it was. Probably a wrong number. Or an emergency. What could *that* be? A plunge in profits two hours after midnight? An order that hadn't come in, seven hours before the office opened? The saleslady from Gucci calling to say the bag she'd ordered had just arrived? Maybe M. Pierre of Poussin d'Or calling back to confirm the lunch reservation for tomorrow. She grinned; one thing she could rely on herself for, Marty thought, was an answer to everything.

When the ringing began again, she picked up the receiver and barked crossly, "Hello, what is it?"

"It's me, only me. Nobody you ever heard of."

"Nick?" she asked, sitting upright.

"You've got to save me, I'm drowning."

"Well, turn the bathwater off, for Chrissake."

"Marty. . . ." The voice was thick, heavy with a night of drinking, and his words slurred. She could picture him weaving in the phone booth, wherever he was.

"You're drunk. Go get some sleep. Do you know what time it is?" she asked angrily, ready to hang up.

"Marty. Please. I've got to talk to you."

"Call my secretary in the morning. She'll set something up."

"You're hard, baby. You're the hardest damn bitch I've come across. . . ."

"I'm not going to be insulted at two in the morning." She put down the receiver firmly, before she could hear him finish his sentence: ". . . and I love you."

She got out of bed and went to the kitchen to make coffee, as she always did when she couldn't sleep. Coffee might stimulate others; on Marty the hot drink worked as a pacifier. She made it strong and drank it black, puffing on her cigarette and thinking about the infuriating call, the impertinence of the man daring to rouse her out of sleep to call her a bitch. But her anger was feigned even to herself. In that drunken, sloppy voice she'd heard a sharp appeal. Despite what he'd said, she knew he'd called out of need for her, and despite herself, she smiled. Marty was used to commanding people and dominating them, but having someone need her was a new sensation. She realized she liked it. She liked it so much that she even let herself imagine what it would be like to have a person of her own, someone so bound to her that she could shed the invulnerability she wore so tightly around herself.

"Stupid bitch," she cursed aloud. "That's what you are, going soft and gloppy." She refilled the cup and carried it into her bedroom, where she lit another cigarette from the one she'd smoked down to the butt. She didn't know why she felt tears behind her eyes or why she couldn't stop imagining what it would be like to depend on someone other than herself.

When Vie finally got to sleep, near morning, she'd resolved not to think further about Hubert's offer until she'd spoken to Josh Manning. She'd been putting it off, hoping for a miraculous product to appear suddenly before her, like a bottle from Wonderland, saying, "Dab Me."

But now she had to take the chance. She couldn't consider working for someone else until she'd tried every avenue to establishing her own domain again, however small. No matter how farfetched, a possibility remained that Manning would be willing to invest seed money in her, and there seemed little reason to wait any longer.

On Monday she called for an appointment. The secretary asked her to hold, and a man's voice came over the phone. She recognized it easily from the few sentences they'd exchanged at the bank. "Is it really you?" he asked. "I've been waiting so long. Can you come in this afternoon?"

She laughed, flattered by his interest, relieved by the lighthearted flirtation after her encounter with Hubert. But this afternoon! She hadn't expected to get in to see him for a week at least, possibly a few weeks. Busy investors weren't people you called on a moment's notice. She'd thought she'd have a long time to prepare for the interview—but his immediate availability, the fact that he'd come to the phone himself made her hopeful. He obviously wasn't playing games, and neither would she. "Yes. What time?"

"Let's see. Four? No, make it five, and we can have a drink afterward."

"But you don't know what I called to see you about! Suppose we don't reach an agreement?"

"Don't worry about it, princess. I can't picture myself

not agreeing with you on anything. But," he added, showing his business side, "even if that happens, you'd have the chance to butter me up and make me go against my better judgment."

She liked his candor. "OK. Five o'clock, then."

Vie arrived at 230 Park Avenue in a cream-colored suit cinched by a wide brown suede belt. She'd chosen the outfit after trying on and rejecting many others, none of which conveyed exactly the right message. It had to be feminine and businesslike, attractive without any overt suggestion of sex. The Chloé suit proved perfect. Though not new, it was set off by the Dior belt to look like this month's fashion. Her scent was subtle. Instead of *Taj*, which remained her favorite always, she wore the lighter *O! de Vie*. Her shoes were brown, her bag was tan, and the only jewelry she wore was a finely sheaved silver necklace. Vie knew that clothes conveyed a statement about one's sense of self; they announced whether or not you regarded yourself as a person of influence.

Josh Manning stood up when she entered and rushed forward to shake her hand. "Hope you didn't take it as an insult when I called you princess," he said, smiling. "It's obvious that you're the queen."

She smiled back, acknowledging a compliment she'd heard too often. By now she was usually irked by it, but from Josh Manning it sounded original. He led her to a chair and held it out for her as she sat down. He drew one up for himself, facing her. She noticed the point he was making: they were talking as equals, not across a desk that belonged to him.

He was easy to talk to. He listened attentively, giving no indication of approval or disapproval, as he tried first to get the facts and figures of her proposal clearly in mind. She couldn't help noticing how attractive he was, how his eyes seemed to hold depths of understanding that made her words almost superfluous.

When she finished, he said soberly, "Thank you for coming to me. I'm afraid I'll probably disappoint you, Vie. It's not the degree of risk that deters me. We've entered into very high risk ventures. But they've got to be—how shall I put it?—flashy. That's the word, even though it connotes something vulgar. But flashy it is, all right. Highly visible, with a chance of stupendous profits; innovative, startling. I'd even go so far as mind-boggling. So, even though your proposal sounds solid, my company can't invest in it. We project a certain image, and that's our identity, which we can't afford to lose or even to play around with."

She'd feared, and half-expected, this answer. Now I have to take a job, she thought bleakly, getting up.

"You haven't forgotten your promise to have a drink with me?"

"Thank you. But do you really think I could persuade you otherwise?"

"No," he said bluntly. "But it gives us a chance to know each other better, and I think we both deserve that. Don't you?"

She looked up at him and the depression suddenly lifted. She recognized the irony: Josh Manning was the only one who could cheer her up after her meeting with him. "Let's go," she said.

Over drinks he confessed that after he'd met her at the bank, he'd made instant inquiries to discover who she was. A week or so later Don Garrison told him she might be coming in to talk to him about a possible investment. "I gave you exactly a month to get in touch with me. If you hadn't, I would have called you."

He was a different man outside his office, looking at her with even greater interest than before.

"In exactly three days from now, if you hadn't phoned, I would have."

"Why?"

"Because that short meeting with you stayed in my mind. I felt a kinship with you, and I knew I had to see you again to find out why."

"Have you found out?"

"Vie, even if I were a genius—which I may be—I couldn't presume to know you in a few hours! You're a complicated, intricate personality." Josh moved his face closer to hers. "It's going to take me years."

She smiled at his presumption of a future together. He moved too fast, but it felt lovely, like being swept up into

the clouds. "Nice of you, Josh, but I haven't figured myself out yet," Vie said flippantly, adding, "And I'm not
sure it's worth the effort. I know myself in what I do, and
right now I'm going to have to do something about my
business."

"Let me take you to dinner, Vie. There's a terrific place
just opened. Le Chat au Toit, means cat on the roof—
you'll love it."

"I like the sound of it already," she said. Josh was
smiling, turning to summon the waiter. "But some other
time, all right?"

"Please, Vie." His eyes were beautiful and intense. Josh
was a wonderfully attractive man. She felt flattered, made
more interesting and charming by his attentions, and yet
she had a sense that his words, even the way he was
looking at her, were rehearsed. What had Don Garrison
called him? A Don Juan? A ladies' man—that was it. Josh
was gazing at her as though she were the only woman in
the world for him. She almost believed it; her breathing
was shallower, her palms moist. She wanted to go with
him, to be taken over by him.

"Sorry, it'll have to wait," she said with an effort that
her tone disguised. She'd had an image of his sitting with
some other woman, a day from now, two days, turning
that same ardent gaze on her.

"It can't wait! This is too important. We owe it to
ourselves, Vie," he said in a low voice. "Please. Cancel
whatever appointment you've made for this evening."

"I'm afraid that's impossible." She smiled, getting up.
Impossible because she had nothing to cancel. "Thanks
for being so open with me about the business. And I
enjoyed the drink." She loved being in his company, but
she didn't want, didn't *dare*, to have dinner with Josh
Manning. Not yet, anyway. He moved too quickly, he was
flash and fire. Though he'd rejected her proposition, she
was sure she wouldn't be able to resist his; the attraction
was too powerful. She didn't want to throw herself into his
arms before she'd had time to think.

Vie walked out on the street. By the time she reached
Madison Avenue and turned south, her thoughts had already shifted to their customary ground. She'd think about

Josh at a future time, when it became necessary. Now she had business on her mind.

What next? Accept Hubert's offer? Go on trying to find a backer, or backers, for Nouvel? She'd take it in steps, and the immediate one, she realized, was dinner. It was after seven, she was hungry, and the cocktails had increased her appetite. Dinner with a friend was what she needed now, Vie told herself. A close friend who'd listen to her problems and options and would offer advice she could rely on.

At the corner pay phone, she had to look up his number in her diary. The office number was stamped firmly in her memory, but Vie rarely called Mike at home.

To her enormous relief, he was in. "Are you free?" Vie asked. "Will you come have dinner with me?"

"You like roast duck, Chinese style? Bit of ginger, lemon, soy? You do! Good. It's in the oven now, be ready within the hour."

"Thanks, Mike, but I'm really not up to a party tonight. I . . ."

"Since when do you call two hungry people and a dead duck a party?"

"Oh. But why were you making such an elaborate feast?"

"I get hungry, and I like good food. The wine's chilled, and we'll have steamed dumplings for appetizers. See you in a few minutes."

Vie replaced the receiver, shaking her head in amusement. Her own dinners for one never required more cooking than could be done in her toaster oven. She'd never known Mike was a cook—chef, by the sound of it—but now she remembered how precisely he'd identify ingredients of dishes they ate together in restaurants.

The taxi brought her to the door of his apartment building on Riverside Drive. "Mr. Parnell," she told the doorman. "I'm afraid I don't know his apartment number."

The doorman nodded. "He's expecting you. Take the elevator up to the eighth floor. It's on the left."

It was the top floor, the elevator opening on a small hall with Delft-type wallpaper. The doors to the two apartments were separated by a marble table, on which stood a large vase filled with an enormous bouquet of fresh flowers.

As she bent to smell them, Vie heard the door to the left open. "Welcome, princess! You're up to your nose in business, I see."

She straightened, smiling, and went over to give him a big hug.

"Welcome to my modest home," he said bowing. "Will you be taking the grand tour or the special condensed one for busy executives?"

She laughed, walking in. "What's the difference?"

"Inestimable. The condensed one leaves out the contents of the refrigerator and the dishwasher."

"That would never do, would it? I'll have the grand tour, please."

"Would you like to rest first, have a drink? Remove your shoes or any other articles of constriction?"

"Mike," said Vie laughing. "Stop your palavering and get on with it. Though you might take your apron off first."

"What? Oh." He looked down and, discovering himself to be enveloped by a large work apron down to below his knees, yanked it off and threw it on a chair. Taking Vie gently by the elbow—"As though I'm one of those blue-haired rickety ladies sightseeing in Venice," she complained happily—he led her through the five-room apartment, spacious but simply furnished, with a grand view of the Hudson.

"Why have I never been here before?" she wondered. "How long have you had this place?"

"Nearly nine years," he told her. Vie had visited his former apartment in the Village a few times, during the days before their aborted Vermont weekend. "You never invited yourself before," he said.

"I didn't! Mike, you know I asked you out for dinner."

"Relax, beauty, I know. Just thought a nice home-cooked meal might be the way to win your heart. You know what they say, though I've always found the image of reaching a woman's heart through her stomach bloody surgical."

"That's because it's a man's heart you're supposed to be digging for."

"That explains it," Mike said, leading them back to the kitchen. "What'll you have to drink?"

"White wine, please, if you have some."

"French, Austrian, or Californian?" he offered, opening the door of his refrigerator.

She asked him to choose, and he brought a glass of Austrian wine to her in the living room. "Lovely bouquet," she said, tasting and inhaling. "It's dry and fruity, reminds me of a brook starting to burble again in the spring."

Her thoughtful expression told Mike that Vie was working again, as always: defining the sense impression for herself to store in her memory bank for later easy withdrawal. A dedicated person, he thought. Not complicated so much as committed. If she ever decided to love a man, she'd give him the full force of her attentions. If she could love him. . . .

Vie leaned back against the soft pile of the rust-colored sofa. The way Mike was looking at her reminded her of Josh. She could have been dining with him now, in a fashionable new restaurant, fussed over by waiters. "I'm glad to be here," she told Mike warmly.

"Wait till you've had dinner," he said in embarrassment.

They moved to the small alcove off the kitchen, Mike's dining room, where the table was set with cloth napkins, two delicate wine glasses at each plate. Vie praised the meal abundantly, saying it was the best duck she'd ever tasted. "You're an artist, Mike!" she told him. "I had no idea you could do something like this."

"There's a lot about me you don't know," he said with a touch of bitterness.

They turned back to the food and ate in silence, until Vie said suddenly, "That's true." The Mike Parnell who lived in this apartment and cooked exquisite meals was almost a new person to her. She was curious about him. "That picture in your bedroom—the blond woman. Who is she?" Vie asked, trying to sound casual.

"My sister."

"Oh." Curiously, she felt relief. "Are you two very close?"

"I wouldn't say that. She's back in Missouri, in a home. I'm not sure she knows exactly who I am."

"I'm sorry," Vie murmured. What secrets lay behind that open, dear face? "Would you mind," she asked timidly, "telling me something about yourself? I know that sounds ridiculous," she added with a nervous laugh. "We've known each other seventeen years, but I guess we haven't been alone together often, have we?"

"No, Vie, we haven't."

"And I guess I was always wrapped up in business." She now remembered why she had called him tonight. The only reason she'd wanted to see him was so that he could listen to *her*. That could wait, she decided now. "Do you enjoy the work you're doing? You've got a marvelous reputation as a lawyer."

"Thanks. Yes, I enjoy it. Maybe I've finally come to terms with it. Do you remember, princess, when we first met in New Haven? I think I told you about my father, a local doctor who brought his services to the Eskimos every summer? He was a good man, and a model to me. My mother, too. She came from a German family, wasn't well educated, but she brimmed over with goodness. No one could get sick or suffer a loss without her trying to help. Food, comfort—sometimes she'd just go over and *be* there."

"Wonderful," said Vie, envying him a little.

"Yes, both of them were wonderful. Both of them were able to feel someone else's pain as though it were their own. When I got to law school, I was determined to use my knowledge of the law so that I could help people. I saw myself as the white knight"—he chuckled—"coming forth on my charger of law and precedents to dispense justice. I planned to start out as a legal-aid lawyer when I passed the bar.

"But I was immediately nabbed by the Peter principle—pushed upstairs to my level of incompetence. That's not completely right, but I managed to be at the top of my class, and the offers I got were all for very high-paying corporation work.

"At that time my sister was in an institution. She'd had an accident at fifteen and suffered irreversible brain damage. My father died while I was at Yale, and the money was running thin. I felt I couldn't afford to turn down a salary that would guarantee Mary's security.

"I accepted the offer of Earnest, Bernbach & Shields, an old respected firm that appealed to me particularly because of their work in the 1950s, defending victims of

McCarthyism. But I told myself the job was temporary. I'd make so much money in a few years that my investments would take care of Mary for the rest of her life. After that, I promised myself, I'd get back on my charger and bring justice to those who'd never known its sweetness. The poor, mainly; blacks, the old—anyone dispossessed by society."

He stopped to drink his wine. Vie reached over and lightly stroked the side of his cheek. Mike caught her hand and kissed it. "Let me clear this and make the coffee," he said.

"No," Vie stated firmly. "You've got to continue." The new aspects of himself that Mike was showing her moved Vie strongly. She'd never met anyone like him in her whole life, Vie realized, except maybe Chandra. But Mike was young, handsome, and—"You're a *good* man," Vie said wonderingly.

"Not up for sainthood by a very long shot, beauty." He loved the way she was looking at him and couldn't understand why a woman like her would be interested in his unexciting life. "Now you know it," he said. "My sophomoric dreams of changing the world. I had poor vision then, I couldn't see the future realistically."

"Because, of course, it wasn't possible to step out of that world after I'd entered it. Within three years I was a junior partner. But I still couldn't save enough money, living in New York City, to guarantee the future of a mouse. The fees for Mary's care kept going up. Even when I was given raises, I'd just squeak through with the payments."

"I always assumed you had a lot of money," Vie admitted. "Lawyers are rich, I thought. And because you were a bachelor, nobody to support. . . ." She remembered the many evenings when she'd let him pay for everything. "I was even surprised that you didn't have a house in the country."

"Or a yacht. I don't have even a very small one. So you see, lovely," he said, taking her hand in both of his, "my life has been drab compared to yours. I've always admired the courage in you, to pursue the profession you love and to make your life the way you wanted it to be."

Vie stood up and went to his chair. She took hold of his hands and helped raise him to a standing position. Then she put her arms around his neck and brought his face down to hers.

When their kiss ended, she said: "I've *followed* my life, Mike, the way you have yours. And it's been closing in. My life has become narrow."

They were still holding each other. "You mean love?" he asked softly.

She nodded, and their lips came together again.

At midnight they were sitting on the sofa sipping brandy. Vie's head rested on Mike's shoulder, and he stroked her hair with his large hand, his movements loving and awkward.

They'd cleared off the dishes quickly and come to the living room for coffee and brandy. They sat with their bodies touching, as comfortable as married lovers, though they hadn't ever made love. They kissed often, sometimes as a light punctuation to their words, sometimes passionately, with open mouths. Mike had suggested they go to bed after their first kisses standing in the dining alcove, but Vie held back. In Mike's embrace she'd thought of Josh, then of Hubert. With those men she'd felt instant fire, her body in the thrall of need. A few hours earlier this evening she'd known she wouldn't have had the strength or desire to resist Josh. In Mike's arms Vie felt a deep tenderness. She felt an excitement, too, or the beginnings of it, but she couldn't be sure that the feeling wasn't simply being transferred onto him. After all, she'd never thought about Mike sexually in seventeen years, except during one short period near the beginning of their friendship, when she'd felt lonely and had fantasized a possible affair with him. But it evaporated, he'd found someone else, and she'd never thought about Mike in that way again.

Tonight he aroused her interest. But how could she rely on these feelings? He was too important to her to simply make love with him as she had with a few others over the years. He didn't take her breath away, as Hubert could still do, despite everything.

When she declined his offer of bed, Vie said she wanted to talk. "All right," he'd agreed in resignation. That was all she ever seemed to want from him.

On the sofa she told him about her great love for Hubert many years ago, around the time when she'd first met Mike. She talked about the excruciating difficulty in deciding between her work and marrying the man she deeply loved. She told Mike about the darkest days of her life— Armand's terrible death and Hubert's disappearance.

"But that's way back in the past," Mike said, patting her head. "It has nothing to do with you now."

"It does, Mike," Vie said softly. "Hubert came back into my life a few days ago."

Mike's hand faltered and dropped. "Will you marry him now?" he asked stiffly.

"No."

"Then why? What's the problem?"

She told him about Josh, the way she'd felt on first meeting him—the same chemistry she'd had with Hubert. Mike winced. Then he turned and grabbed Vie roughly by her arms. "Little girl," he said, with no kindness in his tone, "why don't you grow up? You talk about 'chemistry' like a teenager. These men want you for their egos, not for yourself. I've loved you from the moment I met you, and I never dared to interfere with your life. But I'm not standing back anymore. I'm the man who knows you and wants you and loves you more than anything else in this screwed-up world." He yanked her to her feet. "And now I'm taking you to bed."

At three in the morning Vie was still crying. Her tears of happiness came more easily than any before, and she didn't want to stop. "Beauty," Mike murmured, gazing at her wet, radiant face. "I wish you could turn off that beauty sometimes; it's unbearable; too much for us poor sinners."

"*You* have the most wonderful face in the world," she said, reaching to touch it. "And I'm an old lady."

"Like Venus." His hand moved gently over her breasts down her belly. "But slimmer. Don't cry, my darling." He kissed her eyes.

"Let me. They're new for me—tears," she said. "I never knew how good they feel. Tears of joy—they must be the most precious liquid in the world."

"They'd never sell."

Vie laughed. "Mike! Mike, why didn't you *tell* me?"

"Tell you what, angel?"

"About this. Us. I don't know."

"Love?"

"Love."

"You never asked," he said.

"I thought I knew. Is it possible for someone to take forty whole years to discover what makes the world go round?"

"Love doesn't make it go round, my darling. It just gives the world a reason to."

Vie laughed and Mike laughed with her. They kissed and then Vie traced his jaw with her tongue, down over his neck, across his shoulders to his armpit. "Mike?"

"Yes, love?"

"You smell better than any fragrance I know."

"Not too strong?"

"For daytime we might have to dilute it. But it's perfect for night."

"Then let the night go on." They turned to each other and began to make love again. Slowly they touched and tasted each other's skin. Mike brought his mouth to her belly and inch by inch moved down, over the mound of tight blond curls, his tongue separating her lips, stroking them until she cried out and thrust her pelvis against his mouth. He found the hard center, sucking gently while she ground against him. Then her hands pulled his head away, up to her face. "Now," she said. "Now. I want to come with you inside me again."

He guided himself into her, thrust slowly, and then stopped. "What is it?" she whispered.

"Hush, darling. I get so excited I have to pause."

"Don't," she begged. "Come into me, please. Come now. I need it. Come."

He closed his eyes and thrust into her, his climax coming immediately, thunderingly, meeting her own.

Afterward, her eyes wide and clear, Vie looked up at him. "It's so simple," she said.

5

When the phone rang next morning, she knew it would be Mike. She'd left his apartment at dawn, smiling radiantly at the doorman. At home she thought she'd sleep a few hours, but she felt too buoyant. It was ten o'clock already and Vie was still wide awake, after a sleepless night more wonderful than anything she'd dreamed.

"Hello?" she purred into the receiver.

"Madame Jolay?"

"Yes," she answered, frowning, changing her tone for the caller. She dimly recognized the voice but couldn't place it.

"Here is Paul Mescaux. I hope I have not disturbed you?"

"No, it's fine," she said, puzzled. "What can I do for you?"

"Please be so kind, meet me today."

"I have another engagement. . . ." Mike had said he'd try to get away for an hour over lunch.

"It is urgent, madame. It is a matter which will be of great interest to you, I give my word."

"About my father?" she asked, remembering his last call.

"That also. And your future company."

"My *what*?" Who was this man? What did he know about her, and from whom?

"I can say no more on the telephone. You will meet me for lunch? One o'clock?"

"All right," she said and wrote down the address of the restaurant. Vie hung up, torn between curiosity and disappointment. She longed to be with Mike. Would business always stand in the way? she wondered. Would she always have to choose between the two most important things in her life?

She loved Mike, and for the first time Vie was absolutely sure she knew what love meant. What she felt for Mike went as deep as her sense of self and soared into possibilities. But they hadn't said anything about the future, nothing beyond today's lunch. Vie was grateful for that. She couldn't imagine her life as other than it was. She was too accustomed to her own ways for even this love—this amazing, deep, wonderful love—to make her think of changing.

In any case, now was not the time, when she had a dragon to slay and a world to conquer. She had to do it alone.

Vie called Mike and told him she wouldn't be able to make lunch. "It's business," she apologized.

"What about tonight, then?" he asked, accepting her cancellation without protest.

"Oh, yes. Come over here the moment you can!"

She heard his low chuckle and felt a rush of happiness. Mike knew that business was her life, and he would never try to compete with it. No one else, not even Hubert, had understood her so well.

Riding to her meeting with Mescaux, Vie felt apprehensive. She knew about her father's enemies in the past. Marty had discovered that, too, in France, but she was no more convinced than Vie that their father had actually been a traitor. They both believed Armand had done no wrong, though they knew that he'd been implicated by circumstances and that he'd been hounded by the Resistance.

If Mescaux was one of those, could he be trying to pursue Armand sixteen years beyond the grave? That didn't seem likely, but then, why did he want to see her? And why was it urgent? And what did he mean by a matter of great interest to her future company?

The Czech restaurant on York Avenue was lined with booths against the wall. A gray-haired man rose from one

of them and came toward Vie as she stood with the headwaiter. "Enchanté, madame," he said, kissing her hand.
"I am Paul Mescaux."

He was an old man with a youthful body. A man in his
seventies, Vie estimated, lean, about her height, with a
full shock of hair, and a thick but tidy mustache. His
smile was warm and his manner so charming in its Old
World courtesy that Vie immediately lost her feelings of
apprehension. "Come, my dear," he said, taking her arm
and leading her back to where he'd been sitting. "I have
chosen a spot that gives us a little privacy. If you will be
so kind, step into my office."

She took the seat opposite him. There were only a few
other customers in the Praha, and none on their side of
the room. "You drink beer, madame? I hope so. Czech
beer is the best in the world, and I am irresistible to their
pilsner."

She laughed in amusement at his precise but incorrect
speech and said she'd love one. "Dva pivo," he ordered
the waiter.

"You speak Czech?"

"Only a little bit. It is not so different from Russian,
and I am a Russian at birth."

"From birth" or "at heart," she wondered; his name
was decidedly French.

"We have met before, dear mademoiselle."

"Yes? Where?" She had no recollection of him whatever.

"At the funeral of your father."

Instantly, an image flashed through her mind.

"You? The man standing on the knoll?"

He nodded. "Yes, it was I, come to respect your dear
father."

"Then you were a friend of his! Why didn't you come
up and introduce yourself to me?"

"I was uncertain, my dear. I am afraid I have been
uncertain with you many times. You see, when your father died, I knew he had been living in America under an
assumed name, but I did not have the knowledge of whether
you knew his real name. I was wanting to greet you and
express my sorrows, but I was afraid you would not
know me if I was a friend of Armand Jolaunay."

"Where did you know him?"

"In Paris. I was an employee in his laboratory. A chemist. That has been my métier for all of my life." The waiter arrived with their beers, and Mescaux remained silent until the man was gone. Then he leaned toward Vie. "But it is of your father I wish to speak.

"When I came to work for him, my name was Pavel Moscowitz. A Jew then and still now a Jew, though your father gave me a new name. He acted on advice from the collaborators."

Vie stared at him. So Armand *was* one of them! "Why are you telling me this?" she asked, suddenly suspicious.

"Armand Jolaunay saved my life, and the lives of my family."

"How?"

He told her that Armand's contacts with the German high command in Paris and with Vichy officials gave him foreknowledge of events, as well as providing special patronage for the factory. On the advice of an officer—Mescaux wasn't sure who—Armand dismissed his Jewish employees.

From the outside, it seemed that Jolaunay was adopting the anti-Semitism of the Nazis. In secret, however, he arranged for passports to be issued with false names to his employees and their families and made provisions for them to escape the labor camps and deportations that awaited them in France by emigration to Switzerland. "He fired me, my dear, with a most unusual parting gift: passports for my parents, my two older brothers, and myself. He also gave me a set of instructions on which route was best to take, the addresses of people in Basel, and two hundred thousand francs."

Vie was dumbfounded by the account of her father's generosity. "Why didn't he tell me?" she wondered aloud.

"That is not the ending of my tale. I fled to Switzerland with my parents and was able to find work as an industrial chemist. My brothers chose to go underground and remain in France. The younger was killed within a week of our departure, but the elder held on to his life throughout the war. When we were reunited afterward, he told me that Jolaunay continued to capitalize on his unique position as a favorite of the Boches to help Jews to escape to other countries. These people were strangers to him."

"But why, then," she asked, shaking her head in bewilderment, "did the Resistance go after him?"

"He killed a member of the Maquis."

"In self-defense. The man was trying to kill him!" She'd learned this much from Marty. "He was being hounded by them before—and my mother too. Is it true that she was German?"

"Not at all. A beautiful girl from Alsace, a true Frenchwoman. Her fairness led people into believing she was German, particularly because they were suspecting your father of collaboration."

"Why? Why?" she exhorted the old man.

He explained that the Resistance movement itself was made up of many elements, from extreme rightists—ardent patriots—through the Gaullists to the extreme left—ardent internationalists. There was suspicion and even warring among the anti-Nazi factions. Armand's reputation was complicated by his obvious fraternization with the enemy, his profits, his apparently anti-Semitic actions. Of course it was precisely because of this reputation that he became as effective as he was in saving lives.

"Why didn't he tell me?" she repeated.

Mescaux gave a little shrug and smiled at her warmly. "That I cannot say. But I know the past is treacherous. You cannot let it in a bit at a time. If you open a crack, if you make the slightest hole in the wall, it will burst out, surging through the dyke of the present and flooding it. You have read the great Marcel Proust? He takes a cup of tea, bites on a little cake called a madeleine, and voilà! the taste and smell restore to him a former time in Combray. Not a simple memory; he finds the entire scene restored, the houses and grass, and the people back in life again. A scent can do that; and so, too, can words."

The food they'd ordered had arrived and was getting cold, but neither of them showed any interest in it. "When he killed himself," Vie started, still finding it painful to talk about, "I thought—not at the time, but later, when I learned who he was—I blamed myself—"

"But you had no reason—"

"No, please. Let me finish. I blamed myself for taking authority away from him, his sense of power. And that is definitely true, I did. I don't know how I could have prevented it, but that was the situation, and we both knew it.

"The more I learned about his past, in later years, the more I understood that the feeling of failure had deep roots. I thought his suicide showed his life had become a burden to him, that he was *ashamed* of it. But he saved people's lives! How could he be ashamed?"

Paul Mescaux placed a hand gently on Vie's and looked at her in silence for a long moment, his face showing concern and hesitation. Then he gave a deep sigh. "It wasn't suicide. I learned from my brother. Your father was murdered by a hired killer working for a neo-Maquis terrorist organization."

"No!" She jumped up. "Oh, my God!"

"I shouldn't have told you," Mescaux rebuked himself.

"Yes, you should have." Vie was trembling. "In a strange way, it's somehow better to know he didn't kill himself. It takes a weight off me. But oh, my God—murdered!" She turned toward the rack where her coat was hanging. "You must excuse me. I need some fresh air."

He was standing and made a move to follow her. "Shall I accompany you?"

"Please, no. I'll be back. I'd like to be alone."

"Of course," he said worriedly, returning to his seat and escorting her only with his eyes until she reached the door.

Vie walked down the avenue, toward the large complex of hospitals. She wished Mike could be with her now, his love offering protection against her shock. More than shock; as her thoughts moved back to that time, reconstructing details, the evidence of hard dates brought terror. Armand died three days before Hubert was due in New York. Hubert never came or sent word. She was sure that the two events were linked by a strong connection.

Mike would help her track down the evidence until they uncovered the bare truth, whatever it was. Maybe Hubert would be exonerated at the end. She remembered his face coming out of the shadows, the vaguely familiar scent that clung to him. She shuddered violently.

"Are you all right?" a woman was asking, and Vie realized she'd stopped dead in the middle of the sidewalk.

She nodded and moved on, sure that Hubert had some knowledge, at least, of the murder. Even if his hands were clean, his silence implicated him. His offer of a job, she felt now, was nothing more than blood money. She vowed to take revenge.

When Vie came back to the restaurant, Paul Mescaux was sitting in the booth, a lonely, frail figure with his half-empty glass of beer in front of him, looking at it morosely. Vie hastened over, knowing he was still blaming himself for being the bearer of his news.

A smile of such gratitude came over his face when he saw her that Vie wanted to embrace him. "I'm all right," she said, taking her seat opposite. "It was necessary for me to hear the truth. Do you know *who* ordered his death?" She held her breath.

"No. My brother said only, 'It is the long arm of vengeance.' He is dead now, too."

"I'll find out one day. Soon," she promised.

"Please, dear child, let the grass grow over the dead. Nothing will return him to life."

"No," she agreed. "It's for my own satisfaction. There's nothing more to say about that, is there? So tell me the other reason why you wanted to talk to me."

"I want to help you. Your father gave me my life, and I can make only a tiny payment in return to his daughter. I have heard of your difficulties in business, and I will propose to you something that will help you over the obstacles."

"Thank you," she said. "It's kind of you. But frankly, all I need to get started again is a private fortune."

"I am afraid I have not that. If I did, it would be yours."

She smiled at him affectionately and understood why her father had chosen this man as a friend.

"But, please," he went on, "let me present for your consideration the following idea."

She waited, still smiling. Vie felt obligated to hear him out—Armand's friend, an old man intent on trying to help.

"It is a fragrance of your father's invention, one he was unable to produce during the war. It has never been made, it existed nowhere but in imagination."

"Then how do *you* know about it?" His concern for her touched Vie, but she suspected Mescaux of trying to pull rabbits out of an old beret.

"I know only some, not all. Armand said to me he had made a formula for his greatest fragrance. 'C'est extraordinaire!' he told me, but it was a double problem to make. Problem number one, he could not procure some of the ingredients, not even through his powerful protectors. Problem number two, it was for a man."

"What?" Vie asked, leaning forward.

"The fragrance. Armand intended it for men. But it would have to be as costly as women's perfume, and no one would be buying it. In the early forties he would have been a laughingstock."

"I don't believe it," she said slowly.

"But you must, my dear, because I speak only truth."

When she told Mescaux about her own plans to develop a men's fragrance from Armand's private-label formula, he was amazed and enthusiastic. "My dear!" he exclaimed. "It is destiny! The muses sing in chorus! You have already set foot on the road to greatness!"

"Maybe. But no one's interested in backing it."

"They will, dear child, they will when you give them the greatest of all fragrances. Jolaunay was the finest perfumer in the world, and this was his glory."

"Even if this scent were as great as you say," Vie pointed out, "we don't have the formula."

"Ah," said Mescaux, "that is not all of the truth. Most of the formula we do have—I have a terrible memory. It locks in numbers and chemical formulas. I remember clearly all the ingredients, though I do not know them by name, only symbols."

"You're saying you do have the formula?" It wouldn't be hard to have the chemical terms translated into generic names.

"Yes and no. I am missing one small piece to the puzzle. I do not know the proportions of each. Armand always retained the final mystery, even with me."

"So then," Vie said with a sigh, "we *don't* have a formula."

"Perhaps—I was thinking perhaps there is a possibility that you have some old notes of your father's. . . ."

"I have his notebook."

"His 'bible'?" asked Mescaux excitedly.

"Yes."

"Fly to it, dear child. It is most possible that you will find the proportions there—though, of course, many of the ingredients would not be written down. For protection."

"Will you help me look?" she invited him.

"But of course! A great honor."

"Can you come back with me now?" It was three thirty already.

"I am afraid I must see my doctor a little later this afternoon," he said regretfully. "But I shall be free this evening. May I call upon you then?"

"Here's my address." As Vie handed him the slip of paper, she felt a sense of inevitability. It could never really have worked with Mike; he was too open, and she had too much in the way.

"It's your sister," Nick said, rolling on his back and reaching the phone to her over his chest.

"Bastard," said Marty. "Who the hell do you—"

"Shh, honey. Big sister's listening."

Marty yanked the phone from him, glaring. Nick blew her a kiss, turned toward her, and began playing with her breasts.

When she ended the call, Marty shoved him away from her roughly. "Who said you could answer my phone? What're you trying to do?"

"Compromise you, so you'll be forced to marry me."

"Oh, Nick!" She laughed. "Are you really just a nice, old-fashioned boy hiding in the body of a sex maniac?"

He bent down to lick the soles of her feet. Then, slowly, he sucked each toe as she lay back, naked, offering him any part of her body to do with as he liked. They'd made love three times since he'd arrived in her apartment at midnight, and now his warm mouth surrounding her big toe, sucking insistently, signaled through her own body's reaction that they were about to launch into lovemaking a fourth time.

"Nick," she groaned. "You're insatiable."

He righted himself and moved his body over hers. Looking into his laughing, desiring eyes, she begged, "Let's have a little rest. I'm exhausted. I'm sore." But even as she spoke, her body was arching up toward him, her legs spread, a warm flush rising on her neck.

He remained without moving, propped up on stiff arms, looking down at her face. He looked at her with such intensity, with such powerful, consuming concentration that she looked away from his eyes to his lips, the top of his chest, and then back to his eyes again, still boring into her and now filling with tears. "I love you, Marty," he said harshly, full of need. "I never want you to go away from me."

"I can't stay under you like this all my life," she protested, smiling. "I'd be crushed."

Suddenly he rolled off her and took her in his arms, as gently as if she were a newborn child. "I don't want you under me except in bed," he said in a new voice. "I think I fell in love with you the moment I saw you. But I didn't know it. All I've known about women is wanting to take them. 'Take,' like a thing. I didn't recognize love when it hit me. Marry me, darling."

"How can I, baby?" she asked, her voice choking. Slowly she stroked his hair, her eyes devouring his face. He was so splendidly good-looking that it made her want to weep. "I'm not a wife, I'm a businesswoman. You're my employee."

He stopped her mouth with kisses, and then he said, "I want us to make a child together."

She shuddered as she felt her body meet that yearning. She could almost feel the child expanding her body, reshaping and filling it with their love. Marty began to cry openly, her tears spilling over his face as he held her very close. "Nick, listen, please. It's all crazy, but I think I love you, too. It's too soon, though—until last night. . . ."

"It was good."

"Yes."

"It was the best."

"Yes."

"And now we'll get married."

"No, Nick! It scares me."

"Me, too." He grinned. "The thought of it scares me shitless. It's not what I bargained for."

"Me either," said Marty, grinning also, her tears stopped.

"We can be scared shitless together and hold hands."

"For the rest of our lives? How'd we get any work done?"

"Marty, baby, we'll do it better. With my brains and your beauty. . . ."

"It's the other way around."

They laughed, kissed, and began making love again. They ignored the telephone and the work awaiting them as they remained in bed until noon, exploring each other with hands, mouths, and words. They wove dreams together, of partnerships in love and business, of travels around the world, of endless wealth and happiness as they made their way through life together, anchored to each other, stronger than each could ever be alone.

As they were dressing, Marty remembered: Vie had said she'd be coming to the office today to tell her something important. About their father, she'd said.

Watching her bend to pull on her pantyhose, Nick wondered if he should tell Marty about his meeting with Vie. He didn't want to hurt her, but he felt, looking at her with a tenderness that made him ache, that he could keep no secrets from her; he wanted her to be the one person with whom he could be honest. She hadn't agreed to marry him yet, and Nick knew that Marty, like himself, could make the commitment only after she'd gotten rid of all mistrust. He wanted her to believe in him, but he also wanted to protect her.

Nick decided he'd go back to Vie, to find out what she was cooking up. He'd be the first to know about a rival company if Vie went ahead and violated the terms of her agreement with Motek. He'd spy for Marty, to make sure no one would do her any harm and to prove to her that she could trust him.

*   *   *

The Motek offices were all lucite and plexiglass. Impressive but unoriginal, she thought, revealing no personality or temperament; simply the authority of technology.

She was led into Marty's private office immediately. Marty looked softer, more beautiful than Vie had ever seen her. She greeted Vie politely, without excessive warmth, but also without arrogance or antipathy, and asked her secretary to bring them each a cup of coffee.

When Vie told her what she'd learned about Armand's death, Marty was silent. Then she asked, "That Montalmont you say is implicated—wasn't he someone important to you? I think there was gossip about that."

"Yes. He asked me to marry him."

"Did he?" she asked with unusual interest. "How did you feel?"

"I loved him. I didn't know what to say."

Marty was next to her in two strides, hugging her. "Oh Vie," she said, "what a terrible thing for you to discover."

"Marty!" She clung to her sister, holding on to the sympathy she offered.

But suddenly Marty drew back. "That bastard killed our father?"

"I'm not sure. All I feel is that he had something to do with it." She realized Marty had said *our*—not *your*—father.

"I'll destroy him," Marty threatened.

"No, please, leave him to me," Vie said in a confusion of feelings. Marty was offering help to her, and Vie didn't know the source of it. She remembered the man's voice answering the phone this morning—she'd been sure it was Nick. If he was living with Marty, had he told her about their meeting? Was Marty pretending to support Vie so that she could then spring an attack? Vie's presence here now had nothing to do with business and their rivalry; they were both Armand's daughters, and Vie had to let Marty know the circumstances of his death, even though it meant exposing Hubert. She hadn't expected the sudden sympathy.

She wanted to go on being comforted by Marty for what Hubert had done. She had an image of what it would be like if they were true sisters, joined in trust. But Marty stiffened. "Why were you involved with Montalmont in the first place? Did *you* want to get rid of Armand? From what I heard, he was threatening your authority. He intended to head Jolay, didn't he?"

Vie stared at her. "You bitch," she said crisply and walked out of the office before Marty could answer.

Vie hadn't seen Mike all week. At first he'd accepted the urgent business she had, assuring her, "I'm used to waiting for you. After all, I've had years of practice."

But later his voice had sounded cool on the phone, and this morning he exploded. "I don't mind sharing you with your work," he told her. "I expected that. But it turns out work is the *only* thing you care about."

"No, Mike. I love you."

"That's what you had me believe earlier this week. Monday, was it? Today's Saturday, and you haven't been able to make time for me once. You're too busy—you and that man you're with."

"Mike, please. He's an old man. . . ."

"Yeah—safe. No risks. You don't have to give up anything at all."

"You don't understand. . . ."

"Maybe not. I've sure as hell tried to. All I can see is that understanding doesn't do me a damn bit of good. I'm not going to call you again, and I'm not sitting around waiting for the phone to ring, either. I'm a grown man, Vie, for Christ's sake. I'm not going to be your toy for if and when you feel like playing."

"You're still my lawyer, Mike, aren't you?" she asked, her voice cracking.

"That, yes," he said in a weary voice. "I don't let pleasure interfere with business either. Good-bye, Vie."

She stared at the phone, and great shudders ran through her. If only she could burst into tears like other women, throw herself headlong into a bout of sobbing—then maybe she could feel relief. But she'd never been able to take refuge in tears. They appeared spontaneously in moments of happiness. But with pain—never. Pain was dry-eyed and stayed locked inside her.

* _ * *

Paul Mescaux was going by a list of figures they'd found in the black notebook—figures strewn throughout the pages in margins or at the corners. Vie had never paid attention to those numbers before, not seeing any significance in them. She'd assumed they represented nothing more than a lack of paper at hand—that Armand had simply jotted down a number here and there to remind himself of something, without reference to the notes on the page. To her they'd been random, but Paul, as she now called him, methodically added them together and found their sum to be exactly one hundred.

The discovery cheered him. "We have here the proportions," he told Vie.

But to her the task ahead still seemed insurmountable. "If these *are* the proportions for the compound," she pointed out, "it'll take years to discover which number refers to which ingredient."

"Not years, my dear. We can use deductive powers with many of them. The musk, for instance, cannot exceed a trace amount. I am nearly sure the figure of zero point five means musk."

Taking her list of chemical symbols, Vie had gone to the largest fragrance suppliers in New York. A few substances were easily identifiable. Others were no longer available—though they could be matched or approximated by some of the new synthetics. Three were rejected as not being possible aromatic chemicals.

Vie and Paul worked with what they had—the aromatic chemicals, including synthetic musk, and natural oils. "I believe," he said excitedly, "that the fragrance is based on *two* accords—a forest blend combined with a spicy blend."

But it remained elusive. On Friday they'd captured something—but only for a moment. The dry-out had lasted five minutes, and then the fragrance was gone from the blotting paper.

Nick Benedetti's genius was their only, desperate hope, Vie decided. But when Nick phoned her late Saturday afternoon, Vie at first refused to see him.

He threatened to tell Marty about their previous meeting. To Vie, the threat meant that he'd withheld this information from Marty to use as blackmail against herself. Vie deliberated. She knew that neither she nor Paul could match the brilliance and intuitiveness of Nick. Only he had the potential to understand what the missing ingredients might be and to sniff out the correlations between numbers and substances.

If he'd join her and Paul in producing the fragrance, and if it turned out to be as spectacular as Paul promised, then Nick would have to become a partner in the new company. If Nick was indeed battling with Marty, he might come over to her, be willing to take a share in profits. His salary now was phenomenal, Vie knew—well over $200,000 a year. But he might be intrigued by the challenge and the offer of partnership.

But why was it Nick—and Vie felt almost sure it had been—who'd answered the phone in Marty's apartment?

All this went through her mind as she stood holding the phone in her kitchen, looking out at her awakening garden. "All right, Nick," she said. "I'll meet you."

When she put down the phone, it rang again. Her breath caught as she recognized Hubert's voice.

He was calling from a pay phone two blocks away, he said, and had to meet her immediately, to explain. Marty had caught up with him yesterday when he was with clients in St. Louis, and he'd taken the first plane back. "I must tell you the whole truth, Vie. Please let me come over right now."

"No," she said icily, cupping her hand over the mouthpiece. For a moment she was afraid Paul could somehow hear the voice of Montalmont, Jolaunay's rival. But he was in another room, sniffing blotters.

"Then meet me in the cafe. You must hear me!" he shouted.

"Why?"

"Because I didn't kill your father! Because I had no knowledge of it until afterward!"

"Why should I believe you?"

"Oh God. Vie! It is the truth. I wanted to protect you, to keep you from knowing about my father."

"*Your* father?"

"You must come and let me tell you all of it!"

He was so agitated, shouting, that she had to hold the phone half a foot away from her ear. When she put it down, trembling, she went straight to the front closet and grabbed a jacket. She called out, "I'll be back in a few minutes, Paul," and left the house before he could question her.

As she entered the cafe, he sprang up and ran over to her. Hubert's face was deathly white, his eyes luminous. He led her to the table without speaking.

"Bless you for coming," he said when they were seated opposite each other. "Now you must listen to me, please, Vie. It is very hard—for both of us. Please, you must hear me out to the end."

She nodded briefly. "Go on. I won't interrupt."

His voice shaking, Hubert told Vie how Armand met his death on instructions from Henri Montalmont. He told her how he'd discovered it, how powerless he'd been to take action against his father. "My world crumbled in that moment, Vie," he said, his dark eyes shining with tears. "I lost everything. My name became a curse to me. On account of it, I had to lose you. You must understand, my darling, how I loved you. But I had no choice. I had to surrender you to the ravages of war, twenty-five years after peace was signed. I knew that if you learned the truth, you would never forgive me. I knew also it would not be possible to maintain a lie forever, and that you would come to curse me as I do myself."

Vie felt his torment. Despite everything, despite what her mind was telling her, the old love bloomed again, and she wanted to hold him against her, comforting him.

But she remained silent, watching him, his face buried in his hands. When he looked up at her again, she saw the weakness in his features, the signs of age. Yet age wasn't responsible for the weakness—Paul Mescaux didn't have it. The old love she'd carried like a pressed flower withered and disintegrated. "I'm sorry, Hubert," she said.

"Vie, my beautiful Vie. So much time has passed. You are still the woman I have loved most in my life."

"Don't think about it anymore."

"You can forgive me?"

"No," she said slowly. "I don't hold you responsible for my father's death. I don't know if there was anything you could have done to prevent it. Maybe not. I can absolve you; but forgiveness is something else. It's not possible without forgetting. And that I can never do."

He shook his head mournfully. "Fate prevented us from being husband and wife. But now we can be partners, we can work together. . . ."

"I can't work for you, Hubert, or even with you. You said it was the ravages of war. Whatever I earned would be reparation payments." She stood up.

"No, I could never, never regard it that way."

"And I could regard it in no other way. Good-bye, Hubert."

He was standing next to her. "Au revoir?" he asked hopefully.

"Good-bye," she repeated and gave him a final handshake.

He didn't follow her out the door. Vie went to the pay phone and spoke to Paul. Then she hailed a cab and gave the driver Mike's address.

6

The first of the missing ingredients was supplied by Tam Ghannikar. He'd worked on the formula, trying out different chains of synthetic molecules, none of which produced an odor. Taking a chance, he'd added two molecules to the chain.

He held out the vial shyly to Vie when she came into the shop. "It's a wee bit medicinal," he explained, as though apologizing. "A bit familiar to me, actually. It's the smell of an ointment we use in India for children when their muscles are sore. Perhaps such an ointment was used in France, too, and gave your father the idea."

"You're sensational, Tam," Vie told him. He was approximately her own age, not as good-looking as his father, and more stilted in manner. But Tam was devoted to Vie, and when she'd come to him with the problem of the missing ingredients, he felt bound in both honor and duty to find them. He knew Chandra had loved her as though she were his own child.

Vie sniffed the vial he'd handed her. "Maybe this scent will turn out to be medicine," she said, only half-jesting.

"It won't be that," Tam assured her. "I am quite certain your father used only a trace of it in the accord—for freshness, perhaps."

She thanked him and took the new ingredient back with her. Before a week was over, Tam had found the other two missing links: one turned out to be an extract from pine cones; the other, an old animal-oil synthetic, formulated before the war.

Now Nick had all the ingredients. He put together accord after accord, not as Paul Mescaux would do as a theoretical chemist, using mathematics to find the answer. Nick worked blindly, leaving his thoughts out of his experiments, following his instincts and his nose. But after two weeks he had nothing to show for it and felt very discouraged. Still, he drove himself to work harder every day, up to the point when he was suffused and saturated with scent, until he could get no impression whatever. Then he'd take a break, and return after an hour or less to try again. He worked constantly, driven by the greatest challenge he'd met in his career, and his conviction that he would be able at the end to come upon the gold that Vie had promised.

Marty knew what he was doing. No details yet, only that he was formulating a "revolutionary product" for Vie. She badgered Nick and tried to extract it from him, but he'd always smile and lay a finger over her lips. "It'll all be yours, baby—ours—as soon as I've perfected it. Ask me questions and I'll tell you lies."

Officially, Nick was on a leave of absence after his hard work on their men's fragrance line. Nick had told Vie the leave was only a feint; he wouldn't go back to Motek afterward, but there was no point in refusing the paycheck by telling them that. He convinced Vie that he and Marty had fought so bitterly that it was impossible to work for her any longer. Vie knew him as a ruthless, ambitious, and dazzlingly brilliant chemist who was eager to join her in partnership because he wanted to be out on his own. Nick worked on giving her that impression. He even hinted that he'd want more of the percentage, that his ambition wouldn't stop until he controlled the company.

Vie believed it. As they fenced over money and shares, he knew that the only threat she saw in him was his desire for personal advancement. She didn't suspect that he was betraying her from the beginning.

Marty had approved his plan immediately. When he'd put together the fragrance he called his gold dust, Nick would give it to her, for Jolay of Motek to bring on the market. Nick would return from his "leave" to a double position as head of the lab and a vice president in the corporation.

Josh Manning had phoned three times since their meeting to set a date for their dinner at Le Chat au Toit. In early June, Vie accepted and said she'd meet him at his office.

"Come up to my place instead," he offered. "We can have drinks on the terrace before going out."

"Thanks, Josh. I'd rather meet you at the office," she told him with a firmness that allowed no contradiction. What a woman, thought Josh admiringly: beautiful, brainy, and tough. She was a challenge to him. He'd recognized on the first day he'd seen her at the bank that the fiercely independent Vie Jolay had a vein of romance running through her. He decided to mine that vein, go for the softness, and make her yield. She was the most exciting woman he'd met in months, and he wouldn't rest until she'd delivered up to him the promise he saw in her eyes and lips.

When she arrived, she took the same seat as last time, when she'd come on business.

"Not there," Josh told her, reaching to embrace Vie, "tonight's for pleasure."

She stayed where she was. "I have something to show you."

He groaned. "Not again."

From her handbag she pulled out a small glass flask. "Not the same." She unstoppered the glass cork and held it out for him to smell. "This is going to be the most expensive perfume in the world—and it's for men."

He sniffed and closed his eyes. Then he sniffed again, cautiously, like someone sipping the first drop of a $500 wine. Vie waited, watching him, holding her breath.

At last he looked at her and smiled. "You've got something," he said. "Never smelled anything like this. The fragrance keeps changing, somehow. It seems to expand, to carry you along some kind of spectrum, or harmonics. Hell, Vie, I don't know how to talk about smells."

"You're doing beautifully," she assured him. "You've gotten the idea. It's like a symphony of fragrances, isn't it?"

"Maybe." He sniffed again. "Or maybe like fireworks, coming up with another burst of color after you'd thought you'd seen the last. Why did you say it was the most expensive in the world?"

Vie could feel his interest, his growing excitement in the fragrance. She'd calculated an appeal to his sense of extravagance, and it seemed to be working. "The ingredients are rare, never before used in a fragrance. They're expensive in themselves. But we're going to do a terrific markup on top of that and promote it as 'outrageous luxury—for a man.'"

"I like it," Josh said simply. "It's going with the trend. Men buying furs. I saw an ad in the paper last week for diamonds, and it was addressed to women. 'Tell him you love him without using words'—something like that. Women are buying things for men that men used to buy for women. The more expensive the better."

"And men will buy it for themselves," Vie assured him.

"Men who go to expensive hairdressers, have facials and manicures. . . ."

"They're gay."

"Not at all," Vie countered. "Do you know who's going in for plastic surgery these days? Men. Executives. Men in the corporate world, in their forties and fifties, who know they have to look young to stay at the top. Men are spending *billions* on their looks. They've been taught it's all right to pamper themselves the way women were always encouraged to do. Also that they're *entitled* to luxury."

Josh felt her enthusiasm. She spoke with passion, her hands flying through the air. She was exciting, glittering, the prize of New York.

"What kind of backing do you need?" he asked bluntly. "I suppose that's why you're showing me this?"

"Ten million dollars," she said evenly.

He whistled. "You've certainly upped your stakes. Who's going to shell out that kind of money for a smell?"

"You'll find them," she said with total confidence. "And it won't be a smell they'll be backing—it'll be an image, an essence of success, luxury, sensual appeal. Mainly it reinforces a man's sense of his own worth." Mike had given her that line, with its overtones of psychology.

Josh was hooked, she could see, though still struggling. It was the moment for her coup de grâce. "We'll sell it by the drop."

"What do you mean?"

She smiled sweetly. "This liquid is so precious that it's sold by the drop, not the ounce."

"I like it!" Josh was now fully infected by her own enthusiasm. "It's wild, its exorbitant—outrageous, as you said. We'll do it, Vie! Together. The men's fashion magazines—hell, we'll advertise in *The Wall Street Journal, New York Times, Forbes.* . . ."

"That's the idea," Vie said, laughing. "Shall we dine on it?" She stood up, and Josh took her in his arms. He kissed her on the lips.

"Please," said Vie, drawing away. He *was* attractive, particularly now, when he sparkled with the enthusiasm they both shared.

He was too happy to mind her retreat. "Dinner now, my

princess. The best the city has to offer. We're about to make history together. I can feel it, princess—you and me."

In the early morning hours Vie was chuckling sleepily. "He was carried away all evening. I never heard such compliments! By the time the raspberry mousse arrived, I could swear he thought it was me we'd be selling, drop by drop."

"Was it made with framboise, the mousse?"

"Oh, Mike! You don't care about other men in my life."

He leaned over to kiss the space between her breasts. "If I thought you wanted him, I'd go nuts. You know that, Vie. If I thought Josh Manning had a chance with you, I'd fall apart. But you went to him for backing, and he gave it to you. How can I think badly of the man? Look how happy he's made you."

"You trust me," she said in amazement, stroking his hair softly with both her hands.

"I told you I love you, didn't I?" Mike answered and let her guide his head to where she wanted it.

The light of day wakened Mike to harsh reality. The lover in him was temporarily displaced by the lawyer, who sat up sharply, feeling the little teeth of anxiety attacking his stomach.

Seeing the expression on his face, Vie sat up too. "You worried?" she asked.

"It'll be a lulu of a lawsuit," Mike said with a grimace. "Thirty seconds, maybe less, after that scent appears in a store, Duane Olcott and all his fire-breathing dragons will be on my neck." He put his hand to the back of it. "My poor neck."

"Are you willing to go through with it?" she asked apprehensively.

"Beauty, I told you before: whatever you do, I'm in it with you. I'd go to the wall for you. But I tell you it would be easier to go *through* the Great Wall of China than to win a case against Olcott. To begin with, you've so clearly violated the terms of your agreement that he could be a deaf-mute imbecile and win. But the man's about as stupid as Satan. He's slick, cold, and very hard. A power drill. Olcott can crack through arguments of other lawyers as though they were no deeper than nail polish. And if that weren't enough to intimidate me, he's connected by marriage to the power structure extending from the city to the federal government. You may have the genius for scent in your family, but Marty sure has the nose for who's best at defending her interests."

"I thought we'd been through this before, Mike. That I'd patent it under a different name. . . ."

"Sure, sure," he said, waving her suggestion away like a troublesome fly. He got out of bed, put on a light cotton robe, and began pacing.

Vie wanted him beside her, to be able to snuff out the world again in his arms. Her eyes lingered on his face, traveled down to his naked legs, and she couldn't think of anything that was important except Mike.

"We'll use everything," he went on. "I know Manning's lawyer, Bob Calcituck—he's a shrewd ally to have. But I tell you honestly, love, we'll be going into battle armed with a teaspoon."

"Do you want me to give it up? At this stage?" Vie was alert and defensive.

"Sure I do. It's the only way to save your life. Mine, too. But I know you won't listen, so what the hell." He came over to kiss her quickly on her lips and neck. "I'll try sharpening the teaspoon into a weapon and go straight for his jugular. And if that doesn't work, we can always pray for the intercession of Saint Alexius, patron saint of beggars. Maybe he'll give us a miracle."

Vie smiled, remembering that Philippa had told her she could only hope to get Josh Manning's support by way of a miracle.

"What's funny?" Mike asked, scowling.

"Miracles may be on the way in," she said enigmatically. "After all, here we are."

Mike smiled. "You're a dear, foolish creature, Vie. Did you know that?"

She nodded. "Yes. And you love me."

"Love solves everything?"

"Who knows? Anyway, I have the best lawyer in the city on my side."

"*At* your side," he corrected, throwing off the robe and coming back to bed, into her welcoming arms.

Two weeks later, in his office, Mike told Vie gloomily, "I'm never praying to Saint Alexius again. He can't tell the difference between a miracle and a bloody mess."

"Sacrilege, lad." She reprimanded him mildly.

He didn't even smile. "The most we can hope for is a Pyrrhic victory." Now that they'd discovered Nick's betrayal in bringing the formula to Motek, they had a countercharge of industrial espionage and theft to pit against Olcott's charge of contract violation. But the prize they were fighting for had evaporated in the contest. The fragrance was as good as lost to Vie.

The case would drag on, Mike explained, especially now, with the new indictments. By the time it was resolved, Marty would have put the scent on the market under the Jolay for Motek label. Even if Vie were permitted to go ahead with Nouvel, Inc., she'd have no sensational product to launch it with. Josh Manning, on behalf of the investors, would be forced to ask Vie to refund their money.

Vie listened bleakly to Mike's projections. She felt she'd come to the end of her road as a businesswoman. The hope of a comeback, of proving herself again, now lay shattered.

Over the intercom Mike's secretary announced, "A Mr. Benedetti is here to see you. He doesn't have an appointment, but he says it's urgent."

"Hold on a moment." Mike asked Vie if she knew anything about this.

"All I know is that he's a traitor." She'd heard that his treachery had earned him a promotion to vice president at Motek. "I never want to see his face again," Vie said firmly.

"I understand, love. But if he's come here to my office by himself, he may have something we want to hear. Why don't you wait next door in my partner's office while I find out what it is?"

"You're going to let him in?" she asked incredulously.

"Love, you've got to trust me. I can handle him."

"Don't be so sure," she glowered, but she let Mike escort her through the side door of his office into his partner's empty one.

She waited half an hour before Mike returned. He was beaming. "An interesting proposition," he told her. Vie looked at him coldly as she walked back to his office.

"He came waving a white flag. Not surrender, but truce. Turns out Motek went thumbs down on the perfume. It goes against their image. Too elitist, expensive—way out of their ballpark. Their key word is 'reliability.' They're pushing honest, down-to-earth products a housewife can trust. No extravagance, no sophistication."

"Which means . . . ?" Vie prompted.

"Basically, that Benedetti has lost a lot of his credibility at Motek. Turns out he'd made a deal to come in as a vice president if he brought them the formula he stole from us."

"Who did he make the deal with?" asked Vie, suspecting the answer.

"Your sister," Mike said grimly. "But for once all that brainpower hasn't led her to success. She was so anxious to defeat you that she lost her usual acumen. She fired way over the heads of Motek, bringing their wrath down on her."

"I'm not sure I understand, Mike."

He took her in his arms and kissed her soothingly, as though to make the hurt go away. "I'm not sure either, lovely," he said when he stopped kissing her. He still held her close. "But this is how it adds up to me: Marty wanted to destroy you. She was determined not to let you come up in business again."

"She hates me," Vie said softly, resting her head against Mike's shoulder.

"She's insanely jealous of you. She forced you out of Jolay, but even that wasn't enough. She had to make sure you'd never compete with her again. So—when she learned from Nick what you were doing, all she could think of was to take it away from you. What she stole was useless. Motek won't have it."

"Worse than useless," Mike reflected, leading Vie to a

chair. "Bringing an extravagant luxury product to Motek discredited her in their eyes. Nick told me *he* had lost credibility, but I'll bet Marty has lost even more. There may be a reshuffling of power over at Motek, and Marty stands to lose. We may be able to make a deal with her and her lawyers."

Vie sat very quietly, her hands holding the arms of the chair. She frowned. "If that's what happened, I still don't see why that man came here to talk to you."

"His main purpose will surprise you, beauty. You always thought he and Marty were mortal enemies. But the truth is, he's in love with her, and he wants to protect her from her own mistakes. He'd like us to settle out of court. Motek doesn't need publicity for a product they're not using and don't want to be associated with. Also, I suspect Nick and Marty will be trying to get out of the corporation now. In any case, I'm calling Duane Olcott."

When Mike got through to him, it turned out Marty was sitting in his office. Mike mouthed the information to Vie and suggested to Olcott that the two sisters have a talk. He added that Miss Nouvel happened to be with him now.

Mike waited, hand over the mouthpiece, while Olcott conferred with his client. Vie remained silent, looking at him. When Mike removed his hand, he nodded and smiled. "That'll be fine," he said. "In about half an hour."

Hanging up, he told Vie, "She's picking you up here, out in the front office. I agreed with Olcott that we lawyers would keep out of it." He shrugged and tried to reassure her with a kiss. But Vie was frightened.

When Vie came into the reception area, Marty greeted her with a tough, unfriendly smile. "Long time no see, big sister."

"What're you up to now, Marty? What's the latest scheme—or is it scam?"

"C'mon, Vie, don't you trust me?"

"No," she answered bluntly.

"And you never have!" The receptionist and the waiting clients looked up as Marty raised her voice. Recoiling, as always, from the public airing of family problems, Vie took hold of Marty's elbow and quickly ushered her out.

On the street, Marty hailed a taxi. "You can come to my apartment," she said. "You've never seen it."

"And you haven't seen mine. We'll go there," Vie said decisively, getting into the cab first and giving the driver her address.

Taken aback by Vie's strength of command, Marty shrugged and accepted their destination. When they got out in front of Vie's door, she said sourly, "At last: the mountain comes to Mohamet."

"Let's go into the garden," Vie said, leading the way. The surroundings of her bushes and plants would help sustain her, she hoped.

"Still living in a state of nature, I see," said Marty. "Got some bourbon?"

"How about us sharing a bottle of wine?"

"I'd rather have bourbon."

Vie went to get it, leaving Marty in the garden. The herbs she'd planted in April had reached a mature green color. Basil and rosemary, tarragon and thyme. Pansies, bordering the herb beds, looked out with their faces of absorbed children. The early roses were in bloom, and the delicate lines etching the walls were studded with morning glory. The fragrant enclosure, in the midst of New York City, never lost its charm on Vie, and she hoped it would blunt Marty's harshness.

She brought out the bourbon, and Marty took it with a nod. "Nick and I are letting you off the hook. Olcott told me you don't stand a chance in a million—you'd be convicted by any judge or jury in the country."

"And what about you—spying and stealing?"

"All part of business," she said with a lazy smile. "The competitive system. You don't have a patent. In any case, it was Nick who developed the formula, and he has a right to do with it whatever he wants."

"He does not!" Vie suddenly changed tack, to catch the undercurrent of what they were saying to each other. "Why are you trying to defeat me? Why have you spent your life working to have me fail? What have I done to you?" Her voice rose, quavering. Marty sipped her drink, the smile still on her face.

"Answer me!" Vie cried. "All our lives I tried to take

care of you. I worked to make it possible for you to go to college, have chances that I never got. . . ."

"And you resented me for it. Don't deny that," Marty said sharply. "You resented everything you gave. Whatever you handed out had strings attached. You wanted me to be grateful. But more than that, most of all, you wanted me to be just like you. You were playing God with me, Vie. My life in your hands, for you to mold the way you wanted to. You never saw who *I* was. You didn't care, weren't interested. I was just the receiver of your bounty, a grateful subject of the queen. A worshiper for the saint."

Vie listened, appalled, as she saw Marty's growing agitation. Her own hands were shaking. "No, that's not how it was. . . ."

"You let me finish!" Marty screamed. "Yes, that's exactly how it was. You were so goddamn high and mighty, you never let me be *myself*. I hated you, Vie. Hated you for taking away the only thing I wanted to have—*myself*." She was crying now as she finished the drink in a long swallow. She choked, coughed, then put the empty glass on the ground. "*He* did that too. He wouldn't accept me. Both of you, you were a couple and I was the hated stepchild. Whatever I did was wrong. You got all Papa's attention and all his love. Nothing left for me. You were like his fucking wife."

"Stop! That's not true! As far back as I can remember, I felt he didn't know me, either. I knew he *did* love me, in his way, but he never saw me. I was just the reflection of my mother for him; he was blinded by her. I felt terribly alone."

"You?" Marty asked in surprise. "You had it all. And when Nina came to live with us, you had a mother, too."

Vie was stirred by an old memory of intense pain. She was silent, trying to recover it, and Marty, seeing the expression on her face, waited, not crying anymore.

When Vie spoke again, her voice was gentle. "A long time ago, we were both quite young, you and Papa had an awful scene, and after it you said he hated you. You hit me and told me you hated me, you hated both of us. In that moment I loved you. I felt how lonely you must be. I wasn't happy at the time, I didn't have any friends except for the cats, and I felt Papa was always looking through me, out to my dead mother on the other side. But you were in deeper distress, in a kind of agony, and I was determined to make it up to you somehow."

Marty stood up. "You felt that? But you were a kid then—still in high school."

"You remember?"

Marty nodded and came over to where Vie was sitting on the white wrought-iron chair. She stopped in front of her sister, head bent, speaking softly. "When I came back from France, after I'd learned the truth about my mother, and that my father had saved my life, I vowed to make him proud of me. It was a kind of memorial, I guess. He'd depended on *you* for as long as I could remember, and looked up to you. You were his star, his Virgin Mary—"

"That's going too far—"

"Please. I came back with one firm goal: to prove I was better than you, that what he'd done for me hadn't been in vain. That I was his true daughter and he could be proud of me." She began weeping.

Vie stood and placed her hand on Marty's shoulder. "But he was dead," she said gently.

"That's the bitch of it, isn't it?" Marty tried to smile. "When you perform for the dead, you don't get much applause."

A wave of enormous pity came over Vie. "That means it'll never have an end, will it?"

"He died without ever loving me."

"Does that mean you'll never stop trying to win his approval?"

Marty nodded silently, in tears.

Vie touched her shoulder. "You've been tremendously successful, Marty. From the time you came back to America, you've conquered everything you set out to do. Don't you feel pride in that?"

"Yes, of course I do. But Vie, I had only one real goal, and that was to defeat you. When I managed that, when I went with Motek and forced you into a contract that prevented you from working again, I felt safe. For the first time I felt really safe. I knew I'd done it, I'd reached the top and kicked you out." Marty turned her face away from Vie so she wouldn't have to see her sister's distress.

"While I was up there, I was able to forgive you. Would you believe it? I'd even toy with the idea of us getting back together again, being partners on our own. I was that secure.

"But when you started coming back the way you did, I felt everything crumble under me. The stuff I was developing for Motek seemed nothing better than detergent. You've always been high class, the very top. When I used to argue with you about holding on to an elite image, I definitely believed it would hurt the company, certainly in the long run. But I was jealous, too. You were the queen, and I was just a smart businesswoman. If I couldn't be a queen, too, I'd force you off your throne.

"So when I heard about your ultra-luxurious scent, based on Armand's formula, I was determined to bury you again, this time for good."

"Nick helped you," Vie said, shaking.

"Yes. When I found out you'd gone to him, I wanted to strangle you. *That* had nothing to do with family history, though." She stopped, took a deep breath. "I love him. I'm wildly in love with him. I didn't know anyone could love someone so much. He needs me, you know? It's the first time in my whole goddamn life that someone really needs me and relies on me." She was crying.

Vie waited. Finally she said, "Then you've found it."

"What do you mean?" Marty looked up at her.

"The love you've been struggling to win from Armand. You wanted to feel love for your father, but maybe you never did. He wanted to love you, too, I'm sure of it, but he failed—himself as much as you.

"Now you've found love—in a man who's alive, a man *you're* able to love. That means you're free."

"You think I can remember that?"

"I'll help you," Vie said.

"Back to mothering me again," Marty answered, reaching for her old tough humor.

"Couldn't I sister you instead?"

Marty tilted her head back and looked at Vie for a long time. "Vie!" she cried at last, and threw her arms tightly around her sister. They clung to each other silently as Marty's choked breathing grew calmer.

Vie said softly, "I didn't want to be a mother when I was a little girl; I wanted to be a child. Later, I kept looking for someone who could take the place of a mother. First it was Nina and then, in a way, Philippa."

"Well, I'll be damned," Marty said with her old grin. "And there was I looking for a father. How long do you think it takes to stop being a child?"

Vie smiled. "I've been wondering about that. Do you think we'll live long enough to find out?"

Marty shrugged and walked over to the flower beds. She came back to Vie holding out a pale yellow rose. "For you."

Vie blinked. "First a white flag, then a rose. What *can* it mean?"

"A new venture maybe?" asked Marty mischievously.

"That's my sister! Business first."

"And always." She took Vie in her arms again and kissed her.

Vie's tears came easily as she returned the kiss and held her sister close.

7

The nostalgic strains of the Blue Danube Waltz trailed away, and Marty's billowing silk skirt settled gently around her. In her hair an antique tortoise comb made a crest for her veil of white Spanish lace. The tight bodice of her wedding dress, lightly strewn with seed pearls, gave her the hourglass figure of Victorian dreams.

"Your sister has never been more beautiful," Mike said.

"She's never been so happy," Vie told him, her own eyes shining.

They watched Marty and Nick making their way toward them.

Marty kissed them both. "You like my dress?" she asked Vie, holding it out and twirling around like a little girl. "I bet you would've never guessed I'd get married in something like this. Philippa knew, but I made her keep it a secret."

"What for?" asked Vie. "It's fabulous!"

"Good. It's, well, partly for you. I mean, I was always telling you how old-fashioned you were. I thought I'd see what it feels like. Feels great," she said, grinning, "but I can't wait to take it off."

"Me either," said Nick, and they all laughed.

Marty had chosen a traditional wedding, complete with bridal train, flower girls, and buckets of rice to be thrown after them when the newlyweds took off in the silver Rolls. The warm September weather permitted the reception to take place outside. The parquet dance floor was ballroom size; the tables were laid out with crystal, silver, and large sprays of white roses. "It's the only wedding I'll ever have," Marty had insisted when Nick protested the extravagance. "Anyway, it's my first." With that she'd opened up a pillow and let the feathers float out, covering both of them.

"I didn't think we should go in for this much of a show," Nick admitted to Vie and Mike. "But the way I'm feeling now, it doesn't seem half enough. White elephants! Camels! Where are the dancing girls and the fireworks?"

Vie laughed. "Never mind, it'll still make all the gossip columns, and you and Marty will probably be voted the most sensational couple of the year."

"Just the year?" he asked, disappointed.

"Don't be greedy," Marty admonished him, smiling. The band struck up a fanfare. Marty looked toward the head table. "The wedding cake! Come on, guys, we've got a job to do!"

They raced past astonished guests to take their places, Vie at Nick's left, Mike to the other side of her. Marty stood between her husband and Paul Mescaux.

With Marty's hand on the knife, Nick's hand over hers, they made the first incision into the four-tiered cake with its bride and groom figurines on top, while the band played a lusty refrain of the Wedding March. The guests applauded.

Paul Mescaux tapped his champagne glass with a spoon until everyone quieted down and he had their attention. He turned to the bride. "My dear Marty," he said, "and you, my dear Nick, I thank you for the honor you have bestowed on me, that I may be here with you on the most important day of your lives. The honor is mine because I was a friend of your father. May I extend to you both the blessings he is not here to give? Marty and Nick, I wish you great happiness together, success in whatever you do, and many good jokes to share." He waited, smiling, while the guests applauded.

"You are beautiful as a queen tonight, Marty. Your father would be very proud if he could have lived to see this day. Nothing that he produced in all his life was as fine as his daughters. To you, Marty, to you, Nick, and to Vie, I raise my glass and give you my heart."

When he finished, Marty kissed him on both cheeks, then again, laughing and crying, unable to say anything. Nick went over to embrace the old man while Vie, herself fighting not to cry, was kneading Mike's hand into a pulp.

Their friends came up to the table to kiss and congratulate. "You know what, ladies?" Murray Schwartzman told Marty and Vie. "You flubbed. The best name for a perfume is *Joy*."

"Nonsense," Philippa boomed behind him, "it's missing the 'la.' Don't look so blank, old thing: *l, a.* It fits in between the *o* and the *y*."

Murray puzzled over that. "Oh. You mean Jolay?"

Philippa kissed him on the side of his chin, the highest point she could reach. "Wonderful. You get an extra glass of champagne for that—*and* the chance to dance with me." She led Murray away, winking at Marty.

Marty whispered something to Nick and then pulled Vie aside. "We both have something to tell you. Can we go inside for a moment?"

Vie looked over at Mike. Marty, catching the look and

interpreting it, laughed warmly. "I guess he can come, too. It seems Mike's become a permanent attachment."

The four of them went into the house, a colonial mansion rented for the wedding, with rooms for guests to stay overnight. The small library on the second floor was empty. They went in, and Marty closed the door behind them.

"What's the secret?" Vie asked.

"It's a wedding present."

"You don't like it!" Vie wailed. The Coleport goldplate set from England was one of its kind. She'd paid a small fortune, hoping Marty would be as delighted as she by the delicacy and artistry of it.

"I *love* your present. We both do. I'm talking about our present to you. Nick and I bought back Jolay from Motek."

"What does that mean?" Vie asked, her eyes growing wider.

"It means we made the offer two months ago. They've finally accepted it, providing they retain all rights to everything we'd produced or formulated under Motek auspices. We agreed, and I think everyone's happy. They're buying into a pharmaceutical firm and hope to combine a health line and a grooming line into one. Turns out we really scared them with Armand's fragrance, and they wanted to phase us out, or at least cover us up under health products. So we were able to buy the name back cheaply."

"What's cheap?" Mike asked.

"One million. All it meant was selling a few Motek shares." Marty giggled. "We're not paupers, yet. Vie, the name is yours. You can bring out the new fragrance under the name you created. I had no business taking it from you. That is," she corrected herself, "a lot of business, but no right. Anyway, *you* were Madame Jolay, and now you'll go on being Madame Jolay."

"One of them," Vie said. "The Jolay sisters means *two* Madame Jolays."

Marty nestled against Nick. "Tell you what," she said, beaming broadly. "You take it over. You can go first, try out the waters. While you're doing that, I'll be getting my feet wet in another career."

Vie stared at her. With Marty, the only thing you could

be sure of was that she'd surprise you. It was Mike who asked, "Are you thinking of going into a new line of business?"

"Not quite. I want a tough career this time. As wife."

"You're giving up . . ." Vie began, but Marty raised her hand for silence.

"*And* mother." She turned to Nick and kissed him. He brought his hand to the front of her skirt and held it there.

"Do you mean . . . ?"

"Yes. Three months pregnant."

"The only way I could get her," said Nick, grinning. "I forced her into marriage to make an honest father of me."

"Wonderful!" Vie clapped her hands. "But can you really give up on business, Marty? It's been your life all these years, as it has mine."

"I've taken it as far as I can. You asked me a few months ago, Vie, if I wasn't proud of my accomplishments. I'm not proud of all of them, but I know I proved to you that I could do it. And to myself. Yes," she said softly, "I've proven it to myself. As for Armand—let him rest."

Vie held her a long time. "Amen," she said when they drew apart.

"I won't be completely out of it, I hope. Nick will let me know what's going on—and you, too. Nick will be applying to you for a job in about a year's time."

Vie looked questioningly at Nick. "I'll be back—if you'll have me, Vie. Right now we're taking off for a year's honeymoon. I've never traveled, and Marty promised to show me France. From there—around the world! Our daughter's going to be born in some faraway country. I always wanted at least one exotic relative."

"Daughter?" asked Marty.

Nick kissed her again. "That's what I'm hoping. If I were a better chemist, I could arrange to have you cloned."

"Back to the workbench," Mike told him, smiling.

Nick put his arm around Marty's waist and pulled her so tightly against him that she gasped in protest. "Ain't chemistry grand?" he asked of no one in particular, looking deep into the eyes of his beautiful wife.

*   *   *

On October first, *Le Seul* by Jolay, Inc., was launched at Magdahl-Hoffman and simultaneously in many other stores around the country. Its French name had put off some buyers at first, but Vie refused to change it. "Le seul," meaning either "the one" or "the only," struck her as an ideal name, and the return to French after decades of American-sounding names reinforced its aura of luxury.

The test sales were unprecedented. Even outside major metropolitan areas the "drops" of men's perfume—encased in a glass pouch that rested on red silk lining inside a small silver snuff box—sold instantly at $50 a drop. The larger snuff boxes, containing ten glass pouches, in layers of five each, sold for $400.

Fashion photographers and journalists were milling around the store, but none of them recognized Vie. In slacks, with a scarf over her head and sunglasses hiding half her face, she blended in with the working crowd. From her position near the front door she held Mike's hand as they stood watching the commotion.

Paul Mescaux came up to them, and Vie hugged him in greeting. "You see what we've created, Paul? A runaway, trend-setting marvel."

He nodded. "It is done. The greatest fragrance of Armand Jolaunay has become a reality, more than forty years after he was formulating it. You have made something wonderful, dear child."

"Not me, us. And Tam, and Nick, of course. Nick doesn't want to join the company—not yet, at least. So that leaves the three of us, Paul—you, Mike and me, partners in Jolay."

He shook his head. "I have come to say au revoir." Paul bent to kiss Vie's hand. "I am returning to my adopted Switzerland, where I shall live in contentment."

"Please."

"You cannot offer temptation, dear one." He smiled. "The chocolate in this country is quite horrible." He kissed her on both cheeks, shook hands with Mike, and walked away.

They watched him go, an old man with a youthful gait. "It's just you and me, Mike," Vie said softly. "We're the only partners in the company now."

"Isn't it time, my beauty, that we become partners in

more than that?" He turned her around to face him. Her eyes were shining. Her lips found his and stayed there.

"Darling," she said when she'd caught her breath, "Do you think we've found the secret formula?"

"Maybe." He shrugged. "But really I think it's all due to my cooking."

CATCH A RISING STAR!
JOHANNA KINGSLEY

With her first million-copy bestseller, SCENTS, Johanna Kingsley burst upon the publishing scene. Now she is back with her next bestseller FACES. Enter the dazzling and passionate world of Johanna Kingsley:

☐ SCENTS
26583-0 $4.50

They knew their power, their money and their men. But they did not know each other. They were the fabulous Jolays, half-sisters, bound by blood. Daughters of a powerful French perfume magnate, their rivalry grew as their fragrance empire grew.

It was Vic, the ice goddess that many men desired but few possessed, who created an empire.

But it was Marty, the dark and sensuous beauty that knew how to use her body as well as her mind, who was determined to control it.

☐ FACES
25418-9 $4.50

FACES is the enthralling story of Eugenia Sareyov, who leaves Russia as a frightened child to begin a new life in America with a wealthy but forbidding guardian as her only mentor. As she grows into a beautiful and brilliant young woman, she is sought by men and driven by ambition.

FACES is the story of the young girl and the passionate woman. It is the story of Eugenia's search for family, love and her pursuit of the dream that is her deepest desire.

Look for them at your bookstore or use the coupon below:

The #1 Bestselling Sequel to
A Woman of Substance

Barbara Taylor Bradford's
☐ **Hold the Dream**
(25621 • $4.95)

Ablaze with all the sweep, grandeur, and dynamic characters that made A WOMAN OF SUBSTANCE a legend worldwide, Barbara Taylor Bradford's spellbinding sequel begins as fiery Emma Harte shocks the world once again by relinquishing her fifty-year reign, entrusting her vast holdings to her granddaughter, Paula McGill Fairley. Paula, with Emma's iron-willed support, must confront family betrayal and boardroom warfare; must face her greatest love and her deepest loss before she can triumph and make Emma's dream her own.

Also from Barbara Taylor Bradford

a magnificent and unforgettable drama that spans twenty-three years and sweeps from London, to the Bavarian Alps, to the Riveria, to New York and Hollywood

☐ *Voice of the Heart*
(26253 • $4.95)

Ravishing actress and star, Katharine Tempest was the captivating woman whose face became a legend of beauty and whose astonishing rise to fame became the world's fantasy. But her greatest role became her life, her audience became her friends . . . until Katharine betrayed them all.

Now, perhaps too late, she seeks the one thing she needs most: forgiveness.

Look for them both at your bookstore or use the coupon below: